LINK

A DARK & DIRTY SINNERS' MC: TWO

SERENA AKEROYD

Copyright © 2021 by Serena Akeroyd

All rights reserved.

No part of this book may be reproduced in any form or by any electronic or mechanical means, including information storage and retrieval systems, without written permission from the author, except for the use of brief quotations in a book review.

❧ Created with Vellum

LINK

DEDICATION

TO MY COUSIN.

Kristian, you died so young, cuz. Too young. If there's any relief to be found, it's in knowing you're no longer in pain and are at peace. But it's small comfort.

Until we meet again,

Love

Gem <3

SOUNDTRACK

If you'd like to hear a curated soundtrack, with songs that are featured in the book, as well as songs that inspired it, then here's the link:

https://open.spotify.com/playlist/4OGQnhcrYN7miGQAoXIjcE?si=b013410d43bd4da9

WARNING

Please be advised this book may contain scenes that are disturbing to sensitive readers.

A YEAR EARLIER...

I blew out a breath as the ache in my body made itself known, and using a few sheets of toilet paper, I rolled it in on itself, creating a tiny barricade I hoped would hold.

Shoving it between my ass cheeks was enough to bring on a panic attack, because I hated my ass. Hated. It.

Not for any normal reason, like because it had cellulite. Not because it was just a smidgen too much of a bubble butt. Not because it was bony or flat—I didn't give a crap about how it looked.

I hated it because *he* used it.

Shuddering as I stood, the paper lodged there, collecting blood he'd spilled, I dragged my panties up high and lowered my skirt.

When I approached the vanity, I looked at myself and was, as always, surprised to note I looked normal. So fucking normal. Not like I'd just been used—*abused*. Not like the walking wreckage I was.

My body was one big ball of pain as I washed my hands and launched myself into an upright position.

Smile firmly fixed in place, I headed on out, then winced when I saw Tiffany, my best friend, had let herself in. She was flat on her stomach on the bed, phone in her hand, her legs swaying from side to side.

"Did you see what Lourdes just posted on Instagram? I mean, my God, did she get dressed in the dark?"

"Maybe she did."

Tiffany scowled at me, her eyes squinting as she processed my remark and judged whether I was joking or not. Then, because she couldn't tell—I had a damn good poker face—she grumbled, "Who gets dressed in the dark?"

"It would explain the past few choices she's made," I conceded.

"Fashion disasters you mean." She huffed, rolled off her stomach, and straightened up into a standing position. Her eyes drifted over me. "You look like you're in pain." Her brow puckered. "Got another headache?"

That was the excuse I used when I was feeling this way.

"Yeah. I'll be okay though."

My smile didn't display just how fragile I felt. I'd had a lot of practice in making certain I looked normal.

That was like my family's secondary talent—looking normal when, underneath it all, we were the exact opposite.

Our primary talent, of course, was making money.

Lots, and lots, and *lots* of money.

I'd exchange it all for the ability to lead a regular goddamn life.

"You sure?"

"Positive."

She hummed under her breath as she gave me another scan, then she shrugged. Not because she didn't care—she did.

Sometimes I was positive she was the only person who gave a damn about me period—but because she knew me well.

We'd gone to St. Lawrence Academy in Manhattan together and had been through thick and thin as friends.

She knew I wouldn't let anything stop me. She just didn't know why I was that way.

It wasn't because I was forthright and indomitable—if only it were. But no, it was because the punishment never fit the crime, and I'd learned to adjust my behavior accordingly.

"What's this party about anyway?" she asked, her attention still on our friend Lourdes' post.

"Didn't your dad tell you?" I questioned, amused despite myself.

I headed over to my dressing table and picked up my favorite scent. As I dabbed it behind my ears and along my décolleté, I stared out at the yard where, beneath a blanket of string lights, amid thousands of perfumed flowers and the stirring music from a string quartet, a hundred people were moseying together, appreciating my father's largesse.

One thing could be said about my bastard father—he knew how to throw a party.

"Oh, he did, but I didn't listen." She beamed at me, her green eyes twinkling as she straightened up her tie and sorted out a few flyaway strands of hair. Unlike me, who always wore a dress for these events, she wore pantsuits with ties. Sure, she looked like a sexy newscaster, but hell, she rocked it. "You know I make it my job to ignore my dad on the regular."

"Lies. You're a daddy's girl. Face it."

She stuck out her tongue. "I'm not. He's making us move."

"You're twenty-two, babe. If you want to stay in the city, you can." There was no envy in my tone, even if inside, I was a wriggling, writhing ball of jealousy over her freedom.

"Nah. Not if you're moving there too." Unlike Tiff, I didn't have the freedom of choice. "Might as well see what New Jersey has in store for us." She made a puking sound. "Never thought we'd leave the city."

"Well, that's what happens when people as rich as our parents get tax breaks for moving states," I said dryly.

"True," she admitted.

With another glance out the window, I looked around the crowd, trying to ensure I had the name-to-faces down pat.

At the sight of a man I didn't recognize, a shiver rushed down my spine.

In his forties, he was surrounded by men in black suits that were, quite clearly, packing heat. They had more bulges in odd places than a drug trafficker.

"Who's he?"

She bent forward, peering into the ornate mirror and smoothing her finger around her lips in an effort to keep the line of her lipstick crisp. "Who's who?"

"The guy with the guards."

"Which one?"

"That one," I stated, pointing to him when she peered out the window too.

She shuddered. "Gianni Fieri. Isn't he creepy?"

Creepy wasn't the word.

He was, truthfully, quite handsome. In a young Al Pacino kind of way. But he was dark on dark. Black hair, black eyes, black shirt, black tie, black suit and shoes.

Like a walking shadow, the way he stood there as if he ruled the roost put me on edge.

No one dominated a party in my father's presence. Not without living to tell the tale. Yet he was permitting it.

Beneath my bewildered gaze, my father even wandered over to him, laughing at something before evidently getting down to business.

Well, Father *had* laughed.

Fieri's lips hadn't so much as twitched at the bad joke he'd just heard.

"Whoa, he isn't ass-licking your dad," Tiffany whispered, sounding as shocked as I felt, and for a reason.

Everyone licked my father's ass.

Everyone.

That's what ninety billion in the bank did to you—got you rimmed on the regular.

"No." An uneasy feeling settled in my stomach. "That's weird."

"Weird? It's unheard of. Wonder why he's here."

"He must have invested in your dad's property development."

She frowned. "I guess. Shit. I wish I'd listened in on all those boring conversations over dinner now."

Even though I was so envious of her that I couldn't contain it sometimes, not just because she had loving parents and a familial relationship that looked like it belonged in a rich man's version of *The Walton's*, I had to smile at her.

"You should listen anyway. You know your father wants you to go into the business."

"All the more reason to ignore him." She pulled a face. "What use would I be in property development? I'm a therapist."

"You'd be fantastic at anything you put your mind to."

Tiff, though I loved her, was one of those annoying people who got A grades all the time without even studying.

"Prefer to be married to the property developer. Would save me wrinkles in the long run," she joked, elbowing me in the side. Though she hadn't meant to, she connected with one of my bruises and I flinched. "Sorry, love. God, your head really is killing you, isn't it?"

I gave her a faint smile even as I rubbed my side, pretending that was what hurt. "Yeah. It's all good."

I looked down at my father then jerked when I saw I had Fieri's attention. He was glowering at me to an extent that I jolted back in surprise, which set off a tsunami of aches in my battered body.

His glower deepened, then he grabbed my father's arm, whose attention flashed up to me.

The second I felt his focus, I drifted back and away from the window. The last thing I wanted was to be in his crosshairs.

"Luke's making a fool out of himself," Tiffany pointed out, her attention having shifted, something I was glad for.

"When doesn't he?" I muttered.

"True. Not sure why your dad puts up with him." She trembled again—which put Fieri and Luke in the same league in her mind.

Jesus Christ.

What that said about Fieri, I didn't know. As for Luke? He was a psychopath. Pure and simple.

"He's the golden boy," I mumbled, staring at myself in the mirror one last time to make sure I looked perfect before I stuck on a smile. "Ready?"

She whistled as she turned to give me a quick scan. "You look hot. In pain, but hot." Then she squinted. "You sure you're okay to do this? Nothing worse than feeling shitty when you have to talk to these morons for an entire evening."

Tiff was right. I wasn't in the mood for it, but my choices, my wishes, weren't important. Never had been.

Never would be.

So I gritted my teeth and got on with it.

I'd have my day.

"I'm fine. Promise." I tucked my arm through hers. "Let's get this over with."

She snorted. "Preach, sister. Preach."

ONE

LILY

I WINCED the second the beauty blender collided with my cheekbone. The wince morphed into an extended hiss as I let the pain flush through my system, only to be bombarded by it yet again as I carried on patting on the foundation.

The bruise was shockingly bright against my creamy skin, but I was pretty good at hiding the aftermath of a run-in with my father's fist now and could hide it with the clever application of makeup.

What I couldn't hide was how his ring had torn into the skin, leaving behind the faintest cut, which stung every time I touched it.

There was no hiding that.

A fact, I was sure, that would irritate him to no end. But then, I irritated him period. Always had, always would.

And I would never *not* be proud of that.

Ever since I'd learned the truth, I lived to irritate my scum-sucking father.

I burned for it.

I took his wrath and let him reap it on me, because I loathed him and he loathed me, but I was blood, and now I was his only heir.

It was just time that would make that official, and I couldn't wait for that day.

Wincing yet again as I dabbed on the makeup, my attention was caught by my screen lighting up in the corner of my eye.

I'd set notifications on Google for anything related to my brother's case, and the fact that the cops were in my father's pockets and were trying to spin it so the woman my brother had tried to rape was somehow the attacker hadn't escaped my attention.

I just didn't know how to go about rectifying things.

Which was why I was hiding a bruise caused by my father's fist.

I'd tried, and failed, to put things in some semblance of order, and he wasn't having it. But then, he'd always thought that prick walked on water.

Just because Luke was a boy, he'd received an automatic free pass to do whatever he wanted.

And when you had money like we did, *whatever* took on a different connotation.

Luke was sick. Rabid. I was glad he was dead, because it saved me from having to do it at some point in my life.

The past twenty-two years had been spent working up the courage to kill my father and my brother, and I was ashamed I'd achieved neither.

In another world, in another life, I'd be a good daughter and a good sister, but this wasn't another world, and this was my life.

My family was evil.

My father was one of the malicious, fat white men who ran the world from his ivory tower, and my brother had been born in his image. They were both bastards, and even in death, Luke was being one.

Quickly scanning the news alert, I saw the victim, Giulia Fontaine, had been brought in for questioning. Again.

My mouth tightened, even as I focused on covering up the bruise. It took me an extra forty minutes to achieve what I could usually do in ten, but when I took a step back from the vanity, I was impressed despite myself.

I looked as I always did.

Pristine except for that tiny cut, which I could reason away with ease.

I thought an accident while playing tennis would easily explain it.

'*I tripped and fell against the grass, and there was a tiny shard of glass there.*'

At that point of the conversation, if someone asked, I'd laugh and tell them I'd fired a gardener over their inattention to detail, and everyone would laugh with me.

Because *that* was the world I lived in.

In that world, it was okay for fathers to beat daughters and for daughters to come up with random excuses that everyone accepted even though they *knew* what said father was like.

Donavan Lancaster was the biggest cunt around.

Everyone knew it.

But he had billions in the bank and, therefore, he got away with murder. Literally.

That was why my mom was in the family mausoleum back in Manhattan, because he'd murdered her when she'd done the impossible and had asked for a divorce.

I gnawed on my bottom lip as I stared at the bouncy blonde waves that danced around my shoulders, took in the blue eyes I'd enhanced with a dark slash of navy eyeliner in the corners, and the cheekbones I'd sharpened with bronzer that led to ruby red lips which gleamed in the light above the vanity.

Taking a step back, I looked at the neat dress that clung to all my slim curves, accepted that the black did things for my skin tone and hair that made me look even more attractive, and sucked in a breath.

I knew I looked like a china doll, and it was an image I played up to. I'd continue to do so until I found my way in and, through that, found my way out.

Today was a step toward that path.

An exit that involved my father's death and not my own because, and this was the God's honest truth, the only way out of this family was through death, and I didn't intend to die. Not for a good long while.

The bathroom around me was a study of marble.

The light beige counter was dotted with open makeup bottles, and the floor beneath my Louboutin heels—that added a good four inches to my height and did wonders for my ass—was a darker gray.

The walls were covered in a creamy white stone that had gold striations throughout which, oddly enough, made my hair appear gold rather than blonde.

As I contemplated the contrast, I realized I looked like my mother.

The thought had me twisting my lips as I turned away from my too pretty features and stepped over the mass of towels I'd left on the floor.

I was messy, and I'd admit to it, but that was one thing allowed of me in this household. I had staff who'd clean up after me, and I took advantage of that.

When I returned later on tonight, this place would look like it was a showroom once more. Now, well, it just looked as if a Tasmanian Devil had whirled around the place, knocking stuff over, and leaving chaos in its wake.

I ignored the rest of my suite and headed over to the patio doors at the front of my room. I had access to the grounds from here, thanks to a set of steps. It was how I was supposed to reach the pool, but I used it to sneak out.

Not that my father cared what I did on a daily basis so long as I followed his rules, returned here every night and slept in my bed, and didn't give my security detail too much of a run around, but I didn't want to come across him even accidentally before I got out of here.

The magnificent vista slipped by me.

I didn't even see it as I headed down the steps. My heels sank into the thick grass, but I strode on toward the garage.

It was a little awkward to approach this way, but it was worth it. I had to step around the pool house where my brother had lived—a pool house that was like a mini mansion because Donavan Lancaster's son deserved only the best—and slip between the two tennis courts.

The ten-minute walk in four-inch heels was one I knew well. Though we were relatively new to the area, I'd left the house via my room every day of the three months we'd been here.

If there was a chance I'd run into my father, I'd find a way around it. Meeting him usually ended up with me slathering on foundation to cover a bruise on my face, and while I was adept at it, I wasn't a masochist.

Staying out of his sight was the key to surviving this hellhole.

When I reached the garage, my heels tapped against the concrete floor. Spotting Luke's Lamborghini, I sneered as I let my fingers drift over the sleek lines.

I was tempted, oh so fucking tempted, to take that car out, but if the news hit my father's ears, I'd have matching shiners. So, instead, I went for another sports car. One my father didn't mind me driving—a Porsche Carrera. It was a few years old, and that was why I was allowed to drive it.

My father believed women drivers were a plague, so we weren't to be trusted with the best in his stable.

Chauvinistic asswipe.

I leaped behind the wheel and reversed out, driving past twenty million dollars' worth of cars on my exit, and only when I was through the gates did I release a sigh of relief.

Getting out of there always felt like I was escaping a looming storm cloud.

It was a weight off my chest that made me feel like I could breathe properly for the first time since I'd made it back here the night before.

When my security detail pulled up behind me, I ignored them. They were always watching, always following, so I just pretended they weren't there.

Tonight, however, I'd need to find a way to make sure they weren't as on the ball as usual.

That would mean endangering their jobs but, truthfully, they were dicks anyway.

I didn't really care if their careers were in the can after the moves I was going to pull tonight.

My brother had security too, and they *knew* what he was up to.

Knew it because they followed him just like they followed me.

Bastards.

Of course, they were probably dead bastards by now. My father had undoubtedly paid someone to wipe them off the face of the Earth, lest they ever think to blackmail him for the shit Luke had pulled.

My hands tightened around the wheel as the ever-present rage washed through me, flooding me with more emotion than I knew what to do with.

I'd been locked up tight since my mother's murder, and subsequently Luke's death—and the shit I'd inadvertently discovered about him—was creating holes in my control. Emotions were spluttering toward me, and I couldn't deal with them. I only knew I had to do something, *anything*, to help.

Making it into town was easy.

We lived just on the Caldwell-West Orange border, but the ride was always smooth, and I enjoyed the wind in my hair and the loud music I let blare through the speakers.

A song was still ringing in my head as I cut the engine when I was parked. Humming to the beat, I climbed out after I grabbed my purse. Once I was standing, I stared at the bar up ahead.

My father had been very vocal in his fight to stop a local motorcycle club from gaining the required licenses to open this particular mall but, for once, he'd lost.

I was curious how that had happened, because it meant the MC had more tokens with local councilors than my dad did, and *that* was impressive.

If I had a hat on my head, I'd take it off to them because, yikes, beating Donavan was nigh impossible.

Dear old Dad had been particularly pissed the day he'd heard of the licenses going through, and he'd been doubly pissed when, barely six weeks later, the club had managed to get some of the businesses up and running.

That, right there, told me they had money to burn.

Nobody got several businesses functioning that quickly; not unless they were willing to hemorrhage cash.

The strip consisted of a diner, a strip joint, a garage, and a bar.

It was the latter, Daytona, that was my intended destination.

The place didn't look trashy. Sure, it wasn't swank, not like the bars at the country clubs I usually haunted, but I wasn't here to get drunk. Wasn't here to have fun. There was a method to my madness, a method I was praying someone within the confines of those walls could help me with.

Sucking in a sharp breath, I took off, crossing the road with such purpose that I almost missed the car that was pulling around the corner.

The sharp honk of the horn had me jerking to a halt, and I was on the receiving end of a glower and a fist shake as the driver, a woman in her seventies, passed me by.

Heart in my throat at my stupidity for not checking for traffic, I tried to ask myself what the fuck was going to happen if I died before the shit I knew could be passed on to people who'd help.

There'd be blood on my hands, that's what.

Blood that would haunt me even into death.

Breathing deeply, I carried on after looking right, then left, and made it, *safely*, to the other side of the road.

Not messing around, I moved into the bar and, once I'd checked it out and had spied a kind of area that was cordoned off with bike parts—what the hell was that about?—I couldn't fail to notice all the men in leather cuts, jeans, boots, and Henleys.

It was like a uniform or something.

Only a few had on wifebeaters that were surprisingly white.

As I wondered if they did their own laundry, or if it was totally like *Sons of Anarchy* and they had women who did it for them, I headed to the bar and placed an order.

"Can I have a vodka, please? Neat."

Though my request got me a funny look, the server just shrugged when I shook my head at his, "Not on the rocks?" and within a few minutes, I'd chugged down the clear liquid and felt it going to my head in a manner I seriously needed.

While I burned from the alcohol, my mouth tingling from it in a way that loosened my tongue, I caught the bartender's eye again. "I need your help."

Frowning, the guy leaned into me and asked, "What's wrong?"

I shot him a tight smile. "Two men are going to come into the bar soon. They'll order lagers. I'll pay you a hundred dollars to pour two shots of vodka into each of their drinks."

"You know that's illegal?"

My mouth tightened further. "They're my security detail. I need to divert their attention."

"I'm not going to lose my job just to help some rich bitch lose her guards—"

"You work for the MC here, right?" I jutted my thumb toward the seating area behind me. "I have information for them. Information I think will help them. I can't give it to them if my guards are watching."

Of course, that was half a lie.

The MC might not give a damn about some innocent women's plight, but I was hoping they'd help just to get dirt on my brother.

Boy, dirt didn't even begin to cover it.

Almost to punctuate my comment, the doors swung open, and I didn't have to turn around to feel the stares of the two guards who followed me around.

They weren't supposed to drink at all, but Paul and Alix knew I was, relatively speaking, a good girl. I never got into trouble, never stirred shit, so they could relax.

When I went to the country club, they took it in turn to be DD, while one always got hammered on my daddy's dime.

The bartender's eyes cut to my security detail, and then his gaze flashed over to the guys in the MC, who were seated in that odd concoction of bike parts.

The place was half Western saloon and half parts shop. I didn't particularly like it with its coarse wooden tables and sleek banquettes, but I didn't have to like it, did I?

This wasn't about to become my local haunt.

"Make it two hundred, and I'll dose them up," the server whispered, as he poured me another shot of vodka.

I'd have paid a grand to get Paul and Alix off my back. "Okay. Make it three shots then. I'll double the money if, every time they order, you do the same."

He hitched a shoulder in what I took to be agreement, then moved forward when he saw me slide some money under my empty glass.

Eyes connected, we both nodded as I retreated, heading over to a corner booth.

I watched as Paul took up a table at the opposite side of the room, his gaze on the door, while Alix put in an order.

The bartender must have told him he'd bring their drinks over, because he soon joined Paul. I found a spot in the mirror behind all the liquor on the back wall of the bar where I could watch them without seeming like I was.

I gnawed on my bottom lip as the server poured their beer. I couldn't see anything from over here, not in the dim lights anyway, and I hoped three shots would be enough to impair them.

They were big men but, as far as I knew, they only drank lager. Would three shots make them tipsy? I had to hope it would. Even better, I had to hope it would give them a thirst for more.

Once the drinks were served and Paul and Alix had sipped at them, I stopped studying them in a mirror.

Though they'd pulled a face at the first sip, it hadn't stopped them from downing the rest of their beer and, thank God, putting in another order.

Tonight's designated driver had evidently decided it was time to get hammered.

The bartender smirked at me as he filled some beer mugs for them, and I darted my gaze away from the bar just in case they thought my interest in their order was suspicious.

As I watched a couple shuffling around a space that was for dancing, I learned two-stepping to Guns and Roses wasn't impossible.

My mouth quirked up in a smile, though, as I took in the couple's tight embrace. They looked happy, relaxed in one another's company, and I'd admit to feeling jealous.

I'd never felt like that around another person.

Not even my mom, and I'd loved her more than anyone else on this planet.

Trust wasn't something you could have in my family. We were all back-stabbers, myself included.

I gnawed on my lip as sentimental nostalgia, undoubtedly aided by my second shot of vodka, made me teary-eyed.

I shouldn't have to do what I was doing tonight, and yet, here I was, trying to get my guards drunk and all so I could speak to men who were the type of guys I actually needed protection from.

The MC brothers were loud, raucous, and rude. That much I'd seen in my forty minutes at Daytona.

They drank too much, laughed too hard, and swore like sailors on coke. I didn't like them, but they were my only hope.

There were around ten of them in the booth, and every now and then I'd let my gaze drift around the red, laughing faces, trying to figure out who was the best to approach for help.

Each time, I caught sight of the guy in the corner because everything about him was like metal to my magnet.

He had his arms slung over the back of the booth on each side, and he was slouched down. Though he laughed, his eyes were alert, and twice he'd caught my gaze with his own, his mouth twitching in a smile a split second before I looked away.

He wasn't drunk, even though I'd seen him down two bottles of beer and a couple of shots, and from the heat in his eyes, I figured he thought I was trying to work out which of the men I was going to fuck.

My stomach churned at the prospect. I knew from my own circle of friends that they'd often come here to, as they called it, 'rough' it.

Fucking one of the Satan's Sinners appeared to be a rite of passage in these parts, but I wasn't here to fuck anyone. The last thing I needed was one of these bikers thinking I was here for a quickie in the restrooms.

Gah, just the notion made me scowl into my vodka.

I'd never understood the desire to have sex in a public restroom. Not only were they gross, but ugh, it was filthy and loaded with germs.

I wouldn't have sex in *my* bathroom, and I knew for a fact that Conchita steamed most of my quarters to keep me happy.

When a loud bray of laughter burst out from the other side of the room, I first thought it was one of the bikers.

They'd been making weird noises for a while now, so it fit, but when I glanced at them, they were cutting a look in another direction—my guards.

Paul and Alix were wasted. Alix was snorting out a laugh as Paul was slapping the table with the palm of his hand as he, too, snickered at whatever inside joke they had going on.

I studied them for a few minutes, watched as they turned toward one another and began arguing over something. It was a friendly argument though, and I figured it had to do with sports.

I knew they both supported the same football team and had often heard them discussing stats and the like when they were on detail.

Getting to my feet, I decided to try and make a move.

The restroom was my first port of call, just to see if they noticed I'd gone. I'd taken note of the signage the second I'd taken a seat so, as I walked past them, maneuvering my way through the roughly hewn tables that were made out of slices of trees, I hitched a breath as I wondered if I'd made it.

When they didn't snap out a hand as I brushed past them, I knew I was good to carry on with my plan.

The second I made it to the hall that led to the bathrooms, I almost crumpled as relief hit me.

For a second, I just leaned against the wall, ignoring the picture frame that dug into my back as I did so.

Pressing my hand to my forehead, I sucked in a breath, calmed myself down, then straightened up. As I did, I jerked in surprise.

The brother from the booth was standing there.

Inches away.

Watching me.

I gulped, tense from surprise and uneasiness.

He was close. Too close. In my space, and I couldn't move back.

He tilted his head to the side, his eyes catching mine before they drifted down to my mouth.

He was big.

Huge, in fact.

And even though he was handsome, as handsome as the Devil himself, he was scary. But I was used to that.

My father wore a mask for the public.

He donned expensive suits and watches that cost more than some people's homes, and he'd wave at the photographers, a big ole smile on his face as he beamed at the world because he owned it.

Or, at least, a chunk of it.

The world was his bitch, and he rode it hard and wet.

It was only when he came home, when the front doors were closed, that things changed.

That smile turned dark.

Twisted.

It was even worse when he'd grab my hair and slam my face into his fist.

Worse still when he'd pushed my mom down the stairs that night, all with that cruel smile on his face.

This man wore no mask, yet there was something going on with him.

He was white blond, but it was natural. Not from a bottle. It was kind of like mine, but more strawberry. Short and spiky, it would be, I knew, a tousled mess without gel, and it looked like silk. Honest to God silk.

He had a broad brow, with dark gold eyebrows that accentuated his bright green eyes. His nose was strong, and it led to a set of lips that would have made a saint want to sin.

Around that wicked mouth, he was stubbled from his moustache to the rest of his jaw. He wore the leather cut all the MC brothers did, a white wifebeater, and a pair of jeans that, from that one quick glance, I knew he filled out well.

Around his neck he wore, of all things, a rosary.

To say the sight surprised me was an understatement. It had wooden beads on it and a crucifix. All of it was rough, and any polish came from him worrying it with his hands.

But for all that he was beautiful, those green eyes of his?

They disturbed me.

I couldn't say why, just that they did.

"What do you want?"

Those four words should have come from me, only they didn't.

Hadn't.

He asked them, and sweet Lord, his voice was just as beautiful as the man himself.

It was raspy and deep, and it seemed to sink into my bones, settling there like mercury, weighing each of my senses down until I had no choice but to press my back harder into the wall behind me.

Turning into a puddle of goo in front of a guy like this would do me no favors. I'd been around enough men like him to know what he was—a predator.

He might think I was prey, but I wasn't.

I was a predator too, but I knew how to play a part.

I was a wolf in sheep's clothing, and I would only reveal that when I was ready.

I cleared my throat. "Why are you asking?"

"Because Cody behind the bar told me what you're paying him to do."

My head tilted to the side at that. I hadn't seen Cody approach the booth. The other server had though. But he'd said Cody, and I distinctly recalled the button on the shirt of the bartender I'd dealt with.

"When?"

His lips curved and fuck, what that did to those eyes? Holy shit. It was like looking into a cat's eyes. They were kind of blank, yet somehow managed to transmit exactly what he was thinking which, I knew, was a paradox. Maybe that was this man. Paradox with a capital P.

"Ever heard of the miracle of phones?" He arched a brow at me. "Text messages are a miracle, aren't they? Now, what do you want?"

My throat tightened as I realized, inadvertently, I'd gotten my wish.

I was speaking to a Satan's Sinner brother, and all without Paul and Alix being able to report it to my father.

For a second, my vocal chords froze.

Words I'd been planning on uttering for days in the aftermath of Luke's death seemed to choke me.

I had so much to say, so goddamn much, but I was speechless.

Until the guy stunned the shit out of me and murmured, "Take a breath."

I stared at him, wide-eyed, then he stunned me further by blowing out a breath then slowly inhaling. I focused on his mouth, rounded and perfect, and followed his lead.

At that moment, everything ground to a halt.

The world itself seemed to stop spinning on its axis.

The music blaring behind me, the noise of a toilet flushing in the near distance, the raucous crowd who was spending the evening getting drunk... it all faded into the ether.

I saw nothing but him.

Felt nothing but him.

His peace in the face of the chaos of my life.

His calm in the presence of the turbulence that brought me here.

I could hear the breath rasp from between my lips, heard his as it gusted from his mouth, and slowly, my heart stopped racing, my lungs stopped burning, and time clicked back into being.

After around thirty seconds of the deepest intimacy I'd ever had with another person, I let my gaze drift to his eyes and whispered the stark, horrendous truth: "I know where Luke kept them."

He tensed, his body turning rigid in front of me.

Distance appeared between us, a distance of my own making, especially when those weren't the words I'd wanted to say, but they were all I was capable of. And the space that suddenly pushed us a state apart made me want to sob.

I longed to reach out, to grab his hand, to get that connection back. The link where I felt the beating of my heart as much as I'd sensed his own, but that was gone now.

I'd cauterized it with my family's evil.

His words confirmed what I'd hoped—the MC had been looking into Luke's past to find a way to undermine my father's desire to pin a murder charge on Giulia Fontaine. "His captives?"

I nodded. Once.

"Who was he to you?"

My mouth twisted, and my throat choked as reality punched me there.

"My brother," I spat, speaking those two words like the curses they were, and he reared back, either because he was surprised I was related to Luke or because my vitriol for that bastard had come through loud and clear.

"Where are they?" he demanded, his voice low, rough. Raspier than before.

Now wasn't the time to be caught up in how his voice made me tingle in places *no one* had ever made me tingle before.

Now, I had to think about those poor women.

Those poor women who my bastard of a brother had—

Fuck.

I couldn't even think about that.

I just had to get them out of the hell he'd placed them in.

"Give me your phone number," I ordered, my voice sounding more like mine again.

I couldn't believe I'd shown weakness to a man like this, but hell, even I was overwhelmed at the depravity my brother had waded through in his short lifespan.

Knowing someone was evil and seeing it were two separate matters entirely.

The guy narrowed his eyes at me but reeled off a number which I input into my phone.

Quickly, I found the email where I'd stored all the information I'd uncovered when I was sneaking through Luke's stuff, copied it into a text, and sent it to him.

"That's all the info I have."

He frowned as he stared down at his phone which lit up with my text. "How long have you known?"

My throat grew tight. Not just at the horror at what my brother had done, but at the threat in the MC brother's tone. I was grateful I didn't have to lie.

"A few days. I didn't know where to turn." I sucked in a breath. "My father would let them rot, and the cops are in his pocket along with the mayor."

"The sheriff isn't." When my mouth worked as I tried to figure out what to say, since I hadn't known that was the case, he merely shook his head. "Why come to us?"

"Because Luke attacked one of your women." My smile was tight. "You protect your own."

He tipped his chin up. "You should have come to us sooner."

"Not as easy as you think when you have security following your every move. They'll report to my father." My throat grew tight again. "I'd hurry. If he decides he needs to get to them first..."

The guy didn't stick around to hear my conclusion. He just walked off, his boots silent against the ground as he disappeared as quickly as he'd appeared.

A breath escaped me as I pressed back into the wall.

My task was over.

I just hoped I wasn't too late.

TWO

LINK

"I BELIEVE HER."

"She had tits and an ass. Of course, you believe her," Steel muttered, snorting as he began shuffling a deck of cards.

It was a nervous tic of sorts, a new one.

That damn deck was in his mitts at all times, had been ever since we'd found out about Luke Lancaster's little harem from hell.

I figured it had to do with the prospect of some innocent women being imprisoned somewhere in the United States of America. Starving to death...

I blew out a breath.

Yeah, no wonder he had a nervous tic. I was getting that way myself.

When I closed my eyes at night, I thought about those poor bitches, locked up, not knowing when the cunt who held the keys to their prison would return. Not knowing that he'd never return.

I thought about how hungry they must be. How cold. How fucking alone, and yeah, I ended up *not* sleeping.

I was a callous son of a bitch. By nature and nurture. You couldn't do what we did and have a big heart, but even the cold stones lodged in our chests were flopping like dying fish at what those women were going through.

Even so, I resented Steel's words. You made one fucking mistake as a teenager, and these bastards never let it drop.

"Could be a trap," Rex concurred, breaking into my irritation, rubbing his chin as he eyed up the way Steel was shuffling those damn cards.

"Doubt it. She was nervous as fuck. Paid Cody behind the bar to dope up her guards' drinks with vodka. Then was antsy all night waiting on them to get drunk. Plus..." I flinched as I dragged my pointer finger along the curve of my cheekbone. "She'd been beaten. All covered up. Well, too. Not the first time she's been hit with makeup skills that good."

Steel's jaw clenched. "She put herself at risk."

At his words—words that were a statement and not a question—I muttered, "Yeah. I think so."

"We can afford to send out a couple of brothers to check this shit out," Rex decided. "Even if she's blowing smoke up our asses, I'd rather be safe than sorry. Don't think I'd be able to fucking sleep at night if we didn't at least look."

Steel winced. "Yeah."

Rex clapped him on the back. "You're watching out for the MC, brother. That's what your job is."

"Feel like a cunt."

"We all do," I retorted, shrugging my shoulders uneasily. "We're all hyped up. Worrying about Giulia, worrying about Nyx worrying about Giulia, and wondering when he's about to break and go on the fucking rampage." I let a breath whistle out from between my teeth. "Then there are those women.

"Dunno about you, but I've slept like shit for the past week."

Rex dipped his chin. "Yeah. I'm going to go and tell Nyx."

"You know he's going to want to come along for the ride," Steel pointed out.

"Which means Giulia's coming too," I said dryly. "No way in fuck he's gonna take his eyes off her."

Rex grimaced. "Because taking her to some fucked up prison in the middle of nowhere is his idea of a date now. Jesus Christ." He scraped a hand over his head. "Last thing she needs to see is that."

"Bet she wants to go. She'll want to help. And she knows what it's like to be vulnerable to that fucker. Maybe it will help them?"

"Won't help her though, will it? And I have to think of Nyx."

Despite myself, I had to snicker. "You worry about him too much. He's not as vulnerable as you think he is."

"I don't think he's vulnerable," Rex denied instantly, but his glower told me I'd hit a nerve.

"Yeah, you do. He ain't," I countered. "Bro's got brass balls, and even if he was fucked up, Giulia's straightening him up some."

Steel's snickered. "How did you say that without busting your gut laughing? Last thing that bitch is gonna do is straighten a guy like Nyx out. If anything, she'd encourage him."

"Two psychopaths in sweet harmony," I joked, leaning back against the wall and digging my heel into the drywall as I did so. "Did you hear about what she did to her stepfather? Good thing Nyx's balls *are* brass. That's the only thing that'll keep them safe if she goes nuclear."

My words got my brothers smiling, just as I'd intended, then I reached forward, gripped Rex's shoulder, and urged, "Hustle, Prez. We need to get them girls out."

"If they're even there," Steel said.

"Don't be negative," I chided. "Let's hope they *are* there, then maybe we can sleep again."

Rex grunted but moved down the hall to Nyx's room, where he and Giulia were probably sleeping. He knocked and I heard a few thumps as Nyx made it to the door. When it slammed shut a few minutes later, and I heard more thumps, I knew he was getting ready.

Steel cut me a look. "You think this is true? Not BS?"

"Fuck knows. I just hope she wasn't lying."

"I'll slit her throat myself if she is. What kind of sicko—"

Before he could continue, I mumbled, "She's related to Luke Lancaster. A guy who rapes for fun? Let's hope being a psycho isn't a genetic trait in her family."

Steel huffed but shoved the deck of cards away in his jeans' pocket.

About twenty minutes later, Nyx and Giulia were on his hog, Steel was on his, and I was climbing onto the back of mine.

A quick glance at the clubhouse told me everyone was watching, even though this was supposed to be under wraps, and I mock saluted those peering at us from behind the curtains before I kick-started my bike into action.

The roar of the trio of hogs made my blood sing, and even though our end destination might be the definition of a nightmare in the flesh, I felt energy flood my veins as we began the roll down the driveway.

The gates opened the second the Prospect saw us, and we sped up, flying out of the compound like we were using winged chariots.

As the wind smashed me square in the face, I let out a holler, and wasn't surprised when a feminine version that matched my own came next.

I twisted around and saw Giulia was clinging to Nyx, but her hair was whipping around in the wind, her face was tilted to get it full frontal, and her eyes were closed as she gloried in the moment.

If I hadn't known that she came from biker stock, I had proof then and there. This shit was genetic. Passed down from generation to generation.

We were born to ride these beasts, just like our ancestors had lived on horseback. Some people were meant for the constraints of city living, of the rat race, then there were folks like us. Folks who lived on the fringes of society. Who led their lives the way they wanted, not the way the government did.

The three-hour journey was broken up by two breaks at a pitstop.

It was late already, none of us had been sleeping right anyway, and Giulia was sore after what that fucker had put her through.

We each downed a large cup of coffee which, of course, necessitated the next stop.

Fucking coffee.

Lancaster's little sister didn't realize how lucky she'd been coming across me. As Road Captain of the Satan's Sinners' MC, it was my fucking job to lead my brothers into chaos. She hadn't just caught the eye of any brother, she'd caught mine.

But then, looking like she did, I knew every fucker with a dick had seen her walk into the bar when she had.

No one could have failed to spot the elegance she exuded. Everything about her screamed money.

More than that, it screamed 'hands off,' which of course, was more of a challenge than anything else.

Especially to a fucker like me.

The coordinates to our end destination were on my phone as I led us to hell, but along the way I thought about her, thought about how she'd looked around Daytona like it was dog crap on her expensive heels. Then, I thought about the vulnerability in her eyes when I'd had to help her breathe through her panic.

At first, I just thought she was scared of me. Lots of country clubbers approached the MC, wanting to get laid. Wanting to get fucked hard by the local scum.

I'd thought she was one of them until Cody had shared her intentions with us, then I'd learned otherwise.

She'd entered my world with a purpose, one that saw me driving straight through the heart of New Jersey and close to the Pennsylvanian border.

The reason it was so far from the MC was because of a windy motherfucker of a road that brought us to the town itself and took a goddamn age to traverse.

Stewartsheim, according to Google anyway, was home to less than three hundred souls. I had to assume the women being held against their will weren't included in the census so, yeah, more like three hundred plus.

My mouth twisted into a grimace as we approached the township.

Lancaster's sister had given me fucking coordinates.

How the hell she knew them, I didn't know, but I wasn't about to look a gift horse in the mouth, especially when we went off road, driving onto a field, and approaching a body of water I had to assume was a reservoir, seeing as we were in the middle of the goddamn country, and I didn't know about any lakes in this part of the state.

The early morning sun made the body of water gleam and glitter where it hit, but it was still dark enough for me to see that, in the distance, there were rows of homes where the good folks of Stewartsheim lived, and who were slowly starting to wake up.

The coordinates took us past the township, past the reservoir—if that's what it was—and onto slightly higher ground that was surrounded by trees.

When we reached our destination, I didn't even fucking realize it.

The sun had started its rise, sure, but we were surrounded by a chaos of trees that kept us in the shadows.

Only when I braked to a halt did my brothers join me, and Nyx was the one who called out, "Where the fuck are we? Why did we stop?"

"These are the coordinates," I stated firmly, peering at the map and wondering if Siri had failed me. Again.

"Looks like that bitch was toying with us," Steel muttered.

I glared at him, aware he'd see my expression because of the glow from my phone.

He grunted at the sight, and I bit off, "We can't see for shit. There could be a fucking creepy ass cabin right in front of us and we wouldn't know it was there."

"We have our lights on," Steel retorted, as he folded his arms across his chest.

Fucker looked like he was settling in for a fight.

I opened my mouth to give him what he was asking for, then Giulia whispered, "Did you hear that?"

She sounded shaken, and I knew the difference.

She hadn't been around the clubhouse that long, but she was a weirdo who I quite appreciated.

Snarky, Giulia was usually a bitch, and had a wicked right hook. I actually liked that she'd managed to bust her stepfather's ballsack because with a fucker like Nyx in her bed, she'd need to be ready for anything.

Not that *he'd* hurt her, but living our life the way we did? Shit got real *and* weird, fast.

"What is it, babe?" Nyx rumbled, his voice low. His leathers squeaked as he twisted to face her, giving her all his attention.

The second he did, she released a sigh, like she could breathe or something because he was looking at her, *seeing* her. I wasn't sure why that would help, but it did.

Hell, it had helped Lancaster's sister this evening too.

Breathing with her, calming her down, it had felt oddly natural. But then, I'd done it often enough with my ma, helping her climb out of her panic-fogged stupor, for me to be at ease with it.

"I don't know," Giulia admitted. "It was like a cry."

"Probably the wind," Steel muttered, earning himself a glare from both me and Nyx as well this time.

"Why are you trying to be awkward?" I groused. "You want them found as much as we do."

He gritted his teeth. "'Course I fuckin' do."

"Then don't be so damn difficult." I turned my focus to Giulia once more. "I didn't hear anything. The bike's engine is still whistling in my ears."

"Mine too," she admitted, "and it was faint." She reached up, tugging slightly in a way that made me realize Nyx had somehow managed to grab a hold of both her hands. She ran the one he released over her face. "Maybe I'm losing my mind."

Nyx snorted. "No way, baby. You're not losing shit. I'll find you every fucking time. You hear me?"

Her lips curved in a dry smile, and she surprised me by raising their joined hands and brushing her mouth over his knuckles.

That small act of tenderness probably gained more of a reaction out of me and Steel than her getting naked would have.

Women didn't do shit like that around us, but Giulia had because, it figured, she wasn't like any of the women we usually had at the clubhouse.

And weirder still was that Nyx didn't mind.

He didn't pull back. Didn't pull away. Didn't even shoot us embarrassed looks.

Nyx loved her.

He actually fucking loved her.

I mean, I guessed it made sense. He'd given her his brand, she wore his patch. But still, I hadn't thought about love. Love wasn't a thing in this world of ours.

On edge at what I was witnessing, I kept quiet.

I didn't want to be on the end of Nyx's fist tonight, not when there might be some women who needed our help around here.

Last thing they needed was to see their saviors bruised and bloodied after getting into a stupid fistfight but I wanted to speak. Fuck, I wanted to ask questions.

How did it feel to be in love?

Was it weird?

Was it nice?

I'd never felt anything like that myself and I was curious, even if I probably shouldn't be.

Badass bikers didn't fall in love...*supposedly*.

Nyx had, though. He was the biggest, baddest motherfucker I knew.

Demons would cower before Nyx, that was how messed up he was.

The shit I'd seen him do to those sick fucks who messed with kids, I couldn't see Satan himself not feeling squeamish at what Nyx did in his spare time.

But he was in love.

Fucking love.

Giulia sighed, catching my attention once again, and I saw that their hands were lowered and she'd pressed her forehead to Nyx's arm.

Was she crying?

I cut Steel a look again, saw he was just as uneasy as me.

A noise whispered through the trees as I was about to clear my throat, trying to get things moving along.

It was quiet.

Like a shushing sound, but it was high-pitched too.

I tensed and so did my brothers, and my brother's woman, who scrambled off the bike at the noise.

Nyx had her back a second later.

"What was that?" I rasped, even as I started to climb off my bike too. I pulled off my helmet and hung it from the handlebars as I straightened up.

Steel, peering through the trees where only the faintest of light was bleeding through, said, "I heard it too."

"Well, if you heard it, then it must be real," I snarked at him, earning myself the bird he flipped my way.

I took another look around, sweeping my phone's flashlight in the area.

Steel, evidently doing the same, mumbled, "Some kind of truck has been here. SUV maybe. Something heavy."

I stared where his light was directed and saw what he was seeing and agreed, "SUV. I recognize those tires."

"Of course, you do," Giulia mocked.

Nyx tapped her leg. "Link runs the garage for a reason, babe."

My lips twisted. "Just 'cause I hate cages doesn't mean I don't know how to fix them."

I knew how to fix them too fucking well.

Meant most of our customers wouldn't be coming back as often as they should because I knew my craft.

Of course, I'd tried not to work at the garage.

When Rex had dumped the MC's new businesses on the council's shoulders, I'd hoped some other fucker would want to run it.

No dice.

I was stuck getting engine oil in my asscrack for the rest of my natural life.

"That bodes well though, doesn't it? If there are tracks that means someone's come here recently." The hope in Giulia's voice was painful to hear.

I sucked in a breath. "Could be anyone. Could be hunters."

To counter my words, there was that noise again.

I whipped around, my phone with me, trying to fucking see where that goddamn sound might be coming from.

"Never heard a bird sing like that before," Steel complained as he slowly turned, his gaze drifting along the tree line. "Something's here."

"If that isn't the creepiest thing you could have said," Giulia retorted, shuddering as she wrapped her arms around her waist. "This is like the setup for a horror movie."

Nyx snorted and hauled her into his side. "You're safe with us."

"Yeah," I teased. "Giulia, ain't you realized it yet? We're the boogeymen."

Her only response was to huff, which either meant she thought I was full of shit or she was agreeing. Never could tell with Nyx's bitch.

"We're going to have to go into the woods," Steel stated grimly, and I knew he was just as freaked as Giulia but he wouldn't say shit.

I'd have goaded the motherfucker for being a pussy but hell, it *was* creepy.

It reminded me of the opening scenes of a horror movie too.

When the director was setting shit up to get the audience in the mood.

Even the lighting wasn't on our side. It was bleak and there was a haze to the air.

Plus, knowing that some women might be held in captivity around here didn't exactly make the place fucking cheerful.

Grunting at my thoughts, which were goddamn stupid, I strode forward.

The crunching of grass beneath my feet was a giveaway—there was more crunching when my brothers and Giulia joined me.

Three more streams of light merged with mine as we pushed between the trees and began walking over the soil.

It was pretty peaceful in here, but there was a low mist that made it hard to see the ground.

Okay, so this place was beyond creepy as shit.

I'd admit it.

Even if it was only to myself.

As we walked, our feet making too much noise as we stomped through the forest, it was a miracle we heard that weird ass sound again, but we did.

And we all froze.

I thought about what it sounded like, and could only compare it to the clank of a wrench or something clanging against the body of a car.

Metal against metal.

A dull whine.

Ears pricking up, I peered through the mist, then groaned with relief when a shard of light from the sinking moon pierced the trees.

Giulia whispered, "Oh my God, over there."

I followed the direction where she pointed with her finger and grimaced at the sight of a shack.

Fifteen by fifteen, minimum.

As we processed its sudden appearance, we took off at a run.

The sound echoed again, and my belief that it was metal ringing against metal was reiterated as the dull, shrill whistle seemed to be on repeat.

My heart began to race with hope.

Someone who was being held captive, who'd managed to hear someone in the vicinity, who was trying to call for help—they'd make that kind of noise, wouldn't they?

I heard the click of a gun behind me and dug into the back of my jeans where I kept my weapon.

Knowing Nyx had armed himself made me want my gun in my paw too, and when I heard Steel's safety snick off, I knew we were all feeling the same vibe.

The same hope.

The same concern.

Especially as we slowed down the second we got to the shack.

It was made of wood, almost entirely, except for a window beside the door—four dirty glass panes held together by a cross, loaded with spiderwebs and filth.

There was guttering around the roof that quivered when a gust of wind whispered through the trees.

"Shit, did we bring anything with us? Food? Fucking clothes?"

Steel's remark had me jerking in surprise. I twisted around to glower at him. "You serious right now?"

"Yeah. If there are women in there, we need to help them."

"Yeah, by not shooting the shit," I ground out, even as I strode forward and pulled the door. It was, not surprisingly, locked. "There are space blankets in each of our saddlebags as well as water and protein bars," I informed him absentmindedly.

The door rattled and shook under my grip, the padlock old and rusty, but there was some wear around the hinges that told me it was used.

"When did you do that?"

"When you were taking a leak before we set off," I muttered. Twisting to face Nyx, I ordered, "Hold the light steady so I can shoot off the padlock."

The second the stream of his flashlight hit it, I angled myself so it wouldn't ricochet into my damn face and shot it off.

That clanging sound appeared again, confirming that someone was behind it.

Someone in the fucking shack that belonged in hell.

Breathing in sharply, I pulled open the door, and the second I did, the stench hit me.

Now, I was a hardened criminal.

I'd killed.

I'd watched Nyx torture fucking pedophiles.

I'd even helped torture them.

I would kill and kill again for my MC.

But the smell in the shack had me staggering back with my hand to my face to try to cover it.

"Holy fuck!" Nyx spat, and Steel's curse echoed at the same time.

I wasn't surprised when Giulia dashed off and the sounds of her puking soon followed.

That stench signified one thing only—death.

We were too late.

Too fucking late.

Then the clanging sound came again and fuck, I realized someone had to be alive in there.

Someone had been *living* with that goddamn stench.

The prospect of heading toward the smell made my stomach roil like I'd eaten ten ghost chili peppers, but step forward I did.

I tried to breathe through my mouth, tried not to inhale the scent, but it was impossible.

And then the humming started.

"Coffin flies," I muttered, the words coming out nasally.

"Sweet fuck, someone's down there with a corpse," Steel rasped.

His words shouldn't have been the catalyst, the stench and the flies should have been, but his statement kicked us in the ass.

As one, we stepped into the shack, peering around and seeing jack shit. We swept our lights over the ground, saw the cellar door, and rushed over.

The clanging sound came again, softer this time. Weaker. Like someone who'd either given up hope or who'd lost the strength to carry on.

Heart fucking melting, I scrambled to find the handle, but if the gloom outside was bad, in here it was worse. And with the stench making my eyes water and the flies fucking with my ears, it was a wonder I could do anything.

"Stand back," I roared, the second I found a smaller padlock in the bottom corner of the opening.

Giving whoever was down there a few seconds, I shot the lock off as I braced myself for what I was about to see.

But even as I prepared myself, even as I told myself to man the fuck up and deal with whatever chaos Lancaster had left behind, nothing could have prepared me for what I saw.

Nothing.

Seeing the shit Nyx could do to sick fucks was *nothing* in comparison to this.

It coated all five of my senses.

In comparison to the sight, the smell, the fucking *taste*—I could *taste* it.

The sheer evilness, the fucking horror of what I was witnessing drowned all five of them, making me falter for a few seconds as I tried and failed to process it.

Only seeing the girl slumped over, with some kind of pipe in her hand, twitch, jerked me into action.

As I staggered down the few steps into that pit of hell, I realized there were four cages down here. Four fucking cages I wouldn't have put a goddamn pit bull in.

Half the size of a single bed in both length and width, how the fuck the one out on the floor had escaped was beyond me.

"Go get the blankets and food, Giulia!"

Nyx's command had me jerking in surprise, and it had the women in this pit jolting too.

A woman, filthy, so filthy I didn't even see her eyes at first because she was covered in shit and piss—fucking shit and piss—moaned as she slumped onto her back.

My mouth twisted into a snarl as the desire to string Lancaster up by his balls, to eviscerate him, filled me.

I forced my thoughts away from violence and tried to focus on the women. One of them, at least, was dead. That smell, those flies? Someone had to be dead in here.

I flashed my light over the cages, cringing when I saw more fluids, more insects, more of everything no one ever wanted to see, and finding relief when I heard two sets of moans as the women reacted to the light.

Only one didn't flinch.

The four cages were lined up in a row.

The one to the far left, against the wall, didn't move, and when I trained the light on her, Steel doing the same, I saw—

My stomach roiled once again, and how I didn't puke, I'd never fucking know.

Staggering down the stairs, feeling dazed, I made it to the woman on the floor.

Hauling her up, I lifted her into my arms, wincing as she pretty much goddamn rattled in my hold. She was a bag of bones, and I passed her up to Steel who I knew would pass her to Nyx.

With her out of the way, I approached the cages. My boots had them flinching, and I whispered, "Luke Lancaster is dead. My brother's woman killed him. It was slow. She twisted the knife, made sure he *hurt*, but no amount of hurt is payment for this. My name is Link." I pointed to Steel. "He's Steel, and my brother upstairs is called Nyx, and his woman is Giulia. She's the one who ended that cunt's life."

"He's dead?"

The voice was softer than a whisper, and it was the spookiest shit I'd ever heard. Ghosts were louder than this poor creature.

"Yes. We're here to help."

A cough came from the cage beside the ghost. "Too late for Sarah. Almost too late for us."

"Too late for Sarah, but just in time for you. What's your name?" I asked, even as I stepped into the puddles of human waste and tried to find where the openings to the cages were.

"I'm Tatána," one woman replied, her voice stronger than the ghost's. "She's Alessa, and the one you carried out is Amara."

I hummed at her words, trying to split my attention as I sought a way out for them. It took me longer than I'd like, but there were tiny padlocks keeping them barred.

When Steel stepped forward, I cut him a look, saw he had something from only the fuck knew where, and he smashed it into the padlock.

On the brink of telling him that wouldn't work, it worked, and he handed it to me.

It was a brick.

A fucking brick.

The occupant jerked when I slammed into the metal, and maybe fortitude was on my side too, because within five slams, the padlock was broken and I could open the door.

I crouched down, then peered inside. "You're going to have to crawl out, honey. I can't get you out. It's too small for me."

It was too small for her too.

She was crouched on her side in a fetal position, but her legs were relaxed in a way that told me this was as far as she could stretch.

"Too tired," she mumbled.

"You're not too tired," I countered, my throat thickening with tears. Tears! Me. I hadn't cried at my momma's goddamn funeral, yet here I was, ready to bawl. "We just got here. You gotta help me help you."

I flickered a glance at Steel and saw he was chivvying the other girl out.

Grabbing her arm, he was half dragging her out of the cage, and although I wanted to shout at him, I knew these women were on the brink of death.

If they couldn't help themselves, we'd have to do the heavy lifting.

Wishing there was more fucking light in here so I could see what I was doing, I reached in, grunted when I touched something wet, and tried not to think about it.

Fuck.

Every moment of these past five minutes were going to stick with me for a lifetime, so there was no forgetting any of what was currently going down.

Shoving the thought aside, I grabbed something soft and frail, and started hustling the woman, Alessa, toward the opening.

She cried out in pain, and I understood, I did, but fuck, what choice did I have? I had to get her out of there.

Sweat beaded from every single pore as I strained to get her out. She wasn't struggling, but she was a dead weight, making the job ten times harder.

When I managed to maneuver a part of her out of the opening, I wanted to crow with delight, but she slumped, and suddenly, I knew what a deadweight truly felt like.

My heart in my throat, I shook my head, unable to believe we'd come so close only to fucking lose her.

Rage filled me, it burned me from the inside out, and though I was pretty strong anyway, a level of power I'd never tapped into hit me at that moment.

It helped me haul Alessa out of the tiny space, helped me drag her onto the filthy floor, and it helped me carry her out of that poisonous prison and into the outside world, where there was only the vague scent of death, rotting flesh, the pungency of a mass wave of insects, and human shit.

Giulia was there immediately, and I wasn't surprised when she retched, even as she held open the space blanket so I could wrap Alessa in it.

"I-I think she's dead," I bit off, even as I pressed the bundle to the ground.

"No. She just fainted," Giulia rasped, as she pressed a hand to Alessa's chest. "Feel. There's a slight vibration. She's breathing."

Hope swirled inside me. "She needs help."

Giulia nodded, but after she licked her lips, she whispered, "But how?"

These women needed medical attention, but I knew why Giulia was at a loss.

If we got involved, somehow the cops would make it so that we were the ones who'd abducted the women.

They'd squirrel into our lives, into our world, ruining it because they could Capone us—get us on a charge that had nothing to do with our business to shut down our operation and jail us, even if we'd done nothing wrong to these women.

"Can you drop us off somewhere?"

I jerked in surprise at the ghost's voice. It was a gentle susurration of sound that whispered along my ears, filling me with relief that she was awake again.

"You're too weak to move. You need help. A lot of it."

The ghost's laugh was eerie. "You'd be surprised what we can do. We've survived this far."

Gutturally, I responded, "I know you have. You're warriors, but now's the time to heal. You've done the fighting, now you need to rest."

"I know your MC. I heard of them when I was working over in Newark." She smiled, her brutally thin lips pulling taut against her jaw.

That smile told me she knew something about us, something she probably shouldn't know.

I twisted around so I could look at her, and when her eyes caught mine, there was a stillness there that, oddly enough, calmed me.

Whatever had happened to her in that pit, and it didn't take much fucking guessing, she knew that sometimes, self-confessed sinners weren't all in possession of midnight souls.

"I have a burner phone," Nyx inserted from his crouched position at Amara's side. "We could place you somewhere and you could make the call for help."

Steel disagreed, "No. We need to keep this shit under wraps. Giulia's already in enough shit because of that Lancaster cunt.

"Last thing we need is to have the cops sniffing around us over this. You know as well as I do that they'll pin this shit on us." He sucked in a breath, one that sounded oddly shallow. "We need to bring Stone in."

My eyes widened at that. "Fuck me, has the world just come to an end?"

He scowled at me. "What?"

"You heard me. Thought the only time you'd even fucking breathe her name was if Bruce Willis was stuck on a meteorite above us." I peered up at the sky. "Where's Aerosmith? They gonna burst into song?"

He flipped me the bird. "Fuck you."

I just shrugged. "Too many ladies want to fuck me for me to waste my fine self on my fist."

A soft snort escaped the ghost, and I peered down at her and grinned. Maybe now wasn't the moment for a conversation about classic movies—and fuck yeah, I considered *Armageddon* a golden oldie classic—and maybe I shouldn't be joking when these women had been laying in their own shit for only fuck knew how long, but Christ, that smile on the ghost's face? I knew Steel was right.

Stone could help.

If she'd agree to come to the clubhouse, that is. We all knew Steel and Stone hadn't parted ways as friends.

He slipped his phone out of his back pocket. The screen lit up and he put in the code—don't know why he bothered. Everyone knew he used Marilyn Monroe's birthday for all his fucking passwords—and started scrolling through his contacts.

"You don't have to do this, brother," Nyx rumbled, sounding, as usual, dark as fuck.

"Yeah. I do. For the MC."

I pulled a face at that, because even if it was best for us, I wasn't sure if it was best for the women.

"Stone can't do all that a hospital can for them," I pointed out softly, and I wasn't even joking when I said, "Save the sacrifice for another time, bro. These ladies need proper medical attention. They're starved, their bodies are—"

"Please. Don't take us to a hospital."

Ghost's words had me rearing back in surprise. If anything, I'd have thought she'd want to go back to civilization. "Huh?" I asked, dumbfounded.

"Please." When she started shifting on the ground, moaning as she moved, I realized she was trying to sit up. "Don't take us to the hospital."

I considered myself a dumbass because, just that second, I heard the accent. "You're an illegal, aren't you?"

She sagged against the ground. "We all are."

"That changes things." Nyx cut Steel a look. "Get Stone on the line. I'll talk to her."

"Ain't no one gonna mention that it's fucking weird as shit you still have her number?" I questioned.

"I keep an eye on her," Steel rasped, even as he connected the call and put it on speaker.

"Have pigs started flying? Or has hell frozen over? As far as I know, that was the only time you said you'd talk to me again."

Steel's top lip snagged into a snarl, but he turned his face away at the sound of Stone's voice and left it to Nyx.

Never thought Nyx would be the rational one in a situation like this, but fuck, these were trying times.

"Stone, it's Nyx."

"Nyx?" Stone sounded confused. "Oh my God," she rasped. "Oh, God. I'll be right there! Don't you let that fucker die, do you hear me? I'll drag him back from hell if I fucking have to. Do you hear me, Nyx?" she screamed, making the ghost jolt on the ground in surprise.

"I hear you, honey," he replied, tone soothing as he shot me a wry look. "We'll keep him going until you get here."

"Good," she barked, then cut the call.

I blinked at Nyx before we both turned to Steel.

"She thinks I'm dying?" Steel growled. "And that's the only way she'll come back?"

"Look on the bright side, she doesn't want you to die."

He didn't appreciate my help because he glowered at me.

"At least she's coming to the compound."

"Because she thinks I'm dying," he reiterated.

"Some men would think that was a compliment," the ghost whispered, but again, I heard a sliver of amusement in her voice.

How the poor woman could find anything humorous about this fucking situation, I didn't know. But sweet fuck, I was just grateful she wasn't sobbing and was coherent.

"Stone always did know how to fucking insult me," Steel grated out.

"Not sure it's an insult. She doesn't want you to die, bro," I pointed out. "I mean, she wasn't all, 'let me roll up so I can spit on his grave.' She wants you to live. Ghost's right, that's pretty much as big of a compliment as someone can give to another person."

"If she's on her way, we need to be on ours too," Nyx stated, putting an end to the conversation with a firm tone.

Just because the dude was a sick motherfucker didn't mean he wasn't the bomb at being the Enforcer.

"They can't ride on the back of a bike," Giulia breathed weakly, and I cut her a look, unsurprised to see she was close by but had propped herself up against a tree.

This situation would traumatize *anyone*. But someone who'd only recently been traumatized herself? Fuck, it was a wonder she wasn't catatonic.

When Nyx glanced at her, I knew he saw that too and his face darkened in a way that, usually, he dedicated to the bastards he slaughtered. This one was only softened by the love in his eyes.

Yeah, that goddamn love again.

Giulia didn't burn to nothing at the sight.

Didn't disappear into a puddle of ash at the foot of the tree.

If anything, she shot him a shaky look and rasped, "I'm okay."

"You're not," he instantly countered.

"I'll *be* okay then." She blew out a breath. "We need transport. The MC is too far away to help."

"It's three hours away, Giulia. Not Mars."

"Look at them and tell me we have time to fuck around?"

Ghost cleared her throat. "If we could just eat something, maybe that would help?"

Steel winced. "Don't you need, like, fluids or something?"

"You got sports drinks in those Mary Poppins bags of yours? Or just water?" Nyx questioned.

"Just water," I hissed under my breath. "Dumb of me to forget."

"Water would still be nice," the ghost whispered.

I flinched, because of course it fucking would be.

"I'll go get the bags."

"Nyx brought them already," Giulia murmured, as she began to riffle through the saddlebags that were at her side. Bags I'd only just seen.

In my defense, it was still gloomy as fuck around here. Couldn't see for shit, and trust me, there was enough shit around this place for that to be true.

The dawn light was too weak to make that much of a difference on the forest, and it was a reminder that even though I felt like I'd aged a good two years since I'd first entered these woods, it had probably only been sixty minutes from start to finish.

Sixty minutes from hell, and fuck, if a Satan's Sinner said that, he meant it.

THREE

LINK

IT TOOK four hours to get shit sorted.

A quick Google search told us there was a rental place a thirty-minute drive away, and Nyx and Giulia took off to pick up a van and a fuck ton of water and sports drinks from the nearby Walmart.

I didn't want to know what Giulia had to do to help the women, but giving them some privacy to do it had been hard enough.

There'd been cries of pain, moans of discomfort, and each and every time I heard their hurt, I wanted to grind Lancaster's dick into dust.

That my violence would never be able to come to fruition pissed me off all the more.

I was glad the fucker was dead, but you could only die once, and that bastard? He needed to die a thousand times.

With our backs to the women as they cleaned up using the baby wipes Giulia had also brought with her, I wasn't entirely sure how they thought they could scrape off what appeared to be weeks' worth of grime with some wipes.

I mean, baby wipes were good, but *that* good?

Hell, I wasn't even sure if a good old soak would get the crap off their skin.

But, try they had, and though they didn't look *or* smell much better when Giulia came to us to let us know they were done, the women appeared a bit perkier, and by perky, I meant they didn't look like they were going to die on us.

Which, considering we were leaving Sarah behind until we could return with the appropriate gear to bury her, was too apt.

Death was on the horizon if we didn't make it home and fast.

Amara was the weakest, and I figured that was because she'd expended the most effort by escaping her cage—I wasn't even sure how she'd done that, but I was grateful she had.

Only that clanging noise she'd been making had given us a clue as to their location. She'd made all the difference in our search.

Ghost was weak too, but she had a smile on her face which I didn't particularly understand, but fuck, if she could find something to smile about then I was glad for it.

She'd curled into me as I hauled her into my arms and sighed when I walked her through the forest.

"We're going to be okay," she'd told me, and I really fucking hoped she was right.

"'Course you are," I'd replied gruffly.

"No. I mean it. We'll be okay. Now that we're out of that place... we've survived worse."

Worse?

Sweet fuck.

I couldn't have this conversation.

Couldn't. Have. It.

But the ghost went on, killing me softly with every spoken word.

Telling me about the ship that had brought her over from Europe, followed by a truck ride where they hadn't seen the light of day for eighty hours.

Holy fuck.

What these women had been through had me wanting to scream.

Then, something occurred to me. "He didn't kidnap you, did he?"

Ghost rocked her head on my shoulder. "He bought us."

Fuck.

I blew out a breath as my brain started rattling around inside my skull. I couldn't focus on that, couldn't focus on anything other than getting them back to the clubhouse where Stone could sort them out.

She'd bitch about it at first, but she was one of us, knew the score, and knew how shit worked so she'd help. Even if that involved her cursing us to hell as she went about her business.

I could deal with that, I could, mostly. I just wanted the women to get help. I couldn't imagine what they'd been through, couldn't begin to understand how someone could imprison them the way they had.

"It's okay," the ghost soothed, making me flinch because if anyone needed soothing, it was her. Not me.

"No, it's not," I'd retorted, managing to control my tone enough not to bite at her.

I wasn't feeling soft and gentle, wasn't feeling tender and easy. None of those were my usual state of play, but I had to be all four of them because Ghost and the other women deserved no less.

"It is," she tried again.

"Ghost, it's the exact opposite of okay."

She tilted her head to the side. "My name isn't Ghost."

"You whisper like one," I countered, like it made total sense and maybe it did to her because she snickered.

"I like this name."

"You do?" My lips curved despite themselves. "I aim to please."

She snorted. "This I doubt."

"Then you'd be wrong. Got the best rep in the MC," I boasted, but I wasn't really. I didn't give a fuck about rep, didn't give a shit about what the club bunnies thought about me. I liked what I liked, took what I needed, simple.

But if it made Ghost laugh?

Yeah, I'd talk smack all damn day.

"Will we cause much trouble for you?"

My brow puckered at that. "Don't worry about that. Just worry about getting better."

"A dead body will cause *more* trouble," she muttered in that soft voice of hers, a tone so quiet that it made me strain my ears to hear it.

"I didn't say that," I chided, even if she was right.

"You didn't need to. It's true. But I know that isn't why you're helping. I didn't mean it that way."

"If we wanted you dead, we'd work to that end. We want you to live, Ghost. Didn't come all the way to the border just to stick our thumbs up our asses and gawk at you."

"That sounds uncomfortable."

My lips twitched and I was on the brink of making a joke about how she'd be surprised, but if anyone knew what it meant to be uncomfortable, it was her.

Inside, I wriggled.

I knew that sounded weird.

A thirty-plus-year-old guy fucking wriggling? But I was internalizing my fidgeting because I couldn't do shit about it at the moment.

I was used to wanting to fidget on my bike, so I forced it inside, just like I did now.

I focused on that and split it with getting us back to the van Giulia and Nyx had rented.

The vehicle was a big one with three rows of seating where we each placed one of the women.

We'd probably have to set fire to the damn thing and lose our deposit because there was no way the upholstery wasn't ruined after this trip, but that was neither here nor there.

Storm, our VP, was good with shit like that, so he'd be the one to dispose of the vehicle when the time came.

Giulia handed them all something, and I saw they were bags of trail mix and a large bottle of sports drink.

When she passed them bottles of pills next, I wanted to wince at the amount of pain they had to be in, but I took a step back and muttered, "Giulia, drive safe."

"Of course." She sniffed. "I'm a good driver."

Nyx chucked her under the chin. "Gonna be hard with that smell. They're gonna moan and cry and... It ain't gonna be easy," he finished, tone heavy.

"I could have been one of them. If he'd managed to get me out of the bar, if he'd managed to get me into his car, only fuck knows where he'd have taken me, what he'd have done." Her chin tilted impossibly higher. "I'm good. We need to get going."

She reached up on tiptoe and kissed him real fast before she spun around and headed for the driver's seat.

Without waiting on us, she began the slow reverse down the rough track and I had to admit, she did a pretty good job of getting them out of there.

Nyx, his body tense as he stared at his woman in the driver's seat, grumbled, "Fucking hate cages."

I smiled. "You just hate that she's riding in one."

"Should be riding bitch on the back of my hog."

I clapped my hand on his back, amused at his grouchy tone despite the situation. "You gonna piss on her and mark your territory? I wanna be there to watch you do it because she'll fuck you up, brother."

He shot me a scowl. "What does that have to do with me hating that she's not riding back with me?"

"Because you're gonna blow your wad with her if you try and hold on too tight."

Nyx growled under his breath. "Do I have to remind you what she's just been through? And what she's currently doing as she transports more of her attacker's victims across the goddamn state?"

"The woman kicked a guy hard enough to rupture his fucking balls, dude. She attacked Luke *back*. She came out the victor. You forget that and you'll underestimate her." I shrugged. "It's no skin off my nose if you suffocate her to death by trying to keep her safe, but—"

Nyx raised a hand. "Enough, Link. I'm not in the mood."

I shrugged again, watching as he took off for his bike, climbed astride the beast, and set off.

The second he did, and the second Giulia saw him, she drove off from where she'd been idling, waiting on us to haul ass.

"Why you needling him?"

Shooting Steel a look, I muttered, "I'm opening his eyes."

"Why? It ain't like this is a new piece to Nyx's puzzle. He's always been protective of bitches. What he saw in that cabin must have been like a knife to the fucking gut for him."

"Giulia's good for him," I replied softly. "I don't want him to fuck it up by being too Nyx."

"Maybe that's what she likes. She's glued to him enough. Fuck, they're both like squids."

My eyes widened at that. "What the fuck does that mean?"

"Means they've got their tentacles all over another."

That had my nose crinkling. "That's fucking gross."

"True though. They're sucked onto one another. Probably for life knowing Nyx. He ain't one to get serious unless it was hardcore shit."

Because I agreed with him, well, not the fucking tentacle stuff, I just said, "We need to get you a different porn site. You're watching too much hentai."

He flipped me the bird. "Fuck off. Let's get going."

I smiled even as I climbed onto my bike. Nyx and Giulia hadn't waited on us, so it was definitely time to catch up.

Somehow, we had to right the wrongs that had occurred in these woods, a forest that, with the light of morning, was a beautiful, if still eerie place.

It was hard to think of all the monstrosities that had gone down here, harder still to think of the dead woman back in that cabin.

I felt as big of a bastard as Lancaster for leaving her there, in that fucking place, but I didn't have much of an alternative.

It was amateur to bury a body in the woods, and disposing of her remains...I exhaled.

No.

She deserved a sweeter ending than what she was going to get.

As I kick-started my hog, I thought about how I could make that happen and began the journey home. A journey that Sarah would never make again.

FOUR

STONE

WHEN I SAW him roll through the compound gates, that same fucking bright orange hog between his thighs, same old hair whipping all over the goddamn place from under his helmet, I wanted to kick him off the bike.

I wanted to do something, *anything*, to make him hurt as badly as he'd made me hurt.

He'd let me think he was ill.

Sure, Nyx had been behind that, the schmuck, but Steel could have texted me, let me know that he was okay.

Instead, I'd spent two hours racing to West Orange, trying to get here in time to...

What?

Say goodbye? When we should never have said that in the first place?

I gritted my teeth as I stacked my hands on my hips. At the sight, Rex muttered, "Sweet fuck."

I knew why.

I was named after the Rolling Stones—yeah, my mom's imagination was shit—but everyone knew I went stone-cold when I was pissed.

When I started showing emotion, they knew to run for the hills.

I'd been raised with these fuckers. I knew that if Steel had been injured, it would have been doing something the government considered illegal, and I knew that no matter how fast I raced to get to him, it wouldn't be fast enough.

People bled out from gunshot and knife wounds fast.

Nyx had called at the end of a busy shift in the ER. I'd already been hyped up from losing a kid on my watch; a girl who'd come in after a simple car crash. So simple, she hadn't presented anything except for a headache.

A fucking headache.

The department head wanted to send her home, give her some Children's Tylenol but I'd had a bad vibe. My gut had told me something was wrong, but Hyde's reach was too strong.

I'd forged his fucking signature to get her a CAT scan, but it had been too late.

She'd died.

She'd fucking died while I bullshitted around with the bureaucracy that was fundamental in a hospital.

I was amped up, ready for a fight, and the sight of Steel, someone I fucking *loved*, who I'd thought was dying, riding back without a care in the world had me wanting to kick him in the balls.

Badly.

I gritted my teeth when he pulled up, barely even noticing the cage that was braking to a halt alongside him.

"You're not dead," I told him stonily—that was my rep, after all.

He tugged off his helmet. "Disappointed?"

My top lip curled, then Nyx stepped into my line of sight looking, as per fucking usual, too handsome for the good of anyone with ovaries.

"You lied to me," I snapped.

"No, you didn't let me get a word in edgewise. You assumed because I had Steel's phone that—"

"A solid assumption," I barked.

"If you'd let me fucking finish," he growled. "Then, and *now*, I'd have explained."

"Go on then. Explain why you let me think our brother was fucking dead."

He gritted his teeth. "He ain't your brother."

Wasn't that the goddamn truth.

"I grew up in this place too, Nyx. I don't have to have a prick to be a part of this fucked up family."

That had him tilting his chin down in anger. "Family don't leave family behind."

Stung, my eyes flared wide.

He'd hurt me. I was used to that.

But hurting me only pissed me off and I snarled, "Some of us want to do shit with our lives. Rex is paying for my fucking education. What would you have me do?

"Waste my fucking calling as I spread my legs for the MC? Or have me do something I'm good at and learn how to be the best I can be?"

"Nyx?"

The voice sounded soft, but there was steel behind it.

He turned to look at the woman who'd just rounded the fender of the vehicle I'd only just registered. "Giulia, not—"

"Nyx, you take that back."

I jerked in surprise at her tone then, when I studied her some more, I frowned. In my ear, Rex muttered, "She's Lizzie Fontaine and Dog's kid."

My mouth rounded into an O as I processed that. She looked like Lizzie. Crazily so.

Apparently had her temper too.

"She's Nyx's Old Lady, babe." Rex punctuated his quiet update with a grunt.

"She left us behind," Nyx spouted stubbornly.

"What did she leave behind? She's here now, isn't she? You called her and she came. Immediately. Isn't that what family does?"

Nyx's mouth turned stubborn. "You don't know every detail."

"I'm sure I don't, but if Stone's good at what she does and wants to be more, then what's wrong with that?"

"I like you," I declared, uncaring that that had most of the guys snickering around me. "You don't let him get away with any shit and he needs that. They all fucking do."

She tipped her chin to the side. "I didn't remember you until I got out of the car. You always were fixing shit."

"Always plenty to fix around this place." I studied her, then muttered, "What the hell are you doing riding in a cage with these three bozos?"

Her lips twitched. "Got three women who need your help."

"Why?" I frowned, trying to peer into the windows of the van. "What's gone down with them?"

She blew out a breath and it didn't escape me that Rex didn't step up to try to explain shit, nor did any of the other brothers gathered around me.

I knew them as well as I knew my own flesh and blood, but each of them granted Giulia a level of respect I didn't understand.

Normally, that came with blood. The shedding thereof. Especially of an enemy.

That she was Dog's daughter and Nyx's woman told me she wasn't as soft as she appeared, but murder?

I didn't think so.

"I was attacked at Daytona."

Because nothing surprised me where the club was concerned, I merely concentrated on something I didn't comprehend.

"The racing place?" I questioned with a scowl.

"No. Our new bar," Rex muttered, and when I turned to look at him, I saw he was leaning against the railing, arms folded across his chest as he glowered down at his boots.

"A customer tried to rape me but I—" She exhaled loudly, made fists with her hands, and punching the air at her sides, ground out, "Long story short, we found out this was a regular thing of his. At least, hurting women I mean.

"We learned he was holding some women captive and with him dead—"

"You killed him?" I squawked, stunned despite myself.

Her cheeks flushed, and she shot Nyx a welcome glance as he approached and came to stand at her side.

The move was defensive, possessive, protective, *and* assertive. In fact, I wasn't sure how Nyx managed to channel all four at once, but it was better than a burglar alarm.

It declared to one and all, especially one—me—to back the fuck off.

"Yeah. Anyway, we've been hunting the women ever since. He's dead." She shrugged. "If he couldn't care for them, then who could?"

My jaw worked for a second as I bit out, "You found them?"

"There were four. One was dead." Link whistled, drawing my attention his way, and because he was perennially cheerful, the somberness in his eyes blew my fucking mind. "Never seen anything like it. Ever."

"There a reason you didn't take them to the ER?"

"They're illegals. One of them begged us not to take them to a hospital."

At her explanation, I reached up and pinched the bridge of my nose, then I squeezed it harder when Link stated, "He bought them. Bought them. Like they were fucking animals or something."

I knew the MC was into many things, but trafficking humans had never been our bag. I was glad for that because, if they had, I'd have reported them to the cops.

Family or not.

And if that made me a treacherous bitch, then so be it.

The ER was where I wanted to center my future, and it was, in its own way, a front line. I was used to the trauma because of this life right here.

A life where random fuckery happened every day, and you had to take it on the chin or be steamrolled over and flattened like a pancake.

"They were in cages," Nyx said gruffly, his arm coming around to embrace Giulia, who bit her lip as she stared at me. "Living in their shit and piss. The dead girl..." He sucked in a breath. "She was in a cage, along with two of the others."

If what he'd seen had the power to make Nyx turn green, I knew it was fucked up.

Fucked up enough that maybe even I wouldn't be able to handle what was coming my way.

That steam roller I'd mentioned before?

Well, maybe it had turned into a freight train and I was already halfway under it.

Swallowing down my nerves, I knew I had to get a handle on things. Fast. "Let's get them somewhere warm."

"You're going to help?"

I turned to Rex. "Was that ever in question?"

He'd believed in me, had funded my career from the very start. I owed him and the MC everything. But I wasn't doing this for *that*.

Whether it was in an ER or in one of the bunkrooms on the compound, I was born for this. Born to heal.

I breathed in deeply and took a step toward the vehicle. As I moved, headed down to the driveway, Steel grabbed my arm.

He stared at me, forced me to look at him by not letting go of me, and when he knew he had my attention, insisted grimly, "It's bad, Stone. There were rats."

My jaw tensed. "We're going to need gear. A lot of it."

"Get me a list and I'll get you what you need."

That was from Rex.

"You got this?"

Steel's question had me tipping my chin up in defiance.

I stared at him, at that beautiful goddamn face, that gorgeous hair, lips I longed to kiss, eyes I wanted to stare into until the day I died...

Instead of telling him I loved him, instead of telling him I missed him, I spat, "When haven't I been good at cleaning up the MC's messes?"

His mouth tightened but he let me go, and that was exactly what I did and didn't want.

Fuck.

FIVE

LILY

WITH A BORED YAWN, I leaned back into my seat, even going so far as to tip my head against the side of the armchair as I overlooked the situation.

Maybe it was cold of me not to give a fuck, but as Paul and Alix were raked over the coals by my father for getting drunk on the job, I fought hard not to smirk.

"We're only fortunate that my daughter is a good girl and that your dereliction of duty caused no harm in the long run." Daddy dearest snarled, "But there's no way I can allow you to continue with your position—"

I'd known that was coming, and even though I didn't have much pull with my father who, whether I was a good girl or not, usually ignored me, I muttered, "As you said, Father, I know my place. There was no damage done and it was a one-time situation.

"We're all reeling from Luke's death. His loss has hit the entire household hard."

My father froze at that, twisting around to pin me in place with his glare. He was a handsome man, as had been his son. They both shared the thick golden hair that, even at fifty-six, hadn't disappeared with the ravages of time.

He was lined because he didn't believe in Botox or plastic surgery—for himself, but his mistresses were all like blow-up dolls—but he was strong and slim, and his tailored clothes made him look a good ten years younger than his actual age.

His eyes...we shared them.

A rich blue that was close to a glassy royal cerulean, and his mouth was mine too. Full and pouty—on me, it looked fine, but I'd seen pictures of him as a boy and his mouth had been effeminate.

Time had thinned his lips out, but it didn't age him, merely made him look sterner.

And stern was the way of it in the aftermath of Luke's passing. To which he was insistent in finding a way to get the poor woman Luke had attacked, charged with murder.

The lines at his brow, between his eyes, and bracketing his mouth were harder, and I knew he wasn't sleeping well.

His rampages could be heard from my end of the building, and I truly felt for his girlfriend, who had no choice but to deal with him in this mood.

For myself, I could escape.

Penelope... Not so much.

And yeah, my father was *that* guy.

He had a girlfriend, not a wife because he knew any sensible woman would marry him and divorce his ass the second she could and would sue for alimony that would keep her in luxury until the end of time.

He was also in possession of a stable, yup, a *stable* of mistresses that he had on some kind of weird schedule. I'd even met a few, and they were way too good for my father.

But that was money for you.

It talked.

Those eyes we shared were narrowed on me. "Is this true, gentlemen? Are you so grievous of my son's passing that you decided to make a toast in his honor?"

Paul and Alix were standing, awkward as hell, their hands crossed in front of their packages, in the middle of the office as my father cast judgment on them like King Solomon.

Surrounded by the opulence of this room, their cheap suits looked all the cheaper in contrast to the rich walnut paneling that lined the walls, the millions of dollars' worth of art, and the expensive furniture my father had as a standard.

This office had been replicated in each and every single one of his properties. Everything else could change, but this room could not.

I was tired of it because this was where he reprimanded us like a good patriarch did, and bored because I spent a lot of time here being slapped around for misdemeanors my father deemed grave enough to catch his attention.

At his question, however, Paul and Alix stopped shuffling around and straightened up.

I knew they were going to take the life raft I'd offered them, and I crossed my legs, jaded with it all as they fell on the harpoon of my offering.

My father, being the egocentric, selfish asshole that he was, ate it up. I wouldn't know until he made his final judgment if he was falling for it or not, but I had a feeling because I'd brought Luke into it, his golden boy, that things would be okay for my guards.

Sure, I didn't like them.

Sure, they were dicks.

And nope, I didn't mind getting them into shit, but it was a pain in the ass breaking in new security.

The last thing I wanted was new staff who wouldn't know me, wouldn't know how I rolled. If they were fired, so be it. If they weren't, then the next few weeks would be far easier on me.

"Luke's death was a tragedy, sir," Alix rasped, clearing his throat as he darted a look at his boss.

"That it was." My father's mouth tightened as he rubbed his chin. "I never expected the staff to take his passing so hard, but I should have realized how he touched everyone around him."

Ha.

Touched being the operative word.

Not one of the maids had been safe from Luke. Not a single one, and there hadn't been a damn thing I could do to rectify that.

No one was crying over my scum-sucking brother's passing, no one except for my scum-sucking father.

Said scum-sucker snapped his fingers. "Just this once, in Luke's memory, I'll let this slide, but my daughter's security is more imperative than ever.

"Luke was a young man, and I'll admit to being lax with him because he needed to sow his oats. But look where that laxness got him. And me," he tacked on grimly, his mouth turning down at the corners. "You're on a probation of sorts, and I'll be monitoring you. You may leave."

Paul muttered, "Thank you, sir."

Alix flashed me a grateful look, but he parroted his colleague, before they both turned on their heel and went to leave the office.

I didn't hold my breath, not until they'd made their exit, because my father liked to toy with people too.

Only when they'd departed in earnest did I accept that Donavan Lancaster had accepted my bullshit.

With the door clicking to a close, I turned to face him and saw he was studying me. "Luke's death has affected you greatly, child."

I didn't tense up even though I wanted to—fuck, the need to burst out laughing was a desperate one.

"Of course, it has. The house isn't the same without him in it."

Without his poison lacing the air, I could breathe easier.

Father sighed and rocked back in his desk chair. The plush cream leather surrounded by a gleaming walnut frame cosseted him as he comforted himself.

"That's true," he said grimly. "We'll make that slut pay, Lily. Don't you worry about that."

My stomach began to churn at his words because when my father wanted something, it wasn't often he didn't get it.

If anyone didn't deserve 'justice,' it was Luke.

Giulia Fontaine should get a Noble Peace Prize for slaying that monster.

He made demons look friendly, for fuck's sake.

In fact, if given the choice to be locked in a room with a demon or Luke, I'd take Satan's minion every damn time because that was how evil my brother was.

"I know you have everything in hand, Father," I told him softly, not by one word or change of expression revealing my utter hatred of him or my brother.

His eyes sparkled at that. "Such faith."

"Your will is indomitable," I told him, lacing the words with praise when all I truly felt was revulsion.

"That it is." He rubbed his chin as he looked at me, his gaze skating over today's spectacular makeup job. Then he stunned the life out of me. "I'm sorry I took my grief out on you yesterday."

Not once, not a single time in twenty-two years had he ever apologized.

For a second, I could do no more than gape at him. So accustomed to controlling my expression, to showing him only so much, I was at a loss until he started to scowl, evidently pissed that I wasn't rushing to accept his apology.

Quickly, I cleared my throat. "It's my fault, Father. I shouldn't have pushed you as I did."

"No, child, you shouldn't have. I shall endeavor to control my temper more. However Luke's passing is a tragedy we're all feeling. I must remember that, as I lost a son, you lost your brother."

"I miss him," I lied, my tone gentle enough to have Donavan swallowing thickly as he ate up my bullshit.

"I miss him as well."

Was it too soon? Did I dare to tread where angels would have feared?

Carefully, I whispered, "How are you going to make her pay, Father? How will you get justice for Luke?"

Donavan's eyes flashed with anger, but I sensed that it was aimed at Luke's killer and not me. And trust me, I knew when all that potent rage was aimed my way. I'd dealt with it for years and would deal with it until the time was right.

Until my name was in his will.

With Luke's death, I had to think that would be soon.

"You needn't worry—"

"I'm not worrying, Father. I wish to help if I can." *Help fuck things up.* "My influence in town has more reach than yours. Especially in society. What can I do?"

My father rocked forward, and I saw the gleam in his eyes, a gleam that was close to arousal. I knew what that looked like too.

God help me.

"She's being protected by that scum-sucking MC," —Funny how he used the same adjective I had to describe him and Luke for the MC— "so that's where I'm centering my attention. When I take them down, she'll be defenseless."

"How do you intend on doing that?"

"Pulling in markers with the mayor. Making sure the right pockets are full with my cash rather than theirs.

"That mini-mall of theirs has to be laundering money from their ill-gotten gains." He'd know. He had more illegal gains than anyone on this planet. "Investigations into their management leads me to believe they have links to the Five Points in Hell's Kitchen. I'm just not sure how.

"The sheriff is surprisingly deaf to my attempts to twist his arm for more information—"

I tipped my head to the side. "I know Joseph from the Country Club. I could speak with him. Tell him how much his aid in this matter would be useful."

He started to shake his head, then I smiled at him, schooling my features into one of entreaty.

He liked when I pleaded.

So I did.

I pleaded with him to let me help him take down an innocent woman.

As he studied me, he stopped shaking his head and queried, "You'd like to help?"

"Avenge my brother's death? Absolutely!" I told him, my tone strident.

His gaze turned thoughtful. "You're my only remaining child, Lily. You have to know what that means."

I looked him straight in the eye. "That I need to make you proud of me?"

Whatever he'd anticipated hearing from me, it wasn't that. I knew because he straightened in his seat and stated, "Indeed, I must learn to control my temper."

"And I must learn not to irritate you."

He liked that.

His smile revealed those shark-like teeth of his.

"Luke was..." He hesitated. "He was my son and I loved him, but he was headstrong. The business...he wasn't suited to it."

Damn straight he wasn't.

"If I can help, Father, I will."

He drummed his fingers against the desk. "Perhaps your major will finally come into use. I wasn't happy with you studying economics, but maybe everything happens for a reason."

I pressed my knees together and surged upward with an elegance that had been imbued in me thanks to two terms at a Swiss finishing school—yeah, they still existed, God help me—and strode over to his desk.

Standing where Paul and Alix had, I showed none of the weaknesses they did. The school hadn't taught me *that*, my father had.

I maintained eye contact as I declared, "All I've ever wanted is to make you proud, Father."

He blinked slowly. "You just did, Lily."

Smiling, I informed him, "I'll be away to Crosskeys. Perhaps Joseph will be there."

"Tread lightly, child. This requires the precision of a surgeon and not a butcher."

Apt considering that was probably how you could describe me and Luke. I was careful. Luke wasn't.

"I won't let you down."

He hummed. "I'm sure you won't."

But it wasn't a threat, more than anything, it felt hopeful.

Like he wanted to believe in me.

Like he wanted to think I was on his side.

With another smile, I turned on my heel and made my way toward the doors.

I knew he studied my ass, knew it and loathed him for it, and I only really breathed a sigh of relief once I was outside of his office and down the hall, because I knew he had cameras on those double doors.

When I made it to the landing and started down the curved staircase that swirled into the foyer with a flourish, I saw Alix standing there.

"You didn't have to do that," he said gratefully.

It was always useful to have someone's gratitude.

"You did nothing wrong. It's a trying time for everyone."

He didn't say anything, but from the flicker in his eyes, I knew he was more upset about the Chiefs winning the Superbowl than he was about my dick of a brother's death.

I patted him on the shoulder, even as I began moving down the hallway to the west wing of the property where my quarters were.

About twenty steps away, and without turning back, I called out, "I'll be going to Crosskeys within the hour, Paul."

"We'll be ready," he assured me.

I nodded and carried on toward my destination. Not even in here could I relax. Father had cameras in my bedroom too, probably my bathroom as well.

Pervert.

So I maintained my expression and retreated to the space I used as an office. Not that I had much work to do, in fact, I was nothing more than a doll who lived in here, one my father used as a puppet to hang off his arm when the appropriate time came for him to show the image of a family man to the world at large.

The space was simple with a glass desk, a white leather tubular chair that rocked when I took a seat, and a laptop that purred to life when I clicked my mouse.

After I checked my email, I signed out again and reached for my phone that I left beside my mouse. Aware my father could be watching, I tried to do everything in my power to avoid his suspicions.

Only when I'd behaved with what I considered normalcy, I lifted my phone and searched for the number the guy from the MC had given me.

He hadn't replied to the message I'd sent this morning, hadn't told me if they'd found the women Luke had been keeping prisoner there, and truth be told, I was glad because I wasn't sure if my father could access my phone remotely.

A thought that made my nerves churn and, rather than tap out what I wanted to say, I stared at my manicure for a few moments then, sucking in a breath, typed:

Me: *So glad we met.*

Maybe it was a weird way to start a conversation, but if my dad *was* monitoring my phone, then hopefully he wouldn't find this too disconcerting. I met a lot of people, after all. I dealt with a lot of people too.

Friends were encouraged.

Links to other important families were vital to keeping our peak place in society.

Him: *Excuse me?*

I wished I knew his name.

Mr. Green Eyes wasn't going to cut it.

The guy wasn't exactly James Bond.

If anything, with everything about him disreputable, from his cut and patches to that tousled mass of hair, he was more likely to be a villain in a Bond movie than a friend of 007.

Me: *It was a pleasure to meet you. I'd like to meet again.*

There was a pause then as, I figured, he was getting on the same page as me.

Him: *When? Where?*

I licked my lips, thrilled he understood. Or, at least, hoping he managed to discern my intent.

Me: *Crosskeys? Next thirty minutes?*

Him: *Okay.*

Releasing a relieved breath, I gnawed on my bottom lip for a little while, then closed my eyes and hoped this would work out.

I was living by a rule that had existed since the beginning of time.

The enemy of my enemy was my friend.

In this instance, the Satan's Sinners were my allies.

They just didn't know it yet.

SIX

LINK

TINK SCOWLED AT me when I shoved the plug into her ass and told her, "Keep it there until I get back."

"It's cold."

Amused, I informed her, "Your asshole will soon warm it up."

She huffed then rolled onto her front, displaying that fine tushy of hers for me to ogle. And fuck, if I didn't accept the invitation.

She was both small and curvy yet frail with it too, and she wasn't a bitch.

Today, I'd needed that.

We'd screwed but Tink was kind too, and when I'd fucked her to try to forget what I'd seen in the early hours of the morning, she hadn't minded.

She'd just spread her legs and let me find solace between them.

You couldn't fuck your way out of a bad place, but it was better than nothing in my opinion.

I slapped her perky ass cheek after I pulled on my jeans and tugged up the zipper. I had half a boner so it wasn't comfortable, but I'd done worse for the MC than go to some swank as fuck country club and talk to some rich bitch.

Especially when that rich bitch seemed to need to talk to us.

She'd given us those coordinates when we'd been fucked over trying to find any hint of land the Lancaster cunt might have owned, somewhere he could store humans like they were fucking hamsters, but we'd come up with nothing.

Lancaster's sister had been the key.

"Hurry back," Tink whined, and although I didn't like whiners, I just grinned at her because I knew she hated butt plugs and she knew I loved them.

That was the price of fucking me.

I was all about the ass.

Just thinking about it made my dick harden as I strolled out of my room and headed down to the office where I knew Rex would be.

I tapped once but didn't bother waiting on his shout—perk of being on the council—and the second I was inside, scanned it, saw Nyx and Stone were there, and muttered, "Heads up."

Tossing my phone at Rex, he caught it with a scowl, then eyed the text and frowned even harder.

"She wants to meet with you again?"

"You've learned to read at last," I joked, grinning when he flipped me the bird.

That was usually how I was greeted.

Most people got a wave hello, I got told to ram something up my ass.

Yum.

Better than any greeting I knew, that was for fucking sure.

"Lancaster's sister?" Nyx questioned, his brow puckering as he strode around the desk and leaned over Rex's chair to study the screen too.

Why a few text bubbles were causing such confusion, I wasn't sure, but from the way they were analyzing it, it was like they were trying to translate the Rosetta fucking stone.

"Yep. Just texted now. At a really inconvenient moment."

Stone snorted. "Always thinking with your dick, Link. Glad to see some things never change."

"See you've still got a *stone* up your ass, honey," I retorted with a beaming grin. "Wish I'd been the one to put it there. But then, you always were Steel's, weren't you?"

She hissed, her mouth tensing before she surprised the shit out of me by muttering, "Shame he's the only one who never figured that the fuck out."

I arched a brow at that, and so did Nyx and Rex.

If any two people were made for each other, it was Steel and Stone—even their names sounded like a folk band.

A match made in heaven.

Rex cleared his throat and instead of commenting on her bitter retort, asked, "You're going?"

"Told her I would. Just keeping you in the loop." I folded my arms across my chest and turned to Stone, none of the fire in my voice this time as I questioned, "How are things?"

"They could be worse," she admitted. "But they're not at death's door. With all the stuff Rex managed to get in—I want to know how you got that kind of shit so quickly too," she intoned darkly, shooting him a glance to which he just smirked. "Anyway, we kept them alive, but there are a lot of sores to deal with, infections…

"They need IVs with antibiotics, more shit than we have on hand honestly."

"I'll show you our stock," Rex told her softly.

"What stock?"

"Rex has turned into a Doomsdayer," I teased, laughing when Rex glared at me.

"I'm not a fucking Doomsdayer. I keep that shit because our world can turn upside down in an instant. Case in point right this fucking second."

Stone shoved her hands into her jeans pockets, which made the denim cupping her ass tighten delightfully.

Casting her tight butt a longing glance, I focused on her when Nyx, having returned to the other side of Rex's desk, elbowed me in the side.

I knew why.

She was Steel's.

She pretty much had a 'no entry' sign tatted on her pussy. Even if Steel hadn't staked a claim, not officially in the bylaws of the MC at any rate, that didn't mean a claim hadn't been made.

Fuck, it had been made when she was eight.

I rubbed a hand over my face as I thought back to then, thought back to those times when shit had been so much simpler and yet so fucking complicated too.

We hadn't had the weight of the MC's governing on our shoulders, but somehow that made things easier also.

We were in charge now, we answered to no one, and I was big enough to admit that I loved that Rex was the only one who could boss me around.

Rex narrowed his eyes and, utterly unapologetically, stated, "I get my gear here and there."

The answer just irked Stone all the more. "You mean you steal it?"

He shrugged. "I buy it. It's all above board."

"How can it be above board if you have vials of antibiotics?"

"Told you, he's a Doomsdayer," I muttered. "He's got all kinds of shit on hand, and we have contacts now. We're pretty much pharmaceutical reps."

Even though I knew she was pissed, Stone laughed at that. "Don't think pharma reps wear cuts and ride Harleys."

I grinned at her. "They don't know what they're missing out on."

"I'll bet," she said drolly. Blowing out a breath, she muttered, "Guess it's for the good in this case, but I want it known that I'm not happy about it, Rex."

"I'll take note of that, Stone."

"You should," she grumbled. "If I'm gonna be your resident doctor, then you should fucking listen to me."

Despite myself, my shoulders straightened at that. "You're gonna be our doc?"

"Why the hell do you think Rex has paid for my education?" Stone frowned at me. "I'll be working in West Orange the second I get my board certification and relicense to practice in New Jersey, but I'll be on hand for the MC."

Rex was a clever bastard. He'd done pretty much the same thing with Rachel Laker, the MC's attorney. She was homegrown too, her career funded by the Sinners.

We were criminals with a team of white-collar folk to save our asses when shit hit the fan.

"Huh," was all I said to that, because, in all honesty, I never imagined Stone would return home after completing her education.

There was a lot of water under the bridge for her here, and I'd thought she'd just pay Rex back when she was a rich as fuck doctor with her practice.

I reached over to hook my arm around her shoulder though and, squeezing her tight, groused, "You're a pain in my ass, Stone, but I'll be glad when you're back."

"Thanks, I think."

I bumped her side with mine, then asked, "You gonna get them girls right before you leave?"

She sighed. "They need constant attention, so I'm calling in a few favors. I have maybe ten days of vacation time to play with. I know it's not much, but it's all I can afford at this point in the year."

Rex nodded. "I get it, Stone. You'll do what you can and, in the interim, maybe show Giulia how to help? JoJo and Jingles too?"

She pulled a face. If Giulia had made her dislike of the sweetbutts known with broken noses and bald patches from hair-pulling, that was nothing compared to what Stone had done in her time.

"The first few days are critical, so I'm hoping to steer them out of the infections they're all dealing with. But, without more equipment on hand..." A puff of air escaped her. "I can only do so much."

Rex rocked back in his seat, his expression thoughtful. "Might be time for the MC to start thinking about saving up for some kind of private office for you. That's some costly shit so we'll need to prepare a budget."

Her brow puckered. "I haven't got my board certification yet."

"So? You will soon. Rex is right. Can't imagine that shit is cheap." I knocked her in the side again. "I can just see you being the physician in West Orange." I snickered. "Just think, all those fucking brats at school who used to think they could laugh at us...who's laughing when you roll up in a Beamer?"

Stone narrowed her eyes at me, then to Rex, growled, "You can't just change my career plan, Rex. I want to work in the ER. It's where my heart is."

"And we need you to have equipment we can use. Legit equipment," he retorted, waving a hand. "The local ER will be glad to have you working for them, right?"

Her growl deepened. "You're not going to listen to me, are you?" She didn't give him a chance to reply which, I figured, was smart because she already knew the answer.

Rex had invested in her for a reason, and that reason had just been handed down.

He winced when she stalked off, then pretty much thrust herself out the door before slamming it shut. "I thought I was starting to miss having her around the place."

"Famous last words," Nyx drawled. "She was the only bitch who could ever stand up to you."

"I don't know. Giulia's pretty good at that shit too," I mused.

Nyx's smirk was enough to make me chuckle. "Giulia's afraid of no one."

Maybe her own shadow at the moment, but I knew he was right.

Giulia had balls, that was for sure.

She was entitled to be shaky after what went down, but Nyx wasn't the only one who liked her attitude.

Moreover, I liked that she was good for my brother.

Nyx needed somebody strong at his side, someone who'd have his back too.

Giulia was all that and more.

Sure, they hadn't been together for long, but in our world, you lived hard and died young, so you knew how things worked before most people stopped scratching their asses long enough to get on with life.

"Why the fuck Steel let her go, I have zero idea," Rex muttered, his gaze still on the door like it was wobbling with the force of Stone's wrath.

"Because he doesn't know what to do with her," I said dryly. "She isn't an easy lay, she's his friend. Who he wants to fuck. While not wanting to settle down." Made sense to me.

"Having an Old Lady isn't too bad." Nyx leaned against the desk, settling in like we were going to gossip like old fucking bats at the hair salon.

"Not all Old Ladies are created equal," was all I said, cocking a brow at him, watching as he grimaced, knowing what I was saying without me having to say another word.

Our parents weren't exactly people to look up to, and though most of our moms had been Old Ladies, they'd also been sluts who'd cheated on our fathers.

Of course, our fathers had cheated on them too.

Sluts and manwhores. Was it any wonder Nyx had settled down when he was close to forty and with a woman who'd probably lop off his cock if he dared stray?

"Look, I ain't got time for this," I mumbled. "I need to get going."

"What do you think she wants?" Rex inquired, his focus back on me now.

"Dunno. Only one way to find out." I gave him a mock salute—of the one-fingered variety—shared it with Nyx who shook his head, then swaggered out.

Now I'd checked in with my Prez, I could hurry the fuck on.

The second I was on the back of my hog, even though nothing was right with my world, somehow, everything fucking was.

I could blot out the entire clusterfuck that was going down around me when the wind was smashing into my face as I went full throttle, hurtling down the highway to reach one of the swankiest country clubs in the area.

The Originals, the bastards who'd founded Satan's Sinners, must have had a real giggle when they'd broken ground on our compound.

We were smack in the middle of three of the finest elite clubs in the area, and we pissed them off more than they annoyed the shit out of us.

The sun was bleak today, almost like it was in mourning for what had happened over the course of last night, but the wind was bolstering and the threat of rain encouraged me to edge over the speed limit.

It was only because of the dreary sun that I saw a deputy hiding out behind a copse of trees five minutes away from town, so I slowed down to the legal limit, hiding my smirk as I drove past, smug that I'd caught them out in an attempt to hijack drivers.

Fucking pigs.

Huffing to myself, I bypassed the highway which was boring as fuck with nothing more than row after row of fields interspersed with housing estates, and finally made it onto the country club grounds.

They owned a good twenty acres of land, a big plot of that dedicated to a golf course, naturally.

There were all kinds of other amenities here, most of those I knew because I'd worked here as a snot-nosed kid, bussing tables to get some money together for my first bike.

I hated this place, hated everything it stood for. On the outside, it was beautiful, luxurious. Elite. But it was rotten at its core.

Founded on lies and deceit.

Just because something looked pretty on the outside didn't mean it wasn't fugly on the inside, and these places were all like that. Cesspits for cunts like the Lancaster dick to find shelter in.

But, because I knew the layout, I knew which places to avoid.

It was why I pulled up about forty feet away from the club, begrudgingly tucked my cut into my saddlebags, and made my way on foot.

Hated doing without my cut, but in these parts, it would only bring attention to me. That was the last thing I needed inside this place.

There was the front entrance which was patrolled by security, then there was a staff entrance that, though also manned, was easier to sneak through thanks to Fat Tony who'd been on guard here for twenty years and who, I felt sure, had spent at least fourteen years of those two decades sleeping on the job.

Slipping past him was a piece of cake, and the second I was through, I eyed the ass of the building.

It wasn't as fine as the front, but it was bustling with staff. Some carrying dishes, others with laundry. Some with cleaning equipment, others hauling their bags on the way home after a shift.

I slipped in among them, enjoying the commotion as I made my way over the tiled patio toward an area I knew was the kitchen.

When I was in there, I ducked into one of the side rooms that was used for storage, then I grabbed my cell from my pocket and tapped out, *I'm at the club. Where do we meet?*

Her: *The tennis courts. You know where they are?*

I didn't bother answering. The fact that she wanted to meet here was making me suspicious anyway.

What kind of brother would be able to access this place?

It was dumb fucking luck that I was the one who'd approached her last night, and it was more of the same that I knew my way around here.

This had the makings of a trap written all over it, but I knew some of the managers here so, if I got caught, I figured I could talk my way out of it.

They'd been bussing tables and doing all the shitty jobs at the same time as I had, but when I'd cut and run the second I could start prospecting for the MC, they'd made a career out of wiping rich men's asses.

Not fun.

Nope.

Even for me. Who loved a nice ass.

My lips quirked at the thought, but now I knew my destination, I strolled out, keeping to the staff halls which were a boring mixture of dark brown lino and smudged paint where laundry and cleaning carts had scraped against the gray walls.

Knowing the way to the front of the grounds was only accessible by crossing through the club itself, I peered out one of the service doors, saw the coast was clear in one of the themed TV rooms—this one was for the rich fuckers who liked to lose their money on horse racing—a fact I picked up on thanks to the ten TVs that displayed horse races from around the world, and walls that were loaded down with photos of horses with rosettes on their glossy necks and beaming, tiny pricks who'd rode them hard to win.

Though it was empty, and I was tempted to take a splash of their fine whisky and down it, I decided against it. I was already pushing my luck and, any moment, security could spot me. I'd probably end up in jail for the night if I was caught, but since the info Lancaster's sister had given us had proven useful, I was eager to know *why* she wanted to meet again.

She'd had to spike her guards' beers just to talk to a brother, so that told me there were eyes on her too. And I wasn't just talking about the pricks who couldn't handle mixing their drinks.

Darting outside, I headed for the tennis courts. They were clearly visible in the near distance, and the sound of a ball being volleyed and a machine popping out balls so some spineless rich prick could practice their backhand would have given me another clue if I'd gone blind in the past few minutes.

I was, however, grateful for the club's design. The building was on a higher level than the grounds, which meant the veranda I walked out onto gave me a good grip of the layout ahead.

It made spotting the woman who was sitting on a bench by the courts easy.

Now that I was out here, and aware I wasn't dressed for the part even if I had taken off my cut, I stuck to the hedges that bisected every activity in the grounds.

From the pool to the courts to the bowling green, all of it was surrounded by a natural fence.

Using them to my advantage, I moved fast and slipped onto the bench at the woman's side, jolting her because her focus had been on her phone.

Her eyes widened at the sight of me, and I had to admit, bleak sun or the mood lighting in the bar, she was hot.

I didn't want to say that, not when I knew what stock she'd come from, but sweet Jesus, she was a beautiful bitch.

Long, golden hair that curled around her throat and big, blue eyes that were shielded by the thickest fucking lashes I'd ever seen on a woman. None of those spidery things that looked like beetles had been glued on, but thick lashes she used to hide behind—I could see why.

Those blue eyes of hers were expressive. The color shifted with the light, morphing from navy to royal blue into a cerulean.

I had to wonder if each color corresponded to an emotion, but I wasn't here for girl talk, was I?

She had lips that were made for sucking cock, and her tits made me want to groan as I peered down the white blouse she wore before taking in her pencil skirt that showed off every curve she possessed.

Though she was hot as fuck, or hot enough to fuck depending on your inclination, she was dressed for a business meeting.

As far as I knew, most of the women who used Crosskeys weren't here on business. They were either topping up their tans or trying to stay thin so they could catch a rich husband or, if they'd already caught one, keep him interested in them.

A quick glance at her left hand told me she wasn't engaged or married, but when I lingered on the watch lining her wrist, I had to whistle.

Unable to stop myself, I grabbed her hand, tugged out her arm, then twisted it slightly so I could look at the piece.

"Unusual choice for a woman," I commented, not really looking at her, mostly just taking in the watch. "George Daniels Co-Axial Chronograph."

I let the grumpy sun flash over the face, which was a marvel.

Cream inlay with Roman numerals all around the rim, it had gold hour, minute, and second hands, and had two smaller dials at the bottom with a half-moon dial at the top.

It was history in the flesh, fabricated by a revolutionary in the field. "Beautiful."

I finally looked at her and saw she was amused. That had me scowling.

"You know your watches," was all she said.

"I do."

"My grandfather gave it to me." Her lips twisted into a smirk. "Luke was pissed. He wanted it."

I'd just bet he had.

She had over six hundred thousand sitting on her wrist, and her granddaddy had overlooked her brother to give a girl a dude's watch.

Her amusement faded as she stared at the watch which took up most of her wrist. "He wanted everything. That was his trouble."

"And because he's a Lancaster, he could afford to have most of everything anyway."

"Exactly." Her smile was tight. "What's your name?"

"Didn't you see it on my cut last night?"

"I was too nervous," she admitted. "Scared too."

"Why? Think we'd bite?" I bared my teeth at her, but the move had her frowning.

"Of course not. But things are finally on the right path. I didn't want to fuck it up."

Coming from a woman as sleek as this one, the curse word had me arching a brow.

I slouched back against the fancy bench that was made of filigree wrought iron which would probably imprint itself into my ass, and after kicking out my legs, crossing them at the ankle, and slipping my arm along the back of the bench, I muttered, "Name's Link."

"I'm Lily. Lily Lancaster."

"Your parents were fond of alliteration, weren't they?" When surprise lit her eyes, smugness hit me again. "I went to school too."

"Sorry." She blew out a breath. "Of course, you know what alliteration is."

I did. Not because of school, though, that had been BS.

Alex Trebeck had been one of the best teachers under my roof. Learned a lot of shit from him. Some of it random, some of it useful.

Shrugging, I asked, "You bring me here for a reason? Or just to show off that watch of yours?"

"Hardly," Lily replied, then she pursed her lips and stared down at her shoes.

Last night, before she'd been able to utter a word, she'd had a mini panic attack. I was used to dealing with them, and in fact, preferred to handle that than her staring at her shiny heels.

"I ain't got all day. The guards will notice me eventually—"

"I'm sorry I requested for you to meet me here. I'm on a tight leash. All my movements are monitored, but I wanted to talk to you."

"We got the women—"

Lily released a shaky breath. "Thank God."

Her hands moved to cover her face, but she wiped her eyes before rubbing her temples.

"One died."

Pain flashed across her features before she dipped her chin. "That's because it took me far too long to figure out how to talk to you."

I didn't trust the bitch, but she'd gone out of her way to help. I had to figure that deserved something.

"You did what you could."

"Wasn't enough, was it?" she snapped, surprising me when her eyes flashed with anger. Which, coincidentally, made them deepen into a dark navy.

"If it's any consolation, she'd been dead a while."

The coffin flies had been in full force and because I watched too much TV, I knew that meant she'd been dead for a week at least.

Then there were the rats...

Fuck, that was probably what was going to mess with my mind for-goddamn-ever.

Sucking in a sharp breath as the memory swamped me, I focused on the pristine lawns to my side, looked at the orderly tennis courts that belonged at Wimbledon, and the hedges around me that had probably been cut with a pair of fucking scissors.

It was hard to think that this had been Luke Lancaster's stomping grounds.

Harder still to correlate *this* with that shack in the woods.

"I should have killed him when I had the chance," Lily whispered.

Her profile was drawn, her features pale as she stared blankly ahead.

Her statement, however, drew my attention. "You wanted to kill him?" I kept my tone conversational in the vain hope that would make her talk.

"Of course. He was evil. Just like my father."

Unable to stop myself, I reached forward and tapped her chin.

When she turned to look at me, I reached up and gently touched her beneath her cheekbone, running the tip of my finger along the sharp jut.

"He do that to you?"

"Luke? No. That was Father." Her mouth tightened.

"You want him dead too?" I joked, then out of nowhere, my cock hardened when rage had color flushing her cheeks.

It wasn't aimed at me, but at her father, and she silently gave me her answer.

For a second, she breathed hard like she was trying to get a handle on her emotions.

I had to admit, the sounds she made went to my cock too. She was panting like she'd run a race, and all it made me think about was how she'd look when she was coming down from an orgasm.

That thought process wasn't helping my boner disappear, but the show she put on was better than a goddamn lap dance.

She'd gone from elegant and refined to gloriously alive and vibrant with emotion in a handful of seconds. Somehow, I knew that very few people got to see that side of her.

I wasn't sure why I'd been given that gift, but I knew it was exactly that.

"Why did you ask me to come here?" I questioned carefully, when my dick started to pound behind the cage of my fly. I needed to get shit on track before things derailed too far.

"The sheriff is on your side, but you might need to line his pockets some more. My father's reserves are not unlimited, but where Luke's concerned, I wouldn't be surprised if he put himself in fiscal peril to get justice for that bastard."

Her hatred of both men was evident, and because I knew what Lancaster Jr. had done, and as I also knew that Lancaster Sr. was willing to cover that shit up, it made me like her even more.

Which didn't help my boner.

Not in the least.

Nor did the words 'fiscal peril.'

That people actually talked like her blew my fucking mind.

"The mayor's in his pocket," she told me coolly, her attention reverting to the hedge opposite us when I didn't give her much of a response.

The hedge that separated two tennis courts which were empty wasn't exactly fascinating. Not enough to be worthy of her stare.

I let my gaze drift over her cheekbones, which had a gauntness to them that had me narrowing my eyes.

"Knew that," I admitted. "Glad to know the sheriff's still got our backs. What I'd like to know is why you're telling me this."

"Because the enemy of my enemy is my friend."

That had me quirking a brow at her. "Expect me to believe that? You're going against your daddy?"

"You've never met my father, have you?"

"Haven't had the misfortune, no."

"Lucky you." Her smile was cold. "Luke isn't the only person who's been murdered in my family."

My brows rose at that because, what with the enemy shit and talk of murder, this bitch was suddenly a lot more interesting than she had been.

"Who died?"

"My mom."

"Who killed her?"

"My father."

Tension filled me at the words she uttered, words that came with no intonation. She was talking like she was bitching about the weather or something. It kind of fucked with my head.

"Aren't you going to ask me why he isn't in jail?"

Now, there was a softness I understood, one I hated on her behalf.

"I don't need to. Your daddy's rich as fuck. That says it all. He's managing to twist this shit around with Giulia, making your rapist fucker of a brother look like the innocent party, like maybe my MC had some kind of bone to pick with him...

"If he can do that, then I know he can do anything."

"I want him dead." She whispered those words, softer than even Ghost had talked last night.

"We don't do murder for hire," I spat, just in case that was what she was thinking.

Her nostrils flared as she turned to glower at me. "Did I make that request?"

"No. Just making sure I get that out right here, right now. Especially considering this is how you fuckers tend to entrap people like me."

Her top lip cocked in a snarl. "Yeah, well, you've never met anyone like me, and I don't appreciate you thinking that I'm the same as any other—"

"Poor little rich girl?"

Outrage had her nostrils flaring. "You can say that when I just told you my father killed my mother?"

"Happens more often than it should. Doesn't mean that it ain't a fucking pity. It is. But a tragic past is something most of my brothers have in common with you.

"I ain't about to cut you slack just because you think you deserve it."

Her eyes were like slits as she stared at me, then, after a handful of minutes, she surprised me by smiling.

Honest to fuck smiling.

And shit, if the sun didn't peek out from behind the clouds at the same time.

If a guy like me could be *dazzled*, then that was me. Right there. Right then.

"I like that. Most people let me get away with shit because I'm a Lancaster—"

"Well, if you like that, I have more I can give you."

"I'm sure you can." She reached for her cell phone and stated, "I-I have access to funds."

"Good for you," I taunted.

Her eyes flashed, snapping back to anger once more. "I didn't mean it like that. I'm not like my father and Luke. I don't have access to the fortune outside of a credit card he gives me.

"But if Giulia needs financial aid for her legal team, I can figure out a way to help her."

For a second, I wasn't sure what to say about that, then I muttered, "She's part of the MC. We take care of our own."

"Well, the offer's there." Clearing her throat, she whispered, "I'm glad she killed Luke. He deserved to die."

"He deserved to die after he was tortured like he tortured those women," I said grimly, staring back at the tennis courts ahead of me so she didn't see the torment in my eyes, a torment that was founded in what I'd seen last night.

It was like a parallel universe in this place.

So fucking pretty and clean while being the stomping grounds of sick bastards like the Lancasters.

And yeah, I included the daughter in that statement, considering she wanted to kill her daddy too.

My lips twitched at that and I rubbed my hand across my jaw. "What are you waiting for?"

She frowned. "With regard to what?"

"Your father." I sniffed. "You waiting on him to change the will?"

"Of course. I won't do anything until that happens, and not because I'm a greedy, grasping piece of shit either. That money..." She clenched her teeth. "My mom was the rich one.

"He took *her* wealth and made it his own. He was a venture capitalist back in the day, and he married her for her money. In a divorce, he'd have been entitled to half the estate, but—"

"All is better than half." I plucked at my chin. "What you going to do with all those billions?"

"You talk like it will be easy to kill him." Lily narrowed her eyes at me.

"Won't it? You hate him. You want him dead. You're just waiting on the right moment."

She gnawed on her plump lip. "I wish it was that simple."

"It can be," I responded, well aware I was talking about murdering her father as easily as I would order a coffee from a diner.

But then, in my world, death ran hand in hand with life.

Sure, it did for every miserable human on this godforsaken planet, but for brothers in an MC, it was closer than for regular folk.

"I didn't bring you here to talk about that," she whispered a second later, and I saw the haunted shadows in her eyes, saw them and wondered if she'd somehow seen her father kill her mother.

"No, you brought me here to tell me your father had the mayor in his pocket."

"And that he's trying to get the sheriff on his side."

"Knew that already. It's why the mayor brought in some new detectives from across the county line." I grinned at her wide eyes. "This won't be our first rodeo, darlin'. Ain't the first time some rich fuck wants to pin something on us."

She gulped. "Do you know who the Five Points are?"

I stilled at that, interested at long last. "Do you?" I countered.

"No. I just know they're in Hell's Kitchen."

"Well, I can promise you that they're not a takeout place." I cracked my knuckles. "Why'd you bring them up anyway?"

"He's going to target them to get to you too."

She surged to her feet. When I realized she was going to just stalk off, I grabbed her hand and ordered, "Don't lose my number."

A scowl crossed her brow. "Why shouldn't I? I went to great lengths to get this information to you and what? It bores you?"

The shit about the Five Points didn't.

But she didn't have to know that.

"Don't be a stranger," was all I said.

"Why?" Her eyes were cold, like gemstones.

"We're friends, aren't we? Mutual enemies stay in touch, don't they?"

Her jaw clenched. "If you say so."

When she wrenched her wrist from my grip, the difficult bastard in me wanted to keep a tighter hold on her.

Sure, Tink was back at the compound, her ass stuffed full of a plug that I'd put in there, but Lily Lancaster was far more interesting.

"How come you wanted to meet here?"

She frowned. "It's my regular stomping ground and I told my father I'd be coming here in the hope of meeting the sheriff. I'm supposed to turn him to my father's side."

I whistled under my breath. "You fuck with the devil, baby doll, and don't be surprised when he fucks with you."

"He's already fucked with me," she said simply. "Many, many times, but enough is enough."

"I'm sure it is," I murmured, recognizing something in her words that made me want to kill that fucker of a father myself. "But softly catchee monkey."

"What does that mean?"

"It means that if you want the money and the man and don't want to go to jail, then you need to watch your step." I stared her square in the eye. "Or make sure someone has your back."

Her mouth gaped at that, and I didn't blame her.

I was going off script here.

Hell, the script didn't really exist, but I knew that any extensions of help had to be offered by Rex and Rex alone.

Even Storm, our VP, couldn't make offers like this. But I knew, just fucking knew, that this would help us.

Allied with the enemy?

United to take down someone who could champion their rapist scum and twist it around so that my brother's woman was fearing jail?

Yeah, I'd deal with the devil too...but then, I was one of Satan's Sinners.

We were buds, and I came from a family of other fuckers who'd sold our souls to the big guy downstairs a long while back.

"What are you saying?" she whispered.

"I'm saying that we need to talk on *my* stomping ground."

"I can't. My father watches my every move through my guards—they report to him at all times."

"Suppose getting them blistered last night didn't go down well."

"Yeah, you'd be right on that score." She tugged her bottom lip between her teeth, then drawled, "I'll see what I can do."

"Do that."

I let her go then and watched her walk away, that fine ass of hers squirming against the tight fabric of her skirt.

Tipping my head to the side, I let my gaze drop down to her long legs and feet that were shod in expensive heels.

Everything about her screamed class, and everything about me screamed the opposite.

"Lady and the tramp," I muttered under my breath, my lips curving into a wide grin, one that was loaded with anticipation.

There was only one issue with my plan.

I fucking hated spaghetti and meatballs.

SEVEN

KEIRA

"CYAN, please, I need you to focus and stop fidgeting."

My baby girl looked up at me, big green eyes that would melt the rest of the polar ice cap if given the chance.

Most of the time, she melted *me,* and she definitely melted her damn father. And that was the trouble.

She was a handful. Already higher than a lot of the percentiles in school, I knew, pretty soon, she'd be skipping grades.

Which was exactly what I didn't need or want for her.

I'd skipped two grades, and I'd been miserable ever since. It had put me in a bad place, being with older kids when I was so young and had, undoubtedly, shoved me into a life path I'd never anticipated.

I'd thought I'd become a nurse.

Instead, I'd gotten pregnant at nineteen and had tied myself to a jackass. A jackass named Storm.

"Mommy, it's okay. You don't need to do this."

My mouth tightened as I began re-pinning the dress I'd made for her a week ago for the school pageant and, because she was going through some kind of growth spurt, was about four inches too short now.

Because I was used to that, I'd made a long enough hem, but it was still a pain in the ass.

"I do need to, Cyan. No way I'm having them looking down on you."

Of course, that was a pointless endeavor.

They always would because she was a biker brat.

Hell, back when I'd been older than her, *I'd* looked down on the kids who attended Jackson High and were spawned by the Satan's Sinners.

Maybe because I'd been one of those judgmental bitches, I was scared all the more for my baby girl.

She handled it well, and I knew that was because she had more of her father in her than me.

Well, except for the smarts.

Storm was many things, but smart wasn't one of them.

The thought made me wince with guilt. Because, the shit, Storm, wasn't stupid, not outside of our relationship at any rate.

As I began plucking at the hem again, trying to figure out where to let it down to, a soft starfish hand touched my shoulder. "Momma, it's okay."

It wasn't.

It was the exact opposite.

I fucking hated people.

Hated. Them.

And kids?

I hated them even more.

She never complained, never said anything against anyone but damn, I knew what was what. Knew that on the days when she was quiet after school, it was when someone had insulted her.

Worse, her daddy.

Worse still, me.

I blew out a shaky breath as I looked up at her.

She had the glossiest brown hair, and those eyes of hers made a mockery out of her name. All the books I'd read, and somehow, the knowledge had bypassed me that a baby's eyes changed color a few weeks after birth.

Joke was on me, but still, Cyan suited her. It was beautiful, rich, and vibrant, just like her.

She had a pixie face, delicate features, and her bones were like a bird's. *That* she hadn't inherited from me, or Storm.

I wasn't sure why she was so skinny, didn't know why she kept on spurting upward, just knew that when she was a teenager, she was going to give Storm and me nightmares with boys.

"It's okay," she repeated, her voice far too mature for her years.

I didn't say anything. What could I say? Instead, I cupped my fingers around hers and murmured, "Love you, baby."

"I love you, Momma. Thank you for this dress. I really do look like a princess." Her grin told me how happy that made her. "I want a cut like Daddy's, then I can look like a real biker princess just like he calls me."

My lips curved, and I wished Storm was here to hear that. He'd fucking love that his girl wanted a cut.

"I'll talk to—" Before I could finish that sentence, a knock sounded on the door, then the lock jiggled.

The second that happened, I knew who was there and, warily, I got to my feet and headed out of the small kitchen toward the door.

The knock came louder this time, and I wasn't surprised when Storm growled, "What the fuck, Keira? Let me in, dammit."

I headed to the door and unlocked it, but left the latch firmly in place. The second I peered through the opening I'd made, I saw him scowling at me.

I arched a brow. "That how you think you're going to get in here?"

Keira O'Shea was many things, but a fool she wasn't.

Well, not anymore.

I'd been an idiot back in the day, but now, I knew what he was like, knew what was happening and had been happening in the time since we'd parted.

It was how the MC worked, how things rolled, and it was what I loathed about being Storm's Old Lady.

The reason we were here?

The sweetbutts.

The bastard had cheated on me one too many times, and because that was how shit worked in his world, he didn't seem to realize I wasn't cuffed to him.

If I wanted out, if I wanted away from his cheating ass, I could go. So I had.

I wasn't denying him access to his daughter. I wasn't moving out of the county. I'd just moved away from the house we'd shared, had very little to do with the Sinners' MC unless it involved a few of the Old Ladies who helped me out by watching Cyan when I needed to work, and that was it.

Of course, he hated it.

Hated that I wasn't under his thumb anymore, and the truth was, I wouldn't have minded any of it, just the cheating was something I couldn't stand.

The stuff he did for the MC, the laws he broke, the long runs he went on at the drop of a hat, the fact that he could be imprisoned and sent to jail for years...I could handle it. I could.

But cheating?

Nope.

Big. Fat. Nope.

He was a handsome bastard, and that was how he'd wormed his way between my legs all those years before. That and everything about him screamed bad boy, something that had tempted the good girl in me more than I could say.

All that he was had been a temptation, and to this day, I still felt the fire I'd felt all those years ago. Nothing had doused it. Not even what he was.

But that didn't mean I had to accept it.

I wasn't a masochist, after all.

His hair had always been a mix of black and gray, even when he was younger. Back then, it had been more delineated. Almost like a streak of white lightning through the unrelieved black.

It was why he'd gotten his name.

Lightning, he'd jokingly told me all those years ago, wasn't worthy of a road name.

His eyes, Cyan's eyes, stared back at me from the top step of our front stoop, and they were glittering with fury.

His stubborn jaw was set, and the nose that had been broken one too many times was flaring with his outrage.

"You changed the fucking locks?"

I shrugged. "Wasn't about to have you coming in whenever you wanted."

"What the hell does that mean?"

"It means what I said. You're not my man anymore, Storm. You don't have the right to just walk through the door—"

I'd expected a rebuttal loaded with anger at those words, but if anything, he blanched.

"The fuck?" he whispered, interrupting me. "You changed the locks so I couldn't get in?"

He looked like a kid whose puppy had just been kicked.

I firmed my lips, refusing to be affected by that. Refusing, point blank, to relent, I lifted my chin and said, "Yes."

Simple.

Effective.

He swallowed, looking confused and bewildered, like we hadn't argued for months about his behavior. Like this was all coming out of the goddamn blue.

"Why?" he rasped.

"You know why."

I went to close the door so I could release the chain. His eyes flared in astonishment at the move, and I heard him growl under his breath.

Fuck, that sound got to me.

He made a similar noise when he thrust into me, his hardness plowing my softness, and God, it had been so long since that had happened. Since he'd been inside me.

I released the chain the second the door was closed and pulled it open, surprised to note he was halfway down the path to the curb where he'd parked his hog.

"Where are you going?" I queried, leaning against the jamb.

"You shut me out—"

"No. I was unfastening the chain."

He twisted around, glowered at me.

"Cyan wants to ask you something."

I looked over my shoulder and saw our kid watching us from her stool in the kitchen.

I saw the hurt in her eyes, knew the physical distance that I'd put between father and daughter was a strain on her, but I wasn't about to let my baby be raised in an environment where it was okay for a man to treat his partner like her father treated me.

No way, no how.

That was *not* a lesson I was okay with imparting.

My mom had been subservient to my dad. Always doing as she was told. Always behaving. Never acting out because, God forbid, the neighbors might see. He'd controlled her. All the time.

I genuinely believed that my experiences growing up had made me put up with Storm's shit for as long as I had, and with that at the forefront of my mind, I knew I had to show Cyan another path.

Even if she hated me sometimes for leaving her daddy.

Storm's jaw was like it'd been hewn from stone as he rushed back to the door.

He didn't shove past me, but he made sure that his arm brushed against my body, dragging nerve endings to life that would *always* surge into being for him.

And fuck if I didn't resent the shit out of that.

I hated my body some days. Hated it with a passion because the way he made me feel obviously wasn't reciprocated. If it was, then I'd be enough for him, and I never had been.

Ever.

Not from the start.

If I'd started to soften, just thinking about what Kendra had told me, sneering all the while as she ground me into the dirt with her hooker heel, strengthened my resolve.

She'd been sucking his cock while I was carrying Cyan.

He'd been fucking around since he'd claimed me.

The bastard.

Then, just as hate filled me, Cyan squealed as he stormed into the kitchen, hauled her into his arms, and swung her around in a circle that had her laughing as she huddled into him.

Storm was many things, but I couldn't say he wasn't a good dad.

Sometimes, he wasn't as present as I'd like, and that had been before I'd kicked him out.

It was partly to do with his responsibilities at the MC, but more so his *choices* that kept him at the clubhouse longer than I felt sure was required of him.

Still, that didn't take away from the fact that he loved his baby girl and she loved him.

I would never, *ever* get in the way of that.

No amount of bitterness would ever spill into their relationship because what they had was exactly what I wanted for the pair of them.

So, even though it hurt to watch them, I closed the door behind me and smiled as I leaned back and watched them together.

The hard biker.

The little girl in a fairy princess dress.

Incongruent and all the more beautiful for it.

"Now, what's my baby want to ask me?"

Cyan plucked at his cut then she dipped her chin, twisting her head slightly to the side and, peering up at him from under her eyelashes, said, "Well..."

EIGHT

LILY

IT WAS STUPID.

Weird.

Wrong even, considering what was going on in my life, but when I pressed the bullet vibe to my clit and closed my eyes, the first thing I thought of was Link.

That mass of tousled waves on his head.

The cheeky grin that could turn deadly.

Those eyes that could cut then, out of nowhere, could soften and make me realize he wasn't as hard as he liked to make out.

That body, framed by a cut that declared to the world he was a rebel, exuding power, the pecs that were delineated through the wifebeater he wore, those biceps that were burnished with the sun and had glinting, golden hairs dotted here and there...

Fuck!

I pressed the vibe harder against my clit and rocked my hips up.

Frustration worked through me, making me spread my legs under the covers and arch my hips up, frigging the air if I couldn't frig anything else.

A breath escaped me, hiccupping out into the ether as I thought about him, thought about him between my legs, thought about his hands on my body...

"Oh God," I muttered, slightly overwhelmed by the need flushing through me.

I wasn't often aroused, and that was a nasty truth.

Maybe in my situation, it made sense.

I was living among sharks, sharks who bit.

Often.

I was usually stressed, tense, and unhappy. None of those things made a woman feel horny. But today, after having been in that biker's presence?

God.

I shouldn't like him.

Bikers were dirty, right? Gruff and rough, mean and...what?

My dad *wasn't* a filthy bastard?

Rough and mean and violent?

The only difference was, my father had a shit ton of money in his wallet and that smoothed things over, kept the world from seeing exactly who he was and what he was capable of.

Money was a front, and it shored up the façade that he was a good man. He wasn't.

And Link, he wasn't good either. But he *was* delicious, all the same. And he cared. Fuck, he did. He'd been hurt, distressed about Luke's prisoners, making me wonder what my brother had done.

I'd put nothing past him...and shit, there went my arousal.

Wincing, I forced myself to focus on Link.

He'd been on my mind ever since we'd parted ways back at Crosskeys.

I had, indeed, met with the local sheriff, and all the while I'd been thinking about the biker.

How he'd slouched back against the bench, legs splayed, the thin cotton of his wifebeater clinging to his torso in a way that let me see every part of him.

I thought about his hands, big and large, flecks of grease around the nail. Not in a gross way either. I could see he'd scrubbed his fingers hard because they were slightly soiled, and all I'd been able to think about was how those calluses would feel against my body.

How *he'd* feel against my skin.

Boom.

There it was.

My arousal was back.

I thought about his hands on my breasts, rubbing my nipples, slipping down over my stomach, toward my sex.

I thought about him touching my clit, rubbing me there before slipping a finger or two inside me.

My left eye began to twitch and I dug my heel harder into the bed, pressing down firmly and letting my inner muscles strain as I worked toward my orgasm.

The high-pitched throb of the bullet echoed around the room, whining in a way that made me hate it, but I forced the thought aside, thought about Link fucking me with his fingers and there... *Right there!*

I groaned long and low as the pleasure had me tensing, all my muscles freezing into stillness before I released a shaky breath and sank back into the mattress.

Pulling the vibe away from my clit, I switched it off and let the pleasant sensations worm their way around my system.

Grateful that I felt drowsy, I welcomed sleep and actually felt quite rested when I woke up five hours later.

That was a good night's rest for me.

I'd only ever slept longer than that when I was in the finishing school over in Switzerland and at college.

Both times I was out from under my father's roof.

If he was traveling on business and I had the house to myself, I slept better but not that well.

Whenever he *was* here, I couldn't rest. Would you? Knowing the enemy was in your midst?

As I stared at him over the breakfast table, I knew my cover was firmly in place because, *twice*, he smiled at me. Actually fucking smiled at me.

Though my loathing was masked and masked well, it still surprised me. Father wasn't cheerful, but he'd been like a bear with a sore paw ever since Luke's death. More so than usual.

"Did you sleep well, Father?" I queried, as I cut my grapefruit into segments.

My Earl Grey tea was steeping at my side, and I had a bowl of yogurt and granola to my right.

I hated granola, hated grapefruit too.

The only thing I actually liked was the tea, but my father selected my breakfast.

Always had.

Always would.

God, I couldn't wait until he was dead.

As I envisioned how I'd do it, how I'd free myself from him, how I'd eat pancakes for goddamn breakfast whenever I wanted, I waited on his response.

"Knowing that you're eager to avenge Luke soothed me," he imparted.

"Luke and I were bred from the same root. I didn't realize you were too, Lily."

I wasn't.

Thank God.

Maybe I had some of their twisted evil in me, otherwise I wouldn't be counting down the moments until I could kill him, but I *wasn't* like them.

I wanted my mother's money in my bank account so I could do something with it. So I could do *good* with it rather than just try to accrue more and more.

I wanted to help people, wanted to help people like me. Women and children who were trapped in an abusive situation. Who didn't know how to get out, and who, when it came down to it, had to do things that weren't their natural inclination just to survive.

In another place, another time, I wanted to think that I wasn't the sort of woman who could contemplate murder.

But this was here.

Now.

And my family was how it was.

Thankfully, Giulia Fontaine had cut one of our trio out, sparing me a job in the long run.

"I'm proud to be a Lancaster," I told him, keeping a faint smile on my mouth as I lied to him.

I couldn't smile too much, that would give away the fact I was bullshitting him.

He was used to me shielding my expression as it was something he'd bred in me, so to be overexuberant would get me nowhere.

"This pleases me," he intoned, as he sliced into his egg white omelet. "It pleases me greatly. Did you speak with the sheriff?"

I took a dainty bite of grapefruit, letting it slip down my throat even though the taste made me want to gag.

"Indeed."

"How did it go?"

His impatience washed over me, but I ignored it. It was usually why he hit me, because I didn't concede to him, didn't cower before him.

For the first time, I thought he appreciated that because he just cocked a brow when I stirred my tea and took a sip.

"I didn't make it obvious we were courting him, Father. Softly softly catchee monkey," I told him, using the same phrase Link had yesterday.

It had stuck out in my mind because it was the exact opposite of what I'd imagined a biker saying, so I'd googled it.

Turned out it was a quote from *Victoria*, the show about Victoria and Albert.

I didn't have a clue how he'd come to know it, couldn't imagine him watching something like that, but I liked the phrase. Liked what it meant.

Tread softly.

Be careful.

And you'll gain everything you desire.

I *desired* a helluva lot from this bastard.

My father winced. "Haste is imperative in this matter, Lily," he argued.

"I'm sure it is. But you can't treat officials as though they're servants. I ascertained that he was irked by the family's demand that we bring in outsiders to investigate Luke's passing."

He sniffed. "I was well within my rights. Technically, that bar lies on the county line."

Only if you were bad at geography.

Carefully, I hitched my shoulder. "Regardless, he's *irked*." I repeated the word, knowing it was the truth, and knowing, even though I hadn't spoken to the sheriff about my brother's case *at all*, that he was irritated was simply a given.

"Damn peasants," he sneered. "They don't know how lucky they are to have a job."

I hummed under my breath, neither agreeing nor disagreeing, as I partook of my boring morning meal.

"I have to go to Hong Kong tonight."

That had me cocking a brow. "Would you like me to pack your bag for you?"

God, this was like a modern version of *Downton Abbey*.

Tasks like packing his bag, hand-signing invitations, and sending handwritten 'thank you' notes for the birthday and holiday gifts we received fell on my shoulders.

"Yes. I'll be gone three weeks." His jaw tightened, and his knife scraped against the china plate. "It's unfortunate timing, but a merger can't go ahead without my presence."

"I understand, Father. I'll do what I can to ensure that things carry on in the right vein regarding Luke's case."

"It does relieve me to know that you'll maintain things in my absence."

He set his knife and fork on the dish and sat back against the chair. As he did, I felt his eyes on me, felt them because it was like having insects crawl over my skin.

I ignored them, though, as I often did. I had little choice.

We always ate together in this room.

It was how it was done.

Luke had rarely joined us, usually too hungover to function at this time, but Father insisted that I ate breakfast with him, had ever since I was small.

Not for the first time, I missed college.

Sure, I hadn't been in luxuriously appointed rooms within a mansion that would make most envious, but it was better than *this*.

The room itself was unusual for a morning room.

Normally, they were angled to take in the morning sun and were bright and colorful in design. But in this instance, the room, though it had a large window that let in a lot of light, was painted black.

None of this was to my taste.

He'd hired an interior decorator with bad taste but a killer body.

I had to assume the latter was why we had to breakfast in this disastrous decor.

The walls were matte, and that was offset with swag curtains that were a bright magenta in color. Placed atop a blue and cream flecked rug, the glass table was large enough to seat eighteen, and I sat at the head opposite my father. Always had, even if Luke did design to share a meal with us.

Beside the table was a small accent cabinet that was topped with a picture frame of my mother. It showed her laughing and smiling, a sight that was so rare, my father had copied the image, and it was in every single property he owned, in more than one room.

To me, that image was like a 'fuck you.'

I felt like he was sticking his middle finger up at me whenever I glanced upon her, so I never did.

That wasn't my mother.

My mother had been miserable.

Half doped up on Valium, the rest of her had been swaddled in an alcoholic stupor.

That was how he'd gotten away with her murder.

I'd seen him push her down the stairs, but he hadn't seen me watching them argue. He didn't know I *knew*.

In front of the lie that was that photo, there was a votive candle that burned.

You couldn't make this up, could you?

The bastard had murdered her, yet made sure a candle burned at all hours of the day in her memory.

Behind him, there was an ash console table loaded down with a display of flowers that varied every day.

In this mix, Mozart was piped in, a rousing orchestral movement that invigorated.

At least, it did for my father.

For me, it just gave me a headache.

Amid all this designer splendor, we sat, dressed in the same kind of splendor, so beautiful and yet so vile that it was a wonder I didn't choke on every bite I managed to swallow under his beady eyes.

When I'd finished my meal, I placed the golden cutlery on the magenta-flecked china, and stated, "Do you just need the usual, Father?"

"Yes. Pack my tuxedo though. I think I'll be attending the opera while I'm there."

Inwardly celebrating the fact I'd be out from under his thumb for three weeks, I murmured, "Of course. May I be excused?"

"Yes."

I slipped the chair back and, like every other goddamn morning, I rounded the table and leaned over so I could press a kiss to his cheek.

He twisted his head around, moving so that my lips glanced off his cheek and pressed to his mouth.

Swallowing down my revulsion, I acted as though nothing had happened and retreated, slipping out of the room with a simple, "I'll have your things ready soon, Father."

"Good girl."

My mouth tightened as I escaped the monstrous breakfast room and headed deep into the beast's cavern.

I rarely went into his bedroom unless I had to. And even as I made my way there, I hated the necessity.

Going into my dad's room shouldn't have been creepy, yet it was. Really, truly was.

I sucked down a breath as I headed into the wing where he slept. There was no point in delaying the inevitable, plus, when he'd told me he'd be traveling later, I knew he expected me to act immediately.

So I did.

Making short work of it, I packed his clothes, ensured his suits were in the appropriate coverings, and gathered his tuxedo, as well as selecting a range of ties that would take him from a formal meeting to an evening event.

Having chosen his shoes, cufflinks, and confirming that all the studs were present on the shirt he'd wear with his tux, I was done.

All without seeing the bastard.

The second his suitcases were standing beside the doorway to his suite of rooms, I escaped and retreated to my room.

Hitting the intercom, I announced, "I'll be heading to Crosskeys in twenty minutes."

I didn't wait for a reply, just knew I had to give my guards sufficient warning.

Then I changed into a pair of yoga pants, sports bra, and shirt, grabbed my keys, and went on out.

As usual, the guards were only a few moments behind me as I took off, escaping the house that was shrouded in an atmosphere which was positively Addams' family-esque.

Leaving it behind, I decided to stop in town for a quick coffee.

The twenty-minute ride sped by, those few moments the only true private ones I had, and I used them wisely—shouting along to Rag N Bone Man as a means of expressing my constantly internalized anger.

Better that than have an unknown stomach ulcer explode on me.

When I passed the coffee shop I liked, I noticed the collective of bikes outside the joint and wanted to wince when my heart skipped a beat.

As I pulled up, so did Paul and Alix, but because they knew my routine, I knew they'd stay in the car and wait on me to return.

I wasn't a creature of habit by nature but by necessity. By repeating patterns, they trusted me to never deviate from my path, and I used that to my advantage. Even if it was stupid.

After all, if they knew my routine, maybe some potential kidnapper did as well. They'd know when and how to grab me...

Unfortunately for me, I wouldn't mind being kidnapped.

Anything to get me away from this fucking life I was leading.

As was the way, because I didn't mind, it'd never happen to me.

Murphy's law was a real bitch sometimes.

Phone and keys in hand, mouth tight with irritation, I locked my car and crossed the street.

Stepping inside the café, I made my way to the counter and felt my heart skip a beat when I saw a cluster of men wearing those leather vests in one corner of the room.

I let my gaze drift over them, hoping to see that head of wavy hair, and when I did, my heart skipped *two* beats.

It was stupid to feel nervous, stupid to feel antsy, but all I could think about was last night when I'd thought about him, used *Link* to get myself off.

I was weird with sex, thanks to my upbringing. Masturbating in the dark, under the covers, hiding my face from the rest of the room by pressing my forearm to my eyes, was pretty much standard practice for me.

But last night?

I'd wanted to be naked.

Had wanted to feel the brush of the silk sheets against my skin.

I'd wanted his hands on me.

Had needed to feel another's touch, a touch *I* invited. That I wanted. Craved.

It was stupid, impossible.

A crush.

Nothing more, nothing less, but that was how crushes worked, right?

I'd never had a teenage crush before, so I didn't know for certain.

Back when you were allowed to feel giddy just because you saw a man you liked, I'd been deep in mourning and trying to get over what I'd seen my father do to my mom.

My eyes had been opened that day, and I'd been reeling ever since.

I didn't appreciate that the moment I started being normal again was the moment a rough and ready biker came into my line of sight.

Someone who was totally inappropriate for me.

Someone who would never gel with my lifestyle.

Although, when I put it like that, it was no wonder, really, was it?

Talk about the ultimate rebellion.

My mouth watered at just how delicious the idea was.

Biting my bottom lip, I muttered my order to the waitress and forced my attention onto the menu boards.

I knew the list like the back of my hand, but I gave it every ounce of my focus just to stop myself from gawking at Link. It was bad enough that I thought I was an idiot—I didn't need him knowing it too.

Aware my cheeks were pink, I accepted the kombucha Chrissie, the server, handed me, and tapped my card to the reader.

Once I'd paid, I smiled at her then retreated to my regular table in the corner where I could overlook the rest of the coffee shop, and where Paul and Alix could watch me without having to step inside.

Taking a deep sip of passionfruit kombucha, I switched on my phone and began to mess around on Facebook.

When, a few moments later, a shadow moved across the table, I didn't glance up. If I did, one of the guards would pick up on it.

Instead, I looked out of the corner of my eye, saw the phone on the table, saw the hands I recognized from yesterday, and tensed.

"For you. Untraceable."

His voice was just as deep as it had been yesterday. Just as raspy. Just as rumbly. And God, it hit me straight between the legs.

Exactly where I'd held my vibrator last night.

"Why?" I asked, not moving my lips, aware the question was mumbled but unable to help it.

"There's a text message waiting for you."

He moved away at that, and though I wanted to snatch at the phone and read what he'd written, I reached for my kombucha, swiped my phone onto my lap at the same time, then reached for the one Link had given me.

I had to applaud him for his perception, because it matched mine.

Down to the rose gold color.

Everything came with a cost, but still, it thrilled me to have a means of communication that didn't come tied to a bank account my father monitored.

As I swiped toward the messages, I saw he'd input his number already.

Link: *How are we supposed to talk if you can't say what you want to say?*

I bit my bottom lip to hide my smile. Me: *Figured that out, did you?*

Link: *Just call me a fucking genius.*

This time I couldn't stop my lips from twitching.

I already knew Link didn't have a problem with swearing around ladies. Even my dick of a father tried not to curse around me, and only did so in moments of extreme pressure or stress.

I swore he thought I was some kind of shrinking violet when I was anything but that. Hell, he'd made me into the woman I was today, but he didn't seem to figure out that hearing the word 'fuck' wasn't going to make me pass out with horror.

I pulled on the straw, swallowing more of my drink as I, carefully, looked out of the corner of my eye.

When I spotted Link, watching me but without any of my caution, I relinquished the hold on the straw and shot him a careful smile.

He was splayed out as, I was coming to see, was his way.

On the table of four, he had the seat closest to the wall. His back was to it, and his legs were open at what most decent people would consider a vulgar—and unless he was hung like a fucking stallion—totally unnecessary width.

Still, it suited him.

I didn't think he was trying to take up the maximum space to be a dick either. It was like he just needed the room. *All* the room. His eyes were on me, and he was typing without even looking at his screen.

The phone buzzed in my hand.

Link: *I like that smile on you. I get the feeling you don't do that often.*

What amazed me was the lack of typos. Not a single one. That was a talent I needed to pick up. If I didn't look at the screen then I'd write something barely legible.

Me: *Not much to smile about.*

Fuck, that sounded self-piteous, didn't it?

I quickly sent:

Me: *I didn't mean that to sound whiny.*

Link: *Didn't. Sounded fucking miserable.*

Despite myself, and despite the fact he was right, it *was* miserable, I laughed.

Link: *Not sure why you're laughing, sugar tits. I was being serious.*

My eyes widened. Sugar tits?

For a second, I was speechless, then I turned to him, uncaring that Paul and Alix might be watching, and mouthed, "Sugar tits?"

He smirked at me and spread his arm out, resting it against the table.

His fingers began to tap against the surface, and he looked so cool at that moment, so goddamn slick, that I had to shake my head again.

The phone buzzed once more.

Link: *Now you know how to reach me if you need to tell us anything.*

Me: *Might not be much to share at the moment. He's going away. But good thinking. Thank you.*

He shrugged, the gesture effortless.

Something about him made me wonder if he was always so damn chilled, but even as the thought crossed my mind, I recognized that that couldn't be right.

Everyone had their tipping point.

Link included.

Before I had the chance to stare at him like a love-sick teenager—Lord above, I could have stared at him for days like I was at a gallery opening and he was a lost Rembrandt—I forced myself to finish my kombucha then headed on out, my new phone tucked into the waistband of my pants, well aware that Link watched me go.

Shit, I knew things were bad when I was hoping he was checking out my ass in the skintight pants I was wearing.

Once outside, I dipped my chin, acknowledging Paul and Alix in their SUV before retreating to mine.

My phone bleeped, my real one, and as I climbed behind the wheel, I opened the message and saw it was Tiffany.

My lips curved into a genuine smile because Tiffany was the bomb.

Her family wasn't as rich as mine which, in Luke's opinion, had always made Tiffany unworthy of our friendship—yup, he was *that* much of a dick —but she seriously rocked.

My father agreed, too, because he'd never tried to stop our friendship, and he was more than capable of doing so.

West Orange was an unusual enclave for a gathering of the nation's one percent, especially so close to the city, but it was thanks to Tiffany's family in a small part.

On the outskirts, they'd developed a subdivision that had attracted a lot of wealthy families who were tired of the city sprawl, who wanted more room to roam.

Father, also being a dick, hadn't purchased land there, but had, instead, bought up a few parcels beside the subdivision.

His property was like an island surrounded by an ocean of land which, ultimately, connected with the exclusive urbanization.

I knew Father and Richard Farquar, Tiffany's dad, played golf together at least once a week, so I had to assume they were friends too.

Or, as much a friend as my dickhead dad was capable of having.

Tiffany: *Where. Are. You?*

Me: *Just getting a kombucha.*

Tiffany: *That stuff'll kill ya.*

Me: *How? By over-cleansing my gut?*

Tiffany: *Pffft. You attending class today?*

Me: *Yeah. Just driving to the club.*

Tiffany: *Cool. See you there. We'll get our nails done after, okay?*

I rolled my eyes, because we'd only just had our nails done a few days ago.

Me: *I might have a pedi. You'll damage your nails with the amount of manicures you get.*

Tiffany: *Stop preaching. :p I like to change the color!*

Shaking my head at that non-answer, I just tapped out, *I know, babe. On my way.*

I set my phone on the dash, hooking it up to the wireless charger, then placed my new cell on the passenger seat beside me.

Eying it for a few seconds, I wondered if Link understood what he'd actually given me.

Not just a means of communicating with him, but a liberation I didn't think he or many other people would ever be able to understand.

I was rich. Therefore I had it all.

But I was under guard twenty-four seven. All of my purchases were monitored, my activity taken note of. I couldn't take a piss without someone being aware of it.

What kind of freedom was that?

What kind of life was that?

I was a tiger in a cage, a tiger that was just *waiting* to maul its keeper in an escape attempt.

In yoga, they taught you to let go of what you couldn't change, but how could I do that?

How could I relinquish my internal rage over the systematic governing of my existence?

Was I weird that I couldn't?

Or was I strong in my refusal to turn into the Stepford wife my father wanted me to be?

Even as I gnawed on my bottom lip over that, thinking of a day when I would be free to do whatever the hell I wanted, fucking anyone I wanted in the process—rough and tumble bikers included—I felt the shackles around my throat, wrists, and ankles tighten to the point of suffocation before I overcame the sensation of choking and set off.

What I really wanted to do was head back into the café, flirt some with Link, and do something of value. Something of my choice.

But that was for another day.

Another tomorrow.

So I exhaled, relinquished what I couldn't change *today,* and moved my ass.

WEDNESDAY

Lily: *So, am I allowed to text you about non-murder related things?*
Link: *Depends.*
Lily: *On what?*
Link: *If it's interesting.*
Lily: *How do I know if it's interesting?*
Link: *If I reply.*
Lily: *Okay.*
Lily: *What's the farthest you've ridden on your bike?*
Link: *Why?*
Lily: *Why not?*
Link: *Okay…I'm not going to talk about the MC.*
Lily: *Didn't ask you about the MC. Just wanted to know how far you'd ridden.*
Link: *Why?*
Lily: *Wanted to know if it made your butt hurt after a while.*
Link: *:p I don't mind.*
Lily: *You don't mind an aching butt? Hmm. I need to man up then when I'm doing a spin class.*
Link: *That how you stay in shape? Spinning?*
Lily: *Yup. That and a few other ways. I spend a lot of time at the club.*
Link: *Why?*
Lily: *Because it gets me out of the house.*
Link: *Can't blame you for THAT.*

Lily: *No. If I'm not there, I'm at my friend's.*

Link: *Why haven't you moved out?*

Lily: *I can't. Not really. He wouldn't let me. I tried once, but he cut me off before I could do much. I got a job at this clothing store, he bought the building and threatened to shut the store down. The owner was this really nice woman, and it wasn't her fault he wants me tied to him, so I quit... I know he'd do that again and again. *shrugs* Easier to concede than let someone innocent get hurt by our feuding.*

Link: *o.O He bought the fucking store? You know he's a psycho, yeah?*

Lily: *Umm, yeah. Lol. That didn't escape me.*

Link: *Did you go to college?*

Lily: *Yeah, but it was close to home and I was allowed into the dorms for the first year, but after he made me come back.*

Link: *Fuck, that's shitty.*

Lily: *Yeah. I liked it out of there. I slept really well.*

Link: *You have problems sleeping?*

Lily: *Well, not falling asleep, just staying asleep.*

Link: *Nightmares?*

Lily: *No. More like I'm just on edge. There's a lot of tension in the house. Sometimes it's business, but mostly it's just how it is. Things have calmed down now that Luke's dead, but Father's still uneasy.*

Link: *You ever call him 'daddy?'*

Lily: *Would you?*

Link: *No. Lol. Good point.*

Lily: *I'm smart. Surprisingly.*

Link: *Why surprisingly? Some of the smartest people I know are bitches.*

Lily: *You didn't just call women 'bitches?'*

Link: *Yup. Get used to it.*

Lily: *You going to call me a bitch?*

Link: *Depends on whether you act like one or not.*

Lily: *Good point. I'm not a bitch BUT I do have RBF.*

Link: *What the fuck is RBF?*

Lily: *Resting Bitch Face.*

Link: *Hmm. I could see that.*

Lily: *Thanks! :/*

Link: *You're the one who admitted to it!*

Lily: *It's not like it's a crime.*

Link: *Haha. No, I guess not.*

Lily: *My father doesn't like it. Says it's bad for business.*

Link: *Fuck's sake. Is everything business with him?*

Lily: *That's how you get ninety billion in the bank.*
Link: *That and by breaking laws.*
Lily: *I'd imagine.*
Link: *You don't know?*
Lily: *Not for certain. I have my suspicions. But it's hard to look into him. I don't have access. I wish I did.*
Link: *What would you do if you had proof that could take him down?*
Lily: *Celebrate? Have a massive party?*
Link: *Would you change your mind about killing him?*
Lily: *Maybe. I want him dead.*
Link: *Why?*
Lily: *He deserves to die.*
Link: *Maybe he does, but do you want the stain on your soul?*
Lily: *Is that what it is? To kill someone who taints the Earth by walking on it? Aren't I doing people a favor?*
Link: *Hell, yeah. But it depends on who you talk to.*
Lily: *I've only ever wanted to hurt him.*
Link: *Good to know you're not a nutcase.*
Lily: *Oh, I never said I wasn't.*
Link: *Lol. At least you're funny and sexy as well as insane.*
Lily: *Well, a girl's got to try to give a good first impression.*
Link: *Trust me, you did that. We'd been looking for the women for a while. Since the bastard's death.*
Lily: *How did you find out about them? I wasn't even sure if you knew, to be honest.*
Link: *That why you dropped it like a hammer on my toe? 'I know where they are.'*
Lily: *Yeah. I wasn't going to get people involved unnecessarily.*
Link: *Shrewd of you.*
Lily: *See? Told you I was smart.*
Link: *If you were smart, I don't think you'd be trying to talk to me.*
Lily: *Trying? Isn't this us? Talking?*
Link: *Maybe. O.o*
Lily: *Wellllll... if you don't want to talk...*
Link: *Lily?*
Lily: *This is me. Not talking.*
Link: *Nah. It's all good. You can talk.*

THURSDAY

Lily: *You send me that to make me jealous?*
 Link: *Maybe. :P*
 Lily: *It worked.*
 Link: *My dinner.*
 Lily: *Looks good. Where you eating?*
 Link: *The diner. Just off Daytona. You ever been there?*
 Lily: *No. I usually just go to the country clubs.*
 Link: *Shame. You'd probably like it here.*
 Lily: *I would, huh? How do you know that?*
 Link: *You like to think you have a stick shoved up your ass, but you don't. I think you'd like the fact we're not all pretentious assholes.*
 Lily: *Well, you get used to them.*
 Link: *What? Pretentious assholes?*
 Lily: *Yep. Fact of life for me. At least with Luke dead, I don't have to deal with his prick ways too.*

Link: *That's one way of looking at it.*
Lily: *I'm a glass half full kind of girl.*
Link: *Really? Full of what?*
Lily: *Dreams. Hopes. We can try to live a better life than what we're already leading, can't we?*
Link: *Funny...*
Lily: *What is?*
Link: *From the outside looking in, I mean, you look like you'd be happy.*
Lily: *Why? Because I'm rich?*
Link: *Yeah. Isn't that what everyone wants? To be rich and able to buy good shit and do whatever they want?*
Lily: *What about my life makes you think I can do whatever I want? Lol. I just told you I haven't gone to the diner you're in...know why?*
Link: *Because it's not fancy enough for you?*
Lily: *I'm not that much of an asshole. It's because if I gain any weight, my father restricts my food.*
Link: *You shitting me?*
Lily: *No. I wish I was.*
Link: *Why do you put up with it?*
Lily: *Because it's only for as long as I'm willing to deal with it.*
Link: *And how long is that?*
Lily: *I don't know.*
Link: *Seems to me you don't really know what you want. You let him control you, let him get away with the stuff he does because you think, at some point, you'll break and will end him. But I don't think you have that in you. Not really.*
Lily: *That's a lot of guessing from someone who doesn't know me well.*
Link: *What you want to do...I know what that feels like. It's not something just ANYONE can do. You're not just anyone.*
Lily: *Aren't I?*
Link: *No. I think you're kinder than you realize. I don't think you could do it.*
Lily: *Won't know until I'm pushed.*
Link: *Hasn't he already pushed you enough? Wouldn't you have snapped by now?*
Lily: *I don't want to talk about this.*
Link: *The truth hurts. But if it's any consolation, your ass is to die for, and I think it could survive a few of these sammiches.*
Lily: *Thank you. I think. Lol. I'm surprised. Didn't take you for a steak sandwich kinda guy.*

Link: *No? How come?*

Lily: *Thought you'd prefer something the size of a T-Rex on a plate with loaded baked potatoes.*

Link: *Well, I do, but everything in moderation.*

Lily: *Ha! This is you being healthy, is it?*

Link: *Well, this piece of walking heaven has to stay looking this fine, doesn't he?*

Lily: *I suppose, when you put it like that...*

Link: *Haha.*

Lily: *:P*

Link: *Does that mean you think I'm walking heaven?*

Lily: *I wouldn't want to inflate your ego anymore.*

Link: *Shame.*

Lily: **snorts* If you say so.*

Link: *I do. Every man likes his ego being...stroked.*

Lily: *As well as other things? Or just his ego?*

Link: *Other things too. Ego optional.*

Lily: *So, in the grand scheme of things, you'd prefer 'other things' to be stroked than the ego?*

Link: *You stroke those parts of me, the ego purrs.*

Lily: *You're nuts.*

Link: *I try. :P Seriously, you should come down. I'll even share this sandwich with you.*

Lily: *Won't buy me my own? You're a cheap date!*

Link: *The cheapest.*

Lily: *Haha. Thanks for the offer.*

Link: *But?*

Lily: *I can't go into town. Not without my guards, and as fascinating as I'm sure your company is, it's not worth the crap I'd get for it.*

Link: *You know how prisons work, don't you?*

Lily: *Locks? Keys? Guards? Yep, well aware that's my world. Except, I get to drive a fancy sports car so no one realizes it.*

Link: *That sucks.*

Lily: *Ah, but my stomach is full, I have a roof over my head, and I have staff to see to my every whim. Aren't I the luckiest princess in the world?*

Link: *Sarcasm doesn't become you.*

Lily: *Sarcasm totally isn't the lowest form of wit.*

Link: *If it isn't, what is?*

Lily: *I don't know, but sarcasm is the BEST.*

Link: *Crap, you're one of those weirdos who likes Fawlty Towers, aren't you?*

Lily: *Maybe. O.o John Cleese is a legend.*

Link: *Pfft. Only weirdos like that show.*

Lily: *It's got a cult following.*

Link: *Key word there being CULT. Anything that has that attached to it isn't good IMO.*

Lily: *We'll have to agree to disagree.*

Link: *Definitely.*

Lily: *I bet you like facile American comedies, don't you?*

SATURDAY

Link: *Might have downloaded an episode of Blackadder.*
    Lily: *Legit?*
Link: *Legit. O.O*
    Lily: *You won't regret it. Rowan Atkinson is fantastic. I love that show.*
Link: *Why do you think I'm giving it a try?*
    Lily: *Probably to punish me.*
Link: *Haha. You got that right. If I watch an episode of Blackadder, then you need to watch a...what did you call it? A FACILE American show.*
    Lily: *Like what?*
Link: *I'm thinking Seinfeld. That's funny.*
    Lily: *Bleugh.*
Link: *You'll suffer if I suffer.*
    Lily: *Blackadder isn't suffering. Which season did you get?*
Link: *The one with Queen Elizabeth.*
    Lily: *You listened!*
Link: *I did. I remembered what you said about the first season not being that great.*
    Lily: *I can't believe you remembered.*
Link: *I have a good memory. Anyway, today, I need a laugh.*
    Lily: *Why? Bad day?*
Link: *Not one of the best I've had in a while. Lot going on here. As you can imagine. We brought them here and things aren't going well.*
    Lily: *They must need medical attention! Can I do something?*

Link: *It's all taken care of, but they could be doing better. It's a lot of responsibility.*

Lily: *I'm sorry. <3*

Link: *Yeah. I'm not even the one dealing with them, tbh, but it's just... there's like this heavy cloud over us all atm.*

Lily: *Understandable. My asshole father isn't helping. But with him away, he has to let things slide.*

Link: *Why is he away?*

Lily: *He just said business. He doesn't often go to Hong Kong, but when he does, he's usually in a shitty mood when he gets back.*

Link: *Something to look forward to.*

Lily: *Yeah. Not so much.*

Link: *You should get out of that place while you can.*

Lily: *Just because he isn't here doesn't mean he doesn't have eyes on me.*

Link: *I guess not, but I could help you.*

Lily: *Why would you do that?*

Link: *Because I don't like the idea of what you're going through.*

Lily: *I'm okay.*

Link: *No. You're not. Different prisons, different cages.*

Lily: *I can't be compared to them.*

Link: *No. Maybe not. Trust me, I saw where they were. You're definitely living in better circumstances, but that doesn't mean you don't need liberating as much as they did.*

Lily: *I'm here by my own choice.*

Link: *You just said it yourself. You're not. You have eyes on you.*

Lily: *By choice. I know what I'm doing.*

Link: *Said no one. Ever.*

Lily: *No. I really do. I need to do this. I need to be the one who takes him down.*

Link: *And how are you going to do that without spending the rest of your life behind bars?*

Lily: *I'm going to do what he did to my mom. Simple.*

Link: *Not simple.*

Lily: *Maybe not. But I HAVE to do it. I have to make him pay, and I want all my mother's money. All of it. Not just a slice. I want to take it back from him, and I want to dismantle his stupid empire.*

Link: *There's more to life than vengeance, and I say that from the position of someone who'd know.*

Lily: *Who did you want to avenge?*

Link: *Not me. A brother. It burns inside him. I used to think it rotted him away from the inside out, but I was wrong.*

Lily: *Why? I can't see you being wrong on that score.*

Link: *What do you mean?*

Lily: *I think you're quite astute. Adept at reading between the lines, you know?*

Link: *We've barely talked.*

Lily: *Now who can't take a compliment?*

Link: *True. Well, I try my best. But I was wrong because he fell in love.*

Lily: *Did that make him stop needing vengeance?*

Link: *No. I think his focus has just changed.*

Lily: *Onto what?*

Link: *Your father.*

Lily: *Oh. It's Giulia Fontaine's partner? The brother you're talking about?*

Link: *Yeah. He came from a bad situation, his sister killed herself because of it, and ever since, that fire's been burning away inside him.*

Lily: *I know you can't and WON'T say, but did it help him? Whatever he did to find it, did it ease it?*

Link: *No. And that's how I know that doing what you want to do isn't worth it in the long run. Live your life, Lily. Get out of there while he's away.*

Lily: *You don't understand his reach.*

Link: *I can help you. Let me.*

Lily: *You can't. Nobody can. I have to help myself.*

Link: *You're not as alone as you think.*

Lily: *You barely know me. Why would you even try to help me?*

Link: *Because I'm a decent guy. Someone I just met called me astute. You're dying in that place. I can feel it.*

Lily: *I'll be fine.*

Link: *If you say so. When you decide I'm right, I'm here to help. Pinkie promise.*

Lily: *Pinkie promise? Haha. Not scout's honor?*

Link: *Ain't never been a scout and will never be one either.*

Lily: *Now you really do surprise me. Lol. Are you seriously watching Blackadder tonight?*

Link: *I am. Most seriously. Need a laugh. Things aren't going well for another brother of mine.*

Lily: *No? What's wrong?*

Link: *His wife left him. He needs to pull his head out of his ass.*

Lily: *You're obsessed with things being inside someone's butt.*

Link: *Lol. You've no idea.*

Lily: *O.o No. I don't. Do I want to know?*

Link: *Maybe. :P*

Lily: *Okay, I have a question that isn't butt related.*

Link: *You wound me.*

Lily: *Lol. I'll bet. But...you don't take me as a rosary-wearing kind of guy.*

Link: *Was my Grandma's. She pretty much raised me. Mom was useless and as she got older, she got weirder. Couldn't rely on her to make toast without freaking the fuck out about something.*

Lily: *You wear it to honor her?*

Link: *Not really. She wouldn't approve of what I do. So, in her eyes, I'd probably be besmirching the rosary. But I wear it as a reminder. She used to say that if someone dies and you think of them often, then they're never truly dead.*

Lily: *I like that.*

Link: *Me too. So I wear the rosary and think of her. I had a shitty childhood. Lots of crap going down. It made me who I am, made me accept things most decent people wouldn't. But anything inside me that IS decent? Grandma gave me that.*

Lily: *I'll think of her too when I see your rosary next. What was her name?*

Link: *Rosa. Simple name for a simple lady. And she was. We might have been dirt poor but she was a lady.*

Lily: *I believe it. Thank you for telling me that, Link.*

Link: *No big deal. I'm going to watch Blackadder now.*

Lily: *You want to watch it together? Like, over the phone? I have it on DVD.*

Link: *I'd be down for that.*

NINE

LINK

THREE DAYS LATER

"LINK?"

"Hmm?"

Tink scowled at me, then slapped her hand down on my thigh. "You gonna do something with that log between your legs or what?"

I hummed again, my attention on my phone. I had one hand behind my head propping me up enough to see the screen, and the other I used to tap out a message to a woman who—surprise, surprise—I actually fucking liked.

Liked.

As in, she didn't irritate me.

As in, she was amusing.

As in, she had character, a character that she clung to with both hands in the face of forces that wanted to turn her into a robot.

I admired that.

Me.

Admiring someone, and not just for how well they filled out a pair of yoga pants.

Although, she filled hers out to perfection that was for damn sure.

Just thinking about her swaggering out of the coffee shop that morning made the 'log' between my legs twitch at the memory.

Me: *You serious, right now?*

"Link!" Tink whined. "I'm—"

"Don't care what you are, babe," I muttered, too engrossed in my conversation to give a shit. "Go fuck one of the others if you're that desperate for some dick."

A sharp breath escaped her, and not because she was insulted.

It took a lot to insult a sweetbutt, especially if you were a brother.

I wasn't going to say that you couldn't hurt their feelings, because you could, and we routinely did and sure, that made us shits, but that was the life.

That was their choice.

Choice.

Something I didn't realize, until recently, was a precious thing.

"You being serious right now?" she whispered, and her hand came up to touch my forehead. She twisted it around so the back of her fingers tested my temp. "Are you sick?"

I scowled at her, swatting her hand away. "Nope. Just don't want to fuck you. Fuck off, Tink. I'm in the middle of something."

She strode off at that, huffing as she walked that admittedly fine ass of hers out of my room.

I didn't notice. I was too taken aback.

Lily: *Why would I lie? :P*

Me: *Because your truth is fucked up, babe. Like, beyond fucked up. No one, and I mean no one, likes the Chopped judges. They're assholes. I mean, they watch the dudes busting their guts for a measly ten grand, then literally piss on the dishes when they taste them.*

Lily: *You do know what 'literally' means, don't you?*

Me: *Yup.*

Lily: *I think people would stop watching if one of the judges whipped out their dicks or dropped a squat and took a leak on one of the dishes.*

Me: *You think? I think it would make shit more interesting.*

Lily: *Lol. You would. As for me, I think the judges are paid to be mean. That doesn't make them mean.*

Me: *Gah.*

Lily: *:P You don't have to like it to know I'm right.*

Me: *You're wrong, babe. They were born evil.*

Lily: **snorts* Regular Hitlers. God, I wonder what you think of Simon Cowell.*

Me: *Don't get me started.*

Lily: *I'm still getting over the fact you watch Chopped.*

Me: *I'm feeling stereotyped.*

Lily: *Feel it all you want. Do you even cook?*

Me: *Nope. Caught an episode once by accident and that was it. I was done for.*

Lily: *You're crazy.*

Me: *Only just figuring that out?*

Lily: *That's probably why I like you.*

My brows quirked at that, and I was totally aware I was wearing a dopey ass grin.

Me: *You like me, huh? As in, you LIKE like me?*

Lily: *Are we in high school?*

Me: *I'd PAY to see you in one of those private school uniforms. All plaid miniskirts and legs up to your armpits.*

Lily: *Perv.*

Me: *My fantasies are all nineteen and above.*

Lily: *You think I graduated a year late?*

Me: *Nope. Eighteen is too young.*

Lily: *Not according to the law.*

Me: *Fuck the law. Nineteen is when the corruption starts.*

Lily: *Lol. You say the weirdest shit. Explain.*

Me: *Eighteen is when you're trying not to squirm when someone fucks you. Still hurts. Nineteen? You've done all the screwing around, been groped. Probably gagged on a dick a few times. You know the score. Ya get me?*

Lily: *Not sure anyone 'gets' you, Link. But I admit, I find that refreshing.*

Me: *That's me. Better than a cold beer on a hot summer's day.*

Lily: *Your ego is massive.*

Me: *I have the inches to back it up.*

Lily: *Good to know. :P*

I grinned, for some stupid fucking reason, *proud* that she could banter with me like this.

She looked like she had a stick shoved up her ass and fuck, I wasn't averse to the idea of her having her butt stuffed with *something*, just not a stick.

Sticks were pointy.

Not fun.

Lily?

She was fun.

Hell, she was *fucking* fun.

Like, I'd been shooting the shit with her ever since the morning I'd given her the burner cell.

Rex wouldn't have approved of the burner, fuck, I hadn't even asked him if I should give it to her. I'd bought it out of my own money and why?

Because I'd just known something was off by those texts she sent me, and I'd been right.

I wasn't sure how, but someone monitored her cellphone. Read her messages. And it didn't take a fucking genius to figure out *who*.

The apple didn't fall far from the tree where Luke Lancaster was concerned, but Lily was an orange amid those apples. An orange I couldn't wait to peel because there was *definitely* going to be some peeling going on.

A lot of it if I had my way.

She sent a picture, and the sight of her wineglass, her legs crossed at the ankle revealing hot pink toenails, and the vista a pool that was glowing a bright blue, had me damn panting.

Hot pink?

I'd have thought she'd be a dusky pink. Something sedate. Something bland.

Me: *If I were you, I'd be in the pool drinking that.*

Lily: *If you were here, I'd do that.*

Eyes widening at that come back, I felt my dick go from the semi just regular conversation with her caused, a semi that had made Tink think I was locked and loaded and primed for action, to a full-on erection.

That was the first time she'd said anything like that.

Made *any* mention of the fact that she was into me in any small way.

Truth was, I found it incredible that I was into her.

She wasn't my type at all.

I liked 'em wild. Unrestrained. Free of inhibitions.

Lily, hell, she was the exact opposite of that.

She was pretty much a walking mummy. Tied up in inhibitions, forced to conform to someone else's will.

While a part of me wondered why she put up with it, another part got it.

Her brother had bought four women and held them captive in a shack in the middle of nowhere. He'd caged them. Done only the fuck knew what to them when he visited them. Had let them shit and piss in a corner and had *still* done whatever he wanted to them...

Her *brother* had done all that.

Her *father* had killed her mother.

Escaping from a messed up situation wasn't always easy.

Take Keira, Storm's Old Lady.

I loved her like she was my sister, and when one of the clubwhores had told her Storm had been fucking around on her from the start, she'd kicked him out and moved on.

Broke my brother's stupid prick of a heart in the process, but she'd taken action.

Lily couldn't do that.

Maybe a week ago, I'd have sneered at that.

Said that, of course, she had a choice.

Of course, she could run.

She was rich, wasn't she?

She could easily slip out and make a life of her own. I'd even think she was sticking around just for the money, for the lifestyle it could bring. Now, I knew different.

Irony being, of course, that a part of her *was* sticking around for the money.

But I got that too.

It was the principle.

However, she could argue until she was blue in the damn face because I knew, point blank, that she wasn't just there for the money. She was there because she couldn't get out. Because she *was* trapped. So damn trapped that the only way out that she could see was to kill her father.

And that was messed up.

Which was my jam.

I liked chaos.

I liked that it took you to the edges of your control, made you do shit you'd never usually do.

And while most wouldn't be turned on at the idea of boning someone with murder *literally* on their mind—and I knew what the definition of 'literally' was—I wasn't most people.

Me: *I'd take you up on that if you didn't have eyes on you.*
Lily: *Really?*
Me: *Really.*
Lily: *I can't believe I'm asking this, but if I figured something out...*

My lips curved in a grin and I sat up, my dick on red alert now that potential pussy was on the table.

Me: *'Something out' how?*
Lily: *If I visited a friend's place. She lives in a pool house. She'd probably let me borrow it.*

Thank fuck for friends like that.

Me: *You tell me when and where, I'll be there.*
Lily: *Okay.*

Well, that response wasn't as excited as I'd have liked, but I could deal.

Wasn't like you could show a lot of emotion through a text message.

Emojis could only do so much—
Lily: *Link?*
Me: *Yeah?*
Lily: *I should probably tell you something.*
Me: *All ears, babe.*
Lily: *Did you know you're the first guy to call me 'babe?'*
A laugh escaped me.
Me: *Good to know, BABE. But I don't think that's what you wanted to tell me, was it?*
Lily: *No.*

I didn't reply to that, just waited for her to get whatever it was she wanted to share off her chest.

She did this sometimes, and I understood her reticence.

It took a good five minutes of me twiddling my fucking thumbs and ignoring a text from Rex to head to his office for her to tap out a message.

Lily: *I haven't actually done what we're talking about before.*
Me: *Hook up?*

That didn't surprise me. Not with her Nazi of a father and sick fuck of a brother.

She had more eyes on her than the Mona fucking Lisa.

Lily: *Well, that, and what happens when you hook up.*

For a second, I wasn't sure if I was reading that right. Because there was no way in fuck Lily was telling me she was a goddamn virgin, right?

I knew she'd gone to college, knew she preferred her life there over her current one as she had more freedom.

But seriously? Was she for real right now?

Lily: *Link?*

I blinked a few times, then grimaced at a flurry of texts from Rex which told me I needed to get my ass in gear.

Me: *Yeah, babe. It's all good.*

Sucking in a breath, I came to a decision.

I didn't take virgins. That was like the one rule I had.

But Lily?

She was worth breaking that rule over because, fuck, if I hadn't laughed more in these last few days than I had in a while, and the clubhouse made a morgue look cheerful at the moment.

There was jack shit to be smiling about, but Lily had helped cheer me up. And that *Blackadder* shit? Fucking epic. And watching it with her? Double fucking epic.

Me: *Tell me where and when, I'll be there.*

Lily: *Okay. xo*

I grinned at that small 'xo.'

Was this what I'd been reduced to?

Because it amused me, I replied: *xo.*

Was this how people dated now?

Fuck me.

Life with hook-up apps might seem easy, but it was even easier to have a stable of bitches around.

Of course, that was why Keira's heart was fucking broken and Storm was walking around like he'd been kneed in the balls because she'd kicked him out.

I rubbed my chin at the thought, then got to my feet and made my way down to Rex's office.

"You finally decided to show up?"

Because I was in a relatively good mood thanks to Lily, even if the idea of popping her cherry took some of the vibes away from shit, I took a deep bow. "At your service."

Rex scowled at me then he pinched the bridge of his nose, blew out a breath, and grumbled, "God grant me strength."

That had me smirking at him. "Dude, he abandoned us a long time ago."

"Maybe." He narrowed his eyes at me. "What the fuck took you so long?"

"Was on the phone."

"That's your excuse?" The glower deepened.

I shrugged. "It was with Lily Lancaster."

At that, the Prez stilled, then arched a brow at me. "Why you talking to her?"

"Like her." I shrugged again. "She's funny."

"She's funny," he repeated blandly. "Funny?"

"Yeah. You know. Har-har? Surprises me too."

"She's the fucking enemy."

I snorted. "Nope. Not even close. I told you, she wants her dad dead."

"And only you would think she was dating material. Fuck me, I can just imagine how that conversation went down. Her gagging on your dick, and in between you letting her up for air and her telling you that she wants to murder her dad." He rolled his eyes. "And they say romance is dead."

Though I smirked at him, I admitted, "Ain't boned her yet. All her holes are Link-free."

He pulled a face. "You're fucking gross sometimes."

"Proud of it." I folded my arms across my chest. "You pull me away for a reason?"

"Yeah. One of the women wants to talk to you." He waggled his phone then tossed it at me. "Stone sent me a message."

Uneasy, I caught the phone and stared at it.

Stone: *Ghost would like to speak with Link. It'd be a kindness. She's not doing too well.*

"How are they doing?"

"First time you asked me that," Rex pointed out, his head tilting to the side as he leaned back in his desk chair.

While he went by the label 'Prez,' it wasn't like he was a fucking royal.

The decision for him to be our leader was democratic.

Well, as democratic as it could be.

If he started doing bad shit, pulling stuff we didn't agree with, we'd lynch him and set someone else, probably Storm, in charge.

Which, holy fuck, was the last thing any of us needed.

Especially Storm right now. Keira was fucking with his head in a way I was sure she didn't recognize.

Still, that was neither here nor there.

Point was, Rex wasn't royal, but the way he sat there behind his desk, leaning back into his seat, head relaxing against the rest, he looked like he was the king of all he surveyed.

While that might have pissed another guy off, I appreciated it.

Rex was a strong leader, and the Sinners were a rowdy, motley crew of bastards who needed someone to keep their asses in line.

Not that we always obeyed. Me in particular.

"Link?"

I tossed him his phone back. "What?"

"You heard me. You ain't asked after them."

You didn't need to ask. Whispers went around the clubhouse faster than the Clap. I heard how they were doing and knew it wasn't going well.

Stone had almost lost Amara twice, but she'd pulled her back. Tatána wasn't eating and had tried to slit her fucking wrists, and then Ghost? She was weak—dying weak—from some kind of infection she had that the antibiotics weren't curing.

I tightened my mouth as I headed over to the tray of drinks and poured myself a couple of fingers of tequila.

Sinking back a gulp, I let the burn cleanse me. Not that it got far. Too much of me was filthy, and what I'd seen that night was gonna scar me for a goddamn lifetime.

"How's Giulia? Ain't seen her around."

Rex scowled. "She's been helping the women."

"Legit?" My estimation of her soared.

"Legit." He grunted. "What's going on with you, man?"

I cut him a look. "You weren't there."

Three words, and they said it all.

The irritation on his face lessened some, and he exhaled roughly. "No. I wasn't."

"Be glad you weren't," I stated grimly, eying the amber liquid in my glass and swirling it around so it licked the edges. "Never seen nothing like it, and hope to fuck I never see shit like it again."

"Brother, you doing okay?"

I tipped up my chin. "I'm alive and I wasn't caged like a dog. I'm doing fine."

His mouth tightened. "You going to have a problem with seeing Ghost?" His scowl made a quick reappearance. "Why the fuck is she called that?"

"Gave her the nickname. Dunno why she's still using it."

Rex complained, "Only you'd give a woman a nickname like that."

"Had to be there to get it."

My arched brow had him rolling his eyes. "You going to see Ghost?"

"If she's asked me to go visit, I will. Don't know why she has, but I'll go all the same."

"Good." A breath whistled between his teeth. "We need them to live, Link."

Lips pursing at that, I took a bigger sip of tequila because I knew what he was saying without actually saying the words.

We couldn't lose three women, dispose of their bodies, not without something coming back on us.

"I'll do what I can."

"Good. We need to think about burying the other one too." His tone darkened, and I knew he was shifting the topic to something that pissed him off. "How do you think Lancaster knows about our ties with the Five Points?

"If his daughter is right, then the sheriff is on our side which means our backhanders are true."

"There are lots of backhanders that ease the way. Someone might have split."

"Then they need ferreting out. Fucking weak links, hate them."

I dipped my chin. "Nyx and I can do that."

Rex scraped a hand over his chin. "Would prefer to leave him here with Giulia, but I think it needs the pair of you."

"I agree. You know we're effective together."

"One's the jackhammer and the other's the scalpel."

Snickering, I muttered, "You talk out of your ass."

"But I do it so finely," he mocked. "Get in touch with Declan. See if you can deal with things alone. If not, drag Nyx into it." He rubbed his eyes. "We need a council meeting.

"Shit's been up in the air over the last few days, need to get things back on an even keel. We can discuss where we need you to go then."

"When?"

"Day after tomorrow? It's late now, and Storm's already fucking drunk. Won't get any sense out of the prick."

"Didn't you hear?"

"Hear what?" Rex was still scowling.

"The last time he went to Keira's place." My lips twisted into a grim smile. "She changed the locks."

Brows lifting and mouth parting, Rex couldn't have looked more shocked if he tried. "Seriously?"

"Yeah. I heard this from her. Got to assume that's why he's tanked at..." Looked at my watch. "Six PM."

"He said shit to me. The fucker's derailing. Things were much calmer when Keira and he were a couple. Can't you do something to get them back together again?"

I snorted. "Do I look like fucking Cupid?"

"Maybe. Glitter comes out of your ass sometimes."

"I never shove glitter up there."

"Only butt plugs. I know." He covered his face with his hand. "Why does any conversation with you always revolve around the ass?"

"In my defense, you're the one who brought it up this time," I said wryly, earning myself a chuckle from my brother.

"You turned me. You made me asscentric."

"Best way to be," I retorted, after taking another slurp of the tequila in my hand. "But to get shit back on track, Keira's pissed with Storm, and only Storm is going to change that."

"Dumbfuck. Some bitches you just don't mess around with."

"Seems he's figured that out too goddamn late." I pursed my lips, genuinely irritated by the situation.

In the run up to Keira leaving, I'd been telling him to get his head out of his ass. He'd been partying hard, getting home late.

You couldn't do that shit when you had a kid and an Old Lady at home —not unless you wanted to be like our parents, and they hadn't exactly been role models.

Rex sighed. "I heard Kendra stirred some shit between them."

I arched a brow. "Hadn't heard that. Keira didn't say anything to me about her, but I know a sweetbutt told her some things it'd have been kinder if she never knew."

"Overheard Tink and Jingles discussing it. Whatever it was, even they thought she went too far."

"Fucking Kendra," I sneered. "Never did like that bitch."

"Can't disagree with you. They're all cats. I mean, Giulia and Keira *are*. But I fucking hate it when they turn bitchy on one another. We got enough shit going down without infighting from the bitches."

"If Keira had been a bit more like Giulia, she'd probably have had less trouble."

Rex snickered. "No one handles the clubwhores quite like Giulia."

"True." I smiled.

When Giulia had arrived six weeks ago, she'd caused a lot of shit by headbutting Kendra, breaking noses here and there, getting in a lot of the snatches' faces.

She hadn't rolled over and let them kick her while she was down. Nope. She'd faced them, dealt with them, and now they were all wary as hell around her.

"Keira's not like that," I pointed out. "You know that. She's a homemaker, not a trouble starter."

"Why the fuck he wifed her, I don't know." Rex huffed. "I mean, I get it. She's beautiful. But—"

"He was a selfish prick. Wanting it all and hurting her in the process. And I'm the king of selfish. If I say someone's goddamn selfish, that means they're cunts."

"That's one way of looking at it," Rex countered with a laugh. "I'll talk to Storm. See if I can help clear shit up with him."

"Only way you'll do that is if you change Keira's locks back," I pointed out, before I slammed the rest of my tequila down.

"Well, I ain't going to do that, but maybe I can get the dick to wake the fuck up, see he's only wrecking shit for himself and that little girl of his."

"Douche," I muttered, semi-amused when Rex nodded his agreement. Then, sucking in a breath and drawing courage, I muttered, "I'll go see the women now."

I didn't wait for him to reply, just headed on out and down the hall to the front door.

Passing JoJo on her knees slurping down Steel, I shook my head. "Idiot."

I was surrounded by them.

He peered through slitted eyes and focused on me long enough to flip me the bird.

Shrugging, I walked on, hoping to fuck Stone wouldn't leave the bunkhouse where she was looking after the women and head to the compound, because she'd catch him in the goddamn hallway.

That would hurt her like crazy, which was precisely why the fuckwit had done it.

I truly was surrounded by idiots, and today had only confirmed it.

When I was the only one who was making sense?

The day after tomorrow, we wouldn't be having a council meeting, it'd be Armageddon for real.

Shaking my head at just how big of a moron Steel was, I headed out into the early evening.

The compound wasn't unattractive, it was just boring.

Purpose built, it was easy to see a bunch of guys from the sixties had designed it—guys who'd just returned from 'Nam with a hatred for the government burning in their souls. There was none of the flower power shit here. It was heavily utilitarian.

Before Bear had retired and passed on the gavel to Rex, his only brat, the place had been painted a steel gray.

I wasn't sure which sweetbutt had sucked Rex off and asked him to repaint it a more flattering cream, but it gave off fewer prison vibes now, that was for damned sure.

Reaching for my cell, I smiled when I saw it was Lily.

Lily: *I freaked you out, didn't I?*

Surprised by the show of vulnerability, I froze in my tracks.

Me: *Beautiful girl like you? Went to college? Didn't get laid? You shocked me. Not much freaks me out.*

Well, that was bullshit. I'd found my limit, and that had been discovered in Luke Lancaster's fucking *lair*.

Lily: *I made arrangements with my friend. I'll send you a link to her place. Thursday? Morning/night?*

Me: *Thursday. Morning AND night.*

Lily: *Oh. Okay. x*

I snickered at the 'x' as I had earlier.

Me: *x*

I shoved my phone back in my pocket, ignoring the next buzz because I had to suck it up and suck it in. I wasn't looking forward to seeing the women.

This was for Ghost's sake.

It was why Stone had texted Rex to get me to haul ass—I'd ignored her texts for the past few days.

It wasn't their fault that the second I saw them, I was transported back to that place. That time. And I figured by Tatána's and Amara's reactions, they associated me with that moment too.

Ghost, when I eventually saw her, not so much.

She smiled at me, weakly, and without all the shit on her face and body, without the scent of death lingering in the air, I saw she was a beautiful woman.

As were the others.

Luke had fucking taste, that was for sure.

But they were all brutally thin.

They were all pasty and sickly-looking.

And they had more wires and lines coming off them than I knew what to do with.

The bunkhouses were for visiting chapters and other MCs to sleep in. That meant they were like mini apartments, complete with bathroom, kitchen, and bedroom. This was one of the bigger ones and it had two bedrooms.

The bunkhouse had been turned into a mini field hospital, and it was where I found Stone, leaning back against the kitchen counter watching me take it in.

Giulia was there too, but she was seated at the kitchen table, her eyes heavily shadowed.

I bypassed Tatána who was in a nest of blankets on the sofa, her wrists bandaged up, and who immediately flinched at the sight of me.

Because I pretty much felt the same way, I did the kindest thing and ignored her, then headed for the kitchen.

"You got everything you need, Stone?"

"We're out of the woods now. We just have to build their strength up."

My brows rose at that. Rex—the fucker. He'd been speaking like they were dying. Shit, not that I was complaining, but he'd definitely guilt-tripped me into visiting.

Stone yawned, breaking into my internal grousing, and I saw that her work had taken its toll on her. She looked like she needed a good sleep and, though I'd say this to no one, even more, looked like she needed Steel to hug the shit out of her.

Preferably in a bed.

Where they'd sleep together.

Fuck, maybe I *was* Cupid?

Grunting at the thought, I muttered, "When are you going back to the city?"

"Day after tomorrow."

"They going to be okay without you?"

"Giulia knows what to do now. It's not ideal," she murmured, pulling a face. "But it's the best I can do. I've already stayed on longer than I should."

"I can call you if there's a problem, and it's not like you're far away, Stone," Giulia replied, and the respect in her eyes stunned me because Giulia and most of the women from the club didn't get along well.

At first, with all the shit she'd caused with the sweetbutts, I'd figured she was one of those women who just hated other bitches. Which, in a place like the clubhouse, was a fucking nightmare just waiting to happen.

But I soon realized I was wrong on that front. It took a lot to earn her respect, but when you had it, she gave her friendship too.

I liked Giulia.

She was a pain in the ass, had more attitude than sense, and made the best pasta *puttanesca* I'd ever fucking tasted, but more than that, she was good for Nyx.

I liked her for my bro.

Nyx needed something to keep him sane, and while Giulia wasn't the ideal candidate considering she was prone to violence, it fit that she and Nyx would gel well together.

"What are you staring at, bozo?" she mumbled, glowering at me and reminding me of the whole 'more attitude than sense' thing.

"You. You look exhausted. You both do."

"I am. We are. It's been a long couple of days, and it's been fucking hard but we're getting there. Aren't we, Stone?"

Stone's lips twitched, and I saw from the sparkle in her eyes that Giulia had a new friend.

God help us.

I guessed it fit, considering they were both biker brats, but there was a distinct age gap...

Apparently Giulia liked hanging around old fuckers.

Nyx was a lot older than Stone even, so with Giulia, he apparently liked robbing the cradle.

Fuck.

Lily was about Giulia's age.

Shit. I was just as bad then!

Grunting at the thought, even if I was mostly amused by the notion, I twisted around and asked, "Rex said Ghost wanted to talk to me?"

"Yeah." Stone shook her head. "Only you'd call someone in their situation 'Ghost.'"

That was like the third person who'd told me that. "What can I say? It fit. Her voice was so fucking quiet—"

"Still is. Can barely hear her most of the time," Giulia interjected with a wince.

"I think she must have damaged her voice box," Stone inserted, tone grim.

We all shared a look, each of us knowing and wanting to shy away from exactly *how* she'd done that.

See, we were bikers and they were biker spawn. We knew how the real world worked. We did bad shit. Nyx routinely cut up pedos, for fuck's sake. We weren't innocent little lambs.

But this went to a whole other level.

A level that messed with our comfort zones.

Maybe it was a weird kind of logic, maybe it was fucked up to be okay with murdering *some* people so long as they were shitty bastards, but that was how it rolled for us.

And I included myself in that too.

I wasn't a good man. If I got shot up one day, stabbed to death or whatever, I deserved it.

I'd go meeting my Maker well aware I'd been a shitty human being, so coming across a *shittier* human being?

Well...let's just say it took all our breaths away.

Wanting to avoid this conversation, and not really wanting to talk to Ghost even though it was important to her, I got to my feet and headed to the bedrooms.

When I opened the door and saw Amara curled up on her side, I grunted which had her gasping and flinching back like I was going to attack her.

"Wrong bedroom," Stone told me dryly.

"Could have warned me."

"Nope. She's got to acclimatize to the fact there are men here. Men that look like mean motherfuckers, but are putzes where women are concerned."

"You're just full of fucking charm today, aren't you?"

Stone snickered. "You know it."

Shooting her the bird, I headed for the other bedroom and winced when I opened the door.

Ghost was like Amara, wrapped in a cocoon of sheets and blankets, but the drips and shit around her went to a whole other level.

I knew Stone had only been able to do so much to help.

Shit like X-rays and scans and blood tests were beyond us, but she was training to be an ER doc for a reason.

Under pressure, she worked well, and in the end, it was all that was available to these women...unless they wanted to return wherever they'd come from, and considering whoever had brought them over here had sold them to Luke fucking Lancaster, I couldn't blame them for wanting to stay under the radar.

I didn't believe that shit about the US being the land of the free. Not anymore. But for these women, all they'd been given was a handful of chains, not liberty.

"Hey," I rumbled, keeping my voice low as I didn't want to disturb her if she was resting.

"Link?"

Though I'd expected it, it came as no surprise when her voice was soft and gentle to the point where it was hard to make out my own fucking name.

I stepped into the gloomy room, which hadn't been redecorated in way too long—while the outside was utilitarian sixties, in here, it was fucking flower power to the max—and used the faint light coming from the windows at the back of the bed to maneuver to her side.

"Yeah. It's me." I dropped to a crouch beside her. "How you doing, Ghost?"

"Everything hurts," she admitted, but she laughed. Fucking laughed. And that broke my damn heart. "I'm getting better though."

"Glad to hear it, honey." I reached over, cautious because I didn't want her to flinch like the others had.

The last thing I intended was to cause her pain or anxiety.

"I-I'm sorry to disturb you, but you're the only man I've really spoken to and I-I, the others, Stone and Giulia, they seem to like you. I feel like you might be the right person to ask—" She hesitated. "You've already done so much for all of us. More than we could have hoped for."

I reached over and squeezed her arm again. "Ask, Ghost."

"Please, I have a sister—"

"Did Luke get her too?"

"No," she rasped, but her eyes flared wide in terror at the prospect. "Her situation is different."

Inwardly wincing at derailing that conversation and maybe adding to her nightmares, I muttered, "Different how?"

"My mother left the Ukraine when I was a little girl. She came here and got married.

"My sister is American, but our mother died a few years after she was born, and her father passed in a car crash a year ago."

Jesus, how much bad luck did this girl have?

Unaware of my thoughts, Ghost continued, "I was denied a visa so I came a different way." Her smile was tight. "I promised her I'd be there for her, but Luke happened."

I patted her hand. "You have some details for her? I'll find a way to get in touch."

"Really?"

"Really."

"Thank you, Link," she whispered. "I truly appreciate this as well as everything else you've done for me."

"Done nothing more than another human being should do for another. Just because you've been exposed to the worst out there, don't forget, for most people, decency isn't a curse word."

Look at me go—preaching like I was a *decent* person.

If I went into church, I was the kind of guy who would cause the holy water to start bubbling and boiling. Nothing about me was decent in the eyes of the world.

But... sometimes, you just had to compare yourself to the worst cunt out there to realize you weren't that fucking bad.

I got up from my crouch. "Tatána and Amara are scared of me. Why aren't you?"

Her features were delicate from how much weight she'd lost, and her skin had a strange translucency I didn't understand but fuck, after I'd been in a cage underground for however long, I hoped I'd look as good as she did.

Her elfin features were only enhanced by a pixie cut, something I had to assume was a medical decision considering the others all sported the same style when they'd had long hair back in those cages.

Her smile, delicate but beautiful, burrowed into me, making me grateful I hadn't ignored Lily, that we hadn't given up on finding these women, innocents who'd been dragged into a world they didn't deserve.

"You saved us. You went into that basement. You *helped* us out of those cages. They are silly to be frightened of you. You're our saviors."

My nose crinkled at that. "I'm not a good man."

"But you're a decent one."

"Not really—"

She smiled. "I choose to believe what I choose to believe."

That had me sighing and, determined to change the subject, I asked, "Where was your sister last?"

"St. Jude's Orphanage in Cincinnati."

"I'll find a way to get you in touch with one another."

"Thank you, Link," she whispered, this time, her tone so soft, I only heard my name as I headed out the door.

Before I left, though, I muttered, "Concentrate on getting better, Ghost. You hear me?"

"Yes, I hear you, Link."

"Good."

TEN

LINK

THE NEXT DAY

"DECLAN?"

"Link? What the fuck do you want?"

My lips twitched. "Wonderful to hear your voice too, Dec."

A grunt sounded down the line. "If you say so. There a reason for this call, or you just blowing smoke up my ass?"

"If that's what gets you hot under the collar—"

"Okay, fucker," the Five Pointer growled. "Let's get shit on the road. Don't need you talking sweet nothings in my ear. What do you want?"

"Got a few questions about a guy called Donavan Lancaster. You heard of him?"

"Can't not know who that bastard is." Another grunt, then I heard a scrawl like he was making notes. I didn't think it was about this conversation because he sounded absentminded, like he wasn't focusing on what we were discussing. "He built Landis Scraper and has a few other projects that got Finn all riled up when the plans were revealed."

Because I wasn't a total heathen, the name prompted me to inquire, "How is Finn, by the way?"

"Taken to fatherhood like a charm. It's fucking sickening."

My lips curved at that because, even though he sounded partially disgusted, I heard something I didn't think he realized he'd revealed —*yearning*.

I got it. For the first time in my life, I fucking got it. Which kind of blew my mind.

Declan was about my age, after all. When a man passed thirty, he started questioning shit. Shit he probably shouldn't question but did anyway. And when forty was on the horizon? Fuck.

"Glad to hear it." I cleared my throat with the niceties out of the way. "Any reason Donavan Lancaster would know we were working together?"

"We as in the Five Points and the MC?" He hummed under his breath. "Not as far as I know." Another hum. "Wait. Lancaster? Isn't that the fucker Nyx's girl took out?"

"Yeah. His son. Daddy is causing shit for us."

"I'll bet. That fucker was his blue-eyed boy. Saw him around most of the party spots. Even went to a few of our clubs. Didn't like him. Got called in once to deal with him.

"He'd beaten the fuck out of a girl he'd been trying to pick up. Didn't like it when she said no."

"Why didn't you report it?"

"Since when do we go to the police over shit like that? I stuck a gun under his chin, told him if he darkened our doors again I'd blow his brains out.

"Then, I told him I'd blow off his cock if he approached the girl and sent her home with one of our foot soldiers." A laugh sounded down the line. "They just had their second kid."

"You matchmaker you," I joked, amused at that particular irony.

Declan muttered, "Yeah, regular fucking Cupid, that's me." *Maybe the two of us should go into partnership?* "Anyway, no. I don't see why the daddy would know about our mutual interests. Why do you ask?"

"He's trying to use our connection against us. Leverage with the cops."

"Well, let him. It's not like we don't have the pigs in our pockets."

"True." I grunted. "Was just hoping there'd be a reason for him knowing that kind of shit."

"That kind of money, he'll have ears everywhere—" His voice waned. "I see what you mean. Thanks for the heads up, Link. I appreciate it."

When the dial tone clicked in my ear, I grimaced.

Great.

Heads up or heads roll...I wasn't sure which was likely to be going down in the Five Points today.

Dialing through to Rex, the second he picked up I muttered, "Declan doesn't know of a reason why Lancaster would be aware of our connection, but I might have just started a fucking witch hunt."

Rex groaned. "Good going, Link. What was that shit about you being a scalpel and Nyx being a jackhammer?"

I pulled a face. "He didn't give me a chance to get a word in edgewise."

"Fuck." Rex blew out a breath that gusted down the line. "It's not ideal, but leave him to it. Maybe he'll find a snitch, and if he does, we'll have our answers."

"Yeah, I guess." I was proud of my ability to ferret out shit for the club, and couldn't help but feel like I'd let Rex down.

"Where you at?"

"The garage. Need me at the clubhouse?"

"No. Carry on. You going to have the books to me soon?"

My mouth tightened. "I'll get them to you when they're fucking ready."

"It's already mid-goddamn-month, Link—"

"And I told you I didn't want to manage this place. I'm a fucking mechanic. Not management."

"Well, I want you to be both so get your goddamn act together."

For the second time in as little as twenty minutes, someone put the fucking phone down on me. I growled under my breath then threw a wrench at the bulletproof window that linked my office to the workshop.

Pissed when it didn't shatter, even though I knew it wouldn't, I got some satisfaction out of Gunner and Jaxson, a brother and a Prospect, jerking in surprise at the noise.

Ignoring them, I looked at the books in front of me. Rex seemed to think I'd been ignoring them, but fuck, I hadn't.

For some reason, the numbers just seemed to jump off the page at me no matter how hard I worked to keep shit in line.

I'd gone so far as to transfer all the stuff Gunner input into the computers onto a work pad in the vain hope I'd be able to tally shit up, but to no avail.

Back when I'd been in school, I'd probably have been given a fancy name for why I was shit with figures, but that stuff didn't wash in an MC.

Dyslexic or not, I was expected to do my part. Even if that part felt like I was being asked to find a cure for world fucking hunger.

As I glowered at the books, I wondered if there was something else I could do, something else I could procrastinate over...

I picked up my phone. It had been quiet for a while because I knew Lily was in a class at the country club.

Just the thought of her bending in all those weird positions had me corralling a boner.

Still, I'd prefer to pester her than do the shit I was in this office for...

Me: *You still at yoga?*

Lily: *Just out. Why?*

ELEVEN

LILY

I WAS NERVOUS.

Very, very nervous.

Maybe I was doing something stupid, maybe it was reckless, and maybe it would only end in me being hurt, but this wasn't even a rebellion.

This wasn't something I was doing to spite anyone. It was simply because I thought Link was gorgeous. Because he made me laugh. And he had something about him that made me want to know *more*.

We had nothing in common. Our pasts were too different for that and yet, I was showing him the real me, the true Lily, and he wasn't revolted.

Wasn't disgusted.

He liked me.

Liked *me* despite the fact I was a Lancaster, a family who was putting his MC and a woman he cared about through the ringer.

It was depressing to accept that he might be doing this to punish me for what Luke had done and what my father was doing. But even believing that this was just going to end in heartbreak, I wanted to do it.

Needed to do it.

This was my body, and it was my choice what I did with it.

I blew out a breath as I stared out at the pool beyond the terrace. Tiffany had, as promised, made her escape to the main house where her father was out at work and her mother, quite fortuitously, was visiting Las Vegas for a bachelorette party.

This place was, for all intents and purposes, mine. Paul and Alix were none the wiser about what I was doing, and the only potential flaw to my plan was Link not being able to get to the house.

I gnawed on my bottom lip even as I tugged at my shirt. Tiffany had called me insane for not changing my clothes, but this was me.

Yoga pants and all.

The only difference from my regular outfit was that I didn't have a sports bra on, but a pretty lacy one. Matching red panties too.

I wore a light tee, had flip-flops on my feet, and my Apple watch on my wrist, and a pair of gold hoops in my ears. No makeup. No other jewelry. No artifice. Nothing.

Nada.

He was getting me.

Lily Lancaster.

The real me. The one he'd been getting to know. The one who, I thought, he liked.

God, I hoped he did.

I hoped this wasn't one big ploy.

The pool sparkled. Its huge, kidney shape was one big invitation to jump into it and enjoy the chill against my overheated skin.

I was nervous, antsy, and darting around Tiffany's place like an ant on acid as I tried to work off the energy coursing through me.

This was crazy.

We'd only talked via text. Our meetings hadn't exactly been pleasant. But...

Shit, Tinder dates started with less, didn't they?

If I wanted to hook up with a down and dirty biker, then I freakin' could!

Bolstered by that defiant thought, I straightened my shoulders, wiped my palms down against the sides of my pants, and leaned against the veranda door.

It was no punishment to look over the landscaping that had probably cost Tiffany's father a small fortune, what with the fully matured palm trees that were dotted here and there as well as patches of cacti gardens...the shape of the pool and the way the water licked at the sides, with no tiles around the rim, it was like an oasis.

A mirage, even.

A verdant and luxurious one.

I folded my arms across my chest, taking the opportunity to check the time. When I saw it was a few minutes past the time he'd told me he'd be here, I felt disappointment start to unfurl.

Of course, he might not be punctual, but I just had a feeling—a bad one—that this was all going to come tumbling down around me.

I'd shown too much of the real me, I realized. No one wanted to know that much about a woman. It wasn't something that any man—

"Link!" I whispered, straightening up as I saw him round the corner of the main house and stride across the garden toward the pool house like he had every right to be there.

My heart surged into my throat and my stomach bottomed out as I watched his approach.

Everything about him was dangerous.

I saw it in him, just like I'd seen it in my father and brother. It was an energy about them, a chaotic force I didn't understand.

With my family, I didn't want to understand.

Link? Yeah. I did. Call me crazy, but I really did.

I was under no illusions.

I'd googled the Satan's Sinners' MC long before I'd decided to get in touch with them, and I knew what they were involved in.

When Father had mentioned the Five Points, I'd googled them too.

Mafia.

Or, to be more precise, the Mob. The Irish Mob.

Which, according to Father, the Sinners were tied up with.

That 'business' was only the peak of a mountain worth of trouble the Sinners represented, but for all that, I didn't want to hear it.

I was informed, I knew the worst, and I was going headfirst into this anyway because that smile? Those eyes? The long-limbed, loose gait of his as he moved toward me?

How could I say no?

He wore a pair of jeans, his boots, and that cut—his usual uniform—but this time, he wore a Henley.

It was kind of disappointing not to be able to see his biceps because they were delicious, but I comforted myself with the knowledge that I'd be seeing a lot more of him soon.

My stomach throbbed at the thought and my heart started pounding.

God.

I was going to expire before he even managed to touch me!

"Hey, sweetness. Sorry I had to shuffle things a little later. Had some shit to handle."

His greeting surprised me. As did the lazy smile that set fire to my insides. It was affectionate and warm. And I knew it was stupid, but I could see...he liked me. That smile was impossible to feign.

It was senseless, but that made me shy.

Me.

Shy.

A woman who'd eaten dinner with three Presidents of the United States, who routinely attended events with celebrities and politicians. Who was quite at ease in most situations thanks to having a control freak for a father.

Yes. Me. I was shy.

I bowed my head and smiled at him, my gaze on his lips until he chuckled, reached forward, and with his pointer finger, tipped my chin up.

"None of that, sweetness," he stated firmly, but he was smiling.

With his eyes.

My throat felt tight, so I just waved a hand, silently inviting him inside. I wished he'd pushed into me, had kissed me straight off the bat, maybe that would have taken my nerves away.

But he didn't.

He stepped over the threshold and peered around. "Where's the television?"

For a second, I could do no more than gape at him. "Huh?"

"You heard me, sugar tits. The TV?"

My brow puckered—had I mislabeled this? Made him think this was—

"Whatever you're thinking, stop. Women." Link tutted, folding massive arms over his chest as he stared at me. "Always overthinking. I want to watch *Chopped* with you."

"What if it isn't on?"

"It's always on," he scoffed with an eye roll, making me smile.

"You command it, huh?"

"I more than command it."

"Not sure that's possible."

"You going to bring out a thesaurus?"

I laughed. "If that's what gets you hot."

He smirked, then his gaze raked up and down over me, making me flash with unexpected heat. "I'll tell you what gets me hot. Seeing you in yoga pants so tight I can see your camel toe."

Said camel toe pulsed even as I peered down in horror. "I don't have a camel toe!" I argued, but before I could even finish the sentence, he was suddenly there, and his hand was between my legs.

I almost died. My lungs burned as he rubbed along the crevice of my sex.

"There. Just a tiny one. Enough to give me a boner." He quirked a brow at me again. "You gonna argue with that? Or want to make sure I'm telling the truth?"

Biting my lip, I glanced at his mouth and kept my gaze trained there before I muttered, "I think it's only fair that I make sure you're not lying."

"Go ahead, sugar tits. Frisk me in the name of equal rights."

I couldn't stop myself from laughing, not just from his statement, but from the 'sugar tits.'

It wasn't the first time he'd used it, but somehow, it made me smile more than 'sweetness.' Weird, but true.

Grinning all the while, I reached down and cupped his dick through his jeans. He was hard. Thick. Big.

I whistled between my teeth. "You're packing heavy."

That had him winking at me. "You got that right, babe." He reached up, tapped my bottom lip. "Stop gnawing on that or I'll have to do it for you."

Breathily, I whispered, "I wouldn't mind."

"I would. Now, where's the TV?"

Disappointed, I scowled at him. But he just arched that damn brow of his *again*, and with a huff, I twisted around on my flip flop-clad heel and stalked deeper into the pool house.

He whistled, making me jump, then I realized he was *wolf*-whistling, and my cheeks burned but I refused to turn around, refused to look at him ogling my ass, even though I was really glad he was ogling me.

This wasn't going how I'd expected it to go, and maybe I should have anticipated that. Maybe I should have known that Link never did anything the normal way.

Hadn't I seen that in our conversations? Text chats that went on for hours at a time? Sometimes deep into the night?

I'd only had my cell for a week and a half, and we'd already exchanged thousands of texts which gave me an insight into the man himself.

A man who loved his brothers as if they were blood.

A man who swore like a trooper but was capable of talking me down from a panic attack as he had back at the Daytona.

A man who looked like he was mean and nasty, but who was concerned for a brother who'd recently split from his Old Lady.

So, accepting that Link was a weirdo and I liked him anyway, I carried on toward the TV room which was set up like a cinema.

Link whistled again the second he stepped into the room. "Holy fuck. She's got a cinema? In a goddamn pool house?"

I turned around to smile at him. "Tiffany likes her creature comforts, and she's a daddy's girl, which means she gets what she wants. Especially if she doesn't move out."

He frowned at that. "I thought most parents wanted to get rid of their kids. That was how it was for me and most of my friends."

"I wish Father would loosen the reins he has on me."

I grimaced at just how tight those reins were.

Then, determined not to think of him, I decided to get the ball rolling. Having been in this room before, I knew how nearly all of the tech worked —all through one main switch close to the screen which I turned on.

"Most of the people I know and hang around with are close to their family. Or, maybe they're like me and they're putting on a show too."

Link pondered that, then whistled once again when he walked deeper into the space as it morphed into a vivid ambient purple. The light accentuated all the little extras Tiffany had put in here.

The chairs, burgundy in natural light, suddenly looked blood-red—a plus for her considering she loved horror movies. The chairs were one and a half in size, nice and roomy, and there were four situated on a raised dais with an accent table between them all that had a fridge integrated into each. They had their own footstools too, long and wide, and extra plush just like the chairs.

The carpet underfoot gleamed black in the light, and all in all, with the dramatic paintings on the wall, colorful slashes that I knew had the artist's DNA in them so that, in the purple light, they'd glow—yeah, gross, but Tiff was beyond unusual—it was like an expensive bordello, but she loved it, so who was I to argue?

I moved toward the seats just as Link did, his heavy boots not making a whisper of sound, the carpet was that dense, and when I approached my chair, getting ready to take a seat on the armchair that had all the controls, he beat me to it, slinking down before he hauled me onto his lap.

Then, he proceeded to toe out of his boots and socks, and his now sockless feet soon joined my bare ones on the rest.

A laugh escaped me when he murmured, "You didn't think I was going to let you sit all the way over there, did you?" I had. But I didn't need to say that because he snorted. "Absolutely crazy."

"I try," I said dryly, then I leaned over, tensing when I felt his dick against my ass cheeks.

"Get used to that, sugar tits," he informed me, his tone blasé. "Ain't going nowhere when you're around, waving that fabulous ass of yours in my face."

His words were outrageous enough to make me snicker, but I ignored them as I grabbed the control and switched on the massive TV.

"You really want to watch *Chopped*?"

"Yeah. I want to prove you wrong. The judges are assholes."

"They're paid to do a job," I instantly retorted, and I didn't have to see him to know he was rolling his eyes.

"You keep on thinking that, babe," he grumbled.

When I scrolled through the channels, I had to laugh when there was, indeed, an episode of *Chopped* playing. I switched it on, saying, "We only missed the first five minutes. Want me to rewind it?"

"Of course. We have to know their backstory."

As I rewound the show, I had to reason that those six words pretty much summed Link up.

Backstory was important to him, as it should be. It was what made a man or woman be who they were, wasn't it?

Still, it said a lot about him, a lot I was glad to hear. If he was doing this to get back at my brother, to punish him through me in some weird way, then that put my mind at rest.

Because while I was most certainly a poor little rich girl, I was who I was because of my backstory, and I didn't hide from that.

When the show was back at the beginning, I pressed play and settled into his lap. I felt awkward, but I relaxed when he squeezed my waist, muttering, "Chill out, babe. You'll give yourself a hernia."

I had to laugh. "Don't think you can get a hernia from sitting down."

"You can if you do it right," was all he said, making no sense at all, but it made me laugh harder.

Releasing a breath, I sighed into him and forced myself to calm down.

When, for a few minutes, he didn't touch me aside from that arm squeeze, I relaxed further and got into the show with him.

Of course, that was when he struck.

His mouth was suddenly on my neck, his tongue there, plying the muscles, teasing me as he traced all the sinews on my throat.

A squeak escaped me and I rocked back, inadvertently nudging his dick, which had me instantly rocking forward. Then, I hovered, unsure which way to go as he began to suck down on the tender flesh there.

A moan escaped me as he hit a tender spot behind my ear, and it morphed into a whimper as he nibbled.

After biting my lobe and sucking on it to ease the sting, he mumbled, "Hope you're paying attention to the show, sugar tits. There will be a question and answer session on it after."

After what?

That was all I really heard from his words, and even those were forgotten when he moved his hand down over my chest and cupped my breast in his palm.

My hips jolted again, rocking back into him, and of course, his dick. It was there, like a brand of solid heat straight in the center of my lower back. It had to be uncomfortable squished there, but he didn't seem to mind.

I knew if one of my tits had been in that same position, I wouldn't have been happy, but he wasn't complaining, so I wouldn't either.

My vision began to glaze over as he carried on sucking on my throat.

Licking it.

Nibbling it.

Kissing it.

I was pretty much hiccupping with what he was making me feel between moaning and whimpering when he raked over a super sensitive part.

His hand didn't move from my breast, but he just brushed it softly. Reminding me it was there, warming it, but not doing anything to particularly tease me.

His other hand slipped down to my lap and I gulped, even as I spread my legs. His fingers delved between them, right where he'd touched before, and I squirmed as he began to run the tips over that hyperaware flesh.

I was surprised he hadn't tunneled down the front of my yoga pants to touch skin, but again, most of this was a surprise.

I'd expected to be treated roughly, *crudely*, and God help me, I wouldn't have minded. But *this* was a thousand times better. This was something I could never have anticipated. This was exploratory and, as weird as it sounded, tender.

This wasn't Link.

I knew that. Knew it like I knew my damn name. But this was for me. He was doing this for me, and God, if that didn't make me melt and have me sinking into him all the more.

I wasn't used to tenderness from men. I was used to cruelty. Vindictiveness. Spite. But this? I couldn't say it whitewashed twenty-two years of my past experiences, but it sure as hell went some way to making me realize that not every man had to act on his inclinations.

I shuddered as he began to circle his fingers around my clit. The faint pressure, the way the tips danced over me, had me releasing a shaky breath before a sharp cry escaped me when he bit down against my shoulder.

The discomfort and the pleasure swirled together, making my back arch as I spread my legs wider. His other hand moved away from my breast and slid down to my inner thigh, where his fingers dug into the crevice where my leg met my groin.

The move was distinctly grounding, and I enjoyed it all the more when he began to rub harder against my clit. His tongue lashed at the skin he had between his teeth, and as the blood rose to the surface, I moaned as he worked me higher and higher, not stopping until I was hoarsely crying out my orgasm.

Pleasure flooded me, spilling out of me in the noises that escaped my throat. I thrashed against him, my hands coming up, one to cup the back of his neck, the other to grip his hair, to hold him close.

I needed that connection, the union, and it made me soar a little higher as I experienced my first orgasm that wasn't self-appointed.

Even as he stopped petting me, he carried on working that little sliver of flesh he had between his teeth. I knew it was going to be red, knew it would be bruised in the morning, and I didn't care.

Couldn't care.

When I looked at it in the mirror, I'd smile and remember this moment, and probably crave it all over again.

As the sharp pleasure I'd experienced began to ebb, I slumped in Link's arms. They moved, shifted until they were wrapped around my waist.

He held me close, tight, and I let my head rest against him, my temple to his jaw as, dazedly, I focused on the show.

I wasn't ashamed to admit that, twenty minutes later, when he went through that whole Q&A shit, I didn't have a clue who'd even *won* the ten-grand prize.

I was too busy floating...not only from my climax, but from being held by a man as hard and, I knew, as brutal as a brother from the Satan's Sinners' MC.

TWELVE

GIULIA

NYX: *Where are you?*

My lips twitched as I stared at the text, but my smile kinda died as I stared at Tatána who released a quiet sob that broke my fucking heart.

She was on hunger strike, and I wasn't sure why. I mean, okay, I got it. I did. But...

Okay.

No, I didn't.

I got the tears, understood her misery, but starving herself wasn't something I could get behind.

"Please, honey. You need to eat. Just tell me what you want, and I'll make it. Anything." God, I'd even started haunting blogs for true Ukrainian recipes. No matter what I did, she just wouldn't eat.

She twisted on her side, shoving her face into the pillow as she curled into a ball.

I closed my eyes, wishing like fuck I could do something, *anything*, but it wasn't like she knew me or I her. We'd both been tainted by Luke Lancaster, but by comparison, he'd merely touched my hand.

I couldn't even begin to imagine what the women had gone through. What they'd endured. And, God help me, I didn't really want to know why Ghost had forever lost her voice, leaving behind a rasping whisper that was equal parts creepy and soothing.

Knowing she wanted to be left alone, I moved away from the sofa where she was resting in a pile of squashy blankets and retreated to the dining room table where I took a seat.

This place was like the one I'd been living in with my brothers until Nyx had claimed me as his Old Lady, so I was surprisingly comfortable in it, even if it had been modified into a miserable kind of field hospital.

The smell in the air was disinfectant, pure and simple, and I worked hard to keep things under wraps. It had become harder now that Stone was gone, but we kept in touch, and she'd shown me how to give the women injections. It wasn't ideal, but nothing about this was.

The thought had me gnawing on my bottom lip as I replied to my man.

Me: *Bunkhouse. Why?*

Nyx: *Why d'you think?*

Me: *'Cause you're a control freak and you like to keep tabs on me?* :P

Nyx: *Yeah. I'm all of that and more.*

He was, actually, all of that and more, but I could deal with it because it came from a good place.

He wasn't controlling me because he was insanely jealous. Possessive, sure. But fuck if I didn't feel the exact same way about him.

And this shit with Luke Lancaster hadn't eased things for us any.

Nyx was like a poison in my blood, only I was totally okay with not having an antidote.

There was no cure to this kind of love. It burned in me as much as it burned in him, and that was something I felt honored to have.

He was my savior, but my champion too, and in the face of what these women were going through, I felt doubly fortunate to have him at my side.

Me: *You can freak on me later.*

Nyx: *I can, huh?*

Me: *I need some of that* Terminator *dick of yours.*

Nyx: *I'll terminate something...*

Me: *Aren't I lucky?*

The door squeaked as it opened, then there was some more squeaking as the wheels to Maverick's wheelchair connected with the linoleum.

It wasn't the first time I'd seen him here, but it still surprised me. The dude, according to Steel, hadn't left the clubhouse in years, yet here he was, visiting the women for the second time this week.

I watched as he rolled over to Tatána who huddled deeper into herself when he murmured her name in greeting. Her response had him shooting me a look, and I just shrugged a little helplessly.

She'd tried to take her life once, and I had a feeling she was just coasting until she succeeded where we'd managed to save her before.

She needed help, psych help, but I wasn't sure how to give that to her. Wasn't sure how to provide something that was outside of our limitations. Medical was one thing, but psychological was another.

I plucked at my bottom lip as Mav wheeled over to me. He eyed the kitchen, scanning over the half that contained the myriad shit I needed to keep the women healthy.

All the packaged up needles, and the sharps containers, then the rows of vials. I didn't understand what they contained, just knew which went to each woman and when.

He eyed the table and muttered, "Brownies didn't tempt her?"

"No."

I shoved the tray at him, silently offering him a slice. Mav wasn't as skinny as he'd been back when I first returned to the clubhouse after years of being AWOL, but he was definitely still too slim for his frame.

I'd seen pictures of him around the place before his discharge from the military...not unlike these women, he was a shadow of his former self.

A shadow I was trying to bring back into the light.

He clucked his tongue even as he picked up two brownies—he liked my food. I wasn't ashamed to admit I was proud about that.

A moan escaped him as he bit into the treat, and I winced when a sharp, terrified squeal escaped Tatána at the innocent noise he made.

It *had* sounded vaguely sexual.

Mav instantly froze and pushed the cake back onto the tray. "Fuck," he whispered under his breath.

I gave him a sad smile. "You didn't know. They're so sensitive to so many things... It's easy to freak them out."

Because he looked so guilty, I reached over and patted his hand.

"Amara's in no mood for visitors either." This place was like a morgue. And it made me so uncomfortable to think that, but it was true. "Ghost will see you though."

It didn't escape my attention that his eyes lit up at that. "Yeah?" he asked, like he needed my permission.

I figured, in my own way, I was the gatekeeper. Except this gate didn't open often. No one came here apart from me and Maverick from time to time. That was mostly because the women couldn't handle being around men and because I didn't trust the sweetbutts with them.

Maybe Cammie, ironically enough.

The one woman who I didn't like hanging around as she'd been Nyx's favorite before me, but she'd had to go back home for a few weeks—sick dad or something.

"Yeah. Go on. You might cheer her up. Take some brownies. She won't eat much, but she'll eat some."

I put a few on a plate then placed the dish onto his lap. He grinned at me and began the short journey to the bedroom where Ghost was resting.

From my seat, I could see into the open doors that led to Amara's and Ghost's rooms, so I saw Ghost twitch in bed at the squeaking noise from Mav's wheelchair.

But she didn't flinch, which I took as a good sign, and from the low murmurs coming from her room, so low I couldn't hear, I figured she was okay with seeing Mav today.

Though I had to wonder why she didn't mind him and Link but everyone else, Nyx included, made them all cower into their covers.

Was it because he was in a wheelchair? She thought he wasn't a threat?

The thought pissed me off, even if I got the logic of it. Still, Mav in a wheelchair was as lethal as a regular dude who had the use of his legs.

You didn't go into the military to come out as a pussycat.

Not that I was going to tell her that.

Not when she actually seemed to like talking to him.

My phone buzzed, and I glanced down at it. My pussy twanged at the sight of Nyx in our bed...

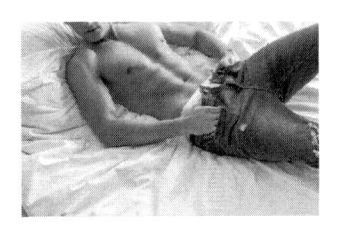

Mouth watering, I tapped out,

Me: *Don't tempt me.*

Nyx: *I was born to tempt you.*

Me: *True dat. Fucccck.*

Nyx: *Yes, please.*

Me: *Think Mav would mind me heading out for a little while?*

Nyx: *If he does, tell him I'll make him suffer later.*

I snorted despite myself, then, with the prospect of being close to Nyx and experiencing some love and comfort and pleasure this afternoon instead of the misery of being locked up inside this room—even if it was by choice and even if it was an honor to help these women come back to their own—I got to my feet and headed to the doorway to Ghost's room.

"Mav?" I called softly. "You good with me heading out for about" — Thirty minutes?— "forty minutes?" Best to be on the safe side. Nyx and that cock of his should have been illegal.

He twisted around. "Sure—" When he looked at me, he broke off, and a cocky smirk made its way onto his mouth. I narrowed my eyes at him, scowling when he stuck his tongue into his cheek. And pulsed it. Twice. *Bastard.* "Have fun."

I sniffed, folding my arms across my chest. "If you consider doing laundry fun, then you have issues," I lied.

"Well, something's going to get wet. That's for sure."

Okay. Point taken. Don't lie to Mav.

Huffing, I muttered, "You sure you're good? They've had all their meds and will be okay for another few hours at least, so there's nothing you'd need to do."

"I'm better than good." His eyes softened. "Go on. Get."

Shooting him a grateful smile, I whispered, "Bye, Ghost."

The whispering and muttering and murmuring was the regular volume in this place.

It was so like the mortuary I'd just classed it as, even if the people inside it were alive if not kicking, that it made me cringe.

"See you, Amara, Tatána," I told them, as I headed past Amara's door and the sofa.

They didn't reply, not that I'd expected them to, and when I was outside, I let the sun sink into my body before I took a deep sigh and cleansed my nostrils from the stench of the sick room.

Tipping my head back, I paused, just for a second, then I felt my phone buzz and knew that was Nyx telling me to move my ass.

Which I did.

With haste.

My body was already heating up with thoughts of what he'd do to me the second I got into our bedroom, and the joy of it was that Luke hadn't wrecked this for me.

He'd wrecked the bar for me though.

I didn't think I'd be good with being in Daytona on my own again for a long while, which I hated. Fuck, weaknesses were made to be overcome, but that was beyond me.

At the moment.

Never say never.

I scurried into the clubhouse, rolling my eyes when I passed Steel boning Kendra—fuck, I hated her the most—on the staircase of all damn places. If I could have sprayed Lysol *everywhere*, I would have done. It'd need it.

Ew.

This place was beyond gross sometimes. I often wondered who was in need of help more—the guys or me for considering this my home.

Rolling my eyes *again* at the thought, I carried on stomping my way up to my room and felt some relief when I made it to our door.

I considered it a good day when I only saw one dick that didn't belong to my man and one pussy that wasn't mine.

Heading inside, my mouth started watering the instant I came across Nyx. He had his legs splayed on the bed, those long, strong, muscled limbs relaxed in rest.

His body was propped up on a stack of pillows I'd bought recently—as well as new bedding, a new mattress, and linens because no way was I sharing anything with clubwhores—and as the door opened, his attention veered off his cell.

The satisfaction loaded in that one look had my lips twisting.

"That sure a bet, am I?" I joked, even as I closed the door behind me, pressing my back against it as I took a second to give him a lonnnnng look.

Trust me, there was a lot to look at.

Not just the log between his legs, which had more metal on it than a cyborg, but everything about him. Just Nyx.

Fuck, he was beautiful.

Like something Michelangelo wished he could ogle as he painted my man.

"Don't just stare," he groused. "Come and touch."

I arched a brow. "I'm showering first."

His eyes lit up. "Y'are?"

"Yep. I need to wash that place off me."

I shivered, and his eyes softened. The arousal in them dimmed slightly, but it was replaced with a tenderness I knew he only ever showed me.

To many people, Nyx would be considered evil. But to me? He was everything I'd never known I needed. He was the dark that made the light in me gleam brighter than it had before.

He made me stronger.

Tougher.

All because he made me feel safe and, until him, I'd never felt that way before.

Which, of course, was ironic considering Lancaster had attacked me recently, but if it wasn't for the brotherhood of men who were linked through shed blood and broken bones, I'd have been raped or worse...been taken to that pit where Tatána, Alessa, Amara, and Sarah had existed.

You knew shit was bad when death was welcome in the face of *that*.

I pursed my lips at the thought, not liking it at all, not when I had this man to come home to.

This man who looked at me like I'd put the stars in his night sky.

His because he was the King of the Darkness.

"Either get a shower or bend over the bed," he warned, making heat flash through me. He was a gruff bastard, but you could never say he wasn't direct.

"Oh, yeah? You gonna make me?" I retorted, daring him when I knew that would get me fucked *without* the shower I really wanted.

He narrowed his eyes at me. "I'll do more than bend you over—"

A giggle escaped me—the giggles were a new development, and I wasn't particularly happy about it—and I darted off to the bathroom before he could say another word.

He growled, making my heart leap as I dashed off, and I heard his feet collide with the floor and his heavy footsteps as he chased me.

Suddenly, the excitement switched into something else.

Something darker.

Something...

My throat choked and my heart, already racing, began to pound.

Chased.

Hunted.

Caught.

Tunnel vision made the darkness spread, but I'd forgotten who owned the dark.

A grumbled, "Giulia," and I was reconnected with the moment. With this day. With my reality.

I caught a glance of myself in the mirror over the sink and saw I looked pale and pasty, my pupils blown, my chest galloping as I tried to catch my breath...and he was behind me. Concerned but calm.

"I'm okay," I squeaked, then he caught me in his gaze, and everything around me stilled.

He wanted to hurt Lancaster.

I felt it.

It throbbed through the room. He wanted to make the person who'd put this fear in me understand what fear truly was, and because I was made to be this man's, because I was his fucking *mate*, I understood, and I fed off that.

Sick, but true.

I tossed my hair over my shoulder as I thought about what I'd just left behind.

A woman who wanted to kill herself, a woman who had almost died from an infection we were barely managing to keep under control, and a woman who was practically catatonic...all that perpetrated by Lancaster.

And 'they' thought my man was evil?

It came in all shapes and sizes, but I'd faced true evil, and I knew Nyx had faced it before and would face it again, only finding relief when he could bathe in someone's blood.

Because I needed the relief, the release, because I *understood* now, I ground out, "Lancaster's gone, but I think it's time we rode."

Because we were in sync, he tilted his head to the side. "We have to be careful. The club's under scrutiny thanks to the investigation."

"We'll ride further. There are sick fucks everywhere, aren't there?"

His mouth tightened. "You don't want to see—"

"I want to do more than see," I rasped, tipping my chin up. "Lancaster can't pay, but other bastards can."

I was talking about murder. About torture. But fuck...that anger in him, the rage in me, it had to go somewhere. We had to burn it off. Between the sheets, on the road, together. We'd burn in the flames we created as a couple.

A breath exploded from him. "I've never wanted you more than I do at this moment, and before here, *now*, I didn't know I could want a woman as much as I want you."

Butterflies exploded into being in my stomach. "I love you," I whispered.

His eyes darkened. "Babe, I love you." His words were a rumble, a thunder that connected with me on a base level.

I swallowed, overcome and hyperaware, and then I took in the bigger picture, saw his dick had softened and, fuck, I wasn't about to have that.

My mood had changed so many times in the past five minutes that I wasn't as horny as I'd been, but I wanted to connect with him, wanted to be at one with him, so I started pulling off my clothes, clothes that had been in a room with the sickness of Lancaster's actions, and I dumped them in the laundry hamper.

When I was naked, his cock was delightfully hard once more, and I smirked at the sight even as I reached up and jiggled my tits, laughing as he scowled at me.

"Get that fine ass in the shower before I make use of that jiggle."

"That supposed to be a threat?" I jeered, but because I really didn't want to smell like a sickroom as we hooked up, I hopped into the shower and turned on the water.

All the while, as it heated up, our eyes were joined, and the fire sparked into being between us in a way that told me there was no chance of this connection ever dying.

This was it for us.

I was his.

He was mine.

I sucked down a sharp breath and broke the connection because the need to get clean was more imperative than before.

Smart man that he was, he didn't join me at first, but I saw his shadow through the curtain once I closed it enough so that the floor wouldn't be drenched.

I washed up, sponged my entire body in his soap, and only after two minutes had passed did he step into the shower with me.

A growl rumbled in his throat once again as he took in my soapy glory, and I reveled in it.

Tossing my head back, I stared at him with defiance. A defiance that told him for all he was the King of the Darkness, I was his fucking Queen.

And if he fucking forgot that, I'd make him pay.

His eyes flashed, his jaw tensed, and in less than a second he was there, he was on me. He pushed me into the shower wall even as he dragged me up, widening my legs so he could step between them while I hooked my thighs around his hips.

His cock was there, a burning brand against tender flesh that still choked on him on a routine basis, and his mouth was on mine.

I felt his hunger. Was seared in his rage. And was reborn in his love.

My eyes grew wet with tears as he thrust his tongue against mine, his hands reaching for my own and pushing them overhead, pinning me to the wall.

The water and soap had taken away my own natural lube, but the pressure of him there, what he made me feel, what he made me *need*, was all that took for me to feel like I was going to die if he didn't get inside me.

Right.

This.

Fucking.

Second.

I squirmed against him, my body slippery as it slid against his hardness, and his cock twitched as I used the lack of friction to get myself off, using all those metal studs and piercings to my benefit.

When he fucked my mouth, I groaned into him and he swallowed it, even as he reached between us, grabbed a firm hold of his dick, and pressed it to my gate.

Slowly, he pushed in.

Slowly, he reclaimed me.

He was too big to take me roughly, even if both our emotions were raging at a fever pitch.

But that he took care, right at this moment, when we were both more animal than our regular selves, was just a reminder of what we were to one another.

As his cock tunneled into me, finally there, thrusting hard and fast as my body took everything he had to give, I felt the peace that had eluded me in the recent weeks.

It was only here, with him, that I could forget everything, that I could focus on him and only him. On *us*, and what we made together.

A muffled moan escaped me as he thrust faster, harder, all those piercings going to work inside me like he was a magician and he was plying my body with magic.

Gravity pulled me down, making him work more, and making me feel fuller, even as he emptied me by retreating only so he could stake another claim and another.

Then, a scream was ripped from me and I tore my mouth from his to release it, to let the bathroom walls around me absorb the sound of true ecstasy as his hard, brutal loving took me exactly where I needed to be.

It was fast, faster than usual for him, but I felt his cum explode into me. His heat branded me, and that was just the icing on the goddamn cake.

Of course, those were famous last words, because when he nipped my bottom lip, hard enough to sting, *that* was the icing on the goddamn cake. And the sprinkles?

Well, they were liberally poured over every-fucking-thing when he grated out, "Mine."

And because I was no shrinking violet, I rasped right back, "Mine," and when I nipped his lip?

I didn't do it to sting.

I did it hard enough to mark.

That single bead of blood was mine.

As was the fire in his eyes and the happiness in his bloodied smile.

"Fucking love you," he ground out, pushing his forehead into mine as the swirls of steam from the shower clouded around us.

"Fucking love you too," I retorted, sliding my arms tighter around him. "Need you, baby. So damn much."

"You'll never not have me," was his instant reply, and if that wasn't a vow, I didn't know what was.

THIRTEEN

LINK

A FEW DAYS LATER

I SUCKED her clit between my lips, smirking as she thrashed around on the sofa. Her hands were gripping my hair, and I knew she didn't give a fuck about making me go bald which I'd admit to appreciating.

She was focused on her pleasure, more so than any other woman I'd ever fucked, and I'd fucked a lot.

Sure, everyone concentrated on climaxing, but Lily did it with a force that stunned me each and every time I pulled shit like this on her because she was uncomfortable with her body, uneasy with being naked, and uncertain when it came time for me to touch her.

I knew *why* even if I didn't understand what had made her this way.

Someone had taught her that sex was dirty. That it was something to be ashamed of. Maybe even that *she* was dirty.

So, when she flung herself into what I was making her experience, it turned me on all the more because she was pushing herself through the shit someone had made her learn and embracing everything I had to give.

I'd grown out of soft, vanilla shit when I was around seventeen, but the truth was, she was already fucked up, *my* kind of fucked up, so the least she deserved was someone leading her into this stuff with kindness.

One of my sex, a bastard, had taught her all the wrong crap. It was my duty to rectify that.

At least, that was what I was telling myself.

My focus fractured as she dug her heels into the soft cushions, arching up and shoving her pussy into my face.

Mouth curving in a Joker grin, I slurped her down, loving her aggression, even more, loving her taste. Because fuck me, she tasted good. Salty, sweet. The best topping for popcorn *ever*.

I almost snickered at the thought, then I ignored the directions she was showing me with her hands and slipped down, tongue fucking her gash, licking up her juices, then doing something for *me*.

I rimmed her asshole, smirking as her butt muscles clenched down, her little rosette tightening, and she released a squeal that was all shock and no pleasure.

Her hands tore at my hair again, but I didn't stop. Even as her legs were clenching down around me, I carried her through the initial wave of disgust, continuing until she was writhing around once more.

When she climaxed, it took her aback, but not me.

Every part of her tautened, her muscles surging up off the sofa as she froze and allowed the power of her pleasure to guide her.

When she returned to Earth, I'd admit to two things.

One, my tongue ached like a fucker because that had taken a while to get her off—my fault. I liked her taste and her responses too much to go easy on her.

Two, my fucking hair ached where she'd almost wrenched it out at the roots.

What I wouldn't admit to was the Cheshire grin I was wearing, or the fact that when I looked at her, legs splayed, pussy juicy and bright pink and right in my line of sight, I knew she was the most beautiful woman I'd ever seen in my life.

Her eyes were closed, her chest rose and fell in deep, jarring movements as she tried to slow her breathing, and the back of one hand rested against her forehead.

A few days of touching her, kissing her, petting her like I was in fucking high school again, had opened her to me in more ways than I'd expected.

Learning she was a virgin had kind of messed with my head. I didn't know anyone who left their teen years nowadays with that label, but she did.

Had.

And I wanted it.

I wanted to own *that* part of her.

Her hymen had my name on it.

Which was beyond fucked up.

I didn't want any part of any woman long term. I liked to fuck 'em and do my own shit. I had a preference among the sweetbutts, but even then, it was fun.

They knew what I was like, knew what I was into, and knew that if they let me do whatever I wanted, I'd make them come so hard they'd be seeing stars for a week.

So, as I stayed where I was, kneeling in front of the sofa, and as I looked over the curves of her body from that angle, I wondered what it was about Lily that was different.

If Rex had been another Prez, he'd have ordered me to get in with her to spy, to see if she was genuine in her admission to help Giulia. But that hadn't been my intent behind getting her.

Sure, I was monitoring shit—no way was Giulia going to get hurt on my watch—but when I looked at Lily, I saw that same fracture deep in her eyes as I'd seen in Giulia.

It was their spirit. Their souls. Someone had hurt them. Ruptured something that belonged only to them. Tainted what should have been pure and damaged it forever.

Now, however, I couldn't use that as an excuse.

How the fuck could I when her calves had settled on my goddamn shoulders?

No, shit had moved past that two weeks ago when I'd felt compelled to get her a burner cell.

When she'd texted me and we'd had a fucking giggle over the shit we'd been sharing with one another.

When she'd asked me, without saying it outright, to be her first.

That shit did something to a man. Sure, most would run for the hills. Some might even stay, fuck her to claim that first time, then ghost her. Others might want to keep what they'd taken...

I had a funny fucking feeling I was going to be the latter.

Just looking at her made everything inside me turn chaotic and chaos—though I liked it in others—for a man like me, was never a good thing.

Because I was feeling irritable, I turned my head to the side and nipped her inner thigh, just above her knee. She jerked and her eyes opened, and she proceeded to drowsily scowl at me.

"What was that for?" she slurred, making me laugh because she sounded like she was drunk.

"Because."

She groused, "Because what?" She began to move her legs, but I reached up and clamped my hands down around her knees so she couldn't move—not in any direction I didn't want her to.

Her eyes flared wide when I hauled her farther down the sofa and shoved my face against the sweetest cunt I'd ever known.

Her sob made me smile when I sucked on her clit, and she nearly fucking suffocated me as she half-shrieked, "No! Link! Nooo, too much, too much."

"Never enough," I ground out against her slit, slurping up that tiny nubbin, dragging it back to life so I could blow her fucking mind and ink on her fucking soul that I was the one to give her this.

That it was *me* focused on her, giving her what she needed, taking what I wanted, to make sure she was ready for what I was going to give her.

She tensed and relaxed all the way through it, moaning and sobbing, hands flailing on the cushions, feet digging into my shoulders as I dragged her tight ass up the path of pleasure, forcing her to come as I focused on fucking that little clit like there was no tomorrow.

The orgasm was hard won, and when she screamed, I had to hope this mini Playboy fucking mansion was soundproofed, because that time?

She made my ears ring.

She yelled until she was hoarse, until she was whimpering, reduced to a moaning mass of nerves that I'd stamped my claim on.

Her legs were limp as I surged off the floor and into a standing position. As I unbuckled my belt, I watched her, amused to note she didn't even notice my change of position. She was in her own world, a world I'd taken her to.

Unfastening my jeans, I shucked out of them. I'd taken off my boots and cut earlier on, and when she'd gotten naked, I'd taken off my Henley, so it took me less than five seconds to strip them off.

When I was bare, I climbed onto the sofa, crawling over her until I could settle my dick against her cunt. Her heat had me hissing, and that was what woke her up.

That noise.

Her eyes flared wide again as she looked at me, took me and my new position in.

Then she fucking broke me.

She swallowed.

The tiniest motion of her throat muscles, followed by the instant shielding of her eyes as she dropped her lashes.

I'd had no intention of fucking her tonight. But if I had? That intention was long gone with that microexpression that was like a stake to my goddamn heart.

"Put your legs around my hips," I muttered, feeling raw after that glimpse into *something* I didn't understand yet, just knew to approach with caution.

She obeyed, and that same stillness was there, making me grit my teeth even as she obeyed. A surprised yelp escaped her when I twisted us over so I was on my back and she was on top of me.

My hands settled on her ass, and I contented myself, soothed myself in truth, by clenching down on that luscious butt of hers and pulling at her cheeks, kneading them for my pleasure more than hers.

"Go to sleep," I grunted, semi-pissed that even after I'd gentled her, she was still scared. Yet I was also aware that Rome hadn't been built in a fucking day, so I needed to chill the fuck out.

"S-Sleep?" she replied, voice shaking with her surprise.

"Yeah. Sleep," I muttered, moving one hand to cup her nape, then shoving her face into my throat so I could rest my head against hers.

"Like this?" she asked, muffled.

"Like this," I confirmed.

When she went boneless, I knew she liked what I'd asked of her. Maybe not just because I wasn't going to fuck her and she wasn't ready for that yet. Maybe because she liked being as close to me as I liked being close to her.

Who the fuck knew?

I closed my eyes, appreciated the silk of her against me, her slick heat cosseting my cock even if it was left out in the cold, the meat of her ass in one hand, my fingers curved inward toward the pucker that was my favorite goddamn place in the whole world, and semi-content, I let myself rest, knowing she was going to as well.

When I awoke, a few hours later I'd guess from the fact the birds were tweeting like shit when it had been pitch-black before, I had to admit that was the best sleep I'd had in a long while.

Even better?

She hadn't moved a goddamn inch.

She was right there where I'd left her.

And fuck if it wasn't epic to wake up like this.

A tiny moan escaped her at what, I assumed, were my minute movements now that I'd woken up, but when she flinched and let out a sharp gasp, I knew she was in the throes of a dream.

Even in this, Lily was a fucking lady. No screams or thrashing for her. Nope. She had to stay composed even in the middle of a nightmare.

That was why I liked breaking her composure when I went down on her.

It made my fucking day to rupture her conditioning, forcing her to give me the real Lily and not the doll she was most of the time thanks to her upbringing.

Because I didn't like that her dream was upsetting her, I stroked along her back, soothing her even as I murmured her name, and alternated between nibbling on her throat and sucking down on the bite mark I'd given her that first night.

It was still bruised, still purple, and would be for a while if I had my way. She hadn't complained about it, and around the edges, I saw stains of makeup which told me she covered it up through the day, then before we met at her friend's place, she removed the gunk to let me see it when we were together.

I kind of liked that.

Weirdo that I was.

"Luke, no! Don't do it. Please!"

The cry was muted, but her heavy intake of air wasn't, and while I was on red alert now because she'd uttered that cunt's name, I processed what that might mean.

What her nightmare might represent.

"Lily," I rasped, urging her awake when she alternated between tensing and relaxing, all her muscles reacting as though they'd been electrocuted before she slumped on me like a vat of goo.

Then, she mumbled, "Link?"

My dick twitched at just how good my name sounded coming out of her when she was half-asleep.

She must have felt it, because she sighed, rocked her hips, then muttered, "You feel good."

I'd have expected her reaction to be negative, especially after last night had shown me she wasn't ready for more, but instead, she wiggled again until I reached down, clamped my hands on her ass cheeks, pulled them apart, and grumbled, "Stop grinding against me, babe. You ain't ready for what my cock wants."

A hum escaped her, but it was in direct contrast to the tensing of her ass cheeks—confirming my theory that she didn't really like her ass being touched.

"Only your cock? Not you?"

I tilted my head until we were connected again. "My penis has a mind of its own. IQ of one eighty."

She whistled under her breath. "Yikes. Your cock is smarter than Einstein?"

"Yup. It's something I've had to learn to live with."

A snicker escaped her. "I'll bet. Nut."

"Literally," I said with a smirk that had her snicker morphing into a chuckle.

She twisted slightly so she could lift her head and look me in the eye. "Hey."

There was a shyness to her tone that amused me, especially in the light of the fact her dried cunt juices were still around my goddamn mouth and my cock was burrowed between her pussy lips, but I let her have it because I liked her like this.

Soft. Playful. Her sense of humor warped—just like mine.

Giving her that phone had changed shit. Not simply because it led us here, to this moment in time, this place. But because it also meant I saw a side of her I wasn't sure I'd have seen otherwise.

Free from anyone checking her phone, she'd been herself. And that 'herself' was someone I liked.

A lot.

"Hey," I repeated, my lips twitching as she looked at me, her gaze drifting over my features. "You making a map of my face or something?"

"I thought it might be a cool thing to have on my wall."

"My face or a map of it?"

"I dunno. You're pretty, but a map would be cooler." She leaned on her hand, which changed the pressure of where our bodies connected, and reached up to rub her fingers over the bump on my nose. "We'll call this Anger Ridge."

"How do you know it was made in anger?"

"Who gets their nose broken outside of a fight?"

"Boys." My tone was dry. "Adrenaline Alley. I fell off a tree."

She narrowed her eyes. "For fun?"

"Who the fuck climbs a tree if it isn't for fun?"

"Not girls," she retorted.

"Well, that's why you're all so much fucking smarter than boys."

"You weren't being chased?"

"Up a tree? I ain't a cat, babe."

"True." She laughed. "I suppose there *are* girls who like to climb trees. I was never one of them."

"Were you always playing with dolls and shit?"

She pulled a face. "No! Ew."

"Dolls trigger an 'ew?'" I arched a brow at her.

"They sure as hell do. I was never a girly-girl. But I wasn't a tomboy either. I liked reading, learning. Mostly I liked being inside. I—" Her mouth worked a little and her smile flashed, disappearing in the blink of an eye. "Never mind."

"Nope. Not never mind. What were you going to say?"

She cringed, then huffed out a breath when I just cocked a brow at her, silently telling her I wasn't going to let her change the subject without her explaining.

"Luke liked being outside," she said.

"And you liked being anywhere he wasn't?" At her nod, I beamed a smile at her. "There's my girl. Had taste, even from a young age."

She snorted, then jolted in surprise when I grabbed her hips and rocked mine up so my dick brushed her pussy. She relaxed, though, when I didn't make another move, just kept us close.

"Your girl, huh?" she questioned after a few seconds.

"See anyone else in the room?"

"No. I don't," she replied dryly.

I got the feeling she wanted me to say more, to add something, and it didn't take a genius to figure out what.

But what could I say?

We'd been texting for a while, petting like we were horny high schoolers for the past couple days...barely any time at all in the grand scheme of things.

Even if I was going to admit to feeling possessive of her, there was too much shit I didn't know about her and that she didn't know about me for us to think about anything deeper.

Plus, I was an MC brother.

Rough and ready.

Raw and crude.

She was the exact opposite.

Every part of her was refined. Every part of her elegant. Even her workout gear was smart and *snazzy*. She oozed money from her fucking pores.

We couldn't have been more opposite, yet here she was. Her virgin cunt inches away from my anything *but* virgin dick.

I'd admit...I liked that she wanted deeper. Even if it was way too soon for that shit. She wasn't like the prissy country clubbers I'd come across in the past. Didn't want a hard fuck on the wild side to rebel against a snooty father.

In truth, I didn't know what she wanted.

Maybe I didn't know what I wanted either.

Except for...well, knowing more about her.

With that in mind, I asked, "What did he do to you?"

Her brows rose. "My father?"

"The cunt."

She tensed. "Nothing."

"Liar," I challenged softly.

When her gaze darted away, she compounded the irritation I felt at her lying. My hand snapped up to grab the back of her neck.

One hand on her ass, the other on her neck, I hauled her up so we were nose to fucking nose. "Don't. Lie. To. Me."

Her eyes went wide, like saucers, and she rasped, "I won't."

I heard the arousal melded with the shock in her words and had to hide a smirk, even as I took a mental note that she liked me being rough with her.

I rubbed where my thumbs had dug in around her neck, and demanded, "What did he do to you?"

Her lashes fluttered. "It wasn't to me."

My brow puckered. "Huh?"

She dropped her gaze to my lips and, focusing on my mouth, whispered, "H-He used to rape the maids."

I tensed. "You're shitting me?"

"N-No. I wish I was." She blew out a breath. "First time I heard…what he was doing, I was five."

My body jolted in rejection of her words. "Five?" I breathed.

Lily dipped her chin. "Yeah."

I let her burrow away, let her hide, because although this wasn't as bad as I expected—the fucker hadn't raped her after all—what he'd put her through was something no one should have to endure.

Psychological torture…fuck.

She put her forehead to my stubbled jaw and whispered, "I didn't understand. Not at first."

"Why would you? You were a baby."

She shivered. "Not for long in my house."

"He didn't do it to you?"

"It's difficult to explain," she muttered, her forehead rocking against my jaw.

I moved my hands again, this time settling them around her waist, holding her against me as I told her, "You're safe now, Lily. Not only because he's dead, but because I will kill any fucker who tries to hurt you. Hear me?"

"I hear you." The words were dull. Wooden.

"You're not hearing me," I retorted, then, in her ear, whispered, "I've killed men, Lily. I know what it is to take a life. You're safe when you're with me."

"You can't always be with me," she rasped. "Nor would I expect you to be." She squeezed my bicep. "I'll only be safe when my father's dead. He's as much of a threat to me as Luke was."

Because I was floating through a puddle of shit, I requested, "Explain, please?"

She released a shaky breath. "Luke was ten years older than me, but worse, he was the only son Mom managed to have.

"There were two kids between me and Luke, both girls. One she lost in a miscarriage, and I'm pretty damn certain my father beat her while she was pregnant and that was *why* she lost my sister.

"The other died of meningitis. Lissa was only three at the time." She bit her lip. "Father thought the sun rose and set on Luke. Always did. He could do nothing wrong, and because he's as warped as Luke, it made sense that he turned a blind eye to whatever he did.

"I mean, I know Father has a few mistresses dotted around the place, but the maids have never been safe from either of them.

"When I had to start hiring people, I always tried to get men, because I knew what they were both like. But Father would just get his secretary to hire some poor woman and—" She gulped. "I knew what they'd do to her. Knew it and couldn't do a damn thing to stop it. It was made very clear what would happen to me if I—"

"If you what?" I demanded, repulsed and disgusted by what she was saying.

"Like I said, I was five when I saw Luke that first time. He was only fifteen. He was weird back then too. It wasn't like it happened overnight, or some trauma made him that way.

"He had the strangest eyes. It was like he knew everything. He could look at me and he'd know if I was lying, or if I was sad, or scared. And if I was happy, he'd know, and he'd do whatever he could to make me unhappy.

"I knew to avoid him, knew it and worked hard to stay out of his way, but he wouldn't always let me. I knew, too, that if I didn't do what Luke wanted, he'd tell Father and Father would punish me."

"Used his hands on you?"

"Hands. Belt. Brush. Shoe, one time. He's better now. Mostly just his hands."

Rage unfurled inside me like a black rose. It surged to the surface and I struggled to keep it under wraps. "He violate you?"

"Yes," she said simply, making me close my eyes to process that answer.

But she was a virgin... "How?" Then I cursed myself for being a dumbass because I knew.

Motherfucker.

"Fucked you in the ass?"

That was why she'd jolted last night and this morning when I gave her butt some loving.

"Yes. My cunt is for sale," she rasped, making me jerk beneath her. "He's always been waiting for the right deal where he can use me as leverage."

As a lot of things slotted into place, I whispered, "He found someone?"

"Before Luke died, there was talk between them."

I sucked in a breath. "Why didn't you run away?"

"I did. Twice."

I fucking hated this dead tone of voice of hers, even as I understood it, I loathed it. I tightened my arms around her and questioned, "What happened?"

"Beatings. Thought he was going to kill me the second time. Almost wished he had." She laughed, but it was mirthless. "The rapes hurt, but it was watching what Luke did to the maids that messed with my head. Sometimes he made me—"

"Made you what, sugar tits?"

She jerked at the nickname, then laughed again. Only this time, it was warmer. "I like that name."

"Know you do."

"It's disrespectful, but I like it."

I squeezed her. "No disrespect between you and me. Everything we do is with the other's permission."

"I know."

"What did Luke make you do?"

"He'd cuff me to a chair and tell me that if I wasn't looking at the maid he was hurting, if I looked *away* for a second, he'd slit her throat."

"He did it, didn't he?"

"I looked away. Once. Never again."

Sometimes, there were answers to questions you wished you'd never asked and while that was the case here, now it was more than that. I wished I'd never asked, because Luke Lancaster was already dead.

I'd already wished I could torture the bastard because of what he'd done to Giulia. Then with Ghost, Tatána, and Amara, I'd wanted to castrate him and make him eat his dick.

Now, I wanted to rip out his veins and choke him with them.

I'd never been a religious man. Never believed in God or the Devil, no matter how hard Grandma tried to instill those values and morals in me...

Now I did.

Now I wanted to believe that some demon was making Luke Lancaster suffer. That he was reaping the years of suffering he'd forced on others. Because if that wasn't happening, then there was no justice.

No justice at all.

I cupped the back of Lily's head, gently played with her hair, and inquired, "Does your father still—"

"He stopped punishing me that way a while ago."

Punishing?

Fuck.

"Why?"

"I have no idea." She wriggled her shoulders. "Didn't stop to ask him why, was just grateful he did."

I squeezed her again. "Sorry. Stupid question."

"Yes," she said. "It was. But it's okay. It might be to do with the man he selected for me."

"Why?"

"My future husband—" Now, didn't those words fill me with fucking rage. "—has bought me. Why would he want a frigid wife who's terrified of sex? Maybe Father is giving me time to get over it."

To get over it?

"It isn't a hill to get over on a bike, babe."

"You don't have to tell me that. *I know.* Anyway...I'm surprised *you* haven't gone running for the hills."

"Why would I?"

"It's fucked up. Everything is fucked up."

"Maybe. Makes sense though."

"What do you mean?"

"Takes a lot of hate to want your father dead. Takes even more to want to kill him yourself. Now I understand why."

"I wanted him dead because of what he did to my mom." She shrugged. "The rest..."

"The rest what?"

"The rest doesn't compare. I'm alive. She isn't."

My eyes widened at that, but I didn't say anything. Couldn't say anything. I mean, that was the worst case of survivor's guilt I'd ever heard, and in the past ten minutes, I'd heard some pretty fucked up stuff.

Plus Mav was my goddamn brother.

He was the King of the Land of Survivor's Guilt.

I rubbed my chin over her hair, aware that the stubble caught on a few of the silk strands but that wasn't going to stop me from comforting her or vice versa.

Fuck.

Whatever I'd expected, it wasn't this whole clusterfuck, and my biggest concern of all wasn't the other shit she'd said. Not the crap about her bastard of a brother even if that was beyond horrendous, not what he'd done to her, or even the nightmare that was her father punishing her by raping her—it was *why* he'd stopped doing that.

That was what gave me pause.

I didn't know Donavan Lancaster, didn't want to know him either, but a man like that didn't just stop doing something without there being a reason why, and giving Lily time wasn't enough of a justification.

Not for a man like that.

So her reasoning had me staring up at the ceiling as the birds fucking twittered through the rising dawn like there was something to be happy about.

See, the world I lived in was fucked up, and the one Lily lived in was too, but they were two separate spheres.

She came from a wealthy family.

Not her fucking father's, but her mom's.

And though my bank account was beyond stuffed, it wasn't from stocks and shares and ownership of a goddamn railroad. It was from the illegal shit the MC did.

So, with that in mind, with the knowledge I had of my corrupt world, I knew virginity wasn't important to the businessmen of Lily's world.

They wanted their wives to be good at sucking cock, not innocent and naïve between the sheets. Only a certain kind of 'businessman,' and I said that loosely, would be interested in a virgin for a wife...

And there was the fact that Lancaster knew about our dealings with the Five Points. Plus the fact that he'd stopped punishing her that way... It had to be because he was frightened of whoever he was intending on marrying her off to.

Who would someone like him be scared of? The bastard, with all his power and influence?

The *Famiglia*.

That had to be it.

There was a whole lot of guesswork and supposition there, but it was plausible. No one except for the competition and the cops would know about our runs for the Irish Mob.

Even though he had the cops in his pocket, I highly doubted he was involved with the task forces that would be monitoring our business.

And the *Famiglia* were evil bastards. Everyone knew that.

A wave of protectiveness flooded through me the more I thought about it. Thought about the why and the how. More importantly, the when. That was what scared the living shit out of me.

"Why me?"

Of all the things I could have asked, I wasn't sure why that was the first question to pop out.

Still, I wanted an answer.

She tensed. "You mean, why did I tell you all that?"

"No. Why do you want me to be your first?"

For some fucked up reason, that mattered to me. I wanted to know her answer. *Needed* to know it.

"You know when I told you where Luke was keeping the women?"

Gruffly, I said, "Yeah."

That moment was probably written in my DNA now. That whole fucking night was.

"I was terrified. It was the first step toward changing my life. Toward..." She released a breath. "Luke's death made him vulnerable for the first time ever.

"Not only because Luke and he made tormenting me a hobby, but because he was mourning. He grieved the sick bastard, and he's willing to do anything, and I mean *anything*, to make someone pay for his passing.

"That meant I had a window of opportunity, but I was still terrified. Still scared that I was going to mess up beyond repair. And I was one hundred percent aware that I only had so much leeway for error.

"You didn't know me, you just knew that I'd asked your bartender to spike my security's drinks, but you calmed me down. You helped me breathe." She peeked up at me. "That meant more than you know. Then... after everything else? Why wouldn't I want you?"

"You know I'm not a good man."

"I know how to measure 'good,' Link," she rasped. "'Good' comes in different shapes and sizes. I'm not stupid. I've read up on the MC. I know you do stuff you shouldn't. I know there are rumors. You said you've killed someone...or some*ones*. But you make me feel safe. You did that night." She burrowed her face into my throat again, and chose that moment to mumble, "Helps that you're pretty too."

Even as she wrecked me, she made me smile. "Pretty?" I scoffed. "I'm a dude."

"Dudes can be pretty," she teased, and I was glad to hear that note in her voice because, for the first time in my life, my mind, heart, and soul were at war.

I wanted her.

More than I had before.

I wanted her to attain her goal...wanted to help her do it.

More than I had before.

I wanted her to be mine.

More than I had before.

She was a survivor, a fighter, and she wanted vengeance, and I was the link in the chain who would bring all those parts together to give her what she desired.

Maybe she'd seen that that night. Maybe she'd recognized someone who would connect the dots for her. Well, I'd do *more* than connect the damn dots.

I'd resented Luke Lancaster's death. He hadn't died with enough pain, with enough torment.

Now, however, I had Donavan Lancaster in my sights and in this instance, the sins of the son would be reaped on the father.

And the father?

The second he'd touched the woman who lay in my arms?

He'd been a dead man walking.

FOURTEEN

REX

"WHAT'S THIS?"

Link peered at the letter I shoved at him, then he frowned.

"Looks like a letter."

His focus returned to his meal, and he hunched his shoulders as he shoveled in some of the casserole Giulia had spent all day cooking.

The scent of rosemary and thyme had perfumed the clubhouse since this morning, and while it wasn't the image I wanted for the Sinners, I wasn't about to complain.

Not when the meal I'd just eaten was better than some of the stuff I'd had in high class restaurants.

"Yeah. It does. Because it is. Why am I getting letters from some Podunk town in Ohio?"

He jerked his head up at that. "Ohio?" He grabbed the envelope from my grasp and tore into it. As he read through the contents, he grinned at me. "I found her."

"Who? Didn't realize someone was lost." I scowled at him, not appreciating being out of the loop.

How the fuck was I supposed to keep an eye on things if I was in the dark about shit?

He waved a hand. "Ghost gave me a mission. Find her sister—she's in the system. Tell her that Ghost is alive." Then he muttered, "Thought I was going to have to ride there, but figured with shit up in the air, it'd be best if I made a few calls at first. They stuck." He fist pumped the air. "Yes!"

My brow puckered once more. "She asked you to do that?"

When I'd gone into the bunkhouse to see if Giulia was managing with all the stuff she had to do without Stone on hand, the women had flinched and turned their backs on me, like that was the only way they could escape me.

Link was lighter hearted than most, but he wasn't a fucking teddy bear.

"Yeah." He shrugged again. "This is the best news. It's going to cheer her up."

Well, it wasn't like it *couldn't*. Fuck, that bunkhouse was the most depressing place in the whole goddamn world. People in prisons in Thailand were happier than those poor three women.

I swore if I could have been the one to slay Luke Lancaster, the piece of shit, I'd have made him truly fucking suffer.

Of course, that was in hindsight.

But from where I was standing, hindsight was the worst fucking place to be. Especially when you knew you'd come close to true evil, and that evil piece of crap hadn't suffered for his sins.

"How did you find her?"

Link beamed his cheerful grin my way as he leaned up to tap his nose. "I have my ways."

I grunted because I knew he wasn't lying, but he didn't have to be such a schmuck about it.

Link had a knack for finding shit.

Be it car parts or, apparently, lost kids, give him something to hunt, and he was better than a fucking bloodhound.

Heavy steps sounded behind me, so when a hand clamped down on my shoulder, I wasn't altogether surprised.

I turned around, saw it was Nyx, and tipped my chin up. "What's wrong?"

"Rachel's here."

I hated that my immediate reaction to that news was to check my fucking hair in the mirror. God help me. That little bit of tail had me all worked up. Always had and probably always would.

"She say why?" was all I asked, because as far as I knew, this wasn't a scheduled appointment and Rachel was very careful to keep things on schedule.

Always.

That was because she felt the livewire that burned between us and was in complete goddamn denial over it.

Still, the MC had paid her way through law school, and now she repped us almost exclusively. As far as I knew, her practice had three clients, and we took up almost seventy percent of her work alone.

I allowed her the other two clients because they were charities. We'd invested in her, just as we'd invested in Stone. That wasn't something my daddy had done.

It was something I'd implemented.

Bear had thought a woman's place was in the kitchen and in bed. Sometimes on the back of a hog. I didn't feel that way.

Clubwhores had their place, and when they were warming my cock, I was mighty appreciative, but women weren't just holes. Back when I'd taken over, of course, I'd been one of the few to believe that.

But wasting home grown talent, people who were dedicated to the club as much as the brothers, was fucking foolish.

Stone was a class A healer. Rachel was a shark in the courtroom, and every year spared one of the men from serving life sentences for the myriad shit we pulled.

They weren't the only ones I'd helped over my time as Prez.

I was putting a few of the kids who didn't want to become brothers through community college.

By the time I was ready to be in my casket, I'd have the MC sorted for life with a team of all kinds of trades loyal to my people.

Plumbers, electricians, lawyers, doctors...I was working on a few cops too, but that was harder.

Most kids round here were raised to hate the lawmen, not respect them.

Normally, I'd be happy about that, but having a pig close to hand would help us out in times like the ones we were going through now with Giulia.

"Says it's to do with the case."

Those two words might as well be capitalized.

Rachel was working on lots of cases for us, but *The Case*? It was to do with the Lancaster bullshit.

"She need Giulia around for the conversation? I can get someone else to sit with the women."

"No. Just you and me. Anyway, Maverick's with her."

For a second, I wasn't sure what the fuck to think.

Mostly, I was thinking it was a goddamn miracle that Maverick had left the clubhouse to go as far as a bunkhouse to be in a sickroom of all places.

But also...

"That doesn't bode well, does it? That Rachel doesn't want her around?"

We shared a look.

"I dunno what to think anymore. She wouldn't say shit without you present, so hustle the fuck on. I need to know what's going on with my woman."

I'd have rolled my eyes at his impatience, but I understood it.

Giulia wasn't my woman, but she was a biker brat whether she hated her father or not, and I gave a shit about her on a whole other level because Nyx, as her Old Man, fuck, I'd never seen him like this before.

There'd always been a kind of mania about Nyx. Not that he was insane which, technically, I guessed he was. But a frenetic kind of energy that made him volatile and quick to stir.

Giulia, even with all this shit they were going through, did something to him. *For* him.

I didn't know what, didn't need to know, was just grateful for this new baseline that was Nyx's current status quo.

"Let's go," I said grimly, and the pair of us stalked off, boots clomping against the ground as we passed through the kitchen into the hall and out toward my office.

I saw Hawk, Giulia's brother and a Prospect, sweeping up a pile of leaves in the hall and shook my head at the sight. "Do I need to ask why?"

"Practical joke," he muttered.

"On who?" I grumbled.

"Me."

"Oh." My lips twitched. "Them's the cards that fall."

He didn't lift his head to agree or disagree, just huffed and carried on clearing shit up.

Literally.

Not that he'd figured that out yet.

As we carried on past him, I kept my ear cocked until I heard it, and grinned at Nyx who, despite the fact Rachel was waiting on us, had also slowed his pace and kept on listening for Hawk's, "Motherfuckers! Who the fuck even does that?"

Snorting even though the hall would be stinking of dog shit for the next few hours, I remarked, "That never grows old. What did Hawk do to earn that particular punishment?"

Nyx scoffed, "Miserable cunt."

Like those two words explained it all.

"Details?" I asked.

"Nothing too bad. Just needs some happy pills. Trust me, I'd have told you if he wasn't cut out to be a brother." He gave me a look. "He's wasted in the clubhouse though."

"Why? Where should I put him?"

"With me."

I arched a brow. "You'd be willing to deal with him?"

"My brother-in-law, ain't he?" He was scowling as he said it.

"Good with security?"

"Giulia said he did some bounty hunting for a while."

"Really?" I pictured Nyx's brother-in-law. "Nah. Too pretty to be a bounty hunter."

That had Nyx snorting. "Well, whether he's pretty or not, he was good at it." He shrugged. "At least, as far as Giulia would have it."

"And she's not exactly the queen of compliments," I stated, which had his lips twitching in a smirk.

"Where I'm concerned, she is."

"Yeah, well, you're the one putting her in a good mood, so I expect no less."

"That I can make her smile at all at the moment is a fucking miracle."

"Miracle dick," I inserted with a laugh. "Your superpower. But then, with all that fucking hardware in it, it's a miracle it doesn't have an engine."

Nyx snickered as he pushed open the door, and I quieted as I saw Rachel sitting in front of the desk, reading something on her phone.

It wasn't the sexiest description in the world, but when I thought of Rachel, I always thought of her as being neat. Not sexy. But she did it so well. All her gear was designer, all tailored, all streamlined and elegant.

When I stood next to her, I looked like a filthy fucking biker, and she looked like she was one of the one percent.

Ironically enough, I was the one who was rich as Croesus, and Rachel had started off as trailer trash, only making it out of there because her momma had fucked a brother, gotten pregnant, and Axel had been too doggone kind to tell her to get the hell out, even after she'd supposedly miscarried that first kid.

That was how I knew Rachel.

She'd been dragged here as a tiny nine-year-old. All skin and bone, in need of a good meal or eight.

Because Axel was a good guy, he'd become a second father to Rachel, not wanting her to be tossed out on the street with that skank ho for a mother, who'd lived up to her rep by eventually running off, leaving Axel with a toddler and Rachel to help out.

The toddler was now a Senior in High School, and Rain was one of the kids I was hoping I could veer into the police academy.

Axel, who'd died a few years back, would be rolling in his grave about that, whereas Rachel would love it.

She'd be happier with her kid brother as a cop than as a Sinner and, God help me, I wanted Rachel to be happy.

At the moment, however, Rachel was *not* happy. She was scowling at her screen, even if she was doing so *neatly*.

In a navy pantsuit that was designed to augment every line of her body, in sleek court shoes that I'd give my left testicle to feel digging into my ass as I screwed her, and a hot pink blouse—the only thing truly feminine about her outfit—that was cut low in front, revealing a pair of tits I wanted to fuck, she was everything I'd ever wanted and the only woman I didn't know if I'd ever get.

She had dark red hair, like a fine burgundy wine, and it was cut in a pristine, longer-length bob that shivered along her shoulders when she moved her head.

Her velvety brown eyes were narrowed on her cell, her coffee brown painted lips were pursed too.

Everything about her screamed irritated, and hell if I didn't want to fuck her into a good mood.

"What's wrong?" I asked as I headed around my desk and took a seat.

Slowly enough to piss me off, she averted her attention from the screen and gave it to me.

"Donavan Lancaster is driving me insane."

"Why?" Nyx demanded, taking a seat on the edge of my desk.

I loved how she didn't flinch in the face of his annoyance. Rachel had guts, and that turned me on all the more where she was concerned.

"Why? Because he's managing to break three sets of state laws and nobody gives a fuck about it." Her nostrils flared, then she blew out a breath and stated grimly, "But I've taught him a lesson his 'Park, Hyde, Lawrence, & Lawrence' lawyers won't forget in a hurry."

I arched a brow—it was either that or smile at her, and I knew if I did that my left ball really would be on the fucking line. "How?"

She curled her top lip. "You don't need to know the intricacies of the game we've been playing. You pay me for results." She jerked her chin up. "I got you them."

"What results?" Nyx growled. "Explain."

"The detectives Lancaster 'brought' in to investigate, every single piece of evidence they've hauled in, can no longer be used in court."

My eyes widened at that and I jerked forward in my seat. "You're shitting me."

"No. I'm not. They were out of their jurisdiction, which we already knew. I thought maybe they were working on the fact the bar is close to the county line, but nope. He just brought them in like they were private fucking detectives. How?"

"How?" I repeated, knowing that was what she wanted from me.

"Because he twisted the mayor's arm." She smirked. "Guess what's happening within the next three months? All because of little old me."

My lips twisted. "Please tell me he's been tossed out and there's going to be an election?"

She grinned. "Yeah. Damn straight." Her phone buzzed and she gave it a quick glance. "Election year wasn't until next year, but did you still want the plans we had arranged put into place?"

"What plans?" Nyx questioned, shooting me a look.

"I want James Lacey for mayor."

Nyx scowled. "Lacey? He's a fucking ass-licking schmuck."

Rachel snorted. "Ass-licking is the word. He's worse than our Link."

"What's that supposed to mean?"

She opened her phone up, did some tapping, then passed the cell over to Nyx. When he saw the images Rachel's team had worked hard to attain, he let out a laugh. "He's into guys?"

"Yup. Can't see that going down well with the sticklers around here, can you?" Rachel retorted, a sniff in her voice because she didn't approve of homophobia.

Her two best friends were gay, and she'd been at their side in high school when most of the fascists in her year gave them hell.

"Not at all," Nyx crowed as he tossed the phone back to her. "Okay, so what's the plan?"

"I have a couple of million I'm willing to donate to his electoral campaign," I told him.

"A couple of million?" Rachel scoffed. "For a penny-ante campaign?"

"You never know what can turn up. We got those pictures, only God knows who else did."

"You're giving them as anonymous donations, right?" Nyx demanded.

"'Course I am. What the fuck do you take me for?"

"Anonymous donations have a cap of ten grand," Rachel remarked.

"They're going through dozens of dummy corporations Mav has set up. When he's elected, then he'll find out *who* his Daddy Warbucks is."

"You should have been governor."

I knew she was being sarcastic, but also knew she meant it. She insisted

I was wasting my life here, and maybe I was, but it was my life to waste, wasn't it?

I caught her eye and didn't stop holding her gaze until her mouth firmed and she ducked down to look at her phone—likely story. She never could out stare me.

"So, what does this mean for Giulia?" Nyx pressed, his attention twitching between me and her.

He knew how I felt about her.

Knew it and hadn't understood it before.

I had to wonder if now, after Giulia, he got it.

The need to care for someone so much that you purposely took a backseat in shit, letting them do what they wanted so they'd be happy.

I'd always been a selfish man, but with Rachel? I was like a fucking saint.

"It's good and it's bad. They'll be reopening the investigation, which means she'll have to be reinterviewed. *But* the investigation will be under the sheriff's jurisdiction, and he's on our payroll."

"Link told me the Lancasters are trying to bring him to their side."

I studied Nyx. "When did he tell you that?"

"He's..." He frowned. "Well, I'm not entirely sure what the fuck he's doing with Lancaster's daughter. Link just said that Lily was supposed to bring him onto their team."

I rubbed my jaw. "Are they dating?"

"Link? Dating?" Rachel mocked. "Have pigs started flying?"

"Maybe. Over West Orange, at any rate," Nyx said. "Haven't you noticed, Rex? He goes out at all hours to meet up with her. She's under lock and key pretty much."

"He's pulling his weight at the garage, right?"

"Of course," Nyx scoffed. "Hell, Link is as dedicated to the MC as any of the council."

Worse still, though a lot didn't see it, Link had a good fucking heart. I thought back to our earlier conversation about Ghost and her sister, and how he'd gone out of his way to find the kid for her.

I thought about how Keira, Storm's Old Lady, confided in him about Storm, and how Link knew almost everyone's business in the MC, and concern flittered through me.

"Nyx? Grab Link. I want to talk to him."

Nyx shrugged but edged off the table. "Two minutes."

I dipped my chin in understanding, then rocked back in my seat, my focus veering onto shit I didn't really need to be thinking about.

"What is it? What's wrong?"

Rachel's voice penetrated my focus, and I let my gaze drift over the office that hadn't changed in a long time and back to her.

She was a damn sight prettier than this room, but I couldn't gape at her without her glaring at me.

I'd have liked to be short with her, wanted to snap at her and ask her why she was interested when she didn't give a fuck about the Sinners, but that was bullshit.

She was made to be my Old Lady.

Born to give a shit about this place.

She was just resistant to the idea, and because I wasn't ready for what we would be together, I was as hesitant as she was for the next step.

Knowing your future while you were still in the present was weird. It didn't smooth shit over, didn't help you along the way.

If anything, it was an inconvenience.

Rachel was my inconvenience and I was hers. Even if I'd kill for her, even if she'd kill for me...we weren't ready for what we'd have.

Not yet.

"Link cares too much. He's soft."

"He isn't the weakest link anymore."

I grunted, hating that she knew the history of this place as well as I did. "I know he isn't."

"You fuckers had to remind him of back then with his road name, didn't you? I mean, God forbid you let sleeping dogs lie."

"Sometimes, it's not a bad thing to be reminded of your most major fuck ups. It keeps a man from wandering."

"If you think that, then why all the concern?"

"Because Link is my brother, and I want to make sure she isn't using him."

"I can see the sense in that."

"Thanks," I said dryly. "Your confidence in me makes me feel so good about myself."

She narrowed her eyes, and I could almost predict the snark that was headed my way when a knock sounded at the door and Nyx trudged in, Link at his back.

"Yo, Rach."

"Hey, Link." She shot him a smile that he returned with a wink that had her smile deepening. Rachel had a soft spot for Link. Fuck, most of the women did.

"What's up, Prez?" Link asked, arms folded across his chest when he came to a halt next to *my* woman. *My* woman, who was anointing my brothers with fucking smiles while all she gave me were goddamn glowers.

"Nothing's wrong, Link, I just wanted to check in. Nyx said something about Lily Lancaster trying to bring the sheriff onto the family's payroll?"

"I've been keeping Nyx in the loop, Rex," Link reported warily. "Ain't been keeping shit secret."

"No. He hasn't," Nyx confirmed. "And most of the stuff I think is important has bled back to you. But shit's been up and down since the attack and since the women came here."

I grimaced, because that was true. "We ain't had church since before Lancaster's death." I pinched the bridge of my nose. "Been working on fumes. Need to get shit back in line."

"Things ain't out of control, Rex," Link said.

"No. Not yet."

It didn't take much for the shit to fall in an MC. So far, things had been okay because I kept everything running on a microlevel, but my attention had been divided between safeguarding Giulia, protecting the MC from the Lancasters, shoring up our business interests, both legitimate and illegitimate, and in between all that, trying to find Luke Lancaster's captives.

Hell, half the MC had been working with Mav and Storm to find the poor bitches whose circumstances would probably be in Link's, Nyx's, Steel's, and Giulia's nightmares for a lifetime.

"Stuff's been up in the air," Nyx replied, his statement as close to soothing as he could be. "We've had shit to do, but business hasn't come to an end. All the storefronts are open and running, and we've a run scheduled next week that we ain't going to postpone."

I had to smile. "It's okay, brothers. I don't need you to make me feel better about the past few weeks. We've all been running around like chickens with their heads cut off. It's time to get stuff back in line now." Tightening my hands about the armrests on my chair, I stated, "What's going on with the Lancaster girl, Link? Nyx says you're heading off to see her whenever you can."

Rachel teased, "Are you in love, Link?"

Link's brow puckered, and though I knew Rachel, Nyx, and myself were expecting a joke for a reply, he didn't give us one.

If anything, he stunned us all by admitting, "I don't know what I feel for her. Just know that—"

When he broke off, Nyx prompted, "Know what, bro?"

Link's eyes narrowed. "She wants her old man dead."

"What? Why?" Rachel blurted out, getting involved in shit she claimed she wasn't goddamn interested in...yeah. *Right*.

He pulled a face. "She has her reasons."

"Reasons I need to know if she's making you side with her over the MC," I warned.

"Fuck that, Rex. You know I don't work like that."

"I know you've got too big a heart for *our* own good," I retorted.

Link's eyes narrowed even as he stood straighter. "The family's a mess. One big fuck up. Makes our world look normal. Lily watched her father push her mother down the damn stairs—she actually died.

"Then, you've got that sick piece of shit Luke raping maids and making Lily watch, and..."

Rachel raised a hand. "Link's right, Rex. This is an invasion of Lily's privacy. That kind of past isn't something—"

"I'm the Prez of the fucking Sinners, Rachel. If we have a threat to our security, then I need to know."

"I'm your Road Captain. Nyx and I work together to make sure nothing happens to us. You think I'm going to jeopardize that?" Link shouted.

"I think if someone tells you a sob story you believe, you'll do everything you can to help them." My tone was softer now. "That ain't a flaw, Link. It means you're a good man. But we have to think of the club."

"How about you bring Lily in, Link? It's her story to share," Rachel soothed, reaching over to grab Link's hand and squeezing it when she pried it off his bicep...a bicep he'd been clenching so he could stop himself from decking me.

"Lily's under armed guard twenty-four seven."

"What the fuck is she? A presidential candidate?" Nyx groused.

Hell if he wasn't wrong.

"How are you seeing her if she's under lock and key all the time?"

"Lancaster's away on business." He scowled at me, his defiance amping up in a way that made me feel like I was his damn father rather than his Prez. What the fuck did they think they were? MC Romeo and Juliet? "She's spending time at a friend's, and that's where we meet up."

Nyx firmed his lips. "She's a potential security breach, Link."

He cut my Enforcer a look. "I know that. Knew it all along. That's why I started shit up with her. Make sure she wasn't a threat. She isn't. She hates her family as much as we do."

"Can't blame her with that scum for a sibling." Rachel sniffed. "Why was Lily trying to turn the sheriff if she hates her family, Link?"

"She's got this idea into her head and she's sticking to her guns."

"What idea?" Nyx inquired.

"Luke was the golden boy. Could do no wrong in her father's eyes by the sound of it. She wasn't going to inherit anything other than what she'd received after her mom's death."

"Now that Luke's dead, she'll be in line to inherit it all."

At Rachel's statement, Link shook his head. "I don't think so. If that was the case, then Lily wouldn't be trying to manipulate him."

"How's she trying to do that? And is it freakin' wise when her father's a goddamn murderer?"

"Seems like she needs to improve the company she's keeping then," Link remarked drolly. "We've all got blood on our hands, Prez. You saying we're not trustworthy?"

Because he wasn't wrong, I sighed. "You know what I mean. We don't mean her any harm, but her father probably does. Especially if he found out that she was actively working against him."

"She wants to inherit it all."

"So she's greedy?" Nyx retorted.

"Says she has plans for the money." Link hitched a shoulder. "I thought she was bullshitting at first, but she really means to kill her father. I can't blame her for the stuff he's put her through—"

"Saying it's one thing, doing is another. You know that," I pointed out.

"True, but she means it." He went on to explain their initial communication, how it had morphed, and what he'd learned that her father had shared with her. "The fact he knows about our dealings with the Five Points, and the fact that Lily says she's pretty much a commodity in a business deal, makes me wonder if Lancaster has dealings with the *Famiglia*."

My ears pricked at that. Hell, so did Nyx's.

"You get in touch with Declan O'Donnelly, Nyx. See if that's true."

"Wouldn't they have shared it with you if they thought that was the case?" Rachel reasoned. "Maybe he just has feelers out in police departments in the city?"

"True. But I'd like to know for sure."

Nyx nodded. "On it."

He pulled out his phone and tapped a message, but I ignored him and switched my focus back to Link.

"You like this girl. Maybe you trust her when you shouldn't. According to her, she wants to kill her damn father. I mean, it would make shit easier for us, but that ain't normal." When he ground his teeth, I muttered, "Calm your horses, Link. Fuck's sake. I want to meet her."

"I already told you she's under guard," he snarled.

"And I don't give a fuck. I want to meet her. Want to hear this straight from her because I know you, Link. You're a bleeding heart to anything with a sweet pussy.

"Hell, Keira isn't even putting out with you, and you take her side over Storm's."

Link's mouth tightened. "Fuck you, Rex. I ain't even *had* her sweet goddamn pussy. She's a fucking virgin—"

"And you're still hanging around her?" Nyx pretty much sputtered the words. "Holy fuck. You are. You haven't screwed her yet, have you? Not even her ass."

Link jerked his chin up. "No. I haven't."

"Jesus," Rachel breathed, and her response just cemented *everything*.

Link was not interested in purity. He preferred dirty sluts who'd take anything he had to give them up the ass. A sweet country clubber virgin was *not* his style.

"Now I definitely want to talk to her. You bring her here, Link," I ordered, aware I sounded like a hard ass, but I didn't give a shit.

Too much about this situation stank, and I needed to get to the bottom of it before Link went on the run next week.

If our dealings with the Five Points were compromised, and I was sending my boys into a stitch up? I needed to know.

If this Lancaster pussy was for real, she'd be able to tell us what we needed to know, maybe more.

"If I do, it will get back to her father."

He was stony, and I got it, but I didn't give a shit. There was more on the line than his dick being tied into knots over a woman with a sob story.

"Then it'll get back to him. She sounds shrewd. She'll either figure out a way to get here or she'll spin it out and reel her father in."

Link's eyes flashed. "You treat her like shit and I'll—"

Nyx leaped up and clapped a hand on his shoulder. "Reel it in, Link. This is Rex. He ain't gonna treat her like shit. You know that."

And that Link cared enough to speak out against me told me just how far gone he was too.

What the fuck was going on?

Maybe pigs really *had* started goddamn flying if Link was falling for a fucking virgin.

FIFTEEN

LILY

OUR POOL HOUSE was territory I'd never dared enter.

See, when someone's brother told them to stay out of their room, most sisters would probably ignore the edict just to be a pain in the ass.

But my brother wasn't like other siblings, and I'd avoided his place like it was Pandora's box.

Of course, only when he'd died, had I realized how the pool house actually *was* Pandora's box.

The second I'd gone in there was the second my eyes had been opened to the reality that was my family.

I'd already *known* to a certain extent, after all my father raped me to punish me.

My brother raped the maids and made me watch.

I was the star of my own horror show, for God's sake.

This wasn't *Little House on the Prairie*, but I'd been curious nonetheless.

With the fear of him gone, knowing he really was dead and buried, I'd wanted to see what his place looked like.

In my mind, I'd imagined blood on the walls, shackles drilled here and there.

That first time, I'd almost been disappointed to find a regular living space.

A nice living room with the requisite massive flat screen and a comfy leather sofa complete with more game consoles than anyone could ever need.

Followed by a couple of simple bedrooms, oak four-posters, plus some dressers. A bathroom, a small kitchen, an office area that looked mostly unused, and French doors that opened onto the pool.

Simple.

Expensive, sure, but simple.

No virgin's blood collected in bottles on the countertops in the kitchen. No whips and chains on the floor.

Just a regular home.

Even while I'd been surprised, I'd known it was a lie. No way could the evil that was Luke not have spread into his living space.

So I'd gone looking.

Even then, I hadn't really known what I was looking for, but I'd been snooping for something until I'd hit a pay dirt so dark, I knew Link and the men who'd helped him recover Luke's captives would never get over what they'd found.

God help me, I'd never get over what I'd found either.

A webcam stream.

A webcam I was going to use in the vain hope I could *do* something to tarnish my brother's name.

As a Lancaster, Luke's memory was protected. Revered, almost. But if I could throw some mud on it, then anything that was endangering Giulia Fontaine's safety was suddenly derailed.

At least, that was my thinking.

And it was why I was entering the belly of the beast once again.

As I slipped behind Luke's desk, eying the expensive piece of equipment like the monster it was, I blew out a breath and tapped in his passcode, something I'd learned from watching him log into his phone, preparing myself for what I was about to uncover.

42—our apartment number in Manhattan. Luke's most favorite of our homes.

33—the floor we lived on.

41—the street of our building.

With the computer unlocked, I eyed the desktop. It was a chaos of folders and screenshots that had landed there, and I found the file that had started it all.

'Heaven Can Wait.'

As a folder name, it had been weird enough to make me click on it, then the link that took me to a web page was the start of a nightmare sequence I'd never forget.

I'd used the coordinates of the webcam to guide Link to the property, but I bypassed it today, not wanting to see where those poor women had been held captive, and instead snooped around the folder.

I was certain there'd be information on the rest of the computer, but in here, I felt sure there'd be something incriminating.

Well, *more* incriminating than everything I'd already uncovered, of course. But it wasn't like I could release this to the cops, not when I was trying to court my dad into believing I was on his side in this war against the MC.

I was only useful if I was playing both sides against each other, and my dad had enough friends to cover this up before it made more than a splash in the cesspit that was his pool of influence.

For a second, I thought about the day he trusted me.

The day he put me into his will.

The day when I got him drunk, seduced him into following me, when I'd push him down the fucking stairs and laugh over his broken body.

The notion made the hairs at the back of my neck stick up on end.

Fuck.

I wanted that.

So badly.

And not just at some random point in the future.

I wanted it today. Now.

Anger washed through me, but there was no point in feeling like that. I needed to make shit happen. So I got on with stuff.

Even if the picture of him lying at the foot of the stairs was at the back of my mind all the while, I rummaged around the folders on Luke's computer, then, I winced when I saw one full of .mp4 files.

Videos.

I closed my eyes as I reached up and rubbed them.

Whatever those videos contained was *not* going to be nice, and if I watched them, there was no guarantee that it would achieve anything other than making me want to vomit and tear out my eyes for the rest of my life.

But...those women had endured what had been done to them. My brother was no longer alive to punish, and my father was intent on castigating an innocent woman, ripping through an MC in the process to get to her.

Now, I knew MCs weren't good news.

I knew the Sinners were involved in shit that made them the opposite of decent people, but, and it was a big but, Link was a brother.

Link who had only ever given me pleasure, even though I'd offered myself up on a plate.

Link who seemed to cherish my innocence, even though I was anything but.

He was a brother to those men for a reason.

To me the term 'good' didn't come with a black or white definition. Just like the term 'bad' didn't. But I knew what evil was. I'd lived with it all my life. Link wasn't evil. And anyone he considered family by choice wasn't evil either. I just knew it.

Like he was aware that I was thinking of him, my burner cell buzzed, and I pulled it out of the slot in my yoga pants to eye the screen so I could see part of his message without opening it.

Link: *Where you at, sugar tits?*

My lips curved at the nickname. Why he insisted on calling me that, I really didn't know, but I was surprised that it didn't insult me.

I wanted to cave in. Wanted to pick up my cell and reply to him, get involved in a conversation that would amuse me, turn me on, and take my mind off what I was about to do, but my father would be home in a week, and I should have already finished up on what I'd started here.

The first time I'd come into the pool house, I'd had to sneak in. Today? I had the freedom of movement that came with my father's absence.

So, once again, I sucked it up and got on with shit.

I clicked into the first file and immediately hit the cross on the video player.

Bowing my head, I clenched my eyes closed and tried not to see what I'd just seen. But unseeing wasn't possible.

My trouble was I had a feeling.

A gut instinct.

And my gut usually wasn't wrong, especially where my family was concerned.

In this instance, I knew my father was involved somehow with what Luke had been doing. The apple didn't fall far from the tree, after all.

Plus, I knew Luke wasn't averse to blackmailing him.

Even though Father gave Luke *everything*, to a man like my brother, everything wasn't always enough. There was always something more, something he might need leverage for.

Which was what I was looking for.

Leverage.

I'd thought that maybe my father might own the land on which this hellhole lay. I thought I'd find some connection that way. I hadn't imagined that Luke would record what he did to the women.

Which, if I was right, meant there might be footage of my father doing stuff too.

My throat grew thick at the prospect of checking out the thousands of files in the folder, and because I couldn't bear to watch a woman enduring what that bastard had put them through, I began to look at the file names.

Videos were separated into folders by women's names. Tatána. Sarah. Alessa. Amara. There were more, but Link had told me there were four, and from the footage, I knew there were four cages.

Cages.

My God.

Bile burned in my throat, making me want to puke as I thought about how many lives Luke had taken. Then, eyes watering from the need to sob, I persevered.

Within each woman's folder, there was less categorizing, so I had to scan through file names. When I saw a series that had our mother's birthday as the title, I frowned, taken aback by that.

When I clicked into it, curious, I almost unclicked when the footage streamed into the pit.

It was a weird kind of camera.

Not clear, not HD quality, but that grainy green light that told me it was either infrared or something that helped cameras record in poor light.

The women's eyes were black from that coloring, and their bodies were contorted in the cages they were contained in as they tried to get comfortable.

I couldn't even imagine what they were thinking, lying there, nude, beaten, starved. *Cold.*

God, just seeing this made me want to wrap them up in blankets and pour grog down their throats.

And the worst thing was, *this* was tame. This horror was before anything bad happened to them for the day.

I sucked in a breath, waiting for whatever Luke had deemed worthy of smearing our mother's date of birth with, and then...it happened.

A little explosion of light fucked with the camera, and I figured that meant the opening to wherever this hellhole was had just been breached.

The women all froze, and a few whimpers of surprise and fear escaped them before they were quickly contained, and then, the echo of footsteps sounded as a pair of boots appeared on the staircase into the pit.

Was I surprised when, with each stair descended, my father was revealed?

Not really.

I just didn't understand why Luke had used Mom's birthday as the code.

Had he also known that Father had killed her?

Would Luke have even cared if Father was behind her murder?

I couldn't imagine it, but who knew how my brother's warped mind worked?

A part of me was praying that Father had gone down there to release the women. Stupid, considering I knew the women had only been saved by the MC who Donavan Lancaster deemed unfit to be in the same town as him.

So when he stepped toward one of the cages and kicked it, I knew I had enough. Knew he was down there with the same intent as Luke's.

I hit stop because I didn't want to see anymore.

I'd felt my father's wrath. I couldn't cope with seeing more of it.

As I stared at the file list, I sagged back into my chair and began to sob. Tears poured from my eyes as my emotions ravaged me.

For a second, I drowned, suffocated in them, and then, like a ray of light peering through the gloom, I knew what was happening.

It was the calm before the storm...A calm that was founded in relief.

I had him.

I.

Had.

Him.

My phone buzzed again and blindly, I reached for it.

Through tear-ravaged eyes, instead of reading the text, I connected a call to Link, and the second he questioned, "Sugar tits?" I started sobbing once more.

Through a bucket load of snot and more tears, I heard him demand, "Lily? What is it? What the fuck's going on?"

I heard his fear *for me*. I heard his concern. *For me.* And that just made me cry even more.

Nobody other than Tiff had ever really given a shit about me, and even then, I'd never been able to truly bring her into the fold because I was hiding so much from her.

Not just because there was so much ugliness to hide in my life either. I had to keep her safe. Had to protect her.

But Link knew the shit I had in my life already.

He knew the good and the bad, worse, he knew that ugly streak too, and he *still* cared.

I could hear him rambling on the other end of the line, and I realized he thought my father had returned and had done something to me, which was what shut me down.

"Link?" I rasped, my voice sounding unlike my own. "I think I have a way to destroy my father."

Silence fell at that.

Then, "Are you at home?"

This wasn't my home. I didn't have a home. But I merely whispered, "Yeah."

"I'm coming to get you."

"Do you know someone who's good with computers?"

"I know a few someones," he said gruffly. "I'll be there soon. Okay?"

"Okay." Then I sucked in a breath. "Can you come in a car? Without your cuts? I don't want anything to stop this from happening. The guards won't let you in if you look like you're from the MC."

He grunted. "You sure you got something to take him down? Or do you just 'think' it?"

I'd been stupid using that word. "No. I'm positive. This is his end."

And somehow, I thought it would be better than him lying dead at the foot of the stairs.

"I'll only ride in a cage for you, babe."

I smiled. "The sacrifice will be worth it."

"It'd better be," he grumbled. "Soon."

"Soon," I whispered back as I cut the call.

Blindly, I stared at the screen for a second, then I reached for my other cell, my legit one, and I patched it through to Alix.

"Ma'am?"

"I have guests coming over. They're Tiffany's friends. She should be over a little later too," I lied. "Let them in."

Alix cleared his throat. "Your father wouldn't approve of a party, Miss Lily."

I knew that better than Alix did, but I appreciated him giving me the heads up. "Can you just not tell him until later?" I murmured. "Please, Alix."

"If they're gone before sundown, I'll just tell him Tiffany came over."

Gratitude filled me. "Thank you."

"You're welcome, Miss."

I cut the call and stared at the computer screen.

My burner cell buzzed.

Link: *In a cage. On our way.*

Me: *Thank you. Try to look like party guests. Message me when you're five minutes away. I'll come and greet you.*

Link: *Party guests...Yeah, that's not going to happen.*

Me: *Just try.*

When I received a bucketload of 'eye roll' emojis, I just smiled. Yeah, I smiled. After what I'd seen, what I'd just found...I smiled.

Maybe that was the miracle from today, a miracle that came in the shape of a gruff biker who managed to take away some of my misery and replace it with amusement.

SIXTEEN

MAVERICK

MY GAZE SWITCHED BETWEEN GIULIA, whose head was on her folded arms, snoring away from her place at the dining room table, and Ghost, who was trying, and failing, to eat a sandwich she'd been given forty minutes ago.

All the women were finding it hard to acclimate to eating regularly, and after being starved, that didn't come as much of a surprise.

In a way, you'd think it would be easier to stuff your face after being denied, but the stomach adapted, and after so long in captivity—not that any of the women knew how long exactly, because they'd had no concept of time where they'd been held—they were simply not used to eating.

Amara would routinely puke if she ate too much, and Tatána wasn't even trying all that hard. Ghost, on the other hand, *was* trying, but she didn't get very far.

I had a feeling Ghost tried for my benefit, and I wasn't about to stop her from doing that—even if she often failed.

There was a time when my past, present, and future had all blurred into one, and for those moments, I'd had nothing.

No one.

Not even the family I'd chosen for my own.

On a roadside in Benghazi, my body broken, my eyes wet from pain, and the sun and smoke burning them, a part of me had died.

Only now, when I looked at Ghost, did that part feel like it was alive again.

I wasn't sure why.

She didn't really talk to me, and when she did, her eyes were always downcast.

I preferred to think she was shy rather than scared of me, because if it was the latter then I'd probably feel like blowing my brains out...and I thought about doing that way too much as it was.

When I looked at her, I felt hope. I felt *something*. And it was weird. Really weird. Really, very weird because I didn't know why.

I hadn't had sex in so long that my cock didn't even twitch at all the shit I saw in the clubhouse.

I didn't think about sex, didn't want it, because my brain was focused on other things. Like the will to carry on. Like the fact I was needed in the clubhouse, by my brothers, my family.

Sex wasn't something I needed because, though my body wasn't broken, my head was.

I accepted it, and I thought the broken parts of me were attracted to the broken parts in Ghost.

Which, when I thought about it, was the most fucking depressing shit I'd heard in like, forever. But it was true.

I didn't mean attracted in the regular sense either. Even if I could see she was a beautiful woman when she wasn't forty pounds underweight.

I meant 'attracted' like with a magnet.

Something about her pulled me in, reeled me toward her like I was a fish on a line, only death wasn't in my future when I looked at her. Life was.

Which was stranger still.

Who looked at a woman and saw all that?

I never had before, and I'd been in love once, back before I'd enlisted, and I hadn't felt that way about Lesley.

Although, now that I thought about it, that was probably wise considering the second I *had* enlisted, she'd gone off the rails during my first deployment.

"You are thinking very hard."

Ghost suited her nickname, even if, with his usual lackadaisical ways, Link had given a woman, near death, the worst name ever. But she was delicate, fragile, and whispered like she was a spirit, so I got it.

She also had a faint accent, but surprisingly not much of one. Just enough to make her roll a few syllables and to go guttural here and there.

I studied her wispy blonde hair, the brittle bones that revealed a woman desperately in need of nutrition, and just felt everything inside me sigh.

"You make me think hard."

My honesty had her brows rising. "I do?" She narrowed her eyes at me. "We don't talk about important things."

"Don't we?" My lips twitched as I curved my hands around the armrest of my wheelchair before I slipped them down to the wheels. I rolled them back and forth in my grip, rocking the seat in place as I eyed her. "I think we talk about important shit."

She frowned. "We talk about people in your house."

"Clubhouse," I corrected.

"Yes, well, those people. We talk about them."

"We talk about politics." I pursed my lips. "As in, should Kendra be allowed to stay when she was pivotal in breaking up Storm and his Old Lady?"

Ghost tutted. "I do not understand this saying. How is she 'old' when she is also young?"

My lips curved. "It's just a saying."

"As you have told me already, but I still don't understand it. Why not 'young lady?' It is far more complimentary."

"It's just how we roll."

She clucked her tongue. "It is still senseless. But then, so is what Kendra did. Such cruelty should not be tolerated, however, she did not make this Storm do the things he did. He is to blame." She shot me a glare. "But because you are a man, you will side with him."

I raised my hands as I grinned at her. "Babe, if you see Kendra and Keira, you'd wonder why the fuck he'd want anyone on his dick other than his woman." I ignored her pink cheeks. "Storm is an idiot. I just don't like that Kendra purposely hurt Keira and hasn't been reprimanded over it."

"Who would reprimand someone like this?" Her brow puckered. "How would it be done? Would she be hurt?"

"Um, nope. This is America, baby. Though we're hard asses, we don't beat women."

Well, some of my numbskull brothers did, and usually Nyx was the one to dole out punishments if that happened.

But adultery didn't fall under Nyx's purview of punishments.

Sadly.

"What would happen?"

"She'd get tossed out of the MC which, to a woman like her, is pretty painful. They live for this life."

She shook her head. "I do not understand this. Why would they enjoy sleeping with so many men all the time?"

"To each their own."

There'd been a time when I'd been pretty fucking grateful for club-whores. Now, not so much. Maybe that was age or my PTSD.

Either way, sweetbutts didn't give me boners anymore.

Not even with the random shit they did to get our attention.

"I figured Giulia would start to curb the bunnies' behavior, but ever since this stuff with Lancaster, things have derailed."

Ghost smiled at me faintly. "You mean, ever since we came into the picture."

"I do," I admitted. "I don't think any of us really expected her to volunteer to do all she has." I peered at her over my shoulder, unsurprised to see she was still sleeping. "I didn't think she had it in her."

"She is very kind."

"Yes, she has been, and that's what I mean. Giulia isn't kind. Yet, here she is."

"People can surprise us."

"That's true. Giulia has surprised us all. She's a good mate for Nyx too."

"Once things get back to normal, she'll keep the bunnies in line until Rex decides to take that stick out of his ass and—"

When my cell rang, I grunted as I reached into my jeans pocket and eyed the screen.

Anyone except for Nyx and Rex, I'd have ignored. Storm included. He might have been the VP, but I only really listened to the Prez and the Enforcer anyway.

Unfortunately for me, it *was* Rex.

Speak of the devil...

"What?"

Rex grunted. "So polite."

"Didn't realize I was on your council because I minded my Ps and fucking Qs."

Another grunt. "We have something that will bring down the Lancasters."

My eyes widened as I glanced at Ghost and saw her watching me with curiosity in hers. When she saw me watching her back, her cheeks grew pink and she ducked her head.

Fuck.

I wished she didn't do that.

She was so pretty, and I liked having her gaze trained on me.

"How?"

I was a man of few words on the phone. Fucking hated them.

"Video evidence that Luke and his father used the women."

Those words tore into me in a way I knew Rex wouldn't understand.

Ghost had been through so much at Luke Lancaster's hands. That alone was bad enough. But to know that two men had used and abused her?

I had to blow out a breath to release my anger. It was either that or start throwing shit, and the women were already terrified without me pulling crazy stunts like that.

"What's the next move?"

Rex rubbed the back of his neck. "Getting Lancaster's ass in jail. We'll be bringing Lily Lancaster into the clubhouse. Can you get Giulia to open up one of the bunkhouses for her?"

"She's resting. Can't someone else do it?"

"Steel? Jaxson? See who's about. I just want somewhere for her to sleep. This score is on her. She found the evidence. I want her nearby for her safety."

I whistled under my breath, taking that to mean psychological and physical safety. "Fuck. That's a nightmare waiting to happen."

"Yeah. Link is going to be with her."

"Can't she just stay in his room then?"

Everyone knew of Link's reputation with the ladies. It wasn't too much of a leap to think he was boning Lily Lancaster too.

"No."

"Why not?"

"It's complicated."

I thought about that, thought about how *un*complicated Link was, and came up with a random guess. "He likes her?"

"Loves her. At least, that's what I'd call it." Rex sniffed. "But that's neither here nor there.

"Just get her somewhere to sleep. It's only for a couple of nights. Until he's arraigned."

"Okay. I'll get that done."

"Mav?"

"Yeah."

"I know you visit with the women."

"Just Ghost. The others don't want me around."

"Could you..."

When he broke off, I prompted, "Could I what?"

"Talk to them about speaking with the sheriff's department?"

"Why's that necessary? If you have video footage I mean." I scowled, and I knew it was dark with anger. "You know their situation is precarious."

"I do, but I'm going with my gut here."

"What, oh great leader, does your gut say?"

"That if there's a woman on the stands, the jury will send his ass to jail forever."

"And they won't if..." My voice trailed off when I remembered Ghost was here, sitting and listening to me talk.

"I don't know. Money talks. Ninety billion has a way of greasing people's palms and getting them to do someone else's wishes. But if a woman is there, crying on the stands, telling the truth? Jurors would listen."

"That's weak ass logic."

"I'm speaking with my gut."

"That's why all I hear are verbal farts."

Rex growled down the line. "Fuck, Mav. Just for once in your life could you do as I goddamn ask?"

"If you were talking logically I would."

Another growl. "Ever thought maybe the women would want the chance to face their attacker in court? To see them burn on the stands? Get the damn bunkhouse ready for guests."

Then he hung up.

I scowled at the screen before I slipped it back into my pocket, and when Ghost asked, "Is everything okay?" I wasn't sure how to answer.

Figuring the truth wasn't a bad place to start, I muttered, "No, not really."

I rubbed my chin as I thought about Rex's logic.

If they had video footage, then I didn't get why they'd need one of the victims to come forward...

Especially when all these women were illegal.

What he was asking didn't make much sense.

At least, not in my opinion.

Pursing my lips for a second, I stared at Ghost and saw that she didn't dart her gaze away the second I looked at her for once, and sighed. "You heard, didn't you?"

"I did." She tipped her chin to the side. "I can hear well now."

"Superhearing is your new superpower. At least you got something out of that fucking episode."

"That and I can see well in the dark." She leaned back against the pillows, and the tray on her lap jostled some as she did.

The level of milk in her glass hadn't altered much, but the sandwich had been nibbled, even if it hadn't been a lot.

"You were angry," she observed simply. "Why?"

"Because what he wants doesn't make sense."

"I have met with your president. He seems like a very sensible man." She smiled. "I think I would like to sit in a stand and see one of the men who hurt me in chains." Her chin tilted up. "I did nothing wrong. He did."

"I know, but—"

"If I get sent back, I get sent back." She shrugged. "My sister would..."

Ghost winced. "Has Link spoken of her? I asked him to find her."

"Link is brilliant at finding people. So am I. If he hasn't found her, then I'll give it a shot, okay?"

"Thank you." She studied me for a second, then murmured, "It is strange, isn't it?"

"What is?"

"I have known you a few days, yet I look forward to you coming and sitting with me. I don't know you, you don't know me, but I feel like I do."

Because I felt the same fucking way, and because I was just as confused by it, I beamed at her. "Yeah, it's weird as fuck."

"Maybe then you will understand why I would be willing to return to my country, even if it meant putting my sister's future in jeopardy just to see that man suffer."

"He wouldn't suffer as you did."

"Men like that are used to too many freedoms," she countered. "Being chained and restrained would be a satisfying sight."

"Babe, I don't even know if things would get that far. Half the clubhouse wants to take down his son."

"But Luke's already dead."

"Yeah, but he's still got a body and he hasn't been interred yet."

"Interred?"

I waved a hand. "Buried." I grimaced. "Got so many men wanting to defile that corpse of his, he'd—"

"What? Get something he deserved?"

I grinned at her, liking this savage side that was coming out. "If we stole the body, would you like to—"

"You could steal it?" Her brows rose. "That is strange."

"We have friends everywhere. What would you do?"

"Everything he did to me." She cleared her throat. "Well, some of the things he did to me."

"Would that make you feel better?"

"No."

"Would seeing the older Lancaster in court make you feel better?"

"Not really. But I'd feel better than if he just carried on living his life."

"That makes sense." I firmed my lips. "Your sister...where is she?"

"I think you call them orphanages."

"Child services, huh? That's shit. What happened to your folks?"

Ghost pulled a face. "My mother was what you call a 'Russian bride.' Her husband paid to have her brought over here. She left me with my grandmother. I don't know who my father is."

"That sucks."

She nodded. "It does. She died, leaving my half-sister behind. She was fine until her father died in a car crash.

"Before my mother passed, she had put us in contact with one another. Her father didn't want us to associate, but when he died and she reached out to me, I promised I'd come for her." She blinked fast enough to tell me she was hiding tears. "That did not work out."

Those broken pieces of me began to throb, *vibrate* with the need to collide with hers.

I sucked in a breath as I rolled forward, needing to connect with her, needing to touch her.

I'd only dared venture in here since a couple of days after they'd arrived. Something in me had wanted to avoid the bunkhouse.

Knowing that Stone had turned it into a temporary medical unit wouldn't have brought back happy memories for me.

Then, I'd heard about Amara almost dying and Tatána trying to kill herself, and...I'd wanted to come by. Wanted to see if I could do anything.

I knew what it felt like to have nothing to live for. I knew what it felt like to feel as though you were living without hope.

Then I'd seen Ghost.

Suddenly, twice daily visits were the norm, and if I could get her to forget about the fact she needed to eat what Giulia put in front of her, I considered that a good goal to have crushed.

I barely knew her.

The length of time we'd been aware of each other could be calculated in hours...

Yet I had no compunction in saying, "I think we can get you your justice while making sure your sister grows up knowing you."

She frowned. "This isn't possible."

I grinned at her, baring my teeth. "Impossible is my favorite word, Ghost." I rolled closer to her. "I can give you what you want."

"How?" she asked, her voice whisper soft as usual, but forceful enough then to tell me she wanted to know.

She wanted justice.

She wanted her sister.

And she deserved to have both.

"Marry me."

SEVENTEEN

LILY

I WAS USED to men's offices.

I'd spent a lot of time in my father's and, before he died, my grandfather's too.

Then, there were the occasions where Tiffany pleaded with her dad for something—like the brat she was, God love her—and she'd hauled me in to wait for her until she was done. There was also the principal's at the academy we'd attended.

None of those offices were like this one.

It was clean, cleaner than I'd expected, to be honest.

Lots of wood paneling, a big, wide desk that was surprisingly neat, a banker's light on one corner that created a warm glow, and a full drink tray on a dresser that was calling to me like you wouldn't believe.

There was a dining room table in a nook where a 'council' had gathered, and behind the desk, there were a couple of Japanese prints that were actually pretty damned nice. Worth a second look, at any rate.

Well, if you didn't look at the men in the corner first, of course.

Bikers were supposed to be rough and coarse. Which these were, I guessed, but no one had told me how gorgeous they were.

All of them.

Link was in good company, and if I was ever going to have a wet dream, then all of them would be in it, because, yikes.

In my world, handsome men wore suits and had eight-hundred-dollar cufflinks on their wrists.

They dared to be brave by going without socks in their hand-tooled Italian leather loafers, and bucked trends by not gelling their hair.

They were as sleek as the women they had on their arms...

Nothing about these guys was sleek.

And that made them all the more beautiful for it.

Link somehow glowed among them, like the sun rising from behind a mountain.

I felt the heat of his energy regardless of the distance between us, even if he hadn't looked at me since he'd half dragged me in here.

It had been an eventful afternoon.

I'd been involved in a shootout when Link had stuffed me into a very nice Mercedes SUV that the men called a 'cage' for some reason, a move my guards hadn't appreciated.

I'd been entangled in a tussle when said highly-paid guards had followed me to the compound, and...well, that was what it had taken to get me to the clubhouse.

I wasn't sure if the guards had been protecting me or the computer Link had been carrying, because knowing my father the way I did, I'd put nothing past him.

But, equally, the bastard would surely have destroyed Luke's computer the second he could, if he'd known there was video evidence that could put him behind bars.

Arrogance made a fool out of a lot of people, my father included, but *this* much of a fool?

I wasn't sure.

Still wasn't.

What I was sure of was that I was about to explode from a surfeit of energy if Link didn't do something.

I was antsy and felt like I had something on my to-do list, something major, and also, I felt like I'd dropped the ball.

My dad would know soon that my charade had been a lie.

All my mom's money gone.

Forever.

So many plans. So many things I'd intended on doing with it. All down the toilet—

"Babe?"

I jerked back when I noticed Link was crouching down in front of me.

That I hadn't realized he'd moved told me how far down the rabbit hole my brain had taken me.

He cocked a brow at my jolt of surprise, and I shot him a sheepish smile. "Sorry."

"Thinking bad shit?" He patted my knee. "Don't worry about it. We'll get him."

"He's still in Hong Kong," I reminded him, as I'd been reminding him since he and his brothers had arrived at my father's estate. "He's ripe for fleeing to a non-extradition country."

Rex grunted. "We got this sorted, Lily."

I frowned at him. "If you underestimate my father, he will make you pay for it. Trust me, I've been there before."

"You'll never be there again," Link ground out, his eyes flashing as he slipped his hands around my waist from his crouched position.

The move put us really close together, like, super close, and a quick glance at the men behind us showed me that this was atypical behavior for Link, because they looked perplexed by his affection.

That didn't bode well, did it?

Having walked into this clubhouse that was 'womanned' by naked ladies called sweetbutts, I'd had a horrendous realization earlier...

Every time Link had come to me and he'd given me pleasure that he hadn't received in turn, he'd probably gone to one of those women with his blue balls.

They were mine.

Mine, dammit.

I wanted to be the one he slaked his lust on. Not some random ho who eked out a living on their backs.

I bit my bottom lip to contain the emotion that was pulling me in two ways—one, cry. Two, scream and pull out Link's hair, if he really had been fucking around with those women instead of doing something with me.

Sure, I wasn't ready for what he needed, but there had to be things we could do together, right?

He could have taught me how to give him a damn blowjob, for God's sake, couldn't he?

"Lily!" Link shook me slightly. "What is it? What's wrong?"

I blinked at him, aware my thoughts had drifted once more.

Oops.

Clearing my throat, I muttered, "Long day."

Maverick wheeled forward.

Of them all, he was probably the leanest of the lot, but a picture above the drinks tray had revealed a younger Maverick.

A god-like Maverick, who made Thor look like an average six out of ten.

"You did good finding that footage." He jerked his chin up. "I'll nail that son of a bitch's ass to a cross. Don't you worry about it."

"I'm not worried," I immediately discounted. "Mostly because I don't think he'll ever return to the States."

Silence fell in the office, and Link's hands tightened around me. Not to the point of discomfort, just a reminder that he was there.

I liked the feeling that I wasn't alone, and Link gave me that in more ways than one. In more ways than he probably knew, to be fair.

"What do you mean?" Nyx rumbled. He was an easy face to remember too. The guy looked like sin and chocolate combined into one devastating package.

"We've got the evidence to take him down, sure, but you don't get to where he is without having contacts.

"The second you give this information to the police is the second he'll make plans to escape arrest."

Link frowned. "I don't get it, Lily. You were so psyched earlier. Why, if—"

I reached down and grabbed his hand. "Because what I found released me from *my* prison. He will never return to the States again." My eyes fluttered to a close on their own volition. "I'll never see him again." A shudder whispered through my frame. "He'll never touch me again."

My eyes were closed, but that didn't mean I didn't feel the way the tension in the room crept up at that.

"He hurt you?"

Nyx.

I forced myself to look at him. "Yes. And though I want him to rot in jail, I'll be quite happy for him never to return home.

"He's a racist, anti-everything that isn't American. He loves this country. Being barred from it will drive him nuts."

"He deserves a worse punishment," Maverick growled, his face white from rage. Did he care that much that my father had hurt me?

I frowned at the thought, then stared at him a little longer...no, there was something personal there. Something that drove him.

Even as I wondered what, he grunted and said, "I'll dig up what I can from Lancaster's files. Let's see if there's something more we can pin on him.

"Something the courts will fight over him for. He's not due back for a while, so we can wait to go to the police when he returns—"

"The second you took me off the estate with that computer, he'll know to change his plans. I told you to leave me there."

Rex slammed his hands down on the table. "What? Like a sacrificial lamb?"

"I've done it before. I could do it again."

"If that isn't the most disturbing thing I've heard all day," a man I knew was called Steel grumbled.

A hiss escaped Rex, then he muttered, "Maverick, call in Lodestar."

"Oh, fuck. Why?"

"Because she can help us. I know you can trawl through that shit and find stuff, but we need to drain accounts." Rex caught my eye. "Let's hit Donavan Lancaster where he really hurts."

"The wallet."

"Exactly. Prisons don't always come with bars."

"They just come without Fendi ties and million-dollar estates." A smile formed out of nowhere. "I approve of this plan."

Rex laughed. "Good to know, sweet pea. Now, I got Maverick to set you up in one of the bunkhouses."

My hand tightened around Link's. "Aren't you staying with me?"

The immediacy of his answer filled me with relief. "Damn straight I am." Link cut Rex a look. "Which bunkhouse?"

"Three."

He hauled himself onto his feet, then for my ears only, muttered, "Come on, sugar tits. Let's get you some fresh air."

I stared up at him, wide-eyed from his words, then was promptly hauled onto my feet too.

When my body collided with his, I released a sigh. The desire to slide my arms around his waist, to hold him tight, was something I fought with.

Men were the source of my problems, always had been and always would be, but there was something about Link...something *safe*. God help me.

I wasn't sure what that said about me. Didn't know if that meant I was weak or pathetic, but if it did, I'd take it.

Two men had made me feel unsafe for the entirety of my life, and I wasn't about to complain if Link could undo all that with not only his proximity, but the fact he could call on only God knew how many bikers to stand at our backs as well...

He grabbed my hand and tucked me into his side. The move had most of the council frowning at our joined hands then darting up to peer at Link's face.

It didn't take a brain surgeon to figure out that this wasn't Link's regular behavior.

Just by sight alone, I knew what he was—a manwhore.

Hell, if I looked like him, I'd be taking advantage of it too. But I took the fact he was acting strangely around me as a good sign.

I didn't really envisage this going far, him and me, even if the notion saddened me. We were too different, and not just in how we'd been raised either. But the way he made me feel was coming to be addictive.

The thought that once my usefulness was over—even if, in the long run, I hadn't been *that* useful—he might move on, had me clinging to his hand a little tighter.

He looked down at me, and what he saw had him frowning, and muttering, "Time to roll."

He half dragged me out of the office, then down a hallway that led to the front door.

In the distance, there was an opening that led to a room filled with couches. There were a lot of guys slouched on them, and a...

"Sweet fuck," I whispered.

Link, frowning at me for braking, peered where I was gawking, and hauled me along even faster.

"Is he fucking her?" I squeaked. "Right in front of everyone?"

Link tugged at his collar. "Yeah, but don't worry about it. It's all consensual."

I hadn't even questioned that. Just the fact that dudes were drinking and shooting the shit while one of their buddies was boning some chick.

As Link towed me down the hallway, I tilted my head so I could swerve and maintain a visual on the weirdest thing I'd ever seen.

And I'd seen some weird shit in my time.

But it was just so...so normal. The guys weren't reacting to it. Weren't even watching, for God's sake. It was like they were bored by the sight!

When Link had dragged me out of the door, I scowled at him. "You're hurting my arm."

He instantly stopped, then rubbed my arm all the way up to my shoulder.

"It doesn't hurt that bad," I muttered, even as I was peeking into the window that led into the same room we'd just walked past.

He reached for me, clutching my chin with his thumb, forcing me to look up at him. "That room isn't for you."

My brows furrowed. "Huh?"

"You don't want to go in there."

"Why not?" I huffed, not liking his tone. "That lady was in there."

"JoJo is the opposite of a lady."

"I guess that's why you like her, huh?"

He cringed—it was minute, but I spotted it. Inside, mortification filled me.

He'd slept with her.

And I wasn't talking about how he'd slept with me either. There'd probably been very little sleeping going down when he was with her.

Because she was normal.

Because she could have sex without shying away from it.

My throat closed up, and I stopped trying to look into the window. Maybe it was weird that I wanted to watch, but it was like a circus act. I just wanted to know what was going down in the big top tent.

"Fuck," he rasped, making me jolt in surprise at his dark tone. Then, his hand was at my nape and he was hauling me against him.

The move was so swift and so abrupt that I yelped before I collided into his chest.

"Don't look like that, Lily. You'll break my fucking heart."

I didn't say anything. What was there to say?

I just carried on looking at him, and he looked at me. He released a breath, bowed his head until our foreheads were touching, then muttered, "I have a past."

"So do I," I whispered.

"Mine's dirty. I've got a reputation." He swallowed. "My entire past is written in those walls. People know stuff about me in there, stuff that might hurt you and I can't protect you from it, because it happened. That was me." When I tried to pull away, he gritted his teeth and firmed his hold on the back of my neck. "No. Dammit. Listen. That was me *then*. But this is me here. Now."

"And what? I'm supposed to think you've changed?"

"Haven't you changed?" he challenged, his voice husky. "Haven't I changed you a little bit? Don't you want my touch now? Where before you were nervous? Don't you want me close?"

I licked my lips. "That isn't fair to ask me that."

"Isn't it? I can't be the only one feeling this way, sugar tits. I want your touch. I like you close. I want you at my side, riding bitch at my back. Never wanted that before. Never needed it. Until you."

My throat felt overfull with emotion. "Link, I'm not right for you."

"Why? Because I'm not good enough?"

His voice lowered at that, but I wasn't sure if I'd hurt him or angered him. "I-I'm...I don't want to say broken, because I'm not. But you say you've got a rep, well, how can I compete with that? There might be things I'll never be able to do for you."

I nipped my bottom lip because the physical pain was better than the emotional pain spearing me.

I hadn't anticipated this conversation, hadn't thought we'd be discussing this after the day's events, and yet here we were, having this talk outside a clubhouse where someone was having sex in a living room just a few feet away.

"Do I make you feel safe, Lily?"

My eyes widened at his question, because hadn't I just been thinking about how safe I felt around him?

"You don't have to answer that, because I know it's true. I know I make you feel safe."

"You do," I admitted, "and that's something I need, but that doesn't mean I'll be able to give you what *you* need."

He bent down, then stunned me by nipping my bottom lip exactly where I'd been gnawing on it.

"That's mine to bite," he declared.

"It belongs to me," I retorted, amused despite myself.

"Me too." He huffed. "People think I'm a soft touch—"

"They do?" I interrupted, stunned by the notion because Link was the opposite of soft in my opinion.

"My name...it means good stuff, but it also has a bad connotation."

"Why?"

His fingers rubbed the back of my neck where he was still holding me tight.

"Before I became a Sinner, I fell for a girl. She told me she loved me and I believed her. I let her in, let her come around."

"Did you love her?"

"Thought I did." His lips twitched. "You don't need to be upset, babe. I just...I felt something for her, and I wasn't ashamed about that.

"Turned out she was an undercover cop. Never heard the end of it ever since."

"Did she get you in trouble?" I inquired, my eyes wide with surprise at the turn the conversation had taken.

"Yeah. You could say that," he rumbled, but there was a trace of amusement that gave me some relief. "My point is, my brothers don't trust me around women anymore, even though they can.

"They think because I'm friends with the clubwhores and the Old Ladies that I'm a pushover. But I'm not." He blew out a breath then, with his spare hand, reached up and tapped my bottom lip. "With you, there's danger."

"What do you mean?" I whispered, my mouth dropping open at his words.

"I mean...you could break me." He cleared his throat. "Please. Don't."

For a second, I could do nothing more than blink at him as I stared up into those beautiful eyes of his, eyes that I felt could see into my very soul.

They knew me somehow, even though we'd only been close for a short while.

His plea was heartfelt, poignant, and I could do nothing less than whisper, "I promise I won't."

He dropped his chin. "Thank you." Another breath escaped him. "Now, as for the other stuff, your father and brother messed you up, and I get that. I'm patient an—"

"No one is that patient, Link."

He rocked his head, making our brows rub together. "You'd be surprised. I've got nothing but time on my hands. I can give you time so long as you give me you."

"What do you mean?"

"I will always stop when you ask me to. I will never take things too far. But I want you. I want to feel you. I want to touch you. I want to taste you. Give me you, and I won't ever take advantage of that gift."

I wasn't entirely sure what he meant, and my mouth worked uncertainly for a second as I thought about what his request might entail.

But then I thought about the fact that he was right—he made me feel safe. I *was* safe around him. And I wanted to give him everything he'd asked for. Him and only him.

"O-Okay, Link."

He sighed, and I knew my ears weren't deceiving me, because I heard relief in that sigh.

"Thank you."

He meant that.

I smiled at him. "You're welcome."

"Come on, let me show you your new place. You ain't gonna like it, but it's only until your dad's no longer a threat, okay?"

I had a feeling he'd always be a threat, but I didn't say that. I'd stay here for as long as I could be close to Link. When things changed, I'd move on.

Fingers crossed, life would be more resolved by then, and until that time, I'd enjoy Link and the pleasure he could give me. And, hopefully, learn to give him that in return.

EIGHTEEN

LINK

THE TINIEST of moans woke me.

It wasn't a good moan which, in my defense, was the kind of moan I was used to hearing. It was a bad moan.

It was Lily.

Who was sleeping at my side.

In the too-small bed in the bunkhouse that was really meant for one person and not two, but somehow, we were making it work.

She was half on, half off me, her body angled off mine to the side. My hands were on her ass, and her thighs clasped one of mine, meaning her pussy brushed my skin.

We were close in a way I'd never really experienced before with another woman, and I wasn't sure why.

A man like me, with my lifestyle, with the pussy all around me, I was used to being with a woman in bed. But shit was different with Lily. Shit was better.

Fuck, shit *wasn't* shit.

Which said a lot.

It surprised me that her tiny moan awoke me, but the second I realized where I was, everything fell into place.

Subconsciously, I wasn't questioning who I was in bed with. I didn't wonder, in my sleepy daze, who had made that noise.

I knew.

It was like something in my fucking soul knew who was with me, and as goddamn weird as that was, it also felt right.

"Babe," I whispered, voice gruff from sleep because, yeah, I found that I slept better when I was being used as a prop for her too. "Wake up."

She twisted her head to the side like she was trying to ignore my command, and I reached over, touched her shoulder, absorbed the hit when she flinched, and blew it out on a deep exhalation that was meant to cleanse me of my anger.

Her fucking father.

That bastard brother.

If I could slice their throats, I would. I'd have bathed in their fucking blood if that was a possibility.

Because she was still sleeping, I rubbed her shoulder, not disconnecting the touch, and murmured, "Sweetheart, it's me. Link. Please, wake up."

A drowsy sigh escaped her. "Link? What's wrong?"

She was slurring too, and that kind of rammed home the intimacy between us.

Weirdly enough, it was like a bridge of trust because Lily had been bred to be perfect. At all times. She'd been punished if she wasn't.

So to hear her like that, to see her less than perfect and sleeping in one of my Sinners' tees was like a golden handshake.

"Nothing, sugar tits." I reached down and patted her on the tush. "Go back to sleep."

I was willing to go the extra mile for her, I was willing to do whatever I had to to keep her safe, but there was no way I could keep my hands off that perfect ass of hers.

Which, I knew, meant slow conditioning. Getting her used to my touch there, because fuck, I couldn't *not* touch the perfection of that butt. It would be cruel to deny an ass man like me that beautiful behind so, slowly, surely, I was touching it but with no other intent. All in the vain hope that I'd gentle her to being caressed there.

Though she tensed for a second when I squeezed, she immediately crumpled into me and began snoozing a second later.

I angled my head down and pressed a kiss to her temple, enjoying the way she snuggled into me.

What was this?

Really?

She was too good for me, and our lives in no way meshed, but I liked this. Liked *her*. I liked her in my arms, my bed. I wanted her hands on my body. I wanted mine on hers.

More, I wanted that virgin pussy around my dick. Christ, more than I probably wanted to play with that ass of hers.

Blowing out a breath as I tried to make sense out of my muddled thoughts, I muttered, "You're playing with my head, Lily Lancaster."

She hummed and rubbed her nose down the ball of my shoulder. "This isn't a game, Link. Nothing about this is fun."

I wasn't sure whether to be insulted by that or not.

"You could hurt me too. Do you know that?" she whispered.

"I don't want to."

I hadn't expected this conversation. I thought she was asleep.

Apparently, I'd been wrong.

"You might not want to, but that doesn't mean you won't." She placed her hand on my hip and patted it. "Don't worry about it."

Don't worry about not hurting her?

"What do you want from me, Lily?" I asked cautiously.

"Things you won't want to give me, and things you probably can't."

She sounded less and less drowsy, and while I hadn't aimed for this chat, maybe it was for the best. Maybe we needed to get things straightened out.

All of this had been forged on a few conversations and dozens of texts. Then a couple of dates that had evolved into fumblings which, I had to admit, were hot as fuck.

Nothing about this had progressed in a way things like this did with me.

I was all about sex. I didn't date. I didn't want a virgin. I didn't text bitches. My mind was on business and my brothers and keeping shit in line in my position as Road Captain and head mechanic and manager of the garage that was owned by the Sinners.

I didn't make out on couches.

I didn't sneak into bedrooms to sleep with country club princesses.

Which meant, all in all, that Lily was different.

But I knew that already.

"What do you want from me?" I repeated, needing an answer.

"What can you give me?" she countered. "Know what I saw when I went to the bathroom earlier?"

My brow puckered. "When?"

"Before we went to sleep." She yawned.

"What?" That yawn had felt relaxed, enough to make me lower my guard.

"Two guys fucking someone against the wall outside."

My eyes widened. "Who?"

She snorted. "How would I know? They were twins, I think."

That had me rolling my eyes. "Fucking Prospects. They ain't supposed to be fucking anyone."

She tensed. "Huh?"

Grumbling because this was going to take us off topic, I explained quickly, "Prospects are like trainees. They want to become full brothers. You can't do that without becoming a Prospect and going through the ropes. Part of that means not having sex with the—"

She laughed. "Yeah. Good time to go speechless, Link."

I winced. "It isn't like you think."

"Isn't it? You have women to fuck and to, what, clean the place?"

It didn't surprise me that she knew what a clubwhore was. Still, I wished she didn't.

Not that she wouldn't have found out soon enough.

Hell, she'd already seen North and Hawk fucking someone they shouldn't around the back of the clubhouse.

God damn them.

With my free hand, the hand that wasn't curved around her, I reached up and pinched the bridge of my nose. Then she surprised me by patting me on the hip again.

"Link, it's okay."

Was it?

Warily, I peered down at her, and the sadness on her face made me wonder what was going on in her head.

It didn't help that I knew how the men in her family treated women, and knowing that she might draw parallels between *us* and *them* pissed me off.

Royally.

But why *wouldn't* she?

We *did* have women hanging around the place with free board and lodging, so long as they fucked whichever brother asked them to bend over. It wasn't like I could escape that fact.

"You told me about Storm and Keira, Link," she reminded me softly. "I already figured out how it rolls."

"If you figured that out, then why did you want to meet up with me, Lily? Why did you want me to fuck you?"

"Because I like you."

"That's it?" I arched a brow. "You like me, and so you thought it was only natural that I might be willing to fuck you?"

"Don't twist this around, Link. You don't understand what I mean." She twisted around, then jerked upright and hunched over in a sitting position before glaring at me.

"Why don't you explain it to me, Lily?" I attempted to soothe.

There was very little light coming in from the window at my back, but there was enough for me to see her scowl.

"Do you know how many men I've liked in my life?"

I scowled at her. "No. Why the fuck would you ask me that?"

"Because, dumbass, I've liked one. You. That's it. That's why I wanted more from you. That's why I... It was my birthday the night before Luke died."

I stilled. "It was? Shit." With a wince, I muttered, "Happy Birthday?"

"Thanks. Know what my birthday present from my father was? Know what had me snooping around my brother's office when he'd died?"

"No. What?"

"Father announced my future husband would be coming for dinner when he was out of jail."

Whatever I'd expected her to say, it wasn't *that*. "Excuse me?"

"You heard me right. My husband is currently in jail."

"You're not married yet," I snapped, enraged at the thought of her belonging to someone else.

Fuck, I was even madder at the thought she'd withheld this from me. We'd talked about this, but she hadn't mentioned anything about the fucker being in jail.

"I'm as good as married in my father's eyes. Probably in Fieri's eyes too."

My mouth rounded because I knew that name... *Famiglia*. "Gianni Fieri is your fiancé?"

"Fiancé isn't the right word, Link," she retorted, folding her arms over her chest. "I told you, remember, that my pussy was for sale. Well, he's the buyer.

"I didn't want him to be my first. That's why I wanted you. Because you're the first man I've seen who I've chosen, who, when I look at you, makes me warm inside.

"You make me laugh, and your eyes are calming, and when you—"

I surged upright, unable to stop myself from sliding my hands around her throat and up to cup her cheeks.

Within seconds, my mouth was on hers and I was thrusting my tongue between her lips.

She moaned the second we connected, and for a little while, she let me play.

I sucked and flicked, teased and enticed, loving that she let me sup from her, adoring the way she arched her head back to give me full access.

I tasted everything she had to give.

But I gave her more than I took.

So many men in her life had taken from her, but I didn't want to be like that. I really fucking didn't.

And that was why I pulled back.

I wasn't like them.

So, even though it pained me, I stopped making goddamn love to her mouth, I stopped teasing her by sliding my tongue against hers—even though I knew she liked it because she dug her nails into my shoulders with each parry—and I drew away.

It hurt.

Fuck, it hurt.

But shit.

A woman tells you that you're her first crush? That she likes you when she's been raped and psychologically abused?

That was the biggest goddamn compliment I thought I'd ever received.

When I pulled back, we were both panting, and I pressed my forehead to hers, needing to retain the connection.

The heat between us was off the charts, and I'd only fanned the flames.

"Why did you stop?" she bit off, each word punctuated by a heavy gulp of air.

"Because I won't take from you."

"It was freely given."

"I know, but I'm different. You just said so yourself."

She froze for a second, then whispered, "I-I could love you, Link. That scares me."

"You think that doesn't scare me? Never loved anyone except my momma, my grandmother, and then a dumb bitch who was only using me." Another breath escaped me. "I feel the same way."

"We're not right for each other. We've got different paths."

"We do, but that doesn't mean those paths can't cross over along the way."

"Just because we were heading in one direction doesn't mean we can't change destinations."

"Would you want to?" she asked sadly.

"For you? For this?" I squeezed her waist. "Yeah. I would." When she shook her head, I sighed and squeezed her waist again. "I have a question."

She bowed her head and pressed it to my shoulder and cemented herself in my memory like no other ever had.

The trust inherent in that move, the affection and intimacy…I'd experienced nothing like it in my almost forty years of fucking living.

"What did you hope to find when you went looking in Luke's office?"

"A way out."

"Of marrying Fieri?"

"Yes."

"You didn't find it."

"No."

"Do you know who he is?"

"A businessman? Obviously, my father and he want to cement ties—"

"Why would your father want to tie you to a criminal?"

She waved a hand. "My father was a banker, Link. Before my mother, that was his trade. Lots of bankers and investment gurus go to jail."

"There's being friends with someone in jail, there's even being associated with someone in jail, but marrying them to your daughter? Bringing them into the family? Isn't that something else entirely?"

She shrugged. "I don't know, and to be honest, I don't care. I was hoping—"

"What? What were you hoping for?"

"That things would change with Luke gone."

"You had the chance of becoming the heiress."

"Yes. It put a deadline on things."

"You mean, you were wanting to kill your father before Fieri was released?"

"Yes. I don't want to marry him," she whispered. "He's creepy."

"He's more than creepy," I muttered, and I squeezed her again, this time to comfort myself as well as her.

Fuck. *Fieri?*

What in God's name was Lancaster thinking? Tying his daughter to that goddamn monster? He made Nyx look like a fucking saint!

His rep preceded him in certain circles all over the country, for fuck's sake.

"Babe, you know *who* he is, don't you?"

"Just one of Father's friends."

"No, love. He's the son of Benito Fieri." When she didn't react, made no other response than a shrug, I had to sigh. "Benito is the head of the Fieri crime family. He's *La Famiglia*, babe. He's mafia."

A long, slow breath escaped her. "He's *mafia?*"

"Yeah. Your dad's obviously more fucked up than—" An explosive breath escaped me. "Sweet fuck, of course."

She jerked back. "What is it?"

"Of fucking course. The *Famiglia* are involved in the skin trade. That's how your father and Luke bought the women."

"The skin trade? Bought? What the hell are you talking about?"

"The women in the videos, the women here, they were bought, Lily. And the *Famiglia* are known for trafficking women and..." My voice waned. "Kids."

"No. No way!" She started off squeaking, then she burst into a shriek that had my ear drums ringing even as she tunneled into my arms, trying to escape what I was telling her.

I hugged her tightly, held her close in a vain attempt at making her feel better.

The more she huddled into me, the more I knew she was trying to overcome what I'd just told her about the kind of man her father wanted her tied to.

I closed my eyes, surprised by the path my thoughts took me down. I wasn't frightened, wasn't even freaked. This was right.

What I was going to do was how it was supposed to be.

"Babe, this changes everything. You know that, right?"

She quivered in my embrace before she whispered, "I need to run away."

The prospect of her leaving had me holding her tighter and, furthermore, it cemented the rightness of my actions.

"No. You're not going anywhere," I told her. "You're going to stay here. With me."

"No, Link, you don't mean that. Your world would..." She pushed her face into my throat and I felt her tears. "I don't want to share my partner."

"And you won't. I wouldn't do that to you."

I meant it too.

Even though the offer stunned the fuck out of me.

"It's a part of your world. Storm didn't stop sleeping with those women for Keira," she pointed out sadly, making me regret sharing that fucking story with her.

"I'm not Storm. I'm not a dumbass. I know what I've got in my arms."

She quieted down, like she was listening, willing to absorb what I had to say.

"You can't run from the Fieris, babe. They'll find you. Wherever you go. The only place you're safe is here. With me. With the MC at your back."

She argued, "I can't bring this to your door."

"I'm asking you to. You mean something to me, Lily. I'm not good with words," I said shakily. "I-I just know that I've never felt this way before, and I don't think I will again.

"Maybe it's nuts, maybe it's been too short a time to really know what either of us wants, and that's good. That's fine. But I want to know you're safe. That's what matters to me."

"W-We might be incompatible," she whispered, the words tickling the tender skin of my throat.

"Of all the stuff you've said tonight, that's the craziest. Baby, we're so beyond compatible my dick is aching from that kiss alone." I squeezed her waist once again. "But we'll take this slow. We'll take this however you need to go."

"That isn't fair to you," she argued, but I heard the yearning in her voice, and fuck me, if that didn't make my dick harder than it already was, I didn't know what could.

"Let me decide what's fair for me, okay?"

"If I stay here, Fieri isn't going to let this drop. He'll come for me."

"Let him," I ground out. "You know those Five Points you mentioned before? When you were trying to keep us in the loop?"

"You mean when I was trying to be your informant and failing?" she countered drolly.

"Yeah, then," I retorted, amused. "Well, they're the Fieris' natural fucking enemies.

"With me at your back, we have a battalion of the Devil's soldiers ready to roll into battle the second you become my woman. And through them, you have the Five Points."

She shifted her head back, her brow furrowed as she stared at me. "What do you mean?"

"Which part? About the Five Points?"

"No. You say 'becoming your woman' like there's a ceremony." She gulped. "You want to get married?"

I had a feeling that one day, sometime soon, I'd wife this woman and tie her to me in all the fucking ways I could, but no. Not yet. She wasn't ready for that, and neither was I.

"There's a process. To come under the club's protection, you've got to be recognized as my Old Lady." I ran my hands up and down her arms.

"Does it involve hazing?" she questioned warily.

My lips twitched. "No. Nothing like that. That's for shit with the Prospects."

Her eyes flared wide. "Oh."

"Yeah. Oh. Best not to ask. And," I released a gusty sigh, "while we're talking about that, there will always be some shit I can't tell you. Shit that you don't want to know because I don't want you to get into trouble."

"I know how that works," she rumbled. "More than I'd like."

"You need to know that I get involved in some shit that no woman would be happy with—"

"Do you sell women and children to men like my father and brother?" she demanded rawly.

"No. I defend them. Avenge them. Well, help avenge them," I whispered back at her.

"Then that's all I need to know. My father is the biggest criminal going. He has his hands in more pies than a baker. I don't even want to know how dirty he is, but because he hides behind companies and umbrella corporations and only God knows what else, he's considered legitimate.

"Well, that's bullshit." She swallowed, and I wasn't surprised when she reached up, her hands cupping my biceps as she dug her nails into my arms, and whispered, "Promise me, Link, that if one day I want to go, you won't trap me here."

The idea that she'd want to leave me didn't sit well with me. I was, by nature, a positive person. I liked to start shit off the right way, with the right frame of mind.

That wasn't what she was asking of me at the moment.

But because of her past, a past I didn't understand but could empathize with, I got it. I really did.

"I promise to do everything in my power to make you want to stay," I conceded, unable to give her the vow she wanted, but giving her an oath I'd stand by.

For as long as I lived.

She bit her lip. "That's a caveat."

"And that's a fancy word."

"I'm an economist and I went to finishing school. What do you expect?"

"True." She was so fucking smart and too good for me. I knew that. "Finishing school, huh?"

"Father insisted."

"Don't you think it's time you stopped calling him that? You won't ever be seeing that fucker again."

She nibbled harder on her lip. "You think?"

"That's a fucking promise."

Her nod was resolute. "Okay. Donavan, then. He insisted I be finished."

"That sounds ominous."

"It wasn't actually. But I had to walk around with a book on my head and learn where to set cutlery on the table.

"There's also a whole damn protocol about where to sit a prince next to an oligarch—tedious as fuck."

My lips curved as I got, more than ever, a sense of the yawning gap between us.

Oligarchs and princes, after all, were *not* a part of my world.

"Babe, you become my woman, my Old Lady, you'll be safe. I will *never* let anyone harm you.

"I will make sure that you're safe from that cunt of a father, and I'll go to war with the *Famiglia* to keep you out of their paws but..."

When my voice waned because she was looking at me like I'd set the planets in the sky, I didn't want to finish my sentence.

I really fucking didn't.

I wanted her to look at me that way.

I wanted this princess, this fucking queen, to look at me, trailer trash, like I was capable of anything. Like I was her knight in goddamn shining armor.

But I wasn't.

My armor was tarnished, and it had been for a helluva long time.

She needed to know that. Lily might think she didn't, but I needed to ram that home because I wasn't doing this with an expiration date in mind, even if she was.

I was going with a gut feeling here.

A feeling that appeared whenever she lay asleep on my chest, whenever she cuddled into me at night.

When she moaned from a nightmare and it pierced my fucking heart like she'd used a goddamn dagger to stab me.

I was going from the smiles she earned whenever she sent me something funny via text, to thinking about how right it would feel when she rode bitch on the back of my bike...

No, this wasn't temporary.

This was, in my mind, permanent.

The fact that I was willing to wait until she was ready, until she wanted me as much as I wanted her, until she was begging for my touch and not tensing up at it, spoke wonders.

"What is it?" she whispered when I didn't continue, when I just looked at her, staring into her starry eyes.

The abused woman finally able to see the broken pieces of herself come together again.

"I'm not a prince. I'm not an oligarch. I don't go to the opera and I don't have a pass to Crosskeys. I used to work there, for God's sake. I don't wear Prada, and my hair? I usually cut it in the bathroom. Nothing about me is fancy, and everything about you *is*—"

Before I could say more, she raised her hand and pressed a finger to my lips. "Do you know how many guys have tried to pick me up at Crosskeys?"

Irritation flashed through me like a tidal wave. "I can imagine," I rumbled.

She snorted. "Don't get jealous—"

Fuck. I was.

Me.

Jealous!

Holy.

Shit.

If I needed proof that this woman was different, I had it.

"I didn't want a single one of them. Dressed in tennis whites, golf vests, Armani suits, or designer casual. I didn't want any of them.

"It was a biker who made me feel safe. One who cuts his hair in the bathroom, one who wears Henleys and ripped jeans and has engine oil in the tiniest creases in his nails.

"You, Link. You. You made me feel safe, you made me feel like I wasn't alone, and when you touch me, I'm not Donavan Lancaster's daughter, I'm Lily. *I'm me.* And I like me around you."

"I like you around me too," I replied huskily, liking her answer so fucking much I thought I'd burst.

"What do I have to do to become your Old Lady?"

"You get a tattoo."

"Is that it?" She released a breath that I realized was relieved.

A laugh escaped me. "What did you think you'd have to do?"

"I don't know. I wasn't sure. I mean, when you join frat houses and sororities they all make you do weird stuff—"

"Well, this is weird enough."

"I've always wanted a tattoo," she mused.

"This one will tell the fucking world what you are to me. What you mean to this club. It's a brand, babe. A stamp of protection that will keep you safe forever. You have my word on that."

Her big blue eyes grew hazy. "You really mean it, don't you? You want me like that. Even though I..."

"Even though you, what? Haven't put out?" I arched a brow. "Don't you realize that's half of what makes me know I need you in my life, sugar tits?" As her eyes widened, I told her, "And don't think that just because I'm taking shit slow, I'm not going to touch you. 'Cause I am.

"I already told you I'm going to glut myself on your fucking taste and give you so many fucking orgasms that you're never going to want to leave me."

A choked cry escaped her as she plunged into my arms, clinging to me as tightly as a fucking spider clung to its web.

And that was exactly where I wanted her.

Cleaved to me.

Body and soul.

NINETEEN

NYX

THREE DAYS LATER

"TELL that moron asswipe that if he brings this shit into me again, I'm telling the sheriff he needs his license revoked," Link snapped, as he wiped his hands on a rag and hollered his irritation at Gunner, one of the brothers who helped out at the garage as Link's right-hand man.

"Ain't gonna tell him dick, Link," Gunner retorted. "Levi Jamieson spends a fucking fortune on this car. Think of how much money he wastes by being a shit driver."

"Yeah, and I made it how it is." Link ran his hand over the sleek, custom-build he'd done last year before we'd moved into these premises, and grunted. "He keeps on damaging it, and I'm going to get a real fucking boner for him."

"Since when were you into dick?"

My lips twitched even as I launched off the side of the wall where I'd been leaning, watching over things without anyone knowing the wiser.

"Yeah, Lily will be surprised to hear you suddenly prefer cock to pussy."

His eyes narrowed at me. "Stop fucking talking about her pussy."

"Wasn't talking about *her* pussy, not specifically anyway."

I pretty much heard his teeth grind as he glared at me, and I almost shook my head at the sight.

Giulia had only last night bet me a hundred dollars that Link would make Lily his Old Lady and, though I'd argued against the notion because

Link was a manwhore, I had a fucking feeling I was going to lose to my woman...

Still, losing to her usually involved her gloating, and I liked watching her gloat. Especially if that included her squirming on my dick as she did so.

"What the fuck are you doing here?" he groused, even as he began packing up tools, tools that were black with the work he'd been doing.

While I liked to think of myself as being pretty open-minded, it still blew my mind that Lily Lancaster, a woman who'd been born with a silver spoon in her mouth, liked a man who got his hands dirty for a living touching her.

I felt shitty for thinking that way, but there was no evading just how different Lily and Link were.

Sure, their names started the same way, but alliteration wasn't the key to a happy future.

And fuck, I cared.

I loved Link.

He was my brother by choice and that was all that mattered to me. I didn't like the idea of this bitch coming in, wrecking his world, and just for...

I blew out a breath.

What?

For what goddamn reason would Lily have done the things she had if it wasn't to cauterize her life from her father's?

I knew that, I did. *Really*. But I was protective, and Link had the worst judgment where women were concerned.

"Thought I was the one in danger of turning," he rumbled, still pissed at me. "Or can I just feel your eyes on my ass because it's wishful thinking?"

A snort escaped me, one that quickly morphed into laughter. The fucker could always make me laugh, even if I was rolling my eyes at the same goddamn time.

"You wish," I retorted.

"Oh, you're right. I do."

He puckered his lips and sent me a kiss that had me wrinkling my nose, and Gunner just shook his head before he tossed a greasy rag at Link's face.

Link, good-natured bastard that he was, snatched the rag, tossed it on the side table where he was working, and asked, "What are you doing here anyway?"

"Lodestar's hit pay dirt."

He stopped tossing tools into a box. I wasn't sure why he bothered when he'd be working on the same vehicle in the morning, but I knew my brother had a routine.

He cleaned the garage and himself down every evening, so that things would be just *so* the next morning when he came in.

He'd fought against running this place, and I wasn't sure why. It was his natural habitat, but I figured it had to do with him not wanting the extra responsibility.

He was already Road Captain, and throw this in? A business that had already been mostly made thanks to his fame with custom work? More responsibility, less time to do what he liked doing—boning chicks and partying.

Something that had seemingly changed since he'd met Lily.

Another reason this entire situation blew my fucking mind.

An old dog couldn't learn new tricks…but was that right? Wasn't *I* an old dog? Hadn't Giulia taught me some new shit? Why couldn't Lily teach Link something new too?

Giulia sure as fuck kept me on my toes, so I couldn't imagine Lily not doing the same for my best friend.

"What? How?"

His urgent tone had me blinking when I realized I'd tuned out of the conversation.

Lodestar was a soldier buddy of Mav's that he'd met overseas. She'd been recruited by the CIA and did shit I really didn't want to know about. For some reason, they kept in touch.

I wasn't sure if Mav had boned her, but had to think that if he had, then it was unlikely she'd still be talking to him and willing to do the illegal shit she did for us.

Not that he asked her often, but when we needed her help, it was usually for something bad.

And she always came through.

Always.

"What did she find?" Link demanded, surging toward me, a storm cloud in his face that told me he really fucking cared for Lily. Enough that this was all he could think of.

Her safety was as imperative to him as Giulia's was to me.

"He's in Hong Kong, which makes Vietnam and Cambodia likely destinations for him if he's going to flee to countries with non-extradition orders with the US."

"Okay, so?"

"She's found some shit that would help persuade those governments to return him to the States."

His eyes widened, glee filling them. "You're shitting me?"

"Nope. I promise I'm not."

"What did she find?"

"Ties to the Triads, more ties to the Fieris." I rubbed my chin. "Lots of trafficking shit, Link. Lots of Vietnamese and Cambodian women..."

"What about them?"

"You know that shit with China? The One Child Law?"

"They could only have one kid per family, right? Population control or something." He scratched his head. "I ain't no historian."

"Yeah. Well... Okay, so that's created a deficit. Lots of dudes, not a lot of pussy."

Link's mouth dropped open. "What? He's transporting women across the border for men to buy?"

"Well, not him in particular. He's the money man."

"Why the fuck has he gotten involved in this? He was legit. He didn't have to go down this road."

"Lodestar found out why." I paused for a second. "He and Benito Fieri were in college together. Benito introduced him to Henry Lindenbourg."

I watched him process that, process a name that was up there with Rockefeller, the Vanderbilts, and the Rothschilds. "I mean, I know who Henry Lindenbourg is, but what does that have to do with anything?"

"Henry is Lily's grandfather."

His mouth dropped open. "Now you really are shitting me."

"No, I'm not. This crap has been tied up for a long time. It's come full circle." I frowned, still a bit confused over all this myself. "But it means we can go to the sheriff with what we've uncovered without fear he'll never come to justice. You ready to ride?"

His jaw worked. "More than fucking ready. Let's take that cunt down."

I caught his eye. "When he's on American soil..."

Mouth tight, he spat, "We'll ride and watch him burn."

We bumped fists and sealed that promise.

TWENTY

LILY

AS I HOVERED in front of the door to the bunkhouse I knew housed the women my brother and father had abused, a door I'd been trying to knock on for the past three damn days, I bit my lip over whether I should go in to help.

I got the feeling that Giulia, the woman Luke had attacked, was working to help them alone, and I wanted to assist.

My family had done this to them, after all. I should be one of the people to do something to make things right.

But I was nervous.

Really nervous.

I deserved their hatred, deserved to have shit thrown at me, and…

I blew out a breath as the roar of bikes suddenly drowned out even the noisiest of my thoughts.

When I twisted around to see where the racket was coming from, I saw about six bikes riding into the yard in front of the clubhouse.

I didn't know any of them, but as I looked over the bikes and the helmets topping the guys' heads, I had a pretty good idea which one was Link.

Whether it was the bike or just the fact that it was Link, my body started to overheat, and when the throb of the engine cut off abruptly, I was reminded of the fact that I really wanted to feel that buzz between my thighs one-on-one.

As the men climbed off their modern-day stallions, I leaned against the wall and watched them strip off their helmets, revealing exactly who they were to the world.

When I saw the same men who'd been around the council table the first day I'd come here, I had to figure they'd gone out to do *something*.

Exactly what, I wasn't privy to, but I had to hope it included my father and his arrest.

Link punched Rex in the arm, which made Rex grab him by the head and give him a noogie.

The sight made me grin—Link was such a jackass sometimes. But I got it. Beneath the gruff exterior was a man who didn't cut himself enough slack.

He was like Puck from *A Midsummer's Night Dream*. Except, his mischief wasn't meant to harm, but to distract.

I didn't think even Link recognized how he acted the fool to make others feel better, but I liked that I was tying myself to a man who did that on the regular. Who thought of others and their feelings before he thought of himself.

What other kind of man would promise a woman no sex until she was ready at our ages?

I wasn't a teenager. I was out of college, for God's sake. And I didn't know how old Link was—Christ, how terrible was that?—but I knew he had to be in his late thirties.

That kind of promise was selfless, and I appreciated him all the more for it.

Not because I wanted to take advantage of him and what he was giving me—safety—but because it made me want to give him the things I wasn't sure I was ready to give yet.

I just knew when I *was* ready, he'd be the one I wanted. Just as he'd been that first time I texted him and asked him to come over to Tiff's place.

The guys strode into the clubhouse, Nyx at their back like a storm cloud. His shoulders and arms were tensed, bunched up like he could throttle something—

"Don't worry about Nyx. He always looks like that."

I jerked in surprise at the voice. Twisting around to find its source, I realized it came from the window to my left.

A beautiful woman of distinct Italian heritage was looking at me like she—

My brow puckered. Like she, *what?*

I couldn't really make it out. Was she angry with me? Distrustful? Disapproving?

Her face was a mixture of expressions, most of them negative enough to make me want to step back because I knew she knew who I was.

Licking my lips, I whispered, "I-I can go."

"Go where?" The other woman sniffed. "Seems like you're cornered."

Was she talking here, now? Or just in life?

I wasn't sure which option was better.

Fuck, I really was cornered. Hell, more than that, *screwed*.

"I'm Nyx's woman. Giulia." She pushed her hand through the window's opening and thrust it at me.

Surprised by the gesture, I grabbed hers and shook it. I wanted to do so gingerly because the polite offering and gesture seemed too banal for this woman, but I made sure to give her a solid handshake. Like I'd give any of my father's associates.

Only by exuding strength and confidence did you show no weakness to a potential foe.

"You're Lily Lancaster."

I could feel my face pucker as a whole, like I'd just chomped on a thousand Atomic Warheads.

Giulia laughed at that, surprising me. "No, we don't like that surname around here either."

I licked my lips. "I loathe everything my father gave me."

Giulia arched a brow. "I wouldn't loathe his millions."

"Billions," I corrected. "Each of them corrupt."

"From what Nyx said, Link thinks you're waiting on that money so it can't be that corrupt."

"I want my mother's original fortune. Nothing more. Nothing less."

"You just gonna toss the rest away?" she countered.

"No, I have plans for it." I tipped my chin up. "Not that I'll get it now. They'll probably freeze all his accounts once he's arrested."

"When they unfreeze them, what will happen?"

"I have no idea. His stakes go far beyond anything he informed me of. I was the useless daughter. He kept me in the dark about most things."

Giulia pursed her lips. "You gonna hurt Link?"

My eyes flared wide. "No! That's the last thing I want."

"Seems to me you and him are pretty close, and it's all very fortuitous on your side."

I snorted, but I wasn't offended. I could appreciate that she was looking out for Link even if, on this occasion, it wasn't necessary.

"Nothing was fortuitous about any of this. It was all bad luck and good timing."

Giulia frowned. "What's that supposed to mean?"

"It all started unfolding when Luke set his eyes on you." My mouth tightened. "You weren't the first, but I'm glad you were the last."

"You don't have a problem with me taking out your bro? Your daddy sure did."

"He isn't my 'daddy.' He was barely my sperm donor, and even then, sperm donors don't do to their daughters what he did to me." Something flashed in her eyes at my words, and I held her gaze, refusing to relent. "My brother was the spawn of Satan. Evil and twisted.

"I'm glad you put him down, and I'm glad that I helped get these women out of the hell he put them into.

"Now, I'd like to help them. Even if it's just, I don't know, sitting with them."

"They're not that big on communicating, Lily," Giulia warned with a wince. "They're mostly on the road to healing now."

"Of course they're fucked up, but most of them are internalizing their shit. I think they're going to need therapy to get them on the right road. Physical healing is only one side of the struggle."

"True. I know where to find a therapist."

Giulia tilted her head to the side. "You do?"

"Yeah. She's my friend. She'll help."

"You trust her?"

"With my life." Tiffany was probably the only person I'd ever trusted throughout my childhood, even if I hadn't been able to share the worst aspects of my life with her.

Giulia hummed. "Let me talk it over with Nyx first. He'll take it up with the council."

"Fine. Whatever. But Tiffany is solid. She'll want to help. Especially when everything comes out."

"You sound excited about that," Giulia mused, her eyes drifting over my face.

"I am. I want to be free of him."

"Maybe you should unchain yourself from that name of yours."

I blinked. "Maybe you're right."

"Usually am."

My lips twitched. "Good to know."

"What's your mom's maiden name?"

"Lindenbourg."

As I'd expected, her eyes widened at that. "Holy shit. You're a Lindenbourg?" Her mouth gaped as she thought about exactly who the Lindenbourgs were. "No wonder you want your mother's stake back."

"I have plans."

"What kind of plans? To buy an island?" she scoffed, then her brow furrowed and I figured she was thinking about Link.

"To protect myself and any other women like me." I jerked my chin up. "I've been chattel all my life. My mom was too. I refuse to be that anymore."

"Hell yeah," Giulia agreed. "Fucking men."

Despite the thoughts flushing through me, and the rage and annoyance they brought, I had to laugh at that. "Yeah. Fucking men."

"What did we do now?"

Giulia grumbled, "For big motherfuckers, you're sneaky as shit."

"All the better for hunting you," Nyx retorted, but he looked smug.

Link just looked confused.

Hell, how had they both approached us without us noticing?

I shot him a shaky smile, and though it took more courage than he probably knew, I held out my hand for him.

He eyed it, then me, then took a step forward.

When our hands were clasped, something inside me sighed, and I twisted my arm under his so I was touching his side.

"You giving Lily shit?" Nyx asked Giulia as he leaned against the bunkhouse wall.

"Just vetting her. Making sure she's good enough for our Link."

"What did you decide? Can Link bone her with your permission?" Nyx drawled.

My cheeks flushed with heat at his crudeness, and Link groused, "Fuck off, man. Don't talk shit like that about my woman."

Nyx's brows arched. "It's like that, huh?"

Link grunted. "Yeah. It fucking is. And you already fucking know it. Stop picking fights you ain't got a chance of winning."

Giulia held out a hand. "You owe me a Benjamin Franklin, Nyxy-poo."

The nickname had me curling my lips inward to hold back a smile. Nyx just grunted, even as he reached into his back pocket and pulled out his wallet.

When he slapped a note on Giulia's still outstretched palm, he looked at me and said, "You've helped the club and I thank you for that. But if you hurt Link, I will end you."

He said it so easily, so casually, that I knew he meant it. And when he said 'end,' I knew he meant a whole other verb.

"Well, that really scared the shit out of her. Jesus, Nyx. You need to work on your bedside manner," Giulia complained, even as she pocketed the money she'd evidently won in a bet.

On us.

What on Earth?

"She's going to hurt me, and I'm going to hurt her. But I'm also going to make her happy and she'll make me happy too," Link rumbled. "Ain't that what happens in a relationship? Ain't there good times and bad times too?"

Giulia's smile was soft, then it turned wicked when she looked at Nyx. "Yeah, babe, ain't that how shit rolls when you're in wuv?" Nyx pulled a face, but before he could reply, Giulia continued, "Lily says she knows someone who's a therapist who might be able to help the girls."

Link turned to me, but it was kind of awkward because I didn't release my odd clasp on his hand. "Who?"

"Tiffany."

His brows lifted. "She's a therapist?"

"Good one." They didn't need to know she wasn't fully qualified. When Tiff got her ass in gear, she'd be the best. So I hedged, "But she doesn't have to do it, so she doesn't."

"Why doesn't she have to do it?" Giulia questioned.

"She's a Farquar," I answered with a shrug. "In our circle, the daughters go to college, but it's not really to get a job."

Giulia made a fake puking sound. "It's to find a husband? Jesus Christ. What is this? 1820?"

"Pretty much." I shrugged. "Not for me now though. I guess not her either, not with everything that's happened."

"No," Link concurred, his hand squeezing mine. "We spoke with the sheriff. Showed him the footage you found. Things are in motion even as we speak."

A shaky smile crossed my lips. "Good."

Giulia's gaze softened on mine once more, then she murmured, "Come back tomorrow. I'll tell the girls about you. If there's a problem, I'll tell them to get over it, but it's good to give them some time to gel with things, you know? They still jump whenever one of the guys comes inside."

"Ghost is stronger than most," Link argued.

"Yeah. True. Plus she's sweet on Mav."

"Still can't get over the fact he's come out to visit with her," Nyx muttered, shaking his head.

Link tugged on my hand. "Come on, babe. Got something to show you."

Giulia snorted. "Don't trust his 'show and tell,' Lily."

Link flipped her the bird, then hauled me along the path back to the bunkhouse I'd been in since the afternoon he, Rex, and Nyx had brought me here.

"What is it? What's wrong?" I queried, breathless at the pace he was setting.

"Nothing's wrong. Nothing at all."

I wasn't sure whether he was speaking truthfully or not, but I figured I'd find out the second I was inside.

The exterior of the bunkhouse was painted a soft cream, and the door and the shutters were a maroon red that gave the place a cozy charm which seemed discordant with their locale.

Still, I wasn't sure why an MC needed little cottages like this on their land, and I wasn't sure I wanted to know either. If only the inside looked as quaint as the outside—hippies would be well at home once they crossed the threshold.

When Link burst into the bunkhouse and slammed the door closed, I wondered what on Earth was the matter, then I found myself pressed against the still vibrating door and Link pressed against me in turn.

Before my heart could leap in surprise, his mouth was on mine and his tongue was between my lips.

Maybe, with another man, I'd have tensed up, maybe I'd have been scared. But this was Link. And I trusted him.

So, with my body in full recognition of who was rubbing up against it, I proceeded to melt into him.

God, my legs almost turned to mush as he took my mouth like he was taking all of me. Like he was absorbing me into him or something.

I'd been kissed before. I wasn't totally hopeless. But this was a kiss. All the others had been posers.

Dear God.

My hands came up to grab a hold of his hair to keep him in place, but he gripped one of them and pinned it over head.

My fingers interlocked with his, and I knew my nails were digging into his knuckles, but he didn't seem to mind as he thrust his tongue against mine, making me think about what it would feel like for his dick to be inside me.

I'd only ever associated sex with pain, and even then, I'd done my damnedest to dissociate myself from most things sexual.

If I was frigid, so be it.

That was my survival technique and, if I did say so myself, I'd done a damn fine job of surviving over the years.

This kiss, however, decimated me.

Tore me down, and snatched all of the teachings that had been forced upon me until he was kissing Lily.

The true me.

I moaned into his mouth as he rocked his dick against my stomach.

When I lifted my leg, hooking it against his hip, he took advantage and moved closer, not stopping until his hardness was pushing into my softness.

The feeling was exquisite.

I didn't have room for fear, didn't have time to tense up. I just felt. And it was simultaneously liberating and mind-blowing.

Not for the first time, I scented sweat and engine oil on him. Scents that came from a day of honest work, and God, it just added to the moment.

Something about the thought of him doing that stuff, of working hard, of getting his hands dirty, made the feel of him against me all the more raw. All the more overwhelming.

I was used to gentle hands, soft, manicured nails. Muscles that were earned solely in a gym. Skin that was tanned from a spray... Link was none of those things, and he was all the more perfect for it.

He rocked his hips, not stopping until every inch of his dick was rubbing down the length of me.

He nudged my clit, prodded at the softness of my opening through my slacks, and made me long to feel him without any of the trappings between us.

When I came, it exploded through me. Bursting into a shower of light I had never anticipated, because who the hell came from just a kiss?

But this wasn't just any kiss. This was Link and me, and when we were together, we made fireworks happen.

The second I screamed into his mouth, he pulled back, and his lips retreated to my throat.

He went to the side, where my neck connected to my torso, and he sucked down hard, nipping until he bit as he rocked his hips harder, faster, grinding into me until he came too.

The long, loud groan was offset by the flesh he had between his teeth and even though it hurt—God, it hurt so badly—it was wonderful.

I rocked my head back against the door, feeling windswept and dazed and, hell, *dazzled* in the aftermath.

He was a heavy weight against me, but I could have dealt with that weight on top of me for the rest of my life.

Fuck.

The words resonated with me in a way that nothing else ever had.

I twisted my head to the side so I could press a kiss to his jaw. "Link?"

He mumbled under his breath, something I translated as, "Whassup, sugar tits?"

"I-I—"

I stared ahead at the shitty bunkhouse that a Lancaster wouldn't be seen dead in.

The dowdy wallpaper, the crappy furniture, all on a compound that was manned by nothing more than modern-day highwaymen. And, Lord help me, my heart squeezed so tight in my chest, I felt certain it would burst.

"Ya okay?" he mumbled again, part of my neck still against his damn lips.

Could I say it?

Could I even begin to enunciate what he made me feel? What he brought out in me?

My mouth trembled as my eyes burned, and I knew I had to say it, I knew it—even if it made things weird. Even if it changed things and made him not want to protect me anymore, though, I did feel certain that that wouldn't happen.

Link wasn't like any other man I'd ever known.

Sure, he had his ways, but he was selfless. He was a protector.

My protector.

I released a shaky breath and whispered, "I love you, Link."

He didn't tense up, didn't even sigh.

If anything, he rocked his head up and back so he could look at me, square in the eye, and with a rueful grin, muttered, "Really glad you feel that way, sugar tits, because if this ain't love, then I don't know what the fuck it is."

My lips curved into a wry smile. "That's how you're going to tell me you love me for the first time?"

His grin widened. "I like to do things a certain way."

"I noticed." I rocked my hips up so I dragged my softness against him. "That was incredible."

"I'd take a bow but my knees might blow out. Hate to admit it, babe, but you do shit to me that no—" He hesitated. "I don't mean sex. Just this. We feel right, sugar."

I'd wanted to pull his hair out for daring to mention other women, but I got the feeling he wasn't just talking about women, but everyone. Maybe even his family. His brothers.

So I nodded. "I understand, Link."

His gaze dropped to my mouth. "Barely know you. Not in the real scheme of things, but I feel like something in me knew you right from the start.

"Saw you walk into the bar that night, all fancy like. Reminded me of 'Uptown Girl,' and I always fucking hated Billy Joel.

"But shit, you got my back up. Especially when you got all cozy with Cody." He cringed. "Wanted to ram his nose into his skull when you leaned into him like that. Then, he sent Storm a message—"

"Storm? I thought he texted you?" I quibbled.

"Nah. Storm's VP. He was there, like he is most nights, getting wasted until he comes back here and gets wasted some more." He reached up and tapped my bottom lip. "You need to meet Keira. I think you'd like her."

I knew her name and the state of her marriage but I hadn't realized they were close.

"She's a friend of yours?" When he nodded, I murmured, "Then she's a friend of mine."

His eyes lit up at that, but he joked, "Got some bad friends, babe, not sure you want to know all of them."

"Can't be any worse than the sharks I've known all my life, Link."

"No, I guess not," he groused. "But Storm showed us the text, and I said I'd deal with it because he was hammered. So I did, I went to you, and I saw you in the hallway.

"You looked like you were gonna have a heart attack or something. Reminded me of my ma, back when she couldn't afford her asthma meds. Used to wheeze and shit."

I swallowed, thickly. "You were—"

"Poor? Dirt poor, babe." His smile was wry. "Not anymore, but I'm still not good enough for you. Better than fucking Fieri though. Fucking scum."

"Don't you think I should get a say in who's good enough for me?" I ran my hands through his hair, letting my nails drag along his scalp, smiling when he groaned at that, tilting his head back so I could scrape all over the curve of his skull. "Everyone has been making decisions for me since I was a baby. I've made my decision. I want you. I love you."

"Done bad stuff in my time," he stated softly. "Weird stuff too. I've got a rep."

"You mentioned that before. What kind of rep?"

He blew out a breath. "Like ass play."

That had me blinking, then cringing. "Oh."

"Yeah. Oh." Another gusty breath. "Not just on you, but on me too."

"On you?" I whispered, unaware that my eyes had dilated at the prospect, but Link, as usual, saw everything.

"Yeah. On me." He grunted. "Fuck, you like the idea of that, don't you? Knew you were a dirty fox the second I laid eyes on you, sugar tits."

A smile crested my lips at his statement. "Your dirty fox?"

"Mine," he rumbled. "Always, Lily. Always mine."

And, Lord help me, I liked the sound of that.

TWENTY-ONE

LINK

THREE DAYS LATER

WHEN I ROLLED into the parking space reserved for customers of Indiana Ink, a hoot escaped the woman riding bitch at my back.

"Oh my *God*, that was fucking epic!" Lily squealed, her arms hugging me so tight that it would have hurt if it hadn't felt so fucking good.

A laugh escaped me. "I'd never have been able to figure it out, what with all the hollering you've been doing back there."

I guided her off the back of my hog, laughing again when she bounced on her feet. "I loved it!"

"I'm glad, sugar tits," I rumbled, reaching out to haul her against me, loving her energy and excitement.

I'd thought she'd be nervous on the bike, wouldn't have thought she'd like it.

A couple of my brothers, Storm and Steel, had warned that it wasn't for everyone, and because she was so fucking dainty, so much a *lady*, she might hate it.

I was glad they were wrong.

Fuck, I was ecstatic myself.

She beamed at me even as she lowered her head to press a kiss to my mouth.

Me being me, I slipped her some tongue, and Lily being Lily—AKA mine—she lapped it up.

A groan escaped her as her hands did that fucking thing she'd started doing, that thing I loved, and her nails scraped over my scalp, digging in in a perfect way.

The only reason I didn't bend her over my bike and make something of this was her goddamn cell ringing.

She tensed at the sound and I figured she recognized the tone. Her tension wasn't the good kind either.

She froze against me, her nails digging into my scalp in a less than perfect way now, and I pulled back, whispering, "What is it, babe?"

"My father." Her voice was hoarse.

"We expected this," I countered.

"Did we?" she whispered.

"You had to know he'd call, babe. Even if it was for help."

"I don't want to answer."

"Then don't."

She clenched her eyes shut, displaying a vulnerability I wasn't altogether used to seeing in her.

But I guessed it made sense.

For all these years, she'd worn a mask, and with him gone, she was safe, and I'd vowed to protect her, so it figured that she'd let the mask slip.

Now, she was regretting that. Regretting it because whatever she thought he'd say, she knew it had to be bad.

She bit her bottom lip so hard that it started to turn purple, and just when I thought she was going to make herself bleed, she released her hold on me and quickly grabbed her cell.

She eyed it like it was an alien gadget, and when I felt certain she was going to toss it on the ground and stomp on it, she connected the call and put it on speaker.

"Father?"

Her voice was different. Fuck. *Talk about a mask!* It was like a different Lily. She sounded so formal, so disinterested and apathetic. So unlike my woman.

I hated it.

"Lilian, I don't have much time," he ground out. "I need you to go into my bedroom and access the safe."

"I'm not at home," she said woodenly. "But I will be later."

"Did they bar you from the house?"

I frowned at that and his concern. Was it self-aimed or for his daughter?

"Why would they?"

"When they pulled the illegal search."

We both shared a confused look. Illegal search? Hadn't her guards told him about us going in and removing Luke's computer?

"Don't worry, my lawyers are working on it. But in the interim," he stated, not letting her get a word in edgewise. "I need you to go home as soon as you can and use the code 07-12-67 to access the safe behind the Picasso above my dresser." He blew out a breath, and in the background, I could hear the sound of a loud speaker that was, unmistakably, in an airport. "When you retrieve the documents, go to my lawyer in Manhattan. The details are all in there." Another burst of sound in the background had him muttering, "Shit, I have to go. I'll be in touch."

He cut the call without even waiting for her to say another word, and she blinked at me, a little dead-eyed even as she whispered, "What the hell is his game?"

"We can reschedule the appointment here?" I suggested, worried by the look in her eyes but I had to admit, I was curious as hell about what was inside his safe that made him call her like this.

"No. I want my tattoo," she grated out. "Whatever he wants can wait." She straightened up, her nose in the air. "I don't care."

"No, but it might be interesting to see what he's hiding. He evidently doesn't think you're involved with his arrest warrant."

"Doesn't surprise me. He knows I'm smart. You don't get the grades I did in school and college without being intelligent, but because I'm a girl, he always discounted it. Well, joke's on him." She tightened her mouth. "I want my tattoo."

"Okay, babe. We'll get it," I told her soothingly, because I felt like she was on the brink of losing control and that was the last thing I wanted.

Seeing her reaction to her father's call made me wonder how long she'd been so on edge, and it made me hug her that bit tighter as I hauled her into my side as we walked into Indiana Ink.

"Yo, Link," Indiana greeted the second we were inside, and I grinned at her, squeezed Lily, and raised my free hand.

"Hey, Indy, how's you?"

She waggled her eyebrows. "I'm good. Real good. This your lady?"

I dragged 'my lady' over to the desk and leaned against it as I smiled at her. "This is Lily."

"Never thought I'd see the day Link would get himself an Old Lady." She beamed at Lily. "I'm looking forward to getting to know you."

Lily's smile was more polite than anything else. "And I you."

Indiana shot me a look that had me holding back a laugh. I thought it was cute as fuck when Lily ended up sounding like she'd come out of an Edgar Allen Poe book, but that was me.

"So, aside from the 'property of' tat, you want anything else?"

"'Property of?'" Lily repeated.

"That's what the tattoo has to say," I told her softly.

"You could have warned the girl," Indy chided. "I mean, dude."

"No, it's okay, I just didn't understand. I'd like a fox tattoo." Her eyes connected with mine and, instantly, I knew we were both thinking back to the other day when I'd called her a dirty fox.

Her cheeks pinkened, but her grin was anything but sheepish. I smirked at her, then at Indy as I hauled my arm over Lily's shoulders, so fucking proud of her right then that I could have goddamn burst.

Indy, not getting the reference, merely shrugged. "Like a real fox? Or some kind of Japanese one? There are some super cool graphic foxes, but I have to warn you, the lines might blur over time."

"Can you show me examples?"

"Of course. Better still, I'll draw you something."

Her hand snapped out, and like it was connected to her, a pencil was suddenly between her fingers.

As I gazed down at the paper she was drawing on, my brows rose as I saw the state of her desk.

There were more sheets of paper everywhere, and her diary was wide open. I didn't mean to snoop, but the second my eyes glanced over a name in the books, I felt my jaw pretty much gape open.

MAVERICK.

In caps.

Maverick? My Maverick? The Maverick who never left the fucking compound? Who hadn't left the clubhouse until Ghost had come to us?

Even as I wanted to choke on that, curiosity making me wonder why the fuck he'd want to come here, the scratching of Indy's pencil grabbed my attention, and I saw she was already on a second example of the fox she could style for Lily.

Because Nyx's sister's imagination was pretty much blooming into being, before I lost her totally, I informed her, "Did Douchebag David tell you that I wanted a tattoo too?"

Indy cocked a brow, but that was all I needed to know I'd grabbed her attention as well. Her pencil stopped, then she eyed me warily.

"David called in sick this morning. Hence the state of the desk. But...*really?*" The word came out over six or so syllables.

"Yeah. Really."

"Long time since you wanted a tattoo." She used the eraser to scratch her chin. "Nyx started another trend, I see."

"You know Nyx?" Lily asked, her surprise clear.

"He's my brother. Blood brother," Indy tacked on. "Not the MC's kind."

"Oh." Her eyes widened. "Really? You're not alike at all."

"I have some Native American in me." To me, she questioned, "Any preference? Location?"

"Over my shoulders."

"Spanning your back?" She whistled. "Gonna be a big one."

"That's how I'm feeling."

"You two are talking cryptically," Lily complained. "What's going on? Is it such a big deal that Link wants a tattoo?"

"That he's asking for it now, at the same time you are, yeah." Indy grinned at both of us. "You'll see."

I rolled my eyes. "There's no secret."

"Not gonna be one for long when someone sees your fucking back," Indy replied with a snort. Then she rubbed her hands together. "Right, let me do my shit, come up with some concepts, and we'll get things sorted."

And that was exactly what she did.

TWENTY-TWO

LILY

MY TATTOO STUNG, but it felt good too.

I'd actually liked the burn, even if it had felt really damn sore by the end, but I'd kind of managed to zen out, and ultimately, I'd been super happy with the little fox on my inner wrist.

The 'Property of Link' part was done in a modern script, and though it was no bigger than a credit card, it felt bigger to me.

Like the brand it was.

Only, I didn't mind.

That tiny tattoo gave me more protection than billions in the bank ever had.

I'd admit to feeling a lot safer once I climbed on the back of Link's bike, and when I thought about what I'd seen unfold when Link had climbed onto the bed Indy had patted for him to get onto earlier, I felt even more secure.

It was clear men didn't need to get branded, but Link was making a choice. He was telling the world I was his—how couldn't I feel more secure than ever?

Surrounded by guards all my life, and followed around like I had professional stalkers, nothing made me feel like this except for my ink and Link's, which declared that I belonged to him as much as he belonged to me.

I hadn't expected that, and when I'd gaped at the rockabilly font, the

LILY and a Japanese fox Indiana had styled for me, he'd just squeezed my hand and muttered, "No going back."

Even now, with the wind in my hair, the scent of gas in my nose, and all the stimuli that came from being on the back of his bike, I was still bowled over by what had just happened.

Throw in my dad's call, I was really feeling the pinch.

But I wanted this over with today. I wanted to know what he thought was so all-important before I destroyed my phone and never gave him the opportunity to talk to me again.

When we made it to my house, the guards let me in without question.

Why wouldn't they?

As far as they knew, I was still Donavan's daughter, even if I'd cut myself off from him. Though, after the way they'd reacted to my leaving, I was surprised I wasn't hustled into the safe room...

When Paul appeared the second I climbed off Link's bike, I raised a hand. "I don't want to know, Paul."

"Your father—"

"Isn't her problem anymore," Link growled. "She's with me."

I didn't like the way he was eying Paul, and while I didn't doubt Link and my ex-guard could really get into it, I didn't want any blood spilled.

Paul frowned at me, and I muttered, "With my father hopefully going to jail, we won't be needing your company's services."

"Fuck that," Paul muttered, his gaze on Link. "The company's severed tied with your father in light of the... well, the situation. But I've been your guard for years, Miss Lily. I want to make sure you're safe."

Despite myself, I was touched. I thought I'd always just been an open checkbook to my guards.

"I am safe," I countered. "Very safe."

He looked at me, then Link, and shook his head, dubious at best.

"I don't have time for this, Paul. I need to do something."

He shoved his hands into his jacket pocket and I tensed, half expecting him to pull out a weapon, but instead he retrieved a card.

I jolted in surprise when he shoved it at me, muttering, "If ever you need a hand."

Link growled under his breath again. "She's safe."

"You're a Sinner," Paul spat. "There's no safety there."

I tightened my hand around Link's. "I want to get this over with," I stated. "Please don't start something."

Link grunted, but his eyes stayed on Paul as we moved forward.

Before we reached the door, I turned back to look at my guard and mouthed, "Thank you."

The second we were inside, I tugged Link to a halt and said, "I don't need this," and gave him the card.

It was a ceremonial gesture, one I figured he'd appreciate. He stared down at the card, then up at me, and frowned.

I could see the desire in him, the urge riding him to grab the card and tear it in two. But he didn't.

"It kills me, but...if anything happens to me, I'd like to know you're safe."

I just gaped at him, taken aback and overwhelmed and completely astonished by the notion that he was—

Fuck. He *did* love me.

I couldn't question it, not when he was willing to put pride and ego aside for me.

My brother, my father, no one I knew would have thought of protecting me in that way, but Link did.

"I love you, Link."

He raised our joined hands to his mouth and said, "Love you too, sugar tits."

I couldn't stop myself from smirking at him, and a laugh escaped me, astonishing me because I didn't want to be here. At all.

Yet here he was, making me laugh, even though I felt the burden of what my father was asking of me like Atlas with the world on his shoulders.

I couldn't even begin to imagine what he had stored within his lockbox, and I didn't want to know, even if I really wanted to know too.

After all, what better way to make sure he was screwed if I had more evidence on him that would get him away from me for a lifetime?

"Where's his room?" he demanded, breaking into my thoughts while proving we were on the same page.

"This way."

As I guided him toward my father's quarters, every now and then, Link would come to a halt to gawk at something.

I couldn't blame him.

Not all of the house had been decorated by the atrocious decorator my father had boned, and some of it was quite lovely, especially the ceiling-wide chandelier in the living room that was made out of thousands of tiny glass balls that looked like stars when they were illuminated and, during the day, were like a blanket of color that warmed the living room through whenever the sunlight hit it.

Aela O'Neill, the artist who'd created the masterpiece, was an exceptional genius.

"This place is fucking incredible," he rasped when, after a while, we made it to my father's room.

"Some of it needs demolishing. Just wait until you see the breakfast room," I muttered as I moved over to the Picasso and pulled it aside to reveal a safe.

It wasn't the first safe I'd seen of my father's, but it was the first time I'd be opening it.

And with my mother's birthday as the code no less.

Bastard.

Absolute bastard.

God, I hated him.

I wanted to ask him how he dared use her birthday when he was the reason for her death, but I wanted nothing to do with him.

My mouth was set in firm lines as I opened up the safe, and when I found nothing more than legalese and documents inside, I was almost disappointed.

"What is it?" Link inquired as I began to leaf through the paperwork.

"I'm not sure," I muttered, recognizing the address of properties my father owned in and around New York.

"Your name's here and here," Link pointed out, as I flipped through the legalese, trying to make sense of what I was reading.

Mostly, I was seeing a lot of my name too.

"Yeah, I see it," I replied, bewildered, "but I don't know—"

"What is it?"

"I-I think these are deeds," I rasped.

"Deeds of property?" Link questioned, and I raised my eyes to him, then nodded.

"Yeah."

"As in, deeds with your name on them, for properties *you* own?"

"Apparently." I swallowed. "He must have put them in my name. As a safety net? Maybe?"

"How did he do that without you knowing it?"

"Fuck knows," I replied, but I didn't really care.

Not if what I held in my hands was *real*, and I had no reason to doubt it wasn't.

Even if the property had been assigned to me without my wherewithal, in a court of law, they'd stand up.

This was why he wanted me to go to his lawyers, and I said as much to Link.

"He wants to dissolve these agreements and have the properties transferred from my name to his so he can access his assets while he's abroad."

"Meaning, if you don't, you own all this stuff and he's penniless?"

My mouth curved into a smile. "I think so."

The MCs plan to ruin him through Lodestar wouldn't be necessary...

Heart pounding and with little aplomb, I sank down on the ground and spread out the documents.

"This is the penthouse on Fifth Avenue. That's for the Juniper Building just off Tribeca, and this one is for the Landis Scraper in the Upper East Side." My eyes felt like they were bulging as I gaped at him. "Link..."

"You're a rich woman, babe."

I let out a happy laugh. "Without having to kill him."

A snort escaped him. "Without even a drop of blood on your hands." He raised his, curled it into a fist, and said, "Worthy of a fist bump."

I knocked my knuckles into his, then went back to the papers.

Giddiness flooded me, but I knew that it was only a matter of time before I found something that burst my bubble and, unfortunately, I wasn't wrong.

I shoved the piece of paper at Link when he was peering at a set of deeds for what looked like some estate I apparently owned in Toronto.

"What is it?"

"Marriage contract. This is going to be a problem," I warned.

He eyed the document, then reached for my hand.

As he threaded our fingers together, he twisted it around to reveal the tattoo. "There is no problem that can't be solved."

I bit my bottom lip. "You need to warn your brothers."

"They're already warned, and now that you're mine, there's no war we won't enter headfirst on your behalf."

My heart was in my throat again. "That's why you want me to keep a hold of Paul's number." My eyes burned. "I don't want you to get hurt, Link."

"I don't intend on going anywhere, babe, but on the off chance I do, I want to know you have someone on your side."

Oddly enough, I figured I did have Paul on my side. Maybe Alix too.

They *had* been my guards for years, and I had saved their jobs—even if I'd been the one to put them in jeopardy.

A part of me wondered if I could trust them because they were my father's men, but... everyone could have that taint.

Only Donavan Lancaster knew how far his money had gone, and I had to put some faith somewhere, didn't I?

But Link was right.

He wasn't going anywhere.

I eyed him, then the marriage contract, and shook my head. "Like I was a piece of meat."

"To him, you were." He untangled our fingers, then reached for it and tore it in two. "Your father misjudged you though. He thought you were mindless and you're not."

"No. I'm not. He mustn't have thought I'd read through these things first."

Did he think I'd just take these blindly to the lawyer after what he'd done?

"Seems there's an advantage to him thinking you're an idiot."

His wry comment had me grinning. "You're right." I peered around the bedroom, with its gaudy colors and horrendous furnishings, and asked, "Link?"

"Yes, babe?"

"Do you have to live at the clubhouse?"

He arched a brow at me. "No. Most councilors with Old Ladies and kids don't."

"Nyx and Giulia do," I pointed out.

"Nyx is a control freak. If he isn't on hand twenty-four seven, he feels like he's letting the club down."

I pondered that for a second, then figured I'd go for broke. "How would you feel about moving in here?" I peered up at him from under my lashes. "I mean, the bunkhouse is nice and all—"

"But it isn't a mega mansion. I think I could deal with this kinda crib." He rubbed his chin. "In fact, I think I could more than deal with it."

I beamed at him. "Want to help me trash this room?"

"That's a Picasso, babe. I ain't trashing that. I ain't that much of a sinner."

"We can keep that safe. I want everything else destroyed."

He winked at me. "I'm down for that." He gathered all the papers together, then reached for my hand and hauled me to my feet. "You got what you wanted, sugar tits. The money and the freedom—"

"I got more than what I wanted, Link. I got you." I reached up and pressed a kiss to his lips.

There were so many things I wanted to do, so many ways I wanted to tarnish this room... But I wasn't about to waste a kiss from Link.

So I gave him all my focus, imbued the meeting of our mouths with all the love I felt for him, and let him know, in no uncertain terms, that he was as much mine as I was his.

When his hands came to my ass, I didn't tense, couldn't. In this room, that kind of touch held bad memories. But this was Link.

I was his.

He was mine.

When he pulled away, pushed his forehead against mine, our breaths mingled.

"You sure about this, sugar tits?"

I frowned. "Sure about what?"

Uncertainty appeared in his eyes, a vulnerability that I hadn't anticipated. It melted me. Turned me into a woman-shaped vat of mush that wanted nothing more than to be in his arms.

"Never question this." I reached up on tiptoe, then gently pecked his mouth. "Mine."

His smile made an appearance at my declaration, only this time, there was a cockiness to it that had me melting some more.

"Well?" he rumbled, prompting me to arch a brow at him. "What are you waiting for? Bring on the destruction."

With a hoot, and needing no more encouragement, I darted off.

Adrenaline buzzed through my bloodstream as I grabbed one of the fancy lamps that graced my father's nightstand and hurled it into the wall of mirrors that lined the panels opposite the bed.

As the glass smashed, spraying in an arc of destruction, I let loose a holler. One that turned into a scream loaded with the freedom I felt as I reached for the cell my father had contacted me on and sent it flying into the window.

Liberty came in many guises, and my shackles were no more.

TWENTY-THREE

TIFFANY

"BABE, YOU GOTTA BE SHITTING ME?"

A snort sounded down the line, making me shake my head. "I'm not shitting you. Anyway, it wasn't me doing the shitting. You found out on the news."

I rolled my eyes. "Exactly. You should have told me first!"

I was actually a bit pissed off at that. Pissed off and *hurt*.

Lily was my best friend, and I was hearing this shit about her dad from the TV? What the fuck was that about?

"I didn't know," she admitted softly. "I didn't realize something was being released so soon." She sighed. "Not to the news anyway."

"It's not true, is it?" I whispered, my eyes on the screen. "I mean, it can't be. Can it?"

I'd known Donavan Lancaster since I was a little girl.

He wasn't the warmest of fathers, in fact, he'd always given me the creeps, but creeps and *this*? They were two different things.

Believing someone to be odd and then finding out they had women captive in the forest? Women they tortured...

My stomach churned.

This had to be a joke.

I mean, we'd had the Lancasters over for dinner. I'd eaten bouillabaisse with Luke and Donavan while I'd been texting under the table with Lily...

"Lily," I whispered, "please. Tell me this is some kind of dream."

"I'm sorry, love. It isn't."

There was something in her voice, something that put me on red alert. "You knew?"

"About the women?" She cleared her throat. "I'm the one who found the evidence to give to the police."

A sharp gasp escaped me. "Oh my God, how the hell did you find that?"

"I snooped around on Luke's computer. He was a sick bastard, Tiffany. I can't even tell you what he did to them. Not without wanting to throw up."

The trace notes of a quiver in her voice made my eyes well with tears. "Did Luke hurt you?"

"In ways no one can ever understand," she rasped. "But I don't want to think about that now. I don't have to."

I shook my head like I'd just climbed out of the pool and was trying to get water out of my ears.

I'd always known things with Lily's family were odd, but this went to another level that was just beyond the extreme.

"Are you okay?"

"I will be." She blew out a breath. "I'm going to go, love. I have things to sort out."

I could only imagine. "Keep in touch."

"Are you sure you want to? Now that you know?"

Anger washed through me. "Lilian Maria Lancaster! How dare you? I stood by you through the Mohawk Disaster of 2015 and the Cheerleading Charade of 2016.

"You aren't getting rid of me, even if your family is starting to look like it belongs on an episode of *Mindhunter*."

"*Mindhunter*?" She snorted. "I don't want to know."

"I swear, how is it you know none of the shows on Netflix?"

"We don't all have a cinema in our pool house," she teased, and I pulled a face at said cinema as I slouched back on my favorite armchair in the room.

"True. Girl, I love you, you know that, right?"

"I do now, Tiff. Thank you, sweetie. I'll speak to you later."

"Do," I urged, suddenly concerned that I'd never hear from my bestie again, and I cut the call so she didn't have to.

For a second, I stared at the ceiling that had faux stars in it that twinkled, then I switched my gaze to the screen that had the news on a loop.

Donavan Lancaster's fall from grace.

Lancaster's evasion of arrest.

The Lancaster Corp throws Donavan Lancaster from their board of directors.

Lancaster's flight to Vietnam.

It felt surreal. But what felt even more surreal was the woman on the screen. A woman who was talking about what the Lancasters had done to her.

Shakily, I switched off the news and clambered to my feet.

My sanctuary felt like it had been violated as I shuffled out into the hall, and I carried onward until I was by the pool.

The garden was neat, manicured precision wherever you looked.

I wouldn't have been surprised if Mom, when no one was looking, dropped a squat and measured the blades of grass on the ground just to make sure they were the perfect height.

Rolling lawns led to a kind of rockery that surrounded the pool where I lived, and surged into the sandy gardens that housed hundreds of succulents and cacti that were my father's pride and joy, even if he didn't do a damn thing to take care of them.

Dad liked to think he was helping the environment even as he was raping it by building these massive developments, and the truth was, I couldn't fault him for trying.

We had more solar panels on our roof than tiles, and we more than did our bit to save the Earth.

I tried to reconcile *that* man with the one who knew Donavan. *How had they been friends?*

I mean, they *had* been friends. We'd gone on vacation with their family. You didn't just do that because your daughter was friendly with another family's daughter, did you?

Had it been business?

As far as I knew, Donavan had never invested in my dad's deals. Just like with the development here, he'd been a prick and had built outside my father's subdivision...

Perplexed and unsure what my brain was even struggling to form, I slouched into the house from the veranda and headed to my dad's office.

The shouts hit me first, which had me pausing and hovering in the hall.

Mom and Dad never argued. At least, I hadn't heard them argue ever since they'd started going to Dr. Leibowitz three times a week.

"You son of a bitch!" she was screaming. "You were friends with that prick! How could you?"

My eyes widened.

How could he what?

Heart stuttering, I wandered closer, trying to pick up on my dad's mumbled retort.

Sliding forward as I strode down the hallway that led to his study, I tried to eavesdrop, but it was just my mom calling him a bastard, an SOB, over and over again.

When she started crying, I almost anticipated the crash and figured she'd thrown one of his whisky bottles against the wall.

Back before Leibowitz, that had been one of her regular weapons.

I made it to the door, eyed the carnage in his office, and saw that my dad was sitting at his desk, back bowed, head in his hands.

My mouth opened, then it closed. I did that a few times before, feeling like a little girl rather than a twenty-three-year-old woman, I managed to rasp, "Daddy, what's going on?"

TWENTY-FOUR

EOGHAN

"GOT a real surprise for your bachelor party, bro."

I eyed Declan, who was grinning at me like a shark.

In my opinion, there was nothing to be grinning about.

Nothing.

At.

Fucking.

All.

Arranged marriages were supposed to be a thing of the past, but in my world, they weren't.

And I was living goddamn proof of that.

In a week, I'd be a husband.

A fucking husband.

And to a Russian.

A fucking Bratva bitch who'd been spawned by a Pakhan who wanted her off his hands.

Our wedding day was her goddamn eighteenth birthday.

Getting married to an eighteen-year-old might be on some weirdo's to-do list, but it wasn't on mine. Not that I had a choice.

The shiner I was wearing was a reminder of why I didn't.

Aidan O'Donnelly was the head of our family in more ways than one.

He was my father, but he was also the head of the Five Points' Mob, and my recent beating was a reminder that *one*, though he was getting old, he could still beat the shit out of me.

Especially when he had some lackeys hold me the fuck down.

Two, I had no say in this. My agreement was not required.

I eyed Declan over the rim of my whisky glass. It was this cool gadget that aerated whisky to perfection, and our elder brother, Conor, was all over his gadgets.

His place looked like it would be a wet dream for any *Star Trek* nerd.

The black, smoky glass meant I couldn't eye the liquid I was drowning my sorrows in, but it didn't stop the liquor from doing its job.

"What kind of surprise?" I asked, dubious to the last.

"Such a cynic," Dec retorted as he slung his elbows onto the bar at my side.

Conor's place was all techno funk with goddamn strobe lightning all over.

It was like a strip joint and a lab combined. The bar was made from tubular steel and glass, which supported some of the finest whiskies and tequilas in the Northern Hemisphere.

The station I was leaning against was made from leather, and it had a nice cushion against my elbows. Swank but sterile.

That should be Conor's slogan, I thought with a snort.

Dec shoved into me. "Fuck's sake, Eoghan. Cheer up. You know we're all on the line, don't you?"

My brow puckered. "What does that mean?"

"Means that if Da can hook us all up through a deal, he will." He grabbed my fancy tumbler and took a deep sip. "Shit, this really does work."

"Fucking told you," Conor hollered from the white leather sofa he was slouched against, having his cock sucked by one of the strippers Brennan had hired for the occasion.

Dec flipped him the bird overhead. "It's not like we're going to get married by our own free will, is it?"

"We might. I might have," I said grumpily, snatching my glass back.

"Yeah, right," he rejoined with a snort. "We're kings in Manhattan, bro. We don't need to tie ourselves down."

Which was bullshit. We all knew he was still grieving Deirdre, his sweetheart.

But even though I was pissed off, I wasn't going to hurt Declan by bringing her up and calling him a liar.

She'd led him around by his dick for the most part, but for some reason, the fucker had loved her.

Which meant, by now, they'd probably have had about ten kids and he'd have been even more whipped than he'd been back then.

Again, I didn't say that. I had the ability to keep my trap shut.

"You're not making me feel better," I slurred. "I don't want to get married. And not to Bratva." I spat, the globule landing on the leather countertop.

"That's just gross," Conor shouted. "No spitting on the leather."

I flipped him the bird this time. "Jerry ain't sucking you off very well if you can focus on your fucking upholstery!" I growled over my shoulder, taking in the sight of debauchery.

Every man I knew, every brother high enough in the ranks, and friends from school, were all here.

Declan and Brennan really had tried.

What amazed me the most was that they'd managed to get Finn here, Finn who was utterly obsessed with his wife.

Because he loved her.

Because he'd had the chance to fall for someone.

A chance I hadn't been given.

Seeing him sitting at the dining room table that was made of what I could only describe as bottle caps—Conor really needed a style overhaul—I asked Dec, "How did you get him here?"

"I didn't," Dec retorted with a laugh. "Aoife did."

I raised a brow at that. "She has to know what was going to happen tonight."

The Five Points didn't have a reputation for being nuns, and on the final night of a man's freedom, we made Roman orgies look tame.

Dec shrugged. "She has faith in him, and she's right to by the look of the prick. Not even given the side eye to any pussy all night, more focused on his fucking phone. Might as well have stayed at home."

"A woman like Aoife is worth ten of these sluts."

"True. But a look, man? What harm would that do?"

"None," I agreed. "But we'd both kick the shit out of him if he did more, wouldn't we?"

Dec grinned. "Damn your sweet ass we would."

"Glad you know my ass is sweet," I muttered, but I was pleased we were on the same page.

Aoife was good as gold.

If Finn had cheated on her, I'd have made him swallow his own dick for it.

She'd given him a beautiful kid that, honestly, I couldn't tell whether it was a boy or a girl, and she made the bastard happy.

The man might not be blood, but he felt like it. He was as much my brother as the rest of my siblings, and that Aoife put a smile on the bastard's face relieved us all.

I wanted that for me.

Fuck, I'd never been sentimental before. Had never given a shit, but that was because I thought I'd had time. Time and choices.

Freedom.

Bullshit.

I might have sold my soul for the land of the free but that didn't mean I got to enjoy any of the goddamn perks of liberty.

"Come on," Dec ground out. "You're about as fucking grim as Finn is."

I scowled. "You're not the one being shackled to scum."

"Have you seen Inessa?" Dec shook his head. "She's beautiful. It's not like Dad is marrying you off to one of the ugly fucking sisters. Which you'd know if you hadn't avoided her every step of the way."

"You like her so much, you have her," I countered.

"Fuck that. She's eighteen. What the fuck would I do with an eighteen-year-old?"

"Because you're so much fucking older than me?" I grunted. "Prick."

"Look, I could have held onto this treat all for myself, but no. I thought I'd give you a present. Maybe put a fucking smile on your face, but if you don't want—"

I narrowed my eyes at him. "What is it?"

He slapped a hand on my back and said, "Come with me."

With another grunt, I stood up, then winced as my body registered exactly how much I'd been drinking.

Still, it did nothing more than give me the whisky equivalent of a brain freeze, and I slouched beside Dec as he guided me through the crowd.

Overhead, there were three balls glittering a bright, luminous blue that created a spotlight where four whores were currently fucking each other for our enjoyment.

I'd never understood the appreciation of scissoring, but to each their own. They had a ringside collection of men watching the party on a makeshift dais that had been crafted for tonight.

Behind them was a large sofa that seated around fifteen, and it was where most of the guys, including my brother Conor, had their dicks out while another team of whores serviced them.

By the table, at their back, was Finn.

He was slouched against the gray leather chair he was sitting on, and he looked like he was at a meeting, except for the fact he wasn't wearing a suit.

He had on a pair of jeans and a thin sweater that would have had him fitting in at brunch at the Four Seasons.

The sight made my lips twitch, especially when I thought about what he was capable of.

Looking at him, you'd never realize the shit he could do with a knife.

As we approached, he lifted his head and frowned at the sight of us.

"I'm not going over there," he snapped. Evidently, this wasn't the first time someone had tried to haul him to the party. "Why would I want a mouth that's sucked a thousand cocks around my own?"

If I'd needed proof Aoife had been a virgin, I probably had it there and then.

Finn, though he didn't realize it, had been bitten by the Catholic bug—whether he liked it or not. A lover of purity in all guises.

I'd never been that bothered about purity, which made it a fucking tragedy that I was getting tied to a chick who'd never been boned in her life.

I squinted at him. "I'd have your dick if you put it in one of those whores' mouths."

He squinted at me, evidently judging whether I was serious or not, and the sicko grinned when he saw I was speaking damn straight.

"Good man," he declared. "Does that mean I can go? No offense, Dec, but I grew out of this scene when I was twenty-three."

"Ready for your pipe and slippers?" Declan sniped.

Finn smirked. "You've seen my wife. Think that's all she gives me when I get home?"

I rolled my eyes. "Yeah, yeah, yeah. We're all really fucking jealous."

"So you should be," he countered, then his gaze drifted over the party, which was more of a communal fuckfest than anything else.

To be honest, I understood why he was bored.

"Couldn't we have gone to Bite? We'd have had a better time, and I wouldn't be starving."

My lips twitched at his complaint. "He has a point. I could handle a steak."

"Everyone's a fucking critic," Dec groused. "Next bachelor party we have, you fuckers get to organize it. Who the fuck eats at a restaurant on an occasion like this?"

"People with stomachs," Finn said wryly. "Bite has a Michelin star. Doesn't that take shit up a notch?"

I thought it did, but Dec didn't agree. He sniffed. "No."

I sniffed back. "Declan has a present for me."

"What kind of present?" Finn inquired, brows raised and finally looking interested. "Not food, I'd assume?"

"Fuck's sake," came Dec's grumble. "Is this what happens when you're shackled? You start thinking with your gut?"

Finn narrowed his eyes, and if Dec wasn't careful, he was about to get his ass reamed.

The way Finn fisted his hands was enough warning, but his words cemented it, "Feel free to test if marriage has made me soft."

Because Finn was a mean fighter when provoked and Declan was my best man—Ma would kill him if he looked beaten to fuck on my wedding day. The shiner I had was accidental, but it was yellowing and fading, and she'd be giving me shit over that this Sunday when I next saw her—I grumbled, "Where's this fucking gift?"

Crisis averted, the distraction worked on both my brothers.

"Come with me," Dec stated, sounding like he was leading us on an adventure.

Finn hitched a shoulder, but evidently bored shitless by the party—I couldn't blame him, pussy wasn't doing much for me tonight either—decided to join in, and he lagged behind me as I followed Dec.

With each step away from the fuckfest, I recognized how unlike Finn I was, and how much good fortune he'd had marrying someone he'd chosen.

Unlike him, this wasn't my last night of freedom. I'd get married, but I could still fuck whoever I wanted because it was an arrangement.

Nothing more.

Nothing less.

And tonight, I didn't want to fuck.

I wanted to drink and...

Well, I couldn't have the latter.

The desire to beat the fuck out of someone, to make them pay for the injustice being handed to me was an urge I'd have to deny myself tonight.

When we made it into Conor's kitchen where it was quieter thanks to the lack of speakers in here, which meant we weren't being tortured with techno, I demanded, "Come on then, what's the gift?"

Declan grinned at me. "Few days back, Link got in touch."

Finn tensed. "The Sinner? What did he want?"

Dec raised a hand. "Told us we might have sprung a leak."

And like that, any haziness from too much whisky instantly disappeared.

"A leak? To the cops?" I rasped.

Finn, his tension clear, spat, "The DEA?"

"*La* fucking *Famiglia*," Declan retorted. "And wouldn't you fucking know it? He was right."

"Who?" I spat.

"Jonny O'Byrne."

My eyes widened. "No fucking way. He's a Five Pointer to his core."

"Nope, he's a junkie," Dec countered, his rage clear as he cracked his knuckles again. "The Fieri cunts snagged him up and reeled us in."

"Been feeding him his highs?" Finn growled, folding his arms over his chest.

"Yeah. Only found out after some digging. You know how tightknit we've been keeping the shipments. Less than a dozen people really know what's going down, and there are maybe a half-dozen more guarding the warehouse—" He shrugged. "I had to investigate and found a fucking rotten apple in our midst."

My mouth curled into a snarl. "Where is he? We going to take him down tonight?"

Dec rubbed his hands together before he strode over the shiny black marble floor, crossed to the station that was topped with more black marble, and pulled a knife from one of the stands there.

This place looked like a pro could cook in it, but Conor couldn't even make a fucking pancake without almost burning the place down.

Still, he had it all fully equipped...

As I eyed a nice cleaver, I asked, "You brought him here?"

Dec grinned. "Surprised?"

My mouth snagged higher into a snarl. "Bet your damn ass I am."

Striding over to him, I grabbed the cleaver, then turned back to look at Finn. "You joining us?"

"Do bears shit in the woods?" he groused. "Why didn't you tell me earlier, Declan? This party wouldn't have been so fucking boring."

Declan snapped, "Fuck you," even as he strode over to a door beside the fridge.

When he opened it and revealed a walk-in freezer, I wasn't surprised at what I saw in there.

We all had special rooms in our places, and most of us had an area where we could sew up a soldier on short notice. Conor was one of the lucky ones.

As I eyed the man who was strung up from the ceiling, his body one big shiver, his eyelashes tipped with icicles and his face blue, I called his name.

His eyes drifted open, and I knew hypothermia was starting to hit him hard, because his responses were dull, slow. But when he saw me, he jerked back and gasped.

I smiled.

It was good to know my rep still preceded me.

EOGHAN'S STORY CAN BE FOUND IN THE NEXT BOOK IN THE *UNIVERSE*: **FILTHY RICH.**
IT CAN BE READ ON KU:
WWW.BOOKS2READ.COM/FILTHYRICH

SIN, THE NEXT BOOK IN *A DARK & DIRTY SINNERS' SERIES,* IS NOW AVAILABLE TO READ ON KU!
WWW.BOOKS2READ.COM/SINSERENAAKEROYD

FILTHY

FINN

Obsessive habits weren't alien to me.

They were as much a part of me as my coal-dark hair and my diamond-blue eyes. Ingrained as they were, it didn't mean they weren't irritating as fuck.

As I rifled through the folder on the table in front of me, staring down at the life of one pesky tenant, I wanted to toss it in the trash. I truly did.

I wanted not to be interested in her.

Wanted my focus to return to the matter at hand—business.

But there was something about her.

Something...

Irish.

I was a sucker for my own people. When I was a kid, I'd only dated other Irish girls in my class, and though I'd become less discerning about nationality and had grown more interested in tits and ass, I'd thought that desire had died down.

But Aoife Keegan was undeniably, indefatigably Irish.

From her fucking name—I didn't know people still named their kids in Gaelic over here—to her red goddamn hair and milky-white skin.

To many, she wouldn't be sexy. Too pale, too curvy, too rounded and wholesome. But to me? It was like God had formed a creature that was born to be my downfall.

I could feel the beast inside me roaring to life as I stared at the photos of her. It wanted out. It wanted her.

Fuck.

"I told you not to get those briefs."

My eyes flared wide in surprise at my brother, Aidan O'Donnelly's remark. "What?" I snapped.

"I told you not to get those briefs," he repeated, unoffended. Which was a miracle. Had I been speaking to Aidan Sr., I'd probably have lost a finger, but Aidan Jr. was one of my best friends, as well as a confidant and fellow businessman.

When I said business, it wasn't the kind Valley girls dreamed their future husbands would be involved in. No Manhattan socialite, though we were wealthy as fuck, would want us on their arm if they truly knew what games we were involved in.

My business was forged, unashamedly, in blood, sweat, and tears.

Preferably not my own, although I had taken a few hits for the Family over the years.

"My briefs aren't irritating me," I carried on, blowing out a breath.

"No? You look like you've got something up your ass crack." Aidan cocked a brow at me, but his smirk told me he knew exactly what the fuck was wrong.

I flipped him the bird—the finger that I'd have lost by showing cheek to his father—and he just grinned at me as he leaned over my glass desk and scooped up one of the pictures.

That beast I mentioned earlier?

It roared to life again when his eyes drifted over Aoife's curvy form.

"She's like your kryptonite," he breathed, tilting his head to the side. "Fuck me, Finn."

"I'd rather not," I told him dryly. "Now her? Yeah. I'd fuck her anytime."

He wafted a dismissive hand at my teasing. "I knew from that look in your eye, there was a woman involved. I just didn't know it would be a looker like this."

I snatched the photo from him. "Mine."

My growl had him snickering. "The Old Country ain't where I get my women from, Finn. Simmer down."

Throat tightening, I grated out, "What the fuck am I going to do?"

"Screw her?" he suggested.

"I can't."

He snorted. "You can."

"How the fuck am I supposed to get her in my bed when I'm about to bribe her into selling off her commercial lot?"

Aidan shrugged. "Do the bribing after."

That had me blowing out a breath. "You're a bastard, you know that, right?"

Piously, he murmured, "My parents were well and truly married before I came along. I have the wedding and birth certificates to prove it." He grinned. "Anyway, you're only just figuring that out?"

I shot him a scowl. "You're remarkably cheerful today."

"Is that a question or a statement?"

"Both?" The word sounded far too Irish for my own taste. My mother had come from Ireland, Tipperary to be precise—yeah, like the song. I was American born and bred, my accent that of someone who'd been raised in Hell's Kitchen but, and I hated it, my mother's accent would make an appearance every now and then.

'Both' came out sounding almost like 'boat.'

Aidan, knowing me as well as he did, smirked again—the fucker. "I got laid."

Grunting, I told him, "That doesn't usually make you cheerful."

"It does. I just never see you first thing after I wake up. Da hasn't managed to piss me off today."

Aidan was the heir to the Five Points—an Irish gang who operated out of Hell's Kitchen. It wasn't like being the heir to a candy company or a title. It came with responsibilities that no one really appreciated.

We were tied into the life, though. Had been since the day we were born.

There was no use in whining over it, and Aidan wasn't. But if I had to deal with his father on a daily basis? I'd have been whining to the morgue and back.

Aidan Sr. was the shrewdest man I knew. What the man could do with our clout defied belief. Even if I thought he was a sociopath, he had my respect, and in truth, my love and loyalty.

Bastard or no, he'd taken me in when I was fourteen and had made me one of his family. I'd gone from being his kids' friend, the son of one of his runners, to suddenly being welcome in the main house.

All because Aidan Sr.—though I was sure he was certifiable—believed in family.

I shot Aidan Jr. a look. "Was it that blonde over on Canal Street?"

He rubbed his chin. "Yeah."

Snorting, I told him, "Hope you wore a rubber. I swear that woman has so many men going in and out of her door, it should be on double-action hinges."

He scowled at me. "Are you trying to piss me off?"

"Why? Didn't wear a jimmy?" I grinned at him, my mood soaring in the face of his irritation. "Better get to the clinic before it drops off."

Though he flipped me the bird as easily as I'd done to him—I was his brother, after all—he grumbled, "What are you going to do about little Aoife?"

I squinted at him. "She's not little."

That seemed to restore his humor. "I know. Just how you like them." He shook his head. "You and Conor, I swear. What do you do with them? Drown yourself in their tits?"

Heaving a sigh, I informed him, "My predilection for large tits is none of your business."

"And whether or not I wore a jimmy last night is none of yours."

"If it turns green and looks like a moldy corn on the cob, who you gonna call?"

"Ghostbusters?" he tried.

I shook my head, then pointed a finger at him and back at myself. "No. Me."

Grunting, he got to his feet and pressed his fists to the desk. "We need that building, Finn."

"The business development plan was mine, Aid. I know we need it. Don't worry, I won't do anything stupid."

He snorted. "Your kind of stupid could go one of two ways."

That had me narrowing my eyes at him, but he held up his hands in surrender.

"Fuck her out of your system quickly, and then get started on the deal," he advised. "Best way."

It probably was the best way, but—

He sighed. "That fucking honor of yours."

I had to laugh. Only in the O'Donnelly family would my thoughts be considered honorable.

"If I'm fucking someone over, I want them to know it," was all I said.

"That makes no sense."

"Makes for epic sex, though," I jibed, and he shot me a grin.

"Angry sex is always good." He rubbed his chin, then he reached over again and flipped through the photos. "Who's the old guy to her?"

"To her? Not sure. Sugar daddy?" The thought alone made the beast inside rage. I cleared my throat to get rid of the rasp there. "To us? He's our meal ticket."

Aidan's eyes widened. "He is?"

I nodded. "Just leave it to me."

"I was always going to, *dearthái*r." He tilted his chin at me, honoring me with the Gaelic word for brother. "Be careful out there."

"You, too, brother."

Aidan winked at me and, with a far too cheerful whistle for someone whose dick might soon be 'ribbed for her pleasure' without the need for a condom, walked out of my office leaving me to brood.

The instant his back was to me, I stared at the photos again. Flipping through them, I glowered at the innocent face staring back at me through the photo paper—if only she knew.

Hers was a building in Hell's Kitchen. Five Points Territory. One of many on my hit list.

Back in the 70s, Aidan Sr., following in his father's footsteps, had bought up a shit-ton of property, pre-gentrification, and it was my job to either sell off the portfolio, reconstruct, or 'improve' the current aesthetics of the buildings the Points owned.

This particular one was something I'd taken a personal interest in.

See, I was technically a legitimate businessman.

This office?

I had views of the Hudson. I could see the Empire State Building, and in the evening, I had an epic view of the sunset setting over Manhattan. This office building, also Points' property, was worth a cool hundred million, and I was, again technically, the CEO of it.

On paper?

I looked seamless.

The businessman who sported hundred thousand dollar watches and had a house in the Hamptons. No one save the Points and my CPA knew where the money came from. I liked that because, fuck, I had no intention of switching this pad for a lock-up in Riker's Island.

Still, this project cut close to home, and the reasoning was fucking pathetic.

I'd never admit it to any of the O'Donnellys. The bastards were like family to me, and if I admitted to this, they'd never let me hear the end of it.

Extortion?

I usually doled that out to someone else's to do list. Someone with a far lower paygrade than me, someone expendable. But the minute I'd heard of the troublesome tenant who was refusing to sell her lot to us? After not one, not two, not even three attempts with higher prices?

Five outright refusals?

The challenge to convince her otherwise had overtaken me.

See, I liked stubborn in women.

I liked fucking it out of them.

Throw in the fact the woman's name was Aoife? It had been enough to get me sending someone out to follow her.

If she'd been fifty with as many chins as she had grandchildren, she'd have been safe from me.

But she wasn't.

She was, as Aidan had correctly stated, my kryptonite. All milky flesh with gleaming auburn hair that I wanted to tie around my clenched fist. Her soft features with those delicate green eyes that sparkled when she smiled and were like wet grass when she was mad, acted like a punch to my gut.

Now?

My interest hadn't just been piqued.

It had fucking imploded.

Yeah, I was thinking with my cock, but what man, at the end of the day, didn't?

I'd just have to be careful. Just have to make sure I put pressure on the right places, make sure she'd bend and not break, and the old bastard in the pictures was my key to just that.

See, every third Tuesday of the month, Aoife Keegan had a habit of traipsing across Manhattan to the Upper East Side. There, at three PM on the dot, she'd enter a discreet little boutique hotel and wouldn't leave until nine PM that night.

Five minutes after she arrived and left, the same man would leave, too.

At first, when Jimmy O'Leary had told me that Senator Alan Davidson was at the hotel, I hadn't thought anything of it.

Why would I?

Senators trawled for donations in fancy hotels every fucking day of the week. It was the true luxury of politics. Sure, they made it look real good for the press. Posing in derelict neighborhoods and shaking hands with people who did the fucking work . . . all while they lived it up large with women half their age in two thousand dollar a night suites.

My mouth firmed at that.

Was Aoife selling herself to the Senator?

The thought pissed me off.

I couldn't see why she'd do such a thing. Not when I'd looked into her finances, had seen just how secure she was. But maybe that was why. Maybe the Senator was funneling money to her.

The only problem was that the lot Aoife owned—did I mention it was owned outright? Yeah, that was enough to chafe my suspicions, too, considering she was only twenty-fucking-five years old—was a teashop in a small building in a questionable area of HK.

I mean, come on. I loved Hell's Kitchen. It was home. But fuck. Where she was? What kind of Senator would put his fancy piece in *that*?

My jaw clenched as I studied the Senator's and Aoife's smiling faces as they left the hotel. Separately, of course. But whatever they'd been doing together, it sure put a Cheshire Cat grin on their chops–that was for fucking sure. Jimmy being a dumbass, hadn't put the two together, had just remarked on the 'coincidence,' but I was no fool.

How did I know they were together in the hotel?

Jimmy had been trailing Aoife for four months—told you I was obsessive—and every third Tuesday, come rain or shine, this little routine had jumped out, and when Jimmy had picked up on the fact Davidson had been there each and every time, I'd gotten my hands dirty, bribed one of the hotel maids myself—and fuck, that had been hard. Turned out that place made even the maids sign NDA agreements, but everyone had a price—and I'd found out that my little obsession shared a suite with the old prick.

My fingers curled into fists as I stared at her. Butter wouldn't fucking melt. She was the epitome of innocence. Like a redheaded angel. Could she really be lifting her skirts for that old fucker? Just so she could own a teashop?

Something didn't make sense, and fuck, if that didn't intrigue me all the more.

Aoife Keegan had snared one of the biggest, nastiest sharks in Manhattan.

She just didn't know it yet.

***

Aoife

"We need more scones for tomorrow. I keep telling you four dozen isn't enough."

Lifting a hand at my waitress and friend, Jenny, I mumbled, "I know, I know."

"If you know, then why the hell don't you listen?" Jenny complained, making me grin.

"Because I'm the one who has to make them? Making half that again is just . . ." I sighed.

I loved my job.

I did.

I adored baking—my butt and hips attested to that fact—and making a career out of my passion was something every twenty-something hoped for. Especially in one of the most expensive cities in the world. But sheesh. There was only so much one person could do, and this was still, essentially, a one-woman-band.

With the threat of Acuig Corp looming over me, I didn't feel safe hiring extra staff. I'd held them off for close to six months now. Six months of them trying to tempt me to leave, to sell up. They'd raised their prices to ten percent above market value, whereas with everyone else in the building, they'd just offered what the apartments were truly worth. Considering this place wasn't the nicest in the block, that wasn't much.

Most people hadn't held out because, hell, why wouldn't they want to live elsewhere?

Those who were landlords hadn't felt any issue in tossing their tenants out on the street. The tenants grumbled, but when did they ever have any rights, anyway?

For myself, this was where my mom and I had worked to—

I brought that thought to a shuddering halt.

Mom was dead now.

I had to remember that. This was on me, not her.

My throat thickened with tears as I turned to Jenny and murmured, "I'll try better tomorrow."

The words had her frowning at me. "Babe, you know I'm not the boss here, right?"

Lips curving, I whispered, "I know. But you're so scary."

She snickered then peered down at herself. "Yeah, I bet I'd make grown men cry."

Maybe for a taste of her. . . .

Jenny was everything I wasn't.

She was slender, didn't dip her hand into the cookie jar at will—the woman had more willpower than I did hips, and my hips seemed to go on forever—and her face looked like it belonged on the cover of a fashion magazine. Even her hair was enough to inspire envy. It was black and straight as a ruler.

Mine?

Bright red and curly like a bitch. I had to straighten it out every morning if I didn't want to look like little orphan Annie.

I'd once read that curly-haired women straightened their hair for special events, and that straight-haired women curled theirs in turn, but I called bullshit.

Curly-haired women lived with their straightening irons surgically attached to their hands.

At least, I did.

My rat's nest was like a ginger afro. Maybe Beyoncé could make that work, but I sure as hell didn't have the bone structure.

"I think grown men would cry," I told her dryly, "if you asked them to."

She pshawed, but there was a twinkle in her eye that I understood.... She agreed with me, knew it was true, but wasn't going to admit it. With anyone else, she might have. She had an ego–that was for damn sure. But with me? I think she figured I was zero competition, so she felt no need to rub salt in the wound, too.

I plunked my elbows on the counter and stared around my domain as she bustled off and started clearing the tables. It was her last duty of the day, and my feet were aching so damn bad that I didn't even have it in me to care.

This owning your own business shit?

It wasn't easy.

Not saying I didn't love it, but it was hard.

I slept like four hours a night, and when I wasn't in bed, I was here. All the time.

Baking, cooking, serving, and smiling. Always smiling. Even if I was so sleep-deprived I could sob.

Jenny's actually a life saver.

My mom used to be front of house before....

I sucked down a breath.

I had to get used to thinking about it.

She wasn't here anymore, but just avoiding all thoughts of her period wasn't working for me. It was like I was purposely forgetting her, and, well, fuck that.

She'd always wanted to have a teashop. It had been her one true dream.

Back in Ireland, when she was a little girl, her grandmother had owned one in Limerick. Mom had caught the bug and had wanted to have one here in the States. But not only was it too fucking expensive for a woman on her own, it was also impossible with my feckless father at her side.

I didn't want to think about him either, though.

Why?

Because the feckless father who'd pretty much ruined my mother's life, wasn't the only father in my life. My biological dad hadn't exactly cared about her happiness, but once he'd come to know about me, he'd tried. That was more than could be said for the man who'd lived with me throughout my early childhood.

"You look gloomy."

Jenny's statement had me blinking in surprise. She had a ton of dishes piled in her arms, and I'd have worried for the expensive china if I hadn't known she was an old pro at this shit. Just as I was.

We could probably earn a Guinness World Record on how many dishes we could take back and forth to the kitchen of *Ellie's Tea Rooms*. I swear, I had guns because of all that hefting. My biceps were probably the firmest part of my body.

More's the pity.

I'd have preferred an ass you could bounce dimes off of, but, when it boiled down to it, there was no way in this universe I could live without cake.

Just wasn't going to happen.

My big butt wasn't going *anywhere* until scientists could make zero calorie eclairs and pies.

"I'm not glum."

"No? Then why are your eyes sad?"

Were they? I pursed my lips as I let the 'sad eyes' drift around the tea room. I wish I could say it was all forged on my own hard work, but it wasn't. Not really.

"I was just thinking about Mom."

"Oh, honey," Jenny said sadly, and she carefully placed all the dishes on the counter, so she could round it and curve her arm around my waist. "It was only seven months ago. Of course, you were thinking of her."

"I just—" I blew out a breath. "I don't know if I'm doing what she'd want."

"You can't live for her choices, sweetness. You have to do what you think is right for you."

I gnawed at my bottom lip again. "I-I know, but she was always there for me. A guiding light. With Fiona gone and her, too? I don't really know what I'm doing with myself."

This business wasn't something that made me want to get up on a morning. It was my mom's dream, her goal. Every decision I made, I tried to remember how she'd longed for a place like this, but it wasn't my passion. It was hers, and I was trying to keep that dream alive while fretting over the fact my heart wasn't in it.

"I think you're doing a damn fine job. You have a very successful teashop. Your cakes are raved about. Have you visited our TripAdvisor page recently? Or our Yelp?" She squeaked. "I swear, you're making this place a tourist hotspot. I don't think Fiona or Michelle could be more proud of you if they tried."

The baking shit, yeah, that was all on me, but the other stuff? The finances?

I'd caved in.

I'd caved where my mom had always refused in the past.

With the accident had come a lot of medical bills that I just hadn't been able to afford. Without her help, I'd had to take on extra staff, and out of nowhere, my expenses had added up.

Mom had been so proud of this place, so ferociously gleeful that we'd done it by ourselves, and yet, here I was, financially free for the first time in my life, and I still felt like I was drowning because my freedom went entirely against her wishes.

"Is this to do with Acuig? I know they're still pestering you."

Jenny's statement had me wincing. Acuig were the bottom feeders who wanted to snap up this building, demolish it, and then replace it with a skyscraper. Don't get me wrong, the building was foul, but a lot of people lived here, and the minute it morphed into some exclusive condo, no one from around here would be able to afford to live in it.

It would become yuppy central.

I'd rejected all their offers to buy my tea room even though I didn't want the damn thing, not really. Mostly I wanted to keep mom's goals alive and kicking, but also, it pissed me off the way Acuig were changing Hell's Kitchen. Ratcheting up prices, making it unaffordable for the everyday man and woman—the people I'd grown up with—and bringing a shit-ton of banker-wankers and 1%ers to the area.

So, maybe I'd watched Erin Brockovich a time or two as a kid and had a social conscience . . . Wasn't the worst thing to possess, right?

"Aoife?" Jenny stated, making me look over at her. "Is Acuig pressuring you?"

I winced, realizing I hadn't answered—Jenny was my friend, but she also worked here and relied on the paycheck. It wasn't fair of me to keep her hanging like that. "They upped the sales price. I guess that isn't helping," I admitted, frowning down at my hands.

Unlike Jenny who had her nails manicured, mine were cut neatly and plain. I had no rings on my fingers, and wore no watch or bracelets because my wrists were usually deep in flour or sugar bags.

I spent most of my life right where I wanted it—behind the shopfront. That had slowly morphed where I was doing double the work to compensate for Mom's loss.

Was it any wonder I was feeling a little out of my league?

I was coping without Fiona, grieving Mom, working without her, too, and then practically living in the kitchens here. I didn't exactly have that much of a life. I had nothing cheerful on the horizon, either.

Well, nothing except for next Tuesday, and that wasn't enough to turn my frown upside down.

The money was a temptation. I didn't need to sell up and start working on my own goals, but that just loaded me down with more guilt and made me feel like a really shitty daughter.

Jenny squeezed me in a gentle hug. But as I turned to speak to her, the bell above the door rang as it opened. We both jerked in surprise—each of us apparently thinking the other had locked up when neither of us had—and turned to face the entrance.

On the brink of telling the client we were closed for the day, my mouth opened then shut.

Standing there, amid the frilly, lacy curtains, was the most masculine man I'd ever seen in my life.

And I meant that.

It was like a thousand aftershave models had morphed into one handsome creature that had just walked through my door.

At my side, I could feel Jenny's 'hot guy radar' flare to life, and for once, I couldn't damn well blame her.

This guy was . . . well, he was enough to make me choke on my words and splutter to a halt.

The tea room was all girly femininity. It was sophisticated enough to appeal to businesswomen with its mauve, taupe, and cream-toned hues, and the ethereal watercolors that decorated the walls. But the tablecloths were lacy, and the china dishes and cake stands we used were the height of Edwardian elegance.

Moms brought their little girls here for their birthday, and high-powered executives spilled dirt on their lovers with their girlfriends over scones and clotted cream—breaking their diets as they discussed the boyfriends who had broken their hearts.

The man, whoever the hell he was, was dressed to impress in a navy suit with the finest pinstripe. It was close to a silver fleck, and I could see, even from this distance, that it was hand tailored. I'd seen custom tailoring before, and only a trained eye could get a suit cut so perfectly to this man's form.

With wide shoulders that looked like they could take the weight of the world, a long, lean frame that was enhanced by strong muscles evident through the close fit of his pants and jacket, then the silkiness of his shirt which revealed delineated abs when his bright gold and scarlet tie flapped as he moved, the guy was hot.

With a capital H.

"How can we help, sir?" Jenny purred, and despite my own awe, I had to dip my chin to hide my smile.

Even if I wanted to throw my hat into this particular man's game, there was no way he'd choose me over Jenny. Fuck, I'd screw her, and I wasn't even a lesbian. Not even a teensy bit bi. I'd gone shopping with her enough to have seen her ass, and I promise you, it's biteable.

So, nope. I didn't have a snowball's chance in hell of this Adonis seeing *me* when Jenny was in the room.

Yet....

When I'd controlled my smile, I looked over at the man, and his focus was on me.

My breath stuttered to a halt.

Why wasn't his gaze glued to Jenny?

Why weren't those ice-white blue eyes fixated on my best friend's tits, which Jenny helpfully plumped up as she preened at my side?

For a second, I was so close to breaking out into a coughing fit, it was humiliating. Then, more humiliation struck in a quieter manner, but it was nevertheless rotten—I turned pink.

Now, you might think you know what a blush is. You might think you've even experienced it yourself a time or two. But I was a redhead. My skin made fresh milk look yellow, and even my fucking freckles were pale. Everything about me was like I'd been dunked into white wax.

But as the heat crawled over me, taking over my skin as the man looked at me without pause, I knew things had rarely been this dire.

See, with Jenny as a best friend, I was used to the attention going her way. I could hide in the background, hide in her shadow. I liked it there. I was comfortable there. Sometimes, on double dates, she'd drag me along, and even the guy supposed to be dating me would be gaping at Jenny. As pathetic as it was, I was so used to it, it didn't bother me.

But now?

I just wasn't used to being in the spotlight.

Especially not a man like this one's spotlight.

When you're a teenager, practicing with your mom's blush for the first time, you always look like a tomato that's been left out in the sun, right?

I was redder than that.

I could feel it. I could fucking feel the heat turning me tomato red.

When Jenny cleared her throat, I thanked God when it broke the man's attention. He shot her a look, but it wasn't admiring. It wasn't even impressed.

If anything, it was irritated.

Okay, so now both Jenny and I were stunned.

Fuck that, we were floored.

Literally.

Our mouths were doing a pretty good fish impression as the man turned back to look at me.

Shit, was this some kind of joke?

Was it April 1st and I'd just gotten the dates mixed up again?

"Ms. Keegan?"

Oh fuck. His voice.

Oh. My. God.

That voice.

It was. . . .

I had to swallow.

Did men even talk like that?

It was low and husky and raspy and made me think of sex, not just mediocre sex, but the best sex. Toe-curling, nails-breaking-in-the-sheets sex. Sex so fucking good you couldn't walk the next day. Sex so hot that it made my current core temperature look polar in comparison. Sex that I'd never been lucky to have before, so I pined for it in the worst way.

Jenny nudged me in the side when I just carried on gaping at the man. "Y-Yes. That's me." I cleared my throat, feeling nervous and stupid and flustered as I wiped my hands on my apron.

Sweet Jesus.

Was this man really looking for me while I was wearing a goddamn pinafore?

Even as practical as they were, I wanted to beg the patron saint of pinnies to remove it from me. To do something, anything, to make sure that this man didn't see me in the red gingham check that I always wore to cover up stains.

And then I felt it.

Jenny's hand.

Tugging at the knot.

I wanted to kiss her. Seriously. I wanted to give her a fucking raise! As I moved away from the counter and her side, the apron dropped to the floor as I headed for the man whose hand was now held out, ready for me to shake in greeting.

There are those moments in your life when you know you'll never forget them. They can be happy or sad, annoying or exhilarating. This was one of them.

As I slipped my hand into his, I felt the electric shocks down to my core. Meeting his gaze wasn't hard because I was stunned, and I needed to know if he'd felt that, too.

From the way those eyelids were shielding his icy-blue eyes, I figured he was just as surprised.

It was like a satisfied puma was watching me. One that was happy there was plump prey prancing around in front of him.

Shit.

Did I just describe myself as 'plump prey?'

And like that, my house of cards came tumbling down because what the hell would this man want with me?

I was seeing things.

God, I was so stupid sometimes.

I cleared my throat for, like, the fourth damn time, and asked, "I'm Ms. Keegan. You are?"

His smile, when it appeared, was as charming as the rest of him. His teeth were white, but not creepy, reality-TV-star white. They were straight except for one of his canines, which tilted in slightly. In his perfect face, it was one flaw that I almost clung to. Because with that wide brow, the hair so dark it looked like black silk that was cut closely to his head with a faint peak at his forehead, the strong nose, and even stronger jaw, I needed something imperfect to focus on.

Then, I sucked down a breath and remembered what Fiona had told me once upon a time. When I'd been nervous about asking Jamie Winters to homecoming, she'd advised me in her soft Irish lilt, "Lass, that boy takes a dump just like you do. He uses the bathroom twice a day and undoubtedly leaves a puddle on the floor for his ma to clean up. I bet he's puked a time or two as well. Had diarrhea and the good Lord only knows what else. Just you think that the next time you see that boy and want to ask him out."

Yeah. It was gross, but fuck, it had worked. Her advice had worked so well I hadn't asked anyone out because I could only think of them using the damn toilet!

Still, looking at this Adonis, there was no imagining *that*.

Surely, gods didn't use the bathroom.

Did they?

"The name's Finn. Finn O'Grady."

My eyes flared at the name.

No.

It couldn't be.

Finn O'Grady?

No. It wasn't a rare name, but it was a strong one. One that suited him, one that had always suited him.

I frowned up at him wondering, yet again, if this was a joke of some sort, but as he looked at me, *really* looked at me, I saw no recognition. Saw nothing on his features that revealed any ounce of awareness that I'd known him for years.

Well, okay, not *known*. But I'd known his mother. Our mothers had been best friends. And as I looked, I saw the same almond-shaped eyes Fiona had, the stubborn jaw, and that unmistakable butt-indent on his chin.

At the reminder of just how forgettable I was, my heart sank, and hurt whistled through me.

Then, I realized I was *still* holding his hand, and as he squeezed, the flush returned and I almost died of mortification.

CHAPTER 2

FINN

GOD, she was perfect.

And when I said perfect, I meant it.

I'd fucked a lot of women. Redheads, blondes, brunettes, even the rare thing that is a natural head of black hair. None of them, not a single one, lit up like Aoife Keegan.

Her cheeks were cherry red and in the light camisole she wore, a cheerful yellow, I could see how the blush went all the way down to the upper curve of her breasts.

She'd go that color, I knew, when she came.

And fuck, I wanted to see that.

I wanted to see that perfectly pale flesh turn bright pink under my ministrations.

Even as I looked at her, all shy and flustered, I wondered if she was a screamer in bed.

Some of the shyest often were.

Maybe not at first, but after a handful of orgasms, it was a wonder what that could do to a woman's self-confidence, and Jesus, I wanted to *see* that, too. I wanted a seat at center stage.

My suit jacket was open, and I regretted it. Immensely. My cock was hard, had been since we'd shaken hands, and her fingers had clung to mine like a daughter would to her daddy's at her first visit to the county fair.

Fuck.

Squeezing her fingers wasn't intentional. If anything, I'd just liked the feel of her palm against mine, but when I put faint pressure on her, she jerked back like she'd been scalded.

Her cheeks bloomed with heat again, and she whispered, "Mr. O'Grady, what can I do for you?"

You can get on your fucking knees and sort out the hard-on you just caused.

That's what she could fucking do.

I almost growled at the thought because the image of her on her knees, my cock in her small fist, her dainty mouth opening to take the tip. . . .

Shit.

That had to happen.

Here, too.

In this fancy, frilly, feminine place, I wanted to defile her.

Fuck, I wanted that so goddamn much, it was enough to make me reconsider my demolition plans.

I wanted to screw her against all this goddamn lace, which suited her perfectly. She was made for lace. And silk. Hell, silk would look like heaven against her skin. I wouldn't know where she ended and it began.

When her brow puckered, she dipped her chin, and that gorgeous wave of auburn hair slipped over her shoulder.

If we'd been alone, if that brassy bitch—who was staring at me like I could fuck her over the counter with her friend watching if I was game—wasn't here, I'd have grabbed that rope of hair, twisted it around my fingers, and forced her gaze up.

Some guys liked their women demure. And I was one of them. I wasn't about to lie. I liked that in her, but I wanted her eyes on me. Always.

It was enough to prompt me to bite out, "Can we speak privately?"

She jerked at my words, then as she licked her bottom lip, turned to look at the waitress. "Jenny, it's okay. I can handle the rest by myself. You get home."

Jenny, her gaze drifting between me and her boss, nodded. She retreated to a door that swung as she moved through the opening, and within seconds, she had her coat and purse over her arm.

As she sashayed past—for my benefit, I was sure—she murmured, "See you tomorrow, Aoife."

Aoife nodded and shot her friend a smile, but I wasn't smiling. There were dishes on every table. Plates and saucers and tea pots. Those fancy stands that made any man wonder if he could touch it without snapping it.

Aoife was going to clear all that herself? Not on my fucking watch.

When the bell rang as the waitress opened the door, I didn't take my eyes off her until it rang once more upon closing.

Aoife swallowed, and I watched her throat work, watched it with a hunger that felt alien to me, because, God, I wanted to see my bites on her. Wanted to see my marks on that pale column of skin and her tits.

Barely withholding a groan, I asked, "Do you often let your staff go when you still have a lot of work to do, so you can speak to a stranger?"

Her cheeks flushed again, and she took a step back. "I-I, you're not—" Flustered once more, she fell silent.

"I'm not what?" Curiosity had me asking the question. Whatever I'd expected her to say, it hadn't been that.

She cleared her throat. "N-Nothing. You wished to speak with me, Mr. O'Grady?"

My other hand tightened around my briefcase, and though seeing her had made my reason for being here all that more necessary, I was almost disappointed. There was a gentle warmth to those bright-green eyes that would die out when I told her my purpose for being here. And her innocent attraction to me would change, morph into something else.

But I could only handle *something else*.

Some men were made for forever.

But those men weren't in my line of business.

I moved away from her, pressing my briefcase to one of the few empty tables. I wasn't happy about her having to do all the clearing up later on, and wondered if Paul, my PA, would know who to call to get her some help.

There was no way I was spending the rest of the night alone in my bed, my only companion my fist wrapped around my cock.

No way, no fucking how.

I paid Paul enough for him to come and clear the fucking place on his own if he couldn't find someone else.

I wanted Aoife on her knees, bent over my goddamn bed, and I was a man who always got what he wanted.

In this jungle, I was the lion, and Aoife? She was my prey.

I keyed in the code and opened my briefcase. The manila envelope was large and thick, well-padded with my documentation of Aoife's every move for the past few months.

It had started off as a legitimate move.

I'd wanted to know her weaknesses, so I could put pressure on her and make her cave to my demands.

Now, my demands had changed. I didn't just want her to sell the tea room we were standing in, I wanted her in my bed.

Fuck, I wanted that more than I wanted to make Aidan Sr. a fucking profit, and Aidan's profit and my balls still being attached to my body ran hand in hand.

Aidan was an evil cunt.

If I failed to deliver, he'd take it out on me. Whether I was his idea of an adopted son or not, he'd have done the same to his blood sons.

Well, he wouldn't have taken their balls. The man, for all his psychotic flaws, was obsessed with the idea of grandchildren, of passing it all on to the next generation. He'd cut his boys though. Without a doubt.

I knew Conor had marks on his back from a beating he refused to speak about. Then there was Brennan. He had a weak wrist because his father had a habit of breaking *that* wrist.

Without speaking, I grabbed the envelope and passed it to her.

She frowned down at it and asked, "For me?"

I smiled at her. "Open it."

"What is it?"

"Leverage."

That had her eyes flaring wide as she pulled out some of the photos. A gasp fell from her lips as she grabbed the photos when she spotted herself in them, jerking so hard the envelope tore. Some of the pictures spilled to the ground, but I didn't care about that.

Leaning back against one of the dainty tables once I was satisfied it would take my weight, I watched her cheeks blanch, all that delicious color dissipating as she took in everything the photos revealed.

"Y-You've been stalking me. Why?"

The question was high-pitched, loaded down with panic. I'd heard it often enough to recognize it easily.

I didn't get involved in wet work anymore. That wasn't my style, but along the way, to reach this point, I'd had no choice but to get my hands dirty. Panic was part of the job when you were collecting debts for the Irish Mob. And the Five Points were notorious for Aidan Sr.'s temper.

He wasn't the first patriarch. If anything, his grandfather was the founder. But Aidan Sr. was the type of guy that if you didn't pay him back, he didn't give a fuck about the money, he cared about the lack of respect.

See, you owed the mob and didn't pay? They'd send heavies around, beat the shit out of you, and threaten to do the same to your family, and usually, that did the trick. You didn't kill the cash cow.

Aidan Sr.?

He didn't give a fuck about the cash cow.

Only the truly desperate thought about borrowing money from Aidan, because if you didn't pay it back, he'd take your teeth, and your fingers and toes as a first warning. Then, if you still didn't pay—and most did—it was death.

Respect meant a lot to Aidan.

And fuck, if it wasn't starting to mean a lot to me. The panic in her voice made my cock throb.

I wanted this woman weak and willing.

I wanted it more than I wanted my next breath.

Ignoring her, I reached for my phone and tapped out a message to Paul. *Need housekeeping crew to clean this place.*

I attached my live location, saw the blue ticks as Paul read the message —he knew better than to ignore my texts, whatever time of day they came— and he replied: *Sure thing.*

That was the kind of reply I was used to getting. Not just from Paul, but from everyone.

There were very few people who weren't below me in the strata of Five Points, and I'd worked my ass off to make that so.

The only people who ranked above me included Aidan Jr. and his brothers, Aidan Sr. of course, and then maybe a handful of his advisors that he respected for what they'd done for him and the Points over the years.

But the money I made Aidan Sr.?

That blew most of their 'advice' out of the window.

The reason Aidan had a Dassault Falcon executive private plane?

Because I was, as the City itself called me, a whiz kid.

I'd made my first million—backed by the Points, of course—at twenty-two.

Fifteen years later?

I'd made him hundreds of millions.

My own personal fortune was nothing to sniff at, either.

"W-Why have you done this?" Aoife asked, her voice breathy enough to make me wonder if she sounded like that in the sack.

"Because you've been a very stubborn little girl."

Her eyes flared wide. "Excuse me?"

I reached into the inside pocket of my suit coat and pulled out a business card. "For you," I prompted, offering it to her.

When she turned it over, saw the logo of five points shaped into a star, then read Acuig—in the Gaelic way, ah-coo-ig, not a butchered American way, ah-coo-ch—aloud, I watched her throat work as she swallowed.

"I-I should have realized with the Irish name," she whispered, the muscles in her brow twitching as she took in the chaos of the scattered photos on the floor.

Watching her as she dropped the contents on the ground, so she was surrounded by them, I tilted my head to the side, taking her in as her panic started to crest.

"I-I won't sell." Her first words surprised me.

I should have figured, though. Everything about this woman was surprisingly delicious.

"You have no choice," I purred. "As far as I'm aware, the Senator has a wife. He also has a reputation to protect. I'm not sure he'd be happy if any of those made it onto the *National Enquirer's* front page. Not when he's just trying to shore up his image to take a run for the White House next election."

She reached up and clutched her throat. The self-protective gesture was enough to make me smile at her—I knew what the absence of hope looked like.

There'd been a time when that had been my life, too.

"But, on the bright side," I carried on, "this can all be wiped away if you sell." As her gaze flicked to mine, I added, "As well as if you do something for me."

For a second, she was speechless. I could see she knew what that *something* was. Had my body language given it away? Had there been a certain raspiness to my tone?

I wasn't sure, and frankly, didn't give a fuck.

There was a little hiccoughing sound that escaped her lips, and she frowned at me, then down at herself.

"Is this a joke?"

"Do I look like I'm the kind of guy who jokes, Aoife?" Fuck, I loved saying her name.

The Gaelic notes just drove me insane.

Ee-Fah.

Nothing like the spelling, and all the more complicated and delicious for it.

"N-No," she confirmed, "but . . ."

"But what?" I prompted.

"I mean . . . you just can't be serious."

"Oh, but I am." I grinned. "Deadly. You've wasted a lot of my time, Aoife Keegan. A lot. Do you think I'm normally involved in negotiations of this level?"

Her eyes whispered over me, and I felt the loving caress of her gaze as she took in each and every inch of me. When she licked her lips, I knew she liked what she saw. I didn't really care, but it was helpful for her to be eager in some small way—especially when coercion was involved.

Aidan had called it bribery. I preferred 'coercion'. It sounded far kinder.

"No. That suit alone probably cost the mortgage payment on this place."

I nodded—she wasn't wrong. I knew what she'd been paying as rent, then as a mortgage, before some kind *benefactor* had paid it all off. Free and clear.

"I had to get my hands dirty, and while I might like some things dirty . . .," I trailed off, smirking when she flushed. "So, as I see it, we have a problem. I want this building. You don't want anyone to know you're having an affair with a Senator. Or, should I say, the Senator doesn't want anyone to know he's having an affair with someone young enough to be his daughter . . ."

If my voice turned into a growl at that point, then it was because the notion of her spreading her legs for that old bastard just turned my stomach.

Fuck, this woman, the thoughts she made me think.

Because I was startled at the possessive note to my growl, I ran a hand over my head. I kept my hair short for a reason—ease. I wasn't the kind of man who wasted time primping. It was an expensive cut, so I didn't have to do anything to it. Even mussing it up had it falling back into the same sleek lines as before—a man in my position had to look pristine under pressure. And very few people could even begin to understand the kind of strain I was under.

The formation of igneous rock had less volcanic pressure than Aidan Sr.

She licked her lips as she stared down at the photos, then back up at me. "And you want me to sell the place to you, even though this is my livelihood and the livelihood of all my staff, and then sleep with you?"

Her squeaky voice, putting suspicion into words, had me crossing my legs at the ankle. "We wouldn't be doing much sleeping."

Another shaky breath soughed from her lips, then, those beautiful pillowy morsels that would look good around my cock, quivered.

"This is crazy," she whispered shakily.

"As far as I'm concerned, all of this could be avoided if you'd just sold to me a few months back. Now you have to pay for my time wasted on this project."

"By spreading my legs?"

Another squeak. I tsked at her question, but in truth, I was annoyed at her using those same words I had to describe her with that old hypocrite of a Senator.

I didn't move, though. Didn't even flex my arms in irritation, just murmured, "Small price to pay. And, even though it's ten percent above market price, I'll stick to the last offer Acuig gave you. Can't say anything's fairer than that."

She shook her head, and there was a desperation to the gesture as she cried, "I need this business. You don't understand—"

"I understand that some very powerful and very dangerous businessmen want this building demolished. I understand that those same powerful and dangerous men want a skyscraper taking up this plot of land. I understand that a four hundred million dollar project isn't going to be put on hiatus because one small Irish woman doesn't want to go out of business . . ." I cocked a brow at her. "You think I'm coming in hot and heavy? These kinds of men, Aoife, they're not the sort you fuck around with.

"Take my check, and my other offer, before you or the people you care about are threatened." I got to my feet and straightened my jacket out. "This suit? These shoes? That briefcase and this watch? I own them because I'm damn good at what I do. I'm a financial advisor, Aoife. Take my word for it. You're getting the best deal out of this."

She staggered back, the counter stopping her from crumpling to the floor. "You'd hurt me?"

"Not me," I repudiated. Not in the way she thought, anyway. "But the men I work for?"

Her gaze dropped to the one thing she'd retained in her hand—my card. "Acuig," she whispered. "Five in Gaelic."

My brows twitched in surprise. She knew Gaelic?

"The Five Points." Her eyes flared wide with terror. "They're behind this deal."

I hadn't expected her to put one and one together, but now that she had? It worked to my advantage.

Nodding, I told her, "Any minute now, there'll be a team of housekeepers coming in here to clear up for the night." When she gaped at me, I retrieved the contract from my briefcase, slapped it on the table, and handed her a pen as I carried on, "I suggest you let tonight be your last night of business."

What I didn't tell her, was that my suggestions weren't wasted words. They were like the law.

You didn't break them, and, like any lawmaker, I expected immediate obeisance.

***

Aoife

SO, the beautiful man just happened to be an absolute cocksucker of a bastard.

Still, this couldn't be real, could it?

The dick could have anyone he wanted. Jesus, Jenny was panting after him like a dog in heat. She would have gone out with him if he'd so much as clicked his fingers at her.

But he'd had eyes for me.

Like he wanted me.

He thought he'd bought me. Or, at least, bought my silence, and yeah, to some extent he had. But . . . why buy me, why not just drop the price on the building if he wanted me to pay for the time he'd wasted on me?

The arrogance imbued in those words was enough to make me pull my hair out, but that was inwardly. I was a redhead. I had a temper. But that temper was mostly overshadowed by fear.

Senator Alan Davidson wasn't my boyfriend, my lover, as this dick seemed to believe. He was my father, and as Finn O'Grady had correctly surmised, he was aiming for the White House.

How could I put that in jeopardy?

My dad was a good man. He'd made a mistake one summer when he'd come home from college, one that only some careful digging by his campaign manager had uncovered. Dad himself hadn't known of my existence, not until his CM had gone hunting for any nasty secrets that could come out and bite him in the ass.

This had been five years ago when he'd run for Senator. Now, Dad's goal was the presidential seat, and I wasn't going to be the one who put a wrench in the works.

When Garry Smythe had approached me back then, I'd thought he was joking. I was out on the street, heading home from work. At the side of me, a black car had driven in from the lane of traffic, just to park, or so I'd thought. As he'd held out his hand with a card, one of the car doors had opened up, and I'd been 'invited' inside.

Had I been scared?

At first.

But when Garry had told me my country needed me, I hadn't been sure whether to laugh or tell him to fuck off. He hadn't shuffled me into the car, though, hadn't tried to coerce me. He'd just asked if I'd voted for Senator Alan Davidson in the elections, and because he was one of the only politicians out there who wasn't a complete douche, and that was the name printed on the card in my hand, I'd shuffled into the back of the car.

Where the Senator himself had been sitting.

Now, when I thought about that day, I realized how fucking naive I'd been to get into the back of a limo for such a vague reason. But I'd been fortunate. Alan *had* been waiting for me. Waiting to tell me a story that still shook me to my core.

I'd made a promise to my dad that I wouldn't tell anyone. He'd offered me money, and I hadn't accepted it. I guess I should have, but back then, I'd been haughty and proud, and because the good guy I'd thought him to be hadn't been so good when he tried to buy my silence, I'd told him to fuck off. I'd been disappointed in him, frightened by the lifelong lie I'd been living, and equally hurt that the man who'd sired me was just concerned that I was a threat to his campaign.

I'd walked out of that car never expecting to see my dear old Dad ever again.

Then, the day after he'd been elected, he'd been sitting in the booth of the cafe where I worked part-time to get me through culinary school.

Seeing him, I'd almost handed that table off to one of the other waitresses, but I hadn't. Not when every time I'd passed the table, he'd caught my eye, a patient smile on his lips, one that said he'd wait for me all day if he had to.

Ever since that second meeting, I'd been catching up with him every three weeks.

And this bastard thought he could use our limited time together against my father? The one politician who could make a difference in the White House? One who didn't have Big Oil up his ass, a pharmaceutical company sucking his dick, or any other kind of corporation so far up his rectum that he was a walking, talking lie?

No.

That wasn't going to happen.

Which meant I was going to have to sleep with this stranger.

Before this conversation, hell, that hadn't been too disturbing a prospect. Because, dayum, what woman wouldn't want to sleep with this guy?

Even with an ego as big as his, he was delicious. Better than any cake I could bake, that was for fucking sure.

More than that, I knew him.

And I now knew that the life Fiona would never have wanted for her son was one he'd been drawn into.

The Mob.

The Five Points were notorious in these parts. Everyone was scared of them. I paid protection money to them, for God's sake. I knew to be scared of them, and having been raised in their territory, it was the height of stupidity to think paying them wasn't just a part of business.

Still, Fiona had never wanted that for Finn, and her Finn was the same as the one standing before me here today. In my tea room, which looked far too small to contain the might of this man.

She'd be so disappointed. So heart-sore to know that he was up to his neck in dirty dealings with the Five Points, and as he'd pointed out, the cost of his shoes, his clothes, and his jewelry, was enough to speak for itself.

If he wasn't high up the ladder in the gang, then I wasn't one of the best bakers of scones in the district.

Like Jenny had said, I had five star ratings across most social media platforms for a reason. I was good. But apparently, this man wasn't.

Before I could utter a word, before I could even cringe at how utterly sorrowful Fiona would be about this turn of events—not just about the Five Points but what her son was making me do—the door clattered open.

Like he'd predicted, a team of people swarmed in.

Finn motioned to the floor. "Want anyone to see those?"

With a gasp, I dropped to my knees and collected the shots, stuffing them back into the envelope with a haste that wasn't exactly practical.

Two shiny shoes appeared before me, followed by two expensively clad legs, and I peered up at him, wondering what he was about. He held out his hand, but I clasped the photos to my chest.

"You're making more of a mess than anything else, Aoife." His voice was raspy, his eyes weighted down by heavy lids.

For a second, I wondered why, then I saw *why*.

He had an erection.

An erection?

I peered around at the staff, but they were all men. Not a single woman in sight, well, except for the seventy-year-old with a clipboard who was barking out orders to the guys in what sounded like Russian.

So that meant, what?

The erection was for me?

The blush, the dreaded, hated blush, made another goddamn appearance, and to cover it, I ducked my head, then pushed the photos and the envelope at him.

For whatever reason, I stayed where I was, staring up at him as he calmly, coolly, and so fucking collectedly pushed the photos back into the torn envelope—it was some coverage. Better than none at all, I figured.

Being down here was. . . .

Hell, I don't know what it was.

To be looked at like that?

For his body to respond to me like that?

It was unprecedented.

I'd had one sexual experience with a boy back in college, and that had not gone according to plan. So much so I was still technically a fucking virgin because, and this was no lie, the guy had *zero* understanding of a woman's body.

Craig had spent more time fingering my perineum than my clit, and every time he'd tried to shove his dick into me, he'd somehow managed to drag it down toward my ass.

I'd gotten so sick of him frigging the wrong bits of me, that I'd pushed him off and given him a blowjob. It had been the quickest way to get out of that annoying situation.

Yeah, annoying.

Jenny, when I'd told her, had pissed herself laughing, and ever since, had tried to get me to hook up with randoms, so I could slough off my virginity like it was dead skin and I was a snake. But life had just always gotten in the way, and I'd had no time for men.

Shortly after *that* had happened, we'd lost Fiona. Then, I'd graduated, and after, Mom and I had set up this place thanks to some insurance money she'd come into after her husband had died. It had been crazy building the tea room into an established cafe, and then mom had passed on, too.

So, here I was. Still a virgin. On my knees in front of the sexiest man on Earth, a man I knew, a man whose mother had half raised me, one who wanted me in his bed as some kind of blackmail payment.

Was this a dream?

Seriously?

I mean, I'd been depressed before Finn O'Grady had walked through my doors. Now I wasn't sure whether to be apoplectic or worried as fuck because he wasn't wrong: you didn't mess with the Five Points.

God, if I'd known they'd been behind the development on this building, I'd have probably signed over months ago.

The Points were....

I shuddered.

Vindictive.

Aidan O'Donnelly was half-evil genius and half-twisted sociopath. St. Patrick's Church, two streets away, had the best roof in the neighborhood and the strongest attendance because Aidan, for all he'd cut you into more pieces than a butcher, was a devout Catholic. His men knew better than to avoid Sunday service, and I reckoned that Father Doyle was the busiest priest in the city because of Five Points' attendance.

"I like you down there," he murmured absentmindedly.

The words weren't exactly dirty, but the meaning? They had my temperature soaring.

Shit.

What the hell was I doing?

Enjoying the way this man was victimizing me?

It was so wrong, and yet, what was standing right in front of me? I knew he'd know what to do with that thing tucked behind his pants.

He wouldn't try to penetrate my urethra—yes, you read that right. Craig had tried to fuck my pee-hole! Like, *why?*

Finn?

He oozed sex appeal.

It seemed to seep from every pore, perfuming the air around me with his pheromones.

I hadn't even believed in pheromones until I scented Finn O'Grady's delicious essence.

It reminded me of the one out of town vacation we'd ever had. We'd gone to Cooperstown, and I'd scented a body of water that didn't have corpses floating in it—Otsego Lake. He reminded me of that. So green and earthy. It was an attack on my overwhelmed senses, an attack I didn't need.

With the envelope in his hand, he held out his other for me. When I placed my fingers in his, the size difference between us was noticeable once more.

I was just over five feet, and he was over six. I was round and curvy, and he was hard and lean.

It reminded me of the nursery tale Mom had sung to me as a child—Jack Sprat could eat no fat, and his wife could eat no lean.

Did it say a lot for my confidence that I couldn't seem to take it in that he wanted *me?* Or was it simply that I wasn't understanding how anyone could prefer me over Jenny?

Even my mom had called Jenny beautiful, whereas she'd kissed me on the nose and called me her 'bonny lass.'

Biting my lip, I accepted his help off the floor. My black jeans weren't the smartest thing for the tea room, but I didn't actually serve that many dishes, just bustled around behind the counter, working up the courage to do what Mom had done every day—greet people.

I wasn't a sociable person. I preferred my kitchen to the front of house, hence the jeans, but I regretted not wearing something else today. Something that covered just how big my ass was, how slender my waist *wasn't*.

Ugh.

This man is blackmailing you into his bed, Aoife. For Christ's sake, you're not supposed to be worrying if he likes the goods, too!

Still, no matter how much I tried, years of inadequacy weighed me down as I wiped off my knees.

"Do you have a coat?" he asked, and his voice was raspy again. "A jacket? Or a purse?"

I nodded at him but kept my gaze trained on the floor. "Yes."

"Go get them."

His order had me shuffling my feet toward the kitchen, but as I approached the door, I heard his strong voice speaking with the old woman with the clipboard: "I want this all cleaned up and boxed. Take it to my storage lot in Queens."

With my back to him, I stiffened at his brisk orders. *Was I just going to let him do this? Get away with it?*

My shoulders immediately sagged.

Did I have a choice?

If it was just him, just Acuig, then I'd fight this, as I'd been fighting it since the building had come to the attention of the developer. But this wasn't a regular business deal.

This was mob business, and it seemed like somehow, I'd become a part of that.

FML.

Seriously, FML.

CHAPTER 3

FINN

SHE WASN'T AS fiery as I imagined.

Did that disappoint me?

Maybe.

Then I had to chide myself because, Jesus, the woman had just been *coerced* out of her business. What did I expect? For her to be popping open a champagne bottle after I'd forced her to sign over her building to me?

Sure, she'd made a nice and tidy profit on her investment—I hadn't screwed her that way. But this morning, she'd gone into work with a game plan in mind, and tonight? Well, tonight she was out of a job and knee deep in a deal with the devil.

Of course, she hadn't actually agreed to my other terms, but when I guided her out of the tea room and toward my waiting car, she didn't falter.

Didn't utter a peep.

Just climbed into the vehicle, neatly tucked her knees together, and waited for me to get in beside her.

Like the well-oiled team my chauffeur and car were, they set off the minute I'd clicked my seatbelt.

The privacy screen was up, and I knew how soundproofed it was—not because of technology, but because Samuel knew not to listen to any of the murmurs he might hear back here.

And if he was ever to share the most innocent of those whispers he might have discerned? We both knew I'd slice off his fucking ear.

This was a hard world. One we'd both grown up in, so we knew how things rolled. Samuel had it pretty easy with me, and he wasn't about to fuck up this job when he was so close to retirement. If he kept his mouth shut, did as I asked, ignored what he may or may not have heard, and drove me wherever the fuck I wanted to go, Sam knew I'd set him and his missus up somewhere nice in Florida. Near the beach, so the moaning old bastard's knees didn't give him too much trouble in his dotage.

See?

I wasn't all bad.

Rapping my fingers against my knee, I studied her, and I made no bones about it.

Her face was tilted down, and it let me see the longest lashes I'd ever come across on a woman. Well, natural ones. Those fucking false ones that fell off on my sheets were just irritating. But as with everything, Aoife was all natural.

So pure.

So fucking perfect.

Jesus, Mary, and Joseph.

She was a benediction come to life.

I wasn't as devout as Aidan Sr. would like me to be, but even I felt uncomfortable thinking such thoughts while sporting a hard-on that made me ache. That made my mental blasphemy even worse.

"Why did you let him touch you? Was it for money?"

I hadn't meant to ask that question.

Really, I hadn't.

It was the last thing I wanted to know, but like poison, it had spewed from my lips.

Who she'd fucked and who she hadn't, was none of my goddamn affair.

This was a business deal. Nothing more, nothing less. She'd fuck me to make sure I kept quiet, and I fucked her so I could revel in the copious curves this woman had to offer.

Simple, no?

She stiffened at the question, and I couldn't blame her. "Do I really have to answer that?"

I could have made her. It was on the tip of my tongue to force her to, but I didn't really want to know even if, somewhere deep down, I did.

"You know why you're here, don't you?" I asked instead of replying.

Her nostrils flared. "To keep silent."

I nodded and almost smiled at her because, internally she was furious, but equally, she was lost. I could sense that like a shark could scent blood in the water. This had thrown her for a loop, and she was in shock, but she was, underneath it all, angry.

Good.

I wanted to fuck her tonight when she was angry.

Spitting flames at me, taking her outrage out on me as she scratched lines of fire down my spine as she screamed her climax. . . .

I almost shuddered at how well I'd painted that mental picture.

"When you're ready, you have my card."

"Ready for what?" she asked, perplexed. Her brow furrowed as she, for the first time since she'd climbed into the car, looked over at me.

"To make another tea room. I've had them move all the stuff into storage."

She licked her lips. "I want to say that's kind of you, but I'm in this predicament because of you."

A corner of my mouth hitched at that. "Honestly, be grateful I was the one who came knocking today. You wouldn't want any of the Five Points' men around that place. Half that china would be on the floor now."

Her shoulders drooped. "I know."

"You do?"

"I pay them protection money," she snapped. "Plus, I grew up around enough Five Pointers to know the score."

That statement targeted my curiosity, hard. "You did, huh? Whereabouts?"

Her mouth pursed. "Nowhere you'd know," she muttered under her breath.

"I doubt it. This is my area, too."

She turned to me, and the tautness around her eyes reminded me of something, but even as it flashed into being, the memory disappeared as I drowned in her emerald green eyes. "Why are you doing this?"

"Why do you think?" I retorted. "You're a beautiful woman—"

"Don't pretend like you couldn't have any woman under you if you asked them."

I wanted to smile, but I didn't because I knew, just as Aidan had pointed out to me earlier that day, that Aoife wasn't exactly what society considered on trend.

She'd have suited the glorious Titian era. She was a Raphaelite, a gorgeous and vivacious Aphrodite.

She wasn't slender. Her butt bounced, and when I fucked her, I'd have some meat to slam into, and her hips would be delicious handholds to grab.

If I smiled, I'd confirm that I was mocking her, and though I was a bastard, and though I was enough of a cunt to blackmail her into this when it hadn't been necessary—after all, before I'd told her who I was, I could have asked her out and done this normally—there was no way I was going to knock this glorious creature's confidence.

"Some men like slim and trim gym bunnies, some men like curves." I shrugged. "That's how it works, isn't it?"

Her eyes flared at that. "But Jenny—"

"Would you prefer she be here with me?" I asked dryly, amused when she flushed.

"Of course not. I wouldn't want her to be in this position."

I laughed. "Nicely phrased."

"What's that supposed to mean?"

Leaning forward, I grabbed her chin and forced her to look at me. "It's supposed to mean that you can fight this all you fucking want, but deep down, you're glad you're here. Your little cunt is probably sopping wet, and it's dying for a taste of my dick. So, simmer down. We're almost at my apartment."

And with that, I dipped my chin, and opening my mouth, raked my teeth down her bottom lip before I bit her. Hard enough to make her moan.

**

Aoife

THE STING of pain should have had me rearing back.

It didn't.

It felt. . . .

I almost shuddered.

Good.

It had felt good.

The way he'd done it. So fucking cocky, so fucking sure of himself, and who could blame him? He'd taken what he wanted, and I hadn't pulled away because he was right. My pussy *was* wet, and even though this was all kinds of wrong, I did want to feel him there. To have his cock push inside me.

Jesus, this was way too early for Stockholm syndrome, right?

I mean, this was . . . what was it?

It couldn't be that I was so horny and desperate for male attention that I was willingly allowing this to happen, was it?

Fuck. How pathetic was I if that was true? And yet, I didn't feel desperate for anything other than more of that small taste Finn had given me.

As a little girl, I'd watched Finn. It had been back in the day when his old man had been around and Fiona had lived with her husband and son. He'd beaten her up something rotten. Barely a week went by when Fiona, my mom's friend, didn't appear with some badly made-up bruise on her face.

I was young, only two, but old enough to know something wasn't right. I'd even asked my mom about it, wanting to understand why someone would do that to another person.

I couldn't remember what my mother had said, but I could remember how sad she'd been.

For all his faults, my dipshit stepfather had never beaten her, he'd just taken all her tips for himself and spent every night getting drunk.

Well, Finn's dad had been the same, except where mine passed out on the decrepit La-Z-Boy in front of the TV, Gerry had taken out his drunk out on Fiona.

And eventually, Finn.

Even as a boy, in the photos Fiona kept of him, Finn had been beautiful.

I could see him now, deep in my mind's eye. His hair had been as coal dark then as it was now, and not even a hint of silver or gray marred the noir perfection. His jaw and nose had grown, obviously, but they were just as obstinate as I remembered. Fiona had always said Finn was hardheaded.

When I was little, I hadn't had a crush on him—I'd been a toddler, for God's sake—but I'd been in awe of him. In awe of the big boy who'd been all arms and legs, just waiting for his growth spurt. Sadly, when that had happened, he'd disappeared.

As had his father.

Overnight, Fiona had gone from having a full house to an empty nest, and my mom had comforted her over the loss of her boy.

To my young self, I'd thought he'd died.

Genuinely. The way Fiona had mourned him? It had been as though both men had passed on, except we'd never had to go to church for a service, and there'd been no wake.

As kids do, I'd forgotten him. I'd been two when he'd disappeared, so I only really remembered that Fiona was a mom and that she was grieving.

We'd barely spoken his name because it could set her off into bouts of tears that would have my mom pouring tea down her gullet as they talked through her feelings.

As time passed, those little scenes in our crappy kitchen stopped, yet Fiona hung around our place so much it was like her second home.

One day, my stepfather died in an accident at work. The insurance paid out, Fiona moved in with us, and Mom had started scheming as to how to make her dream of owning a tea room come true. With Fiona living in, I'd heard Finn's name more often, but the notion he was dead still rang true.

Yet, here he was.

Finn wasn't dead.

He was very much alive.

Had Fiona known that?

Had she?

I wasn't sure what I hoped for her.

Was it better to believe your son was dead, or that your son didn't give enough of a fuck about you to contact you for years?

I gnawed on my bottom lip at the thought and accidentally raked over the tissue where Finn had bitten earlier.

"We're almost there," the man himself grated out, and I could sense he was pissed because the phone had buzzed, and whatever he'd been reading had a storm cloud passing behind his eyes.

"O-Okay," I replied, hating the quiver in my voice, but also just hating my situation.

This was. . . .

It was too much.

How was it that I was sitting here?

This morning, I'd owned a tea room. Now, I didn't.

This morning, I'd been exhausted, depressed about my mom, and *feeling* lost.

Now?

I was the *epitome* of lost.

A man was going to use me for sex, for Christ's sake.

But all I could think was: *did I still have my hymen?*

God, would he be angry if he had to push through it?

Should I tell him?

If I did, it would be for my benefit, not his, and why the hell was I thinking like this? I should be trying to convince him that normal people did not work business deals out by bribing someone into bed.

But, deep down, I knew all my scattered thinking was futile.

I wasn't dealing with normal people here.

I was dealing with a Five Pointer.

A high ranking one at that.

It was like dealing with a Martian. To average, everyday folk, a Five Pointer was just outside of their knowledge banks.

Sure, they thought they knew what they were like because they watched *The Wire* or some other procedural show, but they didn't.

Real-life gangsters?

They were larger than life.

They throbbed with violence, and hell, a part of me knew that Finn was cutting me some slack by asking to sleep with me.

Yeah, as fucked up as that was, it was the truth.

He could have asked for so much more.

He'd have a Senator in his pocket, and to the mob, what else would they ask for if not that?

Yet Finn?

He just wanted to fuck me.

My throat felt tight and itchy from dryness. I wanted some water so badly, but equally, I wasn't sure if it would make me puke.

Not at the thought of sex with this man—a part of me knew I'd enjoy it too much to even be nervous.

No, at what else he could ask of me, that had me fretting.

Was this a one-time deal?

How could I protect my dad from the Five Points when . . .?

I shuddered because there was nothing I could do. There was no way I could even broach any of those questions since I wasn't in charge here.

Finn was.

Finn always would be until he deemed I'd paid my dues. Whether that was tomorrow or two years down the line.

Shit, it might even be forever. If my dad hit the White House, only God knew what kind of leverage Finn could pull if my father tried to carry on covering up my existence. . . .

"We're here."

Something had *definitely* pissed him off.

He'd gone from the cat who'd drank a carton full of cream, to a pissed off tabby scrounging for supper in the trash.

"We're going to go through to the private elevator, and I'm going to head straight down the hall to my living room. You're going to slip into the first door on the right—that's my bedroom."

"O-Okay," I told him, wondering what the hell was going on.

"You're going to stay quiet, and you're going to try to not hear any fucking thing I say, do you hear me?"

"I hear you."

"You'd better," he ground out, his hand tightening around his cellphone. "Coming to Aidan O'Donnelly's attention is the last thing a little mouse like you wants."

A shiver ran through me.

Aidan O'Donnelly was in his apartment?

Fuck, just how high up the ranks was he?

CONTINUE
THE FIVE POINTS' MOB COLLECTION
HERE:
www.books2read.com/FilthySerenaAkeroyd

CONTINUE
A DARK & DIRTY SINNERS' MC SERIES
HERE:
www.books2read.com/SinSerenaAkeroyd

AFTERWORD

What do you think? Did the soundtrack song fit this book or what? ;) Maybe not all the ROUUUUGH sex, but that weird beat? Haha. Link can't be pushed into any mold.

Fret not, Lily and Link *will* be getting down and dirty together over the course of the series, and you *will* have a front row seat! As if I'd leave you hanging like that. ;)

Now, the next book in the Satan's Sinners' MC series is SIN. You can grab him here: www.books2read.com/SinSerenaAkeroyd

HOWEVER, before then, you can catch up with the Filthy Feckers. You've met Finn in FILTHY, you met Declan in NYX and now, again, in LINK, but first up? It's their baby brother, Eoghan's story. You guessed it: he and Inessa are about to get spliced! Grab it here: www.books2read.com/FilthyRich

I hope you're as psyched about this crossover as I am!

For a comprehensive reading order, start here:

FILTHY
NYX
LINK
FILTHY RICH
SIN
STEEL
FILTHY DARK

CRUZ
MAVERICK
FILTHY SEX
HAWK
FILTHY HOT
STORM
THE DON
THE LADY
FILTHY SECRET (COMING NOVEMBER 2021)

    Thank you, so much, for your support. And, while you're here, if you'd like to join my Diva reader group on FB for all the latest news on my releases, especially if it's still release week, there'll be some goodies to grab in there. Join here: www.facebook.com/groups/SerenaAkeroydsDivas

    Love you, guys, and thanks for reading!
    Serena
    Xoxo

FREE BOOK!

Don't forget to grab your free e-Book!
Secrets & Lies is now free!

Meg's love life was missing a spark until she discovered her need to be dominated. When her fiancé shared the same kink, she thought all her birthdays had come at once, and then she came to learn their relationship was one big fat lie.

Gabe has loved Meg for years, watching her from afar, and always wishing he'd been the one to date her first and not his brother. When he has the chance to have Meg in his bed—even better, tied to it—it's an opportunity he can't refuse.

With disastrous consequences.

Can Gabe make Meg realize she's the one woman he's always wanted? But once secrets and lies have wormed their way into a relationship, is it impossible to establish the firm base of trust needed between lovers, and more importantly, between sub and Sir...?

This story features orgasm control in a BDSM setting.
Secrets & Lies is now free!

CONNECT WITH SERENA

For the latest updates, be sure to check out my website!
But if you'd like to hang out with me and get to know me better, then I'd love to see you in my Diva reader's group where you can find out all the gossip on new releases as and when they happen. You can join here: www.facebook.com/groups/SerenaAkeroydsDivas. Or you can always PM or email me. I love to hear from you guys: serenaakeroyd@gmail.com.

ABOUT THE AUTHOR

I'm a romance novelaholic and I won't touch a book unless I know there's a happy ending. This addiction is what made me craft stories that suit my voracious need for raunchy romance. I love twists and unexpected turns, and my novels all contain sexy guys, dark humor, and hot AF love scenes.

I write MF, menage, and reverse harem (also known as why choose romance,) in both contemporary and paranormal. Some of my stories are darker than others, but I can promise you one thing, you will always get the happy ending your heart needs!

Printed in Great Britain
by Amazon